THE HUNGER OF THE DRAGON

DARK VIKING FANTASY

THE FORBIDDEN RUNES SERIES
BOOK 1

R.M. SCHULTZ

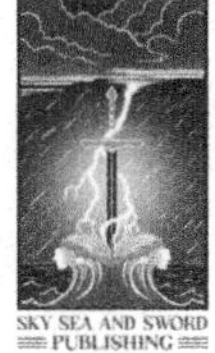

ISBN: 9798262906000

Published by Sky Sea and Sword Publishing

www.rmschultzauthor.com

FOREWORD

Hello, fellow reader!

I wanted to let you know that you're about to embark on an epic grimdark-style fantasy saga full of Norsemen and Norsewomen, monsters, dragons, and magic. This tale is darker than my other fantasy works, and more visceral and real to the time. The characters will grow and change. Many are not inherently good. There is violence and gore and death with frequent curse words as the characters would use, as well as sex without overly detailed descriptions. Issues of child loss, loss of mates and other loved ones, torture, and suggestions of rape are included as would have occurred in such a world during such a time. There is no on-scene rape.

A full glossary has been placed at the back of the book in case you'd like to refer to character names and terms.

Happy reading! I hope this Midgard-inspired world will sweep you away and carry your mind on an epic journey.

This book is dedicated to all those who still dare to read and tread the worlds of imagination.

- Ryan
R.M. Schultz

ULFR
Map of Known
Midgard
(THE NARWHAL'S REMAINS
UNKNOWN LOCATION AT SEA)
THE UNCHARTED
NORTHLANDS
THE MOUNTAIN
OF FIRE
ORMR (DRAGON)
CLAN TERRITORY
THE GHOST
WOODS
ORMR SPINE MOUNTAINS
THE SERPENT ISLES
(JÖRMUNGANDR
TERRITORY)
THE DRAGON'S REMAINS
THE DEAD
LANDS
THE
SERPENTS
REMAINS
THE UNCLAIMED
LANDS
ULFR (WOLF)
CLAN TERRITORY
FJORD
BJÖRN (BEAR)
CLAN TERRITORY
JÖRMUNGANDR
(SERPENT) CLAN
TERRITORY
MOON WOODS
HRAFN (RAVEN) CLAN
TERRITORY
(MUNINN'S
REMAINS)
GOD BREAKER
ISLAND
THE RIVER RED
DURLINN (STAG
CLAN TERRITORY
WETLANDS
ARVAKR (HORSE
CLAN TERRITORY)
DJARKAR (SPIDER)
CLAN TERRITORY
LIMESTONE
CAVERNS
(UNCHARTED)

1

MÄRREN

THE CHILD WAS DEAD.

Märren reminded herself of that fact as her fingers dug into the eye sockets of the child's skull. Her daughter's skull.

Somewhere behind her, trolls were tracking her, the creatures having left the forest to pursue lone prey. These monsters had nearly caught her once already, and she would not be able to engage multiple trolls in a skirmish, not without a pack of her kin.

Märren quickened her pace as she entered the Unclaimed Lands between the territory of the Wolf clan of her people and those of the Dragon clan beyond. The Wolf god would not be pleased with her.

She hefted her double-bladed axe, struggling against the weight of her pack, trudging up the mountain with the typical long strides of her kin, rain spewing from a darkened sky, her feet slipping in the mud, patches of snow, and sodden grass. She grasped the edge of a rock formation, heaving for breath and bracing herself. Her furs soaked up the cold rain but her body was hot, breath steaming, the roar of the downpour drowning out most other sounds.

"She'll never set foot in the lands of fire and ash," one of the voices living inside her head said, its piercing timbre echoing in her ears. The dark shape of a dragon stirring in its lair rose in one corner of her mind. A scarred rune she had carved on the inside of her arm burned.

"She'll die before she finds the people of the Dragon and learns their ways," the deeper voice answered. In her head, the silhouette of a red-eyed wolf stalked through woods beneath a rising moon.

"She's a berserker of the Wolf—the Ulfr," a third whispered, its words quiet compared to the others. The silhouette of a child ran through rowan and tussocks of grass at twilight. *"She won't fall easily. She is strong."*

"But she's alone," the wolf answered. *"The people of the Wolf clan are only strong in a pack."*

Märren glanced back, sensing the presence of trolls slipping closer as she pressed on up the slopes, struggling with treacherous footing, lifting her hand to gaze into her child's empty eye sockets. Rain pounded against the skull, funneling over its forehead and into the gaps of its eyes and nose. Märren brushed back sodden locks of hair that clung to her cheeks, all of it tangled and bronze, her heart aching.

"I'll join you, Eimri," Märren said to the skull. "One day soon." She paused as if waiting for her daughter's response, then said, "I won't die in battle and leave you to the world you now endure, not even if I find the people of the Dragon and harness the powers of their dead god. Only one of their scales can free us of the curse we carry. If I obtain such a treasure, I'll use it against our enemies, but never when I'd likely be killed in war."

Märren tucked the skull into a pouch at her waist and crested the summit where rock cairns were stacked along a ridge. Beyond the mountain, dark sky and clouds carried to the horizon, most of the view blotted out by rain. Somewhere to the west, a flicker of light shone, possibly from the surface of the sea—an inlet. Beyond that flicker, patches of flame danced across a hazy landscape.

The land of fire and ash. Märren was nearly there, as long as she could stay ahead of the relentless trolls and complete the crossing alone. A pack of her people would have been scented by dragons. None of the Ulfr—Wolf—people had ever wielded one of the Dragon's magical scales or ridden such a beast, had never utilized that power. But she would. It was the only answer to the darkness that plagued their lands. Withering crops, raids and battles with other clans, and trolls and unnamed creatures lurking in the woods all led to an increasing number of deaths and droves of bodies.

Märren knelt and placed a stone with a rune carved into its face at the base of a cairn—not for the gods, the humanoid gods had died long ago in a great war, their deaths followed by the deaths of all the beast gods. A version of Ragnarök had already occurred but turned out different than any Seidr man or woman predicted. The rune stone was an offering, a sacrifice, for the land wights and dark elves and dwarves in these parts, to keep these creatures at bay and to persuade them to remain in their own realms. There were no longer gods to ensure that these creatures did not venture to Midgard.

Märren hurried down the far slope, leaning backward to keep her balance as she descended its treacherous terrain. After a few strides, her foot slipped on wet rock, one leg sliding forward, threatening to send her tumbling down the mountain. Her empty hand slapped down against stone, which scraped her palm, tearing her skin with stinging pain. However, she stopped herself from falling and regained her footing, using the head of her axe to steady herself.

"Piss on these Unclaimed Lands and this crossing," she

muttered. A line of scar runes on her thigh stung and lit up in her mind. "But it must be done, Eimri."

A bellow carried over the mountaintop from somewhere not far behind, the call of a bull troll in rut—aggressive, hungry, eager to provide for his mates. He was coming. With only one Wolf woman as his quarry, he was unafraid. He was probably bringing females with him, in case he could not kill Märren by himself.

Märren cursed and picked up her pace, leaning farther back as she descended, slipping over rock, sliding on sodden grass, placing her hands out to steady herself and keep herself from rolling to one side and then tumbling down.

"Never walk away from home ahead of your axe and sword," Märren said to both herself and the voices, paraphrasing a poem from the Hávamál, the great writings of the old gods. "You can't feel a battle coming in your bones."

Another bellow from the bull troll rang out, echoed by his mates.

"She'll be overtaken before she reaches the bottom." The piercing voice of the dragon rang inside her head.

"The trolls will rip her limb from limb and feast on her bowels," the wolf's rumbling voice said, causing Märren's fear to surge.

"She may still evade them," the child added.

"Only if she falls and dies," the wolf replied, his thunderous laughter following.

"By Fenrir's dark fucking blood." Märren glanced over her shoulder toward the mountain's summit. Lumbering figures moved, blending in with stone and drenching rain and grass, only their movement and size making them stand out from the haze. Another threatening troll call echoed off the cliffs.

Märren gripped her axe and lunged down the slope, taking sweeping strides. She again wished she was not shorter than most of her kindred as her feet landed and slid and she fought to keep her footing. Another cry from the troll sounded right behind her, its breath a white cloud over her shoulder. A rush of wind from a swiping hand passed her neck. She fell.

Märren hit stone with a smack and rolled, tumbling downward. Stone outcroppings punched her flesh and bit into her neck. Grass and mud and snow whirled around her. She crashed into a cairn with a crunch and bounced away. A long, spiraling plunge down the slope ensued and did not relent until she hit a mound. Sharp pain radiated across her body. She groaned, her hand reaching to her waist. The pouch there had come untied, the small skull gone.

"No!" Märren struggled against a tilting and spinning world until she dropped her axe and planted a knee in the soft earth, feeling about the ground, her eyes hunting for Eimri. She screamed in outrage, unconcerned with the pursuing trolls. She would not do battle with them. Not now. If she did and was killed, she would cross the soul road and Raven's bridge, ending up in a place for those who died in battle—Valhalla. A place for the glorious dead. Eimri had only been a child. Her daughter would not reside there.

She grabbed at clumps of grass and a divot in the mud that she must have created during her fall, her body throbbing with pain. Nothing. She crawled about, scrabbling along the ground. The skull had to be close. Eimri had to be here.

Märren climbed to her feet, her pain not lessened, although the land did not spin and tilt as much as it had. No bellows erupted, and the trolls did not swarm in from the haze while she was weakened. She paused her hunt for the skull.

Something had stopped the creatures from coming after her.

She glanced around. Other than for the plummeting wet, all was still, the roar of the rain on rock and earth deafening. A flicker of firelight rose in the distance, on a road that wound along the base of the mountains.

Someone was coming through the Unclaimed Lands. Only those who tempted death or were unafraid of its call would wander here. Those with a dark purpose. Those like Märren.

A net flew over her head, landing around her, entangling her arms and legs.

"We got another one!" a man shouted in triumph.

Others stepped out from behind rock formations, warriors veiled by mist that rolled up from the ground. Märren did not concern herself with them. She continued tromping about as best she could under the restriction of the net, scanning the ground for Eimri.

"Take her down," one man said as several ran toward her, wielding spears, bearded axes, and shields.

"She's an Ulfhednar!" A tall, slender man stopped cold. "A Wolf berserker. Her eyelids and cheeks are painted black, and she wears the pelt of Fenrir."

The others halted their advance, their shields rising to better defend themselves, or at least to partially cover their faces.

"Don't let her get that axe." The tallest of her captors used his spear to point at her weapon, which was a short distance away.

"That is not one of Fenrir's furs," a deep voice rumbled behind the men, and they parted. A hulking man with stripes painted across the visible portion of his cheeks—beneath the rounded eye guards of his helm—as well as around his neck and chainmail *brynja*, strode closer. "If it were, you'd feel the pelt's power and fear it. She's alone. A Wolf without her pack isn't as deadly as you sorry lot may believe."

Power radiated from this warrior as he neared, his head and shoulders towering over Märren. A silvery scale dangled from a chain around his neck, and ringing rose in Märren's ears, making her wince. Given the sleekness and color of this scale, it was not draconic, but serpent. Sea Serpent.

Warriors of the Jörmungandr, the Sea Serpent clan, led by a berserker. What the berserker of the Serpent had said was true—Märren did not wear a pelt of Fenrir, did not carry the power of a Wolf berserker, an Ulfhednar. A berserker with proper training could wear the parts of one dead god, but bearing pieces from more than one god would kill them. Many of Märren's people were bestowed with the Wolf's great powers. They needed something more.

"She has already failed," the piercing voice of the dragon, always the quickest, said in her skull. *"These slavers of the Serpent will take her as a thrall and work her till she dies."*

"She failed before she began," the wolf's voice—the deepest and most troubling of the three—added. *"On the day she was born, she was doomed for failure. These slavers will kill her."*

"There's still hope for escape and a return to the Wolf, if not the Dragon." The image of the child darted away.

Märren growled and lunged to the side, searching for Eimri, struggling against the tightening cords of the net.

"She's going for that wicked axe." A warrior stepped closer, jabbing with his spear.

Märren ducked and twisted to the side, avoiding the incoming weapon and preventing it from impaling her. Then she saw a dome of dull white in the grass, a bit farther away than her axe. She leapt as far as she could manage, passing over her weapon before the net restricted her movements and she fell to her knees, landing short of her daughter's skull.

The Sea Serpent berserker blurred, a rush of power sheeting off him while a cloud of fog lifted from the ground to help conceal his whereabouts. In an instant, he solidified beside Märren, the butt of his spear smashing into her ribs—the strike of the Serpent. With another flash of movement and summoning the power of their dead sea god, he materialized on her other side before she could react. The boss on the berserker's shield caught her on the shoulder, sending a blast of pain up her neck. Another blurred movement followed, and a boot sank into her stomach. She grunted in response to a series of strikes that took less than a heartbeat to land and collapsed, reaching out and dragging herself toward Eimri.

The berserker stood over her, scrutinizing her and then her axe. "This Ulfhednar won't fight. Even now she forgets her weapon and seeks to flee by crawling away." He scoffed. "No wonder she travels alone. She's an outcast."

Mutters of confusion and agreement carried from the warriors. Märren would not fight, or she could find herself crossing the Raven's bridge to a glorious afterlife, which terrified her more than anything. If she followed that route, she would abandon Eimri forever.

Märren summoned the last of her strength, her skin burning as the net cut into her flesh. She scrambled toward Eimri's skull, and when her limbs would no longer move, she rolled, colliding with a tussock of grass. Her fingers clawed their way out of the netting, grasping, seeking. They fell onto the smooth surface of the skull, a head she knew as well in death as she had in life.

Märren clutched the skull to her midsection, curling around it, clamping her eyes shut and cursing these men for disrupting her errand. She would not find the Dragon or the Dragon's people, not that the clan would accept her. But now, her plan of sneaking into their temple and taking a scale for herself was ruined. She would not find a way to summon a beast as powerful as a giant.

"She's broken." The berserker loomed over her. "Engrossed with the dead—a child, given the size of the skull she holds. She was probably cast out from her pack. Maybe blamed for their withering crops and disease and failures."

"Do we take her?" a warrior asked.

"She could make a decent thrall or maybe even a sacrifice on the island," the berserker said. "The lightning giant is not particular. He may even prefer Wolf blood."

A warrior sliced through part of the netting and clamped an iron collar around her neck, the mark of a slave, a thrall, and pounded a bolt through its outer rings, sealing it. Strong hands tugged at the netting around Märren and dragged her across stone and grass.

She reached for her axe as she was pulled past her weapon, but the berserker suddenly appeared there in the gray drizzle, bending over and retrieving it first.

"Bring up the carts and let's get to the sea," he said. "There are trolls about." His tongue flicked from his lips and slipped back in. "I can smell them."

2

MÄRREN

THE BARRED CART JOSTLED AS IT ROLLED OVER RUTS IN THE ROAD, heading toward the sea, drawn by black steeds. Rain continued its deluge as Märren mashed herself into a corner of the cart, her muscles cramping, a dozen other slaves wearing collars crowded in around her, which left each of them only enough room to crouch or sit. Their stench was suffocating, the rattle of the locks on the cart a constant reminder of where she was. She hunched over Eimri's skull, the scar of a rune on her shoulder aching.

"One secret may be kept," Märren whispered, summarizing one of the Hávamál's many poems. "But never a second. And if you have three, a thousand people will soon know."

The cart rattled onward.

"The Sea Serpent clan will take her to their isles and make her perform the lowest labors of a thrall," the dragon's voice echoed inside her head.

"When a jarl or karl isn't fucking her," the wolf said. *"And only if they don't offer her as a sacrifice to the giant who plagues their lands."*

"Being a thrall isn't necessarily a death sentence." The child's

optimistic whisper was nearly drowned out. *"Some slaves have a family and live to old age."*

"A half-breed family forced upon them by their male owners," the wolf replied. *"Despised by all free folk."*

Märren winced and pulled at the collar biting into her neck. Beneath its iron link, her skin was raw, but calluses would form. She would become accustomed to it. It was nothing next to what she had already endured. And she would not settle for slavery, could not be a thrall to these Serpent men. Since her capture several days ago, she had witnessed the slavers having their way with some of the women, and each time, she could only clutch Eimri tighter.

She would offer herself as a sacrifice if being a thrall was the only other option. Then she could join Eimri.

A smear of black paint from her cheeks came off on her hand, probably the reason they had not yet touched her. They still worried she could be an Ulfhednar. She glanced through the bars of her cart. The gray haze was darkening, night falling over the far north, the cold bite of the wind tugging at her furs as it howled over the Unclaimed Lands. A line of carts followed hers.

In one of the rear corners of the cage Märren was held in, a woman with hair as black as a crow's feathers sat hunched, her head drooping. She had been there since Märren was taken, withdrawn, silent, and brooding. The rest of the captives huddled together, but they did not crowd around this woman or Märren, as if they knew something—maybe avoiding those who were cursed in the head, different, those who were often blamed for the hardships the gods still managed to rain upon Midgard even after their deaths.

Some of the captives whispered amongst themselves, their voices strained as they sought comfort or information about what was going to happen to them, or maybe they were hoping to unite against their captors.

The blade of an axe banged against the cart's bars, and a slaver sneered. "No talking or I'll gut any who I think might've shared a few words."

The captives fell silent, and the voices in Märren's head grew louder, as they often did. A gust carried the smell of rotting fish, of gull shite and briny air. Soon she would be taken from the land of her people.

"Never to return."

"Not even her bones."

"At least she'll find Eimri."

The woman at the rear of the cage shifted, her head lifting, sodden tendrils of hair plastered against pale cheeks. Her mouth gaped, and she seemed to sniff through her lips. Something poked above the stained neck of her tunic, an object as dark as her locks. It caught the torchlight from the slavers around them, reflecting an orange sheen.

A feather... Märren's blood thrummed, the voices in her head shouting. Did the feather mean something? The woman's striking blue eyes caught Märren's gaze before the woman wiped grime from her cheek and looked away. Beautiful. But not young. She had probably seen a couple more than forty winters, roughly five more than Märren. During their imprisonment, this woman had not been treated well by the slavers but had not been raped, and she ignored their threats and insults.

The cart ground to a halt, the roar of the rain as it struck the roof filling Märren's ears. In the moonlight beyond the line of Serpent slavers, waves slapped at the shore. Longboats settled in alongside a legendary Drakkar ship, and fog rolled in from the sea in clouds. A towering sea serpent on the largest vessel's masthead made Märren feel smaller, causing cold fear to lance through her veins. She nearly soiled herself.

"The Mist Shores."

"A legendary docking place for Sea Serpent raiders. She'll never see her home again."

"She's already suffered more than most."

The horses pulling the carts whickered, fright riding in their tones. The slavers called to the ships, and a man in shining *brynja*—armor—bearing an axe emerged and slogged through the breakers toward the shore. Captives in the carts wailed, their dirt-streaked faces pulling taut, the whites of their eyes opening wide. The leader of the slavers lumbered past Märren's cart, hollering at the ships.

The raven-haired woman shifted, crouching but rising up on her toes, her head brushing the roof of the cart. She reached for something at her neck and grasped it. The feather. Her cloak collapsed upon itself as if she was no longer there.

Märren jolted, gripping Eimri's skull and a bar tighter as she hunched over and planted her feet beneath her. The earsplitting caw of ravens rang out from a murder of the birds who were suddenly inside the cart where the woman had been—no, not a murder. That was the term for a group of crows.

"An unkindness," Märren whispered. That was the term for a group of ravens. Both references had arisen because crows and ravens were regarded as evil and associated with death.

The birds hopped about inside the cage. Märren pressed her back against the bars as the other captives gasped and shouted in terror, some pointing with skeletal arms.

"A dark omen indeed." The dragon's head in Märren's mind perked up, firelight rising in its throat.

A slaver banged on the cart's bars again. "Shut your mouths!"

"You'll be sailing for the Serpent Isles soon," another added.

The ravens squawked and flapped their wings, beaks gaping as they took flight and slipped between the thralls and through the bars, lifting into the air. More slavers yelled as they rushed for their cart, weapons poised.

"The woman, she's Hrafn—Raven. She carries the magics of the dead god Muninn."

"Worthless to us. Her kind have wicked ways."

"If she has turned into an unkindness, then she's a Raven berserker. People now call these berserkers the Knights Black."

"She could've fled the cart at any time." Märren's muscles tensed as she faced the bars and the departing unkindness. "And yet she rode with us. All this way."

The ravens shrieked, and slavers ducked and covered their heads. The birds soared toward a copse of rowan trees, landed, and quickly winged back toward the carts. The unkindness carried something, the lot of them holding a pale blade in their talons.

"Pull yourselves together!" The Sea Serpent berserker's shout was a deep rumble, mist sheeting from him. He appeared to be unaware of the returning unkindness. "We're in the Unclaimed Lands. Load up the slaves, and we'll depart as soon as we're able."

"The ravens." A slaver near him pointed.

The unkindness dropped from the sky, plunging toward the earth. Before they crashed, they blurred into shadow. The shadow's tendrils slowly slid away, revealing the pale woman with black hair and piercing blue eyes. She stood not far from the Serpent berserker, her wet locks stuck to her cheeks and neck. She eyed the berserker, raising a sword with a blade almost as wan as her skin. The hilt was black, a feather forged into it and sticking from the crosspiece, lying alongside the blade. A flight feather—the largest of those from the wings.

"Ah!" The berserker raised his bearded axe, hissing as he crouched.

The woman stood a head taller than most of the slavers but

not the berserker, her frame thin, a shadowy cloak attached to her wrists and reminiscent of wings.

"Certainly a berserker of Muninn." Märren squeezed the wooden bars, trying to bow them outward. The bars gave a little but not nearly enough for her to slip through.

More towering men and women poured from the ships, their boots splashing through the water as they marched to shore carrying bearded axes and shields. Gold and silver rings were tied into their braids and in beards, decorating upper arms and wrists, the precious metals glinting in the torchlight as twilight fell.

Märren clutched Eimri's skull between her shaking hands.

"Why have you come?" the berserker slaver asked the Raven woman as he gripped his axe in one hand.

"To share a few words," the woman answered.

"Caëtin of Muninn?" The hulking berserker regained his composure and stood taller than those behind him. "I did not recognize you at first glance. How did you come to find the Mist Shores?"

"Hithdrein, berserker of the Jörmungandr—the Sea Serpent." Caëtin bowed her head. "I was riding in one of your carts. As a captive. It's good to see you again now that—"

"Spare me your fucking shallow greetings. It's not as if I wasn't expecting you to contact me soon. It's just that your entrance was... startling." The colossal man squinted into the shadows on either side of the road. "Where are your Knights Black and your rangers? I don't want any of your crow magic here."

"Raven magic." Caëtin planted her sword's tip into dirt that was covered by a patch of snow and leaned against it. "And as long as you don't use your Serpent magic to summon a storm, a serpent from the sea, or kraken tentacles to ensnare me, this night should pass smoothly."

"As smooth as the arse of your pretty battle Seidr?" Hithdrein leered. "When whatever this is"—he gestured between them—"is done, I'll find her and squeeze that arse as I thrust my cock inside her."

"This slaver is crasser than Father," Märren muttered.

"Darstrid isn't here," Caëtin replied. "But she probably regrets not hearing your voice and choice of words... I wish I could regret it as well."

Hithdrein arched an eyebrow in confusion. "You wouldn't risk coming to the Mist Shores without her. Not to meet with the people of the Sea Serpent."

"Wouldn't I? And have her miss out on an opportunity to be wooed by you?"

Hithdrein snarled.

Caëtin glanced toward the sea, watching as more Sea Serpent warriors approached. "We aren't here to discuss Darstrid or my people. Let's leave them out of this. I'm here to discuss one thing—the Djarkar."

Märren's blood ran cold. *The clan of the Spider.*

Caëtin continued, "They've escalated their marauding of the lands south and east of ours, and it's past time for summer raids. They're plotting something else."

"I've heard. They've taken territory from some of the lesser clans. Those who weren't blessed by a god dying in their lands."

Caëtin nodded. "Then you're already aware of the situation. Now, only the Horse clan resides between ours and the lands the Spider have claimed."

"But there are other clans still lingering between our lands and those of the Spider. Besides those who wear the mane and tail hair of a dead god."

"Others who are too small to resist our common enemy."

Hithdrein glared at her and then the empty lands behind her before adding, "You seek the aid of the Sea Serpent. You're worried your people could fall now that the Spider clan has become more active. That's why you've come."

"We need each other."

An alliance between clans... None of the clans had gotten on well in longer than Märren had been alive, and most despised each other and fought on sight.

Hithdrein scoffed. "We're strong. The Ravens are not. And the Horse people have never trusted you, not after years of skirmishes and raiding along their borders. Your clan has fewer people than we do, including fewer of those who are trained to wield the remains of a dead god."

"You're certainly a bastard, and I wouldn't trust you with the rats in my cellar, but I'd prefer to share spoils with you rather than with Envinkia and her Spider berserkers, her widows. Acting alone, neither of our people can fend off the Spiders. Not in darkness. Not when they utilize the night to carry out their raids."

"The Serpent people can resist them. I alone carry two of the Sea Serpent's scales."

Caëtin cocked her head and cast the hulking man a sly wink. "Then I'll pray to Muninn that you'll be able to resist their attacks. I've heard they'll come for your lands first."

Hithdrein turned and paced about, shaking his head. "Your threats reveal your underlying fear and eagerness to make an alliance with us." He spread his arms wide. "You've none of your Knights Black with you, then? And all this is a plea for *our* might?"

Caëtin glanced over her shoulders and shrugged. "No berserkers that I can see." She pointed skyward. The cawing of birds sounded, and ravens dived in droves, landing in the grass and shadows around them.

"But why is she *here*?" Märren murmured. "That's the question Hithdrein should be asking. Why ride in a slave cart only to confront your captors before the Mist Shores?"

A man and woman captive reeking of bodily odors and filth crawled closer to Märren and watched through the bars. One by one, men and women wearing black cloaks that resembled wings emerged from the darkness beyond Caëtin and slowly stepped toward her.

"Oh, here are a few of those you were wondering about," Caëtin said.

Hithdrein relaxed rather than grew more nervous. "Then you aren't traveling alone after all." He gesticulated with a closed fist.

Märren tensed. "That's a signal." Two of the captives behind her muttered something lost to the voices in her head.

Hithdrein's warriors moved in closer behind him, their shields preparing to interlace and form a shield wall with jutting spears and axes. The berserkers arriving from the sea quickened their pace, hurrying toward the confrontation. One of the Raven warriors grunted and came slinking up behind Caëtin, as if to stand beside her, but this man moved strangely, awkwardly.

"He's not one of them."

"And yet he is. But he no longer belongs."

"We'll witness more death."

"He's here to cut off the head of the Raven," a man in the cage behind Märren said.

"The slavers have been talking about that," another man replied.

"After the loss of Caëtin and her Berserkers Black, the Raven clan will splinter," the first man said.

"The Ravens now call their berserkers the Knights Black."

"Doesn't matter. The rest of her kin will be easy pickings for the Sea Serpents."

The Raven warrior approaching Caëtin's back continued his

determined advance, his shoulders hunching as he lifted a bearded axe behind her. Caëtin remained facing Hithdrein, unaware of her impending death.

"Watch your back!" Märren shouted, but it was too late.

The sharp whistle of a projectile tore through the night. The Raven warrior approaching Caëtin lurched. An instant later, he cried out. The end of a bolt protruded from his chest as he spun a slow circle, staring at its fletching in disbelief. Another streaking bolt punched into his shoulder. The warrior shuddered and stiffened. He grunted, and three more bolts dropped him into a puddle with a splat.

Märren trembled, the scar runes for death on her calf smoldering in her mind.

"I forgot to mention that our Rangers Black flew in as well." Caëtin continued leaning casually against her sword buried into the earth. She did not glance behind her to witness what had happened, rather threw Hithdrein a wry smirk. "And the possibility of you offering one of your Serpent god's scales to Ningor in exchange for him killing me wasn't unexpected. Uktr has grown suspicious of potential traitors." She sighed. "I was hoping for peace and mutual assistance. A 'common enemy makes others into allies' kind of thing."

Hithdrein regained his composure, brandishing his axe as mist rolled off him and concealed him. In the distance, thunder boomed. Clouds hurtled closer, rain sweeping in from the sea. Hithdrein burst from a cloud of fog, charging Caëtin. The Sea Serpent slavers behind him yelled and stampeded across the narrow road. The Raven berserkers behind Caëtin cried out and plowed forward, gesticulating with axes and shields, steel banging against steel as they came.

Märren squeezed Eimri's skull tighter and rammed her shoulder against the bars of her cage. A fist of pain lanced up her arm as the bars bowed but did not break.

Hithdrein blurred and then appeared before Caëtin, hacking at her head, spitting at her face. A crack sounded, and Caëtin's cloak dropped as it suddenly became empty. Ravens screeched, flapping and flying away in a flurry of beaks and feathers and talons. Hithdrein's axe carved through the cloak, catching its cowl and lifting it as it hung limp on his weapon, his spit steaming as its acid burned through leather. The hulking monster of a man gasped, his eyes gawking. Lightning cracked over the sea, drawing closer. Rain pounded the shores.

The unkindness swirled with thumping wings, landing in shadows off to the side. Bodies and beaks became one, and Caëtin stood, feathers dropping around her, her pale blade jabbing and spearing Hithdrein in the back.

"The beaked strike of the Raven," the captive behind Märren said.

A slash of red flowed out of Hithdrein's *brynja*, and the berserker of the Serpent toppled forward, smacking his face onto the ground and lying still. The rain no longer advanced, and the howling wind and lightning subsided with the death of the berserker who summoned the storm.

The Raven berserkers—the Knights Black—howled and rushed past Caëtin, swinging axes as the slavers paused and stared in surprise before retreating a few steps. The Sea Serpent berserkers rushing in from the shore were nearly upon Caëtin's berserkers, but they halted, only momentum carrying their ranks a few more short strides.

"There doesn't have to be too much more death this night." Caëtin strode toward the berserker arrivals from the sea, brandishing her sword. "But we will not tolerate slavers sailing to the mainland and taking people as sacrifices. Nor making thralls out of farmers and woodsmen. Not people you did not claim in battle. Send word back to your jarl that our offer of allegiance still stands. The Sea Serpent people shouldn't wait till the longships of Envinkia ride the sea and land on your shores. Seek our aid before—"

Caëtin's words faded into the clashing of steel as her berserkers advanced upon the slavers, hammering their own shields with axe heads to create an intimidating din. A half-dozen of the slavers rushed toward the Ravens, jabbing with spears and swinging axes. Weapons clashed with shields and blades. Sparks flew in the night. Most of the charging slavers released death cries and fell, along with one of the Ravens who had a spear protruding from his throat.

Squawking pierced the night as another unkindness soared overhead, the Knights Black holding their line while the birds streaked past and released the contents from pouches in their talons. Liquid plunged onto the remaining slavers' helms and faces.

One slaver near Märren wiped his cheek. "Fuck these birds." He paused, studying the back of his hand before sniffing at the wetness. "It's lamp oil... Why would crows—"

Farther above, another rush of birds tore past, shrieking. Firebrands dropped from talons, spiraling downward and lighting up the night with dancing embers, a wonder of light and shadow. Sheer beauty to behold. A surge of fear and awe struck Märren as she watched.

Blinding flashes stung her eyes as the firebrands struck the slavers, lighting those people up in bright flame. Then burning projectiles whistled across the area, impaling more of the slavers and igniting them in gouts of orange.

Their screams bothered Märren less than any voice in her head.

3

CAËTIN

All eyes were focused on the spectacle created by the Ravens. The Serpent berserker arrivals from the sea stood frozen, watching the slavers crackle like torches before dropping into flaming heaps. When violence was justified, it could not be avoided in favor of less savage tactics.

"Free those who want to be freed." Caëtin pointed to the carts, and her Raven berserkers moved swiftly and silently, using axes and hammers to shatter locks. "Put the others out of their misery."

Filthy men and women emerged from the carts, their backs hunched at first before they stood straighter, eyes wide with fear.

"You're no longer captives." Caëtin strode past them. "Free as birds."

"Where do we go?" a woman asked.

"Home." Caëtin shrugged. "The Knights Black can't carry you. Take supplies from the slavers, but you'll have to cross the Unclaimed Lands yourselves... unless you'd rather catch a ride with the Serpent berserkers." She pointed at the shore.

The woman and several freed captives rushed for the carts and horses and dug through packs, piling up armloads of bread and wineskins. A man leapt onto a horse and kicked its flanks until the beast galloped away.

One person remained behind, a woman whose face was smeared with black paint, her hair like bronze fire but full of muck. She muttered something under her breath, something barely discernible but vaguely familiar, words that had to be from the Hávamál. "Hidden runes shalt thou seek and interpret. Symbols of might and power, painted by the great singer, sculpted by the utterer of gods." She wore the pelt of a wolf but stood shorter than Caëtin, which was atypical of the Wolf people.

"You rode in the same cage as me," Caëtin said. "The slavers were too afraid to touch you. You're an Ulfhednar?"

"I don't wear a pelt of Fenrir," the woman replied, tugging at the iron collar around her neck, which rattled against a short chain. "Never have." Her eyes wandered, and the way she did not focus on Caëtin made Caëtin think she was pondering something deep. Her hands were cupped around a white object.

Caëtin retreated to recover something she had seen Hithdrein carrying on his belt. She waved a hand to dispel the fog that hovered around the berserker's body, although her action did little good. After a bit of searching, she found what she was looking for and retrieved it.

Caëtin held up a double-bladed axe as she returned to the strange woman. "Then you are a warrior of the Wolf?"

"I've been asked to join the pack, but I did not wish to." She gazed at the weapon but did not reach for it.

Caëtin let her hand and the axe fall to her side. "Understandable. It's a dangerous hobby. Better to tend the land and raise children and crops as one of the karls. At least until the other clans come raiding."

"I desire to wear the Dragon's scale."

A rush of air hit the back of Caëtin's throat. She glanced

over her shoulder northward into the night before facing the woman again. "You sought the land of fire and ash. You're mad."

She nodded.

Caëtin offered her the butt of the axe, and the woman accepted it, partially revealing the object she held in her other hand—a skull. A small one. Probably a child's.

"I'm Caëtin Harekrsdóttir. Of Muninn."

"Märren."

Caëtin cocked her head, waiting for more.

"I have no other name. No father."

Strange. "Well, Märren, traveling north only grows more difficult from here, and I'm sure you've heard rumors that the people of the Dragon don't take kindly to outsiders. It's not a lie. If you still believe you must go seeking the Dragon's people, it'd be best to return to your lands for a respite and to replenish your supplies. Enjoy a few more days of life before you throw yourself off the Raven's bridge."

"There were trolls pursuing me." She indicated the mountains behind them.

"And there are many more trolls between here and the land of fire and ash. If you hurry, you can catch up with the rest of those we freed. Traveling in large numbers deters most trolls. Go home. And if you must return, bring companions with you. Trust me. I've flown over this area much of late. You won't survive the crossing. No one would. Not alone."

Märren did not blink.

"Not that the people of the Dragon will allow you to live if you make it beyond the Unclaimed Lands and trespass into theirs," Caëtin added. "They're less welcoming than the bitterest old jarl I've known."

Märren winced and muttered something under her breath, her eyes turning glassy. Her shoulders sagged, and her head drooped. "Your words are reminiscent of what my people have told me."

A flash of movement caught Caëtin's eye. A dirt-smeared boy emerged from under a cart and darted to the body of her slain Knight Black. The boy took the dead berserker's axe, then heaved and rolled the body over, grasped a chain around the berserker's neck, and yanked, breaking its clasp. A small tail feather of Muninn was fastened to the chain. He squeezed it in his palm and darted into the night. Headed north. Toward the land of fire and ash. None of the slaves would be from those lands. The slavers would not have risked traveling there.

Surprise and anger stirred Caëtin's blood. *He is a shite-faced fool.* The sensation of shattering pulled at her limbs and torso as she collapsed into an unkindness and a flurry of wings, taking flight and pursuing the boy. Other ravens were already soaring after him.

Her quarry ran faster, his steps lighter as he dashed across mounds of rock and snow like he was becoming weightless, because power and magic were flowing through his skin and into his bones. He glanced over his shoulder, sneering at the ravens, a bestowed sense of defiance and courage clearly igniting within him, tempting him to turn around and fight his adversaries. But he gripped his forehead, which would be thrumming with power, disorienting him, and he blinked heavily. Darkness would also be flooding his vision, turning his colorful world into black, white, and grays. And the orange of fire. He was on his way to becoming a warrior of the Raven clan, the people of memory and cunning and dreams. Of death.

To possess a piece of a dead god would impart power beyond compare. Even a small feather from a lesser berserker would do so. This boy must have succumbed to temptation, believing that if he could bear such an item, he would be able to slay great enemies.

The boy tripped over a log, which sent him sprawling, his momentum carrying him several horse lengths through the air and into a tussock of dead grass. He scrambled about to regain his footing. The thumping of Caëtin's many wings grew louder as her unkindness landed in the brush and shadows ahead of the boy. The boy's heart hammered so loudly against his breastbone that it rang in her ears. Cold sweat beaded on his forehead as he stood in the night, shivering in terror. Her pursuing comrade had already arrived and approached the boy.

"Where are you off to so suddenly?" Darstrid's voice rose after Caëtin's cawing diminished and then ceased. Darstrid's feet crunched through the brush.

"I am Halvi! I will destroy you!" The boy hefted the axe he took from the berserker, his wrath and power surging as he swung the weapon before him. The Raven's blood—the magic of Muninn—flowed through him. He was strong, and portents of what was to come, and of the past, would be sweeping through his mind. But in the beginning, it was all so twisted. He grabbed at his forehead again, as if a hammer beat against his temples, and swayed.

Darstrid chuckled in an unamused manner, her posture rigid, long blonde hair with dark streaks waving. "You can't simply steal a feather or a tooth or pelt of a dead god and harness their ancient powers without repercussions, Halvi." She stopped an arm's length from the boy, vitriol spewing in her words. "Anyone hoping to control such magic must first dive into another realm, one where Muninn's first temple resides, and travel to as deep a tier as they're able. To claim what power they will before the ever-watching raven hunts them down. And before this, they must be trained to wield magic and might. Otherwise, it'll destroy them. As it will destroy you."

Caëtin strode past Darstrid and grabbed Halvi's wrist, jerking him around to face her as she pried his fingers apart and knocked his feet out from under him. Halvi dropped to the ground. Caëtin wrenched the feather from his grip and held it up in the moonlight, twirling it between thumb and forefinger.

Halvi groaned in anguish as he rolled about on the ground, the effects of losing a divine remnant crashing upon him. The feeling of power and strength, the abilities of a god, would have fled him faster than light after sunset. And the sensation of having a missing piece of himself would linger beneath a yearning to fill its void, an addiction stronger than any in this world, like being trapped and partially crushed by an avalanche and needing to crawl out for air. There would only be one way to satiate such overwhelming desire—bearing another god part.

"You experience the longing now." Darstrid's tone was vengeful, but a hint of enjoyment pitched her words.

"You should've been there, Darstrid," Caëtin said as Halvi sank further into despair. "Hithdrein mentioned you."

"I had an inkling he would, a portent born more out of female sense rather than Raven magic. And I'm glad you finally killed him. I would've done so, but much slower."

Caëtin tucked the feather away beneath her cloak.

"What're we going to do with this young man?" Darstrid asked.

Caëtin tapped her lip with a finger. "We can't trust him enough to make him an altar boy to Muninn. But he has gall."

"The punishment for thievery from the gods is death. Even for children."

Halvi lurched, his gaze whipping back and forth between the two of them as his eyes rolled and he gasped.

"We should carry out the jarl's laws." Caëtin brandished her pale blade, and it shone in the moonlight.

"I only wanted its power," Halvi whimpered. "To become a warrior of one of the dead beast gods. To wield strength unmatched by common fighters."

"You thought the clans would then seek *you* out?"

He nodded. "Once I held such power, they'd beg me to join their ranks."

"And which clan were you hoping to join?" Darstrid asked. "The ranks of the Sea Serpent? Or the Boar or even the Spider? Or maybe you'd choose one of the smaller clans still clinging to their spits of land."

"The Ravens." Halvi's voice cracked with the lie.

Caëtin glared down at him. "So many desire what you do, and we can never allow such thefts to go unpunished. God parts will kill any untrained person who possesses them. And even if I allowed you to join our villagers and assist the karls with farming and fishing, blacksmithing, or wherever else they find a use for your sorry arse, you'll merely bide your time until you can run away."

"N-no!" Halvi said. "I won't. I'll be faithful to the Raven."

Both of the Knights Black contemplated the predicament, knowing by law what they must do.

"If you must, make me into a thrall!" Halvi held up his hands.

"I just freed you from slavery"—Caëtin kicked at the collar around Halvi's neck—"and you already want to join our captives of war and rapists and murderers?" She shook her head. "That's no life. Thralls toil and aid those they despise. They have no rights."

Darstrid raised her axe. Halvi flinched and shrieked, curling into a ball. Caëtin grabbed her comrade's hands, staying her blow.

"At the very least, we must beat him within a hair of his life." Darstrid reared back and kicked Halvi in the side, expelling the air from his lungs so he could not even manage a scream as a few of his ribs cracked. "Then sell him off as a thrall. Make sure he remembers this lesson and what all berserkers and warriors do to god thieves."

"That would surely turn him against us," Caëtin said. "We already have too many enemies. Instilling hate in a child who will one day grow into a man isn't wise." She paused. "Be off, Halvi. Before I change my mind and beat your arse bloody."

A cloud passed over Darstrid's face. "Like Father says—young men only respect strong leaders who punish those deserving. You have to make them fear the consequences and respect us."

Darstrid's boot lashed out with unnatural speed, kicking Halvi multiple times in quick succession, landing blows on his back and neck. His head. Halvi yelped in pain before Caëtin wrapped Darstrid up in her arms and hauled her off him.

"Enough," Caëtin said. "If he works our lands, he'll aid our people for decades." To Halvi, she said, "Go. Now. Join any others who wish to return to Raven territory, you foolish boy."

Halvi struggled to find his feet. One of his ankles twisted beneath him as he clutched his side and limped away, his eyes wild.

His yearning for the power that had been granted by the feather and taken away would already be growing.

4

CAËTIN

CAËTIN HEAVED APART HEAVY DOORS AND STRODE INTO THE longhouse—the great hall. A chill wind whipped in at her heels, guttering the torches lining posts and beams inside. Men and women of the Raven paused their feasting and drinking and fell silent, staring. At the end of a walkway that stretched between tables running the length of the single interior chamber sat Uktr, the jarl of the Hrafn—Raven.

Darstrid, the clan's battle Seidr, waited before Uktr but stepped aside so Uktr could see Caëtin approach. Uktr's gray hair draped over his shoulders, his cloak of Muninn loose around his chest and bound by a gold chain, his face always stern. Old runes were carved into the wooden beams and chairs surrounding him. Silence pressed down upon the chamber, broken only by the scuff of a boot or shuffle of a bowl.

"Mother!" A boy with dark hair who had seen nine winters came running. A girl five winters older and with brown hair, followed him more slowly. The boy wrapped his arms around Caëtin's waist. "You've returned."

Caëtin kissed his head. "I'm safe, Treln." She faced her daughter, Lythi, and smiled. "I missed you both."

"It's good to have you home." Lythi waited until Treln pulled away to embrace her mother.

"Now let me speak with Uktr, and then I'll share nattmal with you two before bed," she said.

Treln hopped up and down until Lythi took him by the wrist. Treln resisted and started yelling, but Lythi forcefully led him away. Caëtin approached Darstrid and Uktr.

"Jarl." Caëtin dipped her head in acknowledgment.

"So the Sea Serpent didn't take to your idea of kinship?" Uktr stared down at Caëtin from his high seat.

He seems of sound mind this day. "It wasn't the meet I foresaw and believed both clans needed. I envisioned drink and merry-making and dancing to music of—"

"Drop your sarcasm." Uktr glanced away, his cloudy eye turning distant before both of his eyes blurred. "The Raven's wings guide mysterious winds. We seek the dreams of Muninn to see through feathers and gods in dark times. In what's foretold, we all shall be. I foresaw this."

He's only sound of mind when he's angry. Once his rage subsides, his gibberish returns. "I also dreamt of the meet while I walked the lands of Muninn with her flight feather in my possession." Caëtin held up her pale blade, displaying the tip of the Muninn feather rising from its hilt. A similar feather was clasped to a chain around her breast. "The vision I saw may not have involved dancing and drinking, but it was more agreeable than what it actually turned out to be."

"Then you do not see the portents clearly." Uktr motioned over his shoulder, as if directing the log steps leading up to the jarl's loft to follow a command. "And thus the flight feather is wasted upon you, my daughter."

Adopted daughter. And you cannot see through whatever fog has taken hold of your mind. Caëtin stopped herself from uttering the thought—the sort of retort that came to her too often and too quickly. She would not speak such words to the jarl. Uktr may not often be kind, but he had been like a father to her after her parents were killed in a raid.

Two Knights Black lumbered forward from somewhere behind the throne, dragging a man between them, a bearded axe in each of the berserkers' hands. They dropped the limp man onto the floor before Caëtin and stepped back, the victim's face bloodied and purple, one eye swollen shut, the other a slit he could probably still see through.

"Another Raven traitor?" Darstrid asked.

"We're nearly certain," Uktr answered.

Caëtin sheathed her sword and knelt beside the man, Jundr, recognizing him despite his battered face. After a skirmish many years ago, when he was a young man, the Raven people had adopted him from the Bear clan. Jundr had never been made a thrall after being taken and had been with the Ravens for decades now. He was raised as one of their own and had become a warrior—a fighter who could carry a small god part and command some of its magics. Berserkers ranked above warriors as the elite fighters of the clans because they could bear larger divine remnants and wield more magical abilities.

"*Nearly* certain?" Caëtin asked. "And yet you did this to him?"

A muscle under Uktr's beard bulged. "Better to stop the hemorrhaging of secrets now rather than allow information to continue to flow to our enemies. Halt the danger until we obtain definitive proof of his loyalties. You, Caëtin, will take his inquisition."

Caëtin glanced up. "Me? I'm no inquisitor. I'm a poor interpreter of portents, but I'm better at that than interrogations."

Uktr glared at her. Darstrid folded her arms across her chest.

"This is your opportunity to make amends for your last orders to the Knights Black while I slept," Uktr said. "For attempting to make an alliance with the Sea Serpent. Disastrous. I hold you to a higher standard than all others. So stop with the fucking mistakes. I fear the day I walk the Raven's bridge, not because of death but because you shall have my seat. No one should *ever* take in those from other clans."

"Some of the other clans do the same," Caëtin said.

"Which ones?"

"The Wolf."

"The Wolves are fools, Caëtin. Do not put your hope in a belief that the clans of the dead gods will one day be united. They cannot. We wield our magics and might to raid, and if need be, to kill the other clans. It's how the gods acted toward each other and how they wanted their people to behave. For glory and honor in battle. We did not create or fashion this world, but we intend to survive in it."

Caëtin found no decent rebuttal. If a legendary throne of a high jarl of all the lands had ever existed, it had long been vacant, before the gods and giants warred and died. But without peace to bind the clans, their lands would splinter and fragment, and blood would continue to flow in rivers until the last people of one clan slayed all others.

"But what becomes of us when more of those invading legions arrive at our shores?" Caëtin indicated those in the hall. "We must seek unity. The numbers of those beyond the seas are endless."

Uktr's upper lip lifted in a snarl. "Then each clan will have to deal with the raiders who are fool enough to come to their lands. As it has always been. As the gods and their dead beast gods left this world for us. Do not ask such foolish questions."

Caëtin hid her irritation and shame, deciding not to further debate the matter or defend her choices. "I'll use Muninn's grace and dive into Jundr's dreams. Make him sign a confession to the jarl of the Raven."

"Not in *my* longhouse." Uktr waved her away. "Not during nattmal. Take him elsewhere. To the temple. Let our people feast here."

Caëtin stepped back, cocking her eyebrow at the woman she considered her sister. They had both been adopted by Uktr. "Darstrid? Will you join me?"

Darstrid approached to speak with Caëtin but gave a quick shake of her head. The berserkers dragging Jundr followed them toward the entrance of the great hall. Conversation and laughter returned, echoing around them as horns slammed onto tabletops.

"If it were up to me," Darstrid said to Caëtin, "I'd behead Jundr and be done with any further risk to our people. Killing him shouldn't endanger trade with the Bear people. They've probably long forgotten about him." She cleared her throat as they neared the doors. "In the end, we all know what you should do, Sister. First, learn what you can, but don't disappoint Uktr again so soon or he may change his mind about who shall take his seat when he's gone."

Caëtin's head lolled back in disbelief before she managed to signal to the Knights Black to drag Jundr outside.

"Mother." Treln ran to her. "Aren't you going to join us?"

"I'll return soon." She flashed Treln and Lythi a smile, knowing they would probably be asleep before she finished her task. Another broken promise. But she could spend the day with them on the morrow. She knelt before her son and kissed his forehead. "Watch over your sister until I'm done."

"I will."

"Good boy. Now go eat."

He looked back once before racing off to a table. Bile churned in Caëtin's guts along with guilt as she led the berserkers outside and walked the ice-encrusted road between houses. Darstrid did not join them.

Their destination was not far. In Aonark—the Raven's largest city—the only location more central and thus more protected than the jarl's longhouse was the temple of Muninn. She headed for it.

The reek of piss and smoke clung to the air, the sound of Jundr's knees dragging along the road close behind. Wings flapped overhead, and a lone raven squawked, circling above Caëtin. She raised an arm, and the raven alighted on her gauntleted wrist, the bird cocking her head and studying Caëtin. The raven clutched something in her talons, and Caëtin held up her other hand.

"What have you got now, Huginn?" she asked.

The raven blinked, cocked her head to view Caëtin with her other eye, and dropped the item onto Caëtin's palm—a few bones stuck together. Probably the remains of some rodent.

No. Caëtin scrutinized them more closely until she was certain of what they were. The bones of a human finger. Given their state of decay, whoever they originally belonged to had either died long ago or at least had lost their finger many years past.

"Where do you find this shite?" Caëtin asked.

Huginn blinked again and flapped her wings before settling.

"I know—it's another gift," Caëtin muttered as the Knights Black behind her grumbled with impatience. "We have pressing matters." She stroked Huginn's cheek, and the bird's beak parted as if she relished her touch. "If you ever find something of dire importance, I believe you'll bring me a piece of it and lead me there."

Huginn cawed, beating her wings and flying off. Caëtin grimaced as she studied the finger, waiting until the raven had gone before chucking it off to the side of the street. Ravens were nearly as intelligent as most people, and more intelligent than some. Caëtin did not want to insult the wild creature who had befriended her by discarding her gifts in front of her.

Caëtin led the berserkers on and soon they stood before blocks of black stone that jutted from the earth. Caëtin approached a set of doors where two women in cloaks waited, hoods shrouding their faces as they looked downward. Without a word, the women drew the doors open.

5

CAËTIN

TWO *GYÐJA*—PRIESTESSES—STOOD BEFORE THE OPEN DOORS TO the temple of the Raven god Muninn. One *gyðja* was lithe, the other voluptuous, both scantily clad beneath black cloaks draped around their shoulders.

"We must perform an inquisition on a suspected traitor," Caëtin said to the *gyðja* as she stepped inside, followed by the Knights Black, who dragged Jundr between them.

Buzzing sounded in Caëtin's skull. The *gyðja* whisked past them, accompanying Caëtin and the berserkers into a circular chamber composed of black stone. The ground level tier. Hundreds of candles hung from the rafters and burned with either violet or emerald flames.

As they walked toward stairs that led downward into the darkness of the temple's descending tiers, their footsteps echoed. Caëtin did not need the *gyðja* as guides, although the women would not leave her and her companions to their own doings. Not here.

After winding down long stairways and passing several dimly lit levels where no one was about, Caëtin and the others stepped onto a lower landing. Here, fewer candles burned, and shadows lived everywhere—around the base of the stairs, the walls, a statue of an enormous raven—the altar of Muninn.

Caëtin mopped at her brow, the air warmer here than anywhere else, the discomforting buzzing in her head growing to a pounding din. The *gyðja* led her and the Knights Black dragging Jundr around the altar and descended another level, spiraling into the depths of the temple and its darkness. The fetid stench of decay wafted around them, an odor not unfamiliar to those of the Raven—men and women of death and memories. Of cunning and intelligence.

They reached the lowest level, a place with few candles, shrouded in shadow. The remains of their dead Raven god lay on a pedestal, her feathers as dark as midnight but as shimmery as water under a splash of moonlight. The feathers had not decayed in the least over the past centuries, the Raven's beak and talons also unaffected by time. However, the rest of her was nothing more than dried bones, her avian body roughly the same size as a tall and broad man.

The power wafting from the dead god caused the din inside Caëtin's skull to rage like clashing steel in battle. She winced in pain. Footsteps shuffled toward her as a cloaked *goði*—priest—of Muninn emerged from the shadows, his bald head bowed, his eyes vacant.

"The sacred oils have been bestowed on Muninn," the *goði* said without emotion as he stopped before Caëtin. "May her feathers ever shine." A chain of vials hanging around his neck caused him to hunch over, and his manner was so sedate that he seemed half dead.

These men and women of Muninn knew things before events occurred. They understood more than Caëtin could ever hope to tease from dreams, even those she experienced within the temple. But the holy people suffered mental and emotional torment from living too close to the Raven's remains, a side effect of the power expelled from a dead god.

The Knights Black behind Caëtin dragged Jundr to the foot of the pedestal, holding him there on his knees. One forced a horn filled with dark liquid into Jundr's broken hand.

"Drink," the berserker said.

Jundr spat at them, and the tall berserker who had spoken grabbed Jundr by the hair, wrenching his head back. The other berserker squeezed Jundr's cheeks and dumped the horn's contents into Jundr's mouth before hammering his jaw closed and covering his lips. Jundr swallowed.

Caëtin took another horn from the edge of the pedestal and downed its bitter contents, then sat on a cot nearby, leaning back and closing her eyes. She spread her arms wide, allowing her cloak wings to unfurl as the darkness took her.

Caëtin's eyes slowly opened, and she sat up in a realm of haze and darkness, of grays and blacks and browns. The Raven's bridge world. Bright white gashes of flame dotted the landscape. Ghostly people floated around her, drifting onward. Farther along, their ranks divided and followed one of two paths. Those bearing weapons in their hands moved faster, pressing back a host of wraiths while other specters accosted those who were unarmed. Ash fell like hot black snow. Jundr cowered there beside Caëtin, his body quivering, his one visible eye darting about in fear.

"We're in Muninn's world?" Jundr's voice cracked.

"Aye. The Raven's bridge, where the soul road divides and crosses into either Helheim or Valhalla. Where the dead walk their allotted path."

Jundr paled. Crows and ravens wheeled overhead in murders and unkindnesses, cawing and screeching, their black forms smattered against a pale sky. A nimbus of ice surrounded a hazy sun, and fire covered ice-cloaked mountains in the distance.

"Can you truly see the past here?" Jundr glanced about, terror dancing in his eye.

"That's what they say. If you don't confess to being a traitor to the Raven clan, we may have to call up images of prior events."

But even the best inquisitors knew that peering into the past was not like watching something happen before them. It too was full of portents and blurred history, open to interpretation, any understanding limited by the ability of the inquisitor.

"Did you betray the Ravens?" Caëtin asked.

Jundr trembled.

"In this world, I can feel your pain." Caëtin indicated Jundr's broken hands and battered face. "I can make it stop. All the anguish. Your turbulent emotions. Your consuming fear. You simply have to sign the confession." She unrolled an ethereal parchment as more of the dead floated past. *Admit to what the jarl wants you to.*

"I didn't... I must confess, mustn't I?"

"If you betrayed the Raven to others, you must."

Jundr stared at the ground as fog rolled around him. "And if I didn't? They won't believe me and allow me to fight alongside our warriors again."

Caëtin waited, considering that this man may indeed be innocent. A woman in a black cloak strode past them, one of Muninn's people. "Darstrid?"

The woman did not acknowledge her or even act as if she heard her. Such things happened when dreaming. Caëtin often dreamed of others, but typically, if they were also dreaming and present here, linked to the Raven's bridge, they could speak with one another. The woman burst into flames and walked on before blowing away as ashes.

Another portent that could mean anything... But the first thing that came to mind was Darstrid's death. Caëtin shuddered.

Jundr tore the parchment from Caëtin's grip and pressed a bleeding finger to its surface, scrawling a blood rune of an admission. "Take it." He shoved the parchment back into Caëtin's hands, crumpling it. "If Muninn were alive, she'd know the truth. Then we wouldn't need this shite."

Caëtin glanced at the bloody scrawl of the rune. "Then this inquisition is sealed. Finished. Even before I explained what the parchment says."

Jundr spat in disgust. "I have a good idea of its meaning."

"You've not only admitted to betraying your kin, but that you did so to benefit another clan. I cannot argue with this admission, and you know what punishment you face."

Jundr sneered and turned away. Discomfort prickled Caëtin's skin. Something was deeply wrong, but Jundr had confessed. Allowing him to live would violate many of the Raven clan's laws.

"You shouldn't have signed unless it was true," Caëtin said. "Uktr wouldn't have believed you, but I may have."

Jundr scoffed. "None will believe me. Not with what's coming. Not with all the souls the Spiders send across this bridge." He gestured at the wraiths gliding past.

Caëtin's disbelief of how this situation unfolded simmered before her wrath crushed her initial emotion. She despised carrying out such orders for Uktr and gritted her teeth, swinging her pale blade and decapitating Jundr.

His head rolled across the bridge.

The passing dead around them wailed and paused, turning shadowy faces with glowing eyes in Caëtin's direction, studying her and the head before shrieking and gliding on. The bridge realm blurred into darkness.

Fear of what she had done stabbed Caëtin, and she blinked

repeatedly, sitting up and rubbing haze from her vision. Violet and emerald flames burned around her with unwavering light. *I've returned to Midgard.*

At the foot of Muninn's pedestal, Jundr's headless body lay in a pool of blood. The Knights Black gripped the corpse by its arms and dragged it away, leaving a smear and the head—a sacrifice and offering to Muninn.

Muninn is dead. Like all the gods. They no longer desired sacrifices.

Caëtin groaned and stood, her jaw clenching as more doubts related to what occurred in the bridge realm plagued her. At least this time, the jarl and Darstrid would approve of her actions. Her head drooped as she stepped away from the divine remains. More *goði* and *gyðja* surrounded her, their black hoods thrown back. They had dark hair and toned figures, and corded muscle protruded beneath cloaks where they wore little else. Feathers adorned their garb, although these were common raven or even crow feathers, not those of Muninn.

A tall man named Igendrn strode forward, his eyes piercingly blue and haunted. "Berserker of Muninn, will you walk me to the night chamber?" He handed her a horn, this one filled with mead. "I'll listen and ease what troubles you."

Caëtin's gaze ran down his sculpted face and neckline to his striated chest, the blocks of muscle on his stomach. Her heart beat faster. Igendrn and the other *gyðja* and *goði* of Muninn were eager to please her and any of the Knights Black when they visited the temple, and this was far from the first time Igendrn had offered himself to her. He was always her first choice. She drank the mead, its sweet and yet bitter liquid washing down her throat as some of her worries about recent events fled her mind. Who was she to refuse the overwhelming desires of the Raven?

Caëtin took Igendrn by the arm and guided him away,

another *goði* trailing behind as they ascended one tier and slipped through the slats of a curtain, passing into a small chamber with a single bed. Caëtin faced Igendrn, looking into his eyes as he dropped his cloak, its folds piling up around his feet. His pressed his chest against hers and stroked her hair.

"What troubles you?" He began removing her cloak, then her tunic and leggings until she stood naked with him, unwilling to recall the events that haunted her. He ran a hand across her bare chest, feeling everything as he went.

"Nothing you can't take away for a few minutes." Caëtin shoved Igendrn, and he fell back onto a feather bed as dark as night. Caëtin landed on top of him, bracing herself with both arms extended on the bed as she took in his eyes, his face, his chest, his stomach, his eyes again. His hands ran up and down her body as the feathers rustled beneath a thin sheet.

6

MÄRREN

Darkness pressed in around Märren even though dawn's light crept in through cracks around the doorway, doing little to banish the shadows. She curled into a ball on the floor of her hut, shivering. Some days were better than others, although when the darkness fell upon her, it usually lasted for days. A new line of runes she had carved into the back of her hand lit up in her mind, outlining the ancient symbols with fire.

She had joined with the fleeing thralls and crossed the mountains without another troll pursuit. Then, last night, she departed the group and reached her home alone.

"She won't get up again," the voice with the twisted timbre that lived in her head said, its words echoing in her ears. A dragon's tail flicked, rattling coin and treasure surrounding it.

"She'll die today," the deeper voice answered. The wolf stalked through a moonlit forest. *"She failed to reach the land of fire and ash. Again. She'll never set foot in that land no matter how many years she waits. No matter how many attempts she makes."*

"Eventually, she'll rise again and conquer each day as it comes," the third whispered. The silhouette of a child peeked out from a hazel thicket.

Märren groaned and pressed her eyes shut, fading in and out of awareness haunted by dreams of the slavers—their bodies burning as they raped their female captives. She spiraled into the shadows.

Sometime later, a fist rapped on Märren's door. She uncurled and staggered to her feet, bumping into a table and chair, spilling a bucket of water and a horn of mead. The visitor pounded again before she peered through a slit in the planks of the door.

A lone man. He had a short beard salted with gray, his frame tall and thin but laced with muscle.

"What does he want?"

"He'll kill her."

"He's here for companionship. Out of concern."

Märren pulled her furs up higher around her neck to hide the thrall collar she still wore. Other captives had probably since traded favors and pounded out each other's locking bolts, removing the irons, but she had traveled home before the others' fears had ebbed enough for them to stop and address the inconvenience.

She unlatched the door and heaved it open. Outside, her cousin, Belfedrn Nvutsson, stared down at her with lupine eyes, the neck of his chainmail *brynja* peeking over the gray fur of Fenrir, a spear in hand, shield and longbow slung across his back. The power radiating from the god-pelt vibrated Märren's skull, causing her headache to lessen and the darkness to flee to the corners. But it was usually this way with company. Being forced into a social encounter pressed back the affliction for a short time, visitors drowning out the voices in her head, but after they departed, or if they lingered for too long, the shadows would hurtle back in and grow all the stronger for the respite.

"Märren Sig—" he started, but she cut him off.

"Don't mention that name."

Belfedrn paused and nodded. "Are you well, Cousin?" A few more wrinkles had worked their way into his forehead and the skin around his lips than when she had last seen him. He was five and forty now, or close to that. Roughly eight winters older than Märren.

Märren met her cousin's gaze. Belfedrn would notice her fiery eyes. He always did, especially when the darkness in her mind had engulfed her. In the distance, his ship waited at the bank of the fjord, its sail furled, a few men hunkered down behind shields lining its sides.

"As well as can be expected." Märren winced as she rubbed her temple and tangled mess of bronze hair. Belfedrn would have no inkling that she had set out for the lands of fire and ash, and that was for the best. If he knew, he may feel betrayed.

"May I come in?"

Märren sidled aside, and Belfedrn took one long step in before pausing and glancing around, his tall and broad frame making the interior feel cramped. He stared in the direction of the hearth. Märren knew what he saw—the hideousness Märren could not live without. Her daughter's skull.

Belfedrn exited and rested his spear against the wall of the hut, his hair lifting in the wind. "Perhaps we should take a walk."

"Aye." Märren squinted against the midday light sifting through the clouds and shuffled beyond her doorway. Dead grass and late autumn snowdrifts rolled over hills dotted with birches and brush. In the distance, a stream wound through the hillocks, runnels of water creeping everywhere and flowing into the fjord at the base of the mountains. Belfedrn walked with the long, easy strides of their people, and Märren kept pace without effort as they headed for the stream. The open-mouthed wolf heads on the face of Belfedrn's shield—the symbol of a Wolf berserker, an Ulfhednar—judged her.

"Will you come home before winter falls?" Belfedrn asked.

"It isn't time."

"No?" Belfedrn studied her. "You've been out here since last winter's end. Is your grief still so thick?"

Märren paced on.

"It's time to come home and wear your piece of the pelt," Belfedrn said. "To take up the might of the hunting god. Of Fenrir. For your people, and the Ulfhednar. Before winter arrives. Before you grow too old."

"I... don't want to wear the pelt."

"Because of the old myth of the Dragon and the Spider—the Ormr and the Djarkar?"

Märren bit her lip until she drew blood, its metallic taste swimming in her mouth. "I'm not holding out for that belief. Not any longer."

"Good. Because you won't be given the parts of a god who isn't your own. You'll never take up a scale of the Dragon and command its power, much less use that power to ride some monstrous beast. Getting the Spider god's chitin is even more unlikely. Your people are there"—he pointed behind them, to the lands beyond his longship—"waiting with pelts and our might as a pack. Our magics may not be as glamorous as that of the Dragon or Spider, but ours are sound. When we work together, none can match our prowess. Alone, you—any of us—are much weaker. You're a fighter. In more ways than one." He indicated her head, referencing her affliction. "Don't you want to join the pack?"

"I want Eimri."

Belfedrn paced with his head down, silent until they reached the stream. To the north, beyond the fjord, a line of birches blended into pines and spruces, stretching away as a forest without end. He knelt and placed a small rock with a rune carved into it along the banks.

"You still leave rune stone sacrifices?" Märren asked.

"Aye."

"Even though the gods are dead?"

He shrugged. "Land wights and dark elves and dwarves still haunt these regions. The offerings are for them."

She pointed at another rune stone lying on the shore nearby. "I leave the same kind of sacrifices. But I'm not certain that it keeps all the dark spirits away. Some of them still haunt me." She tapped her head.

"Leaving sacrifices is all we can do to dissuade creatures from other realms from entering ours. And I'm not sure the darkness in your head is of their making." He motioned with a flick of his chin at the trees filling the lands to the north and running up the mountains. "It's beautiful out here, but there are plenty of trolls still living in those woods. In the winter they'll venture south, hunting."

"Just because I no longer live in the village with the pack doesn't mean that I've forgotten the dangers that lurk in our lands."

"They'll destroy this place. And eat you."

It was true. After the beast gods died, trolls and other monsters had become far more plentiful across the lands. Only the jötunn—giants—were more feared than trolls.

"That's why I have a guardian." Märren tapped the toe of her boot on the stream's surface. "No troll can cross this water without alerting the uisge."

The stream rippled beneath her boot and Belfedrn's jaw tensed as he said, "An uisge? A land wight lurks here? Their kind shouldn't leave the fjord and reside in shallow water. Especially not a stream bestowed with rune stone offerings."

"My rune stone is meant to coax the uisge into remaining here."

He regarded her with skepticism. "It's dangerous to trust such creatures. They'd just as soon eat you as look upon you."

"I saved him from a troll, and I feed him."

"*Him*?" Belfedrn's upper lip wrinkled in disgust as he stalked along the bank, shaking his head and sniffing before calming. "This lone wight isn't why I've come. Out here, you probably haven't heard, but word is the Spider's people are wearing the remnants of their dead god, wielding its magics, and crawling across the lands, creeping northward. Raiding and pillaging. Conquering. And the Raven and Sea Serpent clans recently met at the Mist Shores in hopes of forming an allegiance."

A chill washed through Märren's blood along with an onslaught of memories of the event. Belfedrn would have never expected her to leave her dwelling. "I don't believe the Sea Serpents and Ravens will be able to put aside their differences."

Belfedrn halted his pacing and nodded. "Aye. Your hunch is probably true. For the moment, I don't think we have to worry about them. Their meet seems to have ended badly."

"But if the Spiders invade the lands of other clans and claim them..."

"Then they'll take the pelts and scales of the other dead beast gods." A hint of fear hung in Belfedrn's words. "Their berserkers who wear the chitin won't be able to combine the powers of the Spider with the spoils of their pillaging, but I don't doubt their intentions of controlling more land and people. If the rumors are true, and they've already taken land from some of the lesser clans, then Horse territory could be their next target. And Wolf and Sea Serpent lands border the Horse people's."

Märren nodded her understanding of the situation and its implications for her people while using a knife to slice through a mess of rune scars on her wrist, drawing blood. This time she carved a new shape, one that sprang into her mind, the painful sting of the blade making her arm tremble.

"She cuts herself again."

"To feed the vile water beast with her flesh."

"To befriend the ancients."

Märren turned her forearm over and allowed a runnel of blood to drip into the water. The red swirled within the turbid stream. Bubbles rose.

Belfedrn stepped back from the water, gawking at her. "No one should feed an uisge. Definitely not in such a manner. This is witchery, and you are no völva—no Seidr woman."

Near Märren's blood offering, an arching neck crested the stream, water weeds in its mane along with clumps of mud. Belfedrn yanked his seax from his belt, pointing it at the creature.

"Don't worry, Cousin." Märren shook out the blood on her arm and clamped a hand over her wound. "I won't trust him enough to ride him."

Belfedrn did not take his gaze from the water as an equid tongue lapped at the blood from below the surface. "They have more ploys than making riders stick to their backs and taking them into the deeps to drown them."

"I believe I've befriended him."

"If I return again and find nothing but your liver floating in these waters, I'll know it deceived you. Then I'll kill it."

"If that day comes, I won't stop you."

Belfedrn's eyes narrowed as he studied her and eventually chuckled. "No. Then you surely won't." He stepped farther from the streambank. "Why do you resist taking a pelt and joining your pack? Did I wrong you?"

"No, of course not." Märren squeezed her cousin's arm to reassure him. "I love you, Cousin."

"Then it's the curse your mother carried in her mind. You struggle with the same darkness."

Märren looked toward the fjord.

"Don't you want to see your mate again?" Belfedrn asked. "If you hunt with the pack, you'll be with him. You can bring honor to your family's name, and when you die in battle, you'll live the glorious afterlife of a warrior or berserker."

"If women can enter Valhalla."

"The Seidr men and women agree that women who die in battle have always done so. Just like the men. This fact was only kept secret in the early ages. You know this."

"So I've heard, but my mate wasn't around much. Not too kind or loving either. Not toward Eimri or me."

"He wants to be. But you have this sickness." Belfedrn gestured at her head. "Most don't know how to deal with it."

"Or how to deal with me. Those at Nistreel, and the villagers, probably blame me for their withering crops and the threat of the Spider. They always do. Because of my curse." She took a deep breath. "Tell me true, is the pack pointing fingers in this direction?"

Belfedrn suddenly found great interest in the ground around his feet. "No. Not that I've heard." He paused. "Such curses from the gods cannot haunt you in Valhalla. Join the pack. Show them how you can fight. How you battle evil more often than they ever could, evil that's far stronger than any foe they've faced."

Märren watched the ripples fade as the red wash disappeared from the water. The wolf in her mind made her stomach cramp with fear and loathing. *I cannot embrace the Wolf. Not ever.*

After a few minutes, Belfedrn grunted. "Then you'd rather waste away here only to die alone? To spend eternity in Helheim with those who have passed from disease and old age? You, a clan member of the Wolf? Take up the pelt of Fenrir and become a warrior or berserker."

The creature in the water submerged itself, leaving only bubbles.

"She avoids committing to the pack."

"Following her pitiful desires will kill her just the same."

"She won't succumb to weakness. Her heart longs for Eimri."

"Spend eternity in Valhalla," Belfedrn continued. "Or become a Valkyrie. What else could be consuming you so much? To forget your blood and people?" Belfedrn grabbed her by her tunic and shook her, his eyes seeing some other world, probably what he had glimpsed in the darkness before the hearth. "It's that skull you keep, isn't it? You must let her go. Eimri has already crossed the Raven's bridge."

Märren swung her arm downward, breaking her cousin's strong grip and knocking his hands away. "I never want to enter Valhalla! Or become a Valkyrie. I despise the idea of either." Her spittle showered Belfedrn's face. "I'd sooner die of disease, but if there isn't one that'll take me before my time, I'll accept death by old age. But never in battle. I will join my daughter in Helheim! That's where I wish to spend eternity."

Belfedrn's shock twined with pain, both emotions contorting his expression. He had finally heard his cousin's ire flung into the world, and his anguish from realizing the life Märren meant to live sheeted from him. He probably believed such a life could not include bravery or honor. He stared in unblinking silence as time passed and the wind soughed through the forest. A howl rang from somewhere far away.

"Eimri carried your mother's curse as well, didn't she?" Belfedrn finally asked. "The same affliction that resides in your head."

Märren bit her lip, waiting until her rage abated enough for her to manage a quick nod.

"Eimri's fate doesn't have to be yours, Cousin," Belfedrn said.

"I wish for the same fate. I must end up in the same place as her."

Another spell of quiet lingered.

"Then stay the winter," Belfedrn continued. "I'll check on you again in the spring, and if the uisge and trolls haven't eaten you, I'll ask again if you'll join me and the pack. By then, I hope you've lain Eimri's skull in the earth. Let her return to dirt so she can rest. Even the dead in Helheim find relief."

Märren studied the stream where the uisge had appeared as Belfedrn turned about and retraced their path to the hut.

After Belfedrn had traveled a dozen steps, he paused, faced Märren again, and said, "I came all the way out here because we need all our warriors and berserkers now. For a potential encounter with the Spider clan, but also for something more pressing. The jarl received word that one of our villages along the northeastern border was destroyed. We found troll tracks around the area, and the scent of those creatures hung thick in the air. Such monsters are no longer afraid to leave the woods. Even our ancestors never saw such reckless killing from them. I fear we don't yet understand all that's happening or why. The pack is gathering and will set out to investigate the northlands in two days."

A tempest of emotion—not solely doubt and longing but also gratitude and regret for turning her cousin away—swirled inside Märren. However, the darkness in her head pulled her in another direction. All she could see was Eimri. The thrall collar around her neck seemed to gain weight and drag her down.

Finally, Belfedrn strode toward his longship, but he paused outside her house, retrieved his spear, and hung a pelt on her door. A pelt of Fenrir himself.

"She will never take up the pelt."

"Her cousin is outraged. As he and the pack should be. Betrayed by their own blood, the blood of the cursed. She will be left to die, like all her family."

"She held out for a scale of the Dragon and its powers for too many years, preferring it over the Wolf. Now it's too late for her to wield the power of any god."

7

BELFEDRN

THE STREETS OF THE WOLF CITY OF NISTREEL TEEMED WITH KARLS selling smoked venison and roasted pheasant. Smiths pounded orange-hot iron on anvils. Tanners stretched pelts across racks.

Belfedrn paced toward the sanctuary. The Ulfhednar were preparing for their departure. Two days seemed like too long to wait when trolls may be about Wolf territory, but Belfedrn was not pack jarl—that was Vard—and Vard had many things to deal with in addition to informing those who needed to prepare. Vard needed to weigh their options.

Dark gray pillars and towering archways of stone waited ahead. Belfedrn passed through the entrance, its steel gates open. Beyond, spruces, alders, and elms created an outer ring. Belfedrn waited, sitting against an elm, and he left a sacrifice—a rune stone. Traveling into the sacred grove and laying eyes on or feeling the power of the dead god who resided there was never easy. Not even for an Ulfhednar. Not even after years of training. And memories of those formative years as a trainee, the pains and triumphs alongside his kindred, came flooding back.

It was not long before adolescent boys and girls slipped

through the trees carrying axes and shields. The crunching of foliage under their feet raked Belfedrn's nerves. Their movements would be considered quiet by some, but they still had much to learn before they could become Wolf warriors and carry a piece of Fenrir. Only a choice few could ever hope to become a Wolf berserker, an Ulfhednar, and wear a full pelt.

One boy, taller than the rest and who had pale hair and a scrawny frame, paused as he spotted Belfedrn. The boy veered away from the group and strode toward him, moving quieter than the others. The boy smiled. "Belfedrn Nvutsson."

"Deyja." Belfedrn stood and clasped the boy in a firm embrace. "How's the training?"

A cloud passed over Deyja's face. "I think I'm ready to be tested and take on a piece of the pelt, but the masters won't allow it."

Belfedrn chuckled. "I was just as eager and believed the masters to be too old and cautious."

Deyja looked up at him. "Aye. It seems they haven't changed."

"Except those Ulfhednar who taught me are long dead, and more aged masters have taken their place. They're right. Temper your impatience. You can't become a Wolf warrior overnight."

"Overnight?" Deyja scoffed. "I've been training for over ten years. I can best any other here with the spear and axe. I can hunt with the bow. I move more stealthily than any of them." His cheeks turned red. "I'm ready."

"If you're so far ahead, perhaps you should focus more on working with them. In a pack. The Ulfhednar are only the mightiest of berserkers when we're together, especially in the shield wall. The pack is where our might and stealth and abilities stem from. We're only as strong as our weakest."

Deyja squeezed the shaft of his spear, his knuckles blanching. He exhaled slowly. "I understand." He did not sound convinced.

"Confidence can shatter fear, but arrogance will get you killed."

"Can't you teach us?"

Belfedrn laughed and put his arm around the boy's shoulder, steering him out from under the archway and into the city. "I'm not that old yet, and I don't know the first thing about teaching someone what I went through. It takes many years to learn how to instruct the young."

"But you're Ulfhednar. You survived the Wolf's den in the god's realm. You've been there, and you not only returned, you obtained many of Fenrir's abilities."

"I was scared shiteless the entire time I was in the den." Belfedrn shook his head as dark memories filled his mind. "And I had many more years of training than you do now."

Deyja grumbled something under his breath as they walked. "I don't fit in with any pack my age or younger. They... I got into a fight with a few of the boys. They surrounded me, and I still beat them back. They should fear me, but together, they think they can best me and earn back some of the respect I've taken from them."

"You have to work with them. Don't demean yourself to fit in, but don't make them want to fight you. One day, they'll be your pack mates."

Deyja shook his head and grunted. "Aye. I'll try."

They walked in silence down the street between houses.

"But that's not why I came for you," Belfedrn said.

Deyja tensed. "The only times you've come to visit me after Father died have been when I've gotten into trouble."

"I owe it to him and your mother to keep you safe. May they both be feasting in the great halls of the dead gods." He exhaled.

Memories of his and Kesg's closest friend resurfaced. Years ago, after a raid into Bear lands, both Belfedrn and Kesg had clasped their Ulfhednar comrade's bloodied hand and arm as Belfedrn made a promise to watch over his friend's son. They had been an inseparable trio. Now down to two. Belfedrn felt he owed Deyja more than he would a child of his own. He owed Deyja something that could never be repaid—a father. "I need to ask you about something."

"It wasn't my fault."

Belfedrn held up a hand. "I didn't say it was. I'm just here to ask about it. I don't want to add to your arrogance if you are the highest regarded of the litter, but it must be what made you stand out."

"All I did was travel to the Sea Serpent clan's boundary. I didn't even step foot in their land."

"But they took you anyway?"

"I was alone. The others didn't want to venture so close. I wanted to see the edge of Wolf territory and gaze upon other lands."

"But you *didn't* cross over? Don't lie to me. It's important if I speak with the Serpent people."

"Nay." Deyja swallowed and paused. "I... well, I stood on the boundary, and then a bull elk came bounding through the woods behind me, nearly crashing into me. You should've seen the size of its antlers. I've never seen one so big. I ran after it, but it was only for a few strides before I realized I may've stepped over."

"Did you cross into Sea Serpent lands or not? I need the truth."

"I think I must've. But I didn't *mean* to. A few warriors wearing Serpent scales came out of nowhere. They surrounded me. I backed away, preparing to fight, but they said my presence was nothing, that we were allies and long had been. They understood what had happened with the elk, but they said it would be appropriate if I'd return with them to their village. So their jarl could speak with me. They said it would only take a moment."

Belfedrn's blood ran hot with worry and anger for the boy. "So you accompanied a few Sea Serpent warriors deeper into their territory? Alone?"

"Aye. I felt an underlying threat, although they acted amicably."

"You fool." Belfedrn slapped the back of his head. "If you get yourself killed, I'll have failed your father. You're in no way ready to be a pack member."

Deyja's shoulders hunched as they walked deeper into the city.

Belfedrn's voice turned hard and cold. "Tell me everything."

"The warriors took me to the village. It wasn't far. Not more than an hour's jog. They offered me drink and brought me to the jarl's longhouse. I was worried, but no threats were made. No weapons drawn. I swear it. They were welcoming, like the quiet allies I've been told they are."

Belfedrn's apprehension eased.

"So I entered the longhouse with them. The jarl was friendly. He asked me who I was and what I had been hunting. About my training. I told him I was from the Wolf clan."

Belfedrn gritted his teeth. "And what did this jarl say?"

"Vegask—the jarl—offered me mead and roasted pork. I declined and said I should be getting back and that it was a simple mistake if I crossed the boundary hunting a trophy elk and all. He laughed and drank and tried to make me feel at home, but then it all felt off. He stood from his high seat and showed me around the longhouse and village, acting like we were old warrior comrades who hadn't seen each other in years."

What strange behavior.

"Then Vegask asked me if I had ever imagined becoming a Sea Serpent warrior and wielding the powers of their god," Deyja continued.

A rush of surprise hit Belfedrn like a wall. His fists clenched and unclenched. "He's insulted the Wolf. All of our people. Directly. He tried to play it off as an affable conversation, but this jarl knew what he was doing. Asking one from our litters to switch clans?" He snarled.

"He was no simple village jarl either." Deyja shook his head. "He was a Sea Serpent berserker. The power that radiated from the scales he carried was unmistakable."

Belfedrn reached into a pouch at his waist and toyed with a tiny scrap of pelt he had blackmailed a *goði* into removing from Fenrir's remains, a betrayal to the pack and their deceased god. Given the ceremonious way the strip had been removed, it retained its power, unlike a piece of pelt that had been sliced apart or desecrated—a weakness of the pelt over the parts of some of the other gods.

A mistake... Belfedrn released the scrap and hurriedly withdrew his hand. He could not get caught with it. Ahead of them, an Ulfhednar man who had seen over fifty winters paced before a longhouse, his hair steel gray, his frame broader than most of the Wolf people's.

"Vard," Belfedrn called.

The alpha of the Ulfhednar, the jarl of Nistreel, turned to regard him. "Belfedrn. You're prepared to hunt trolls?" He grinned.

"Aye, but have you heard what happened to Deyja?"

"Indeed. A Sea Serpent jarl opening his maw and showing his fangs. Maintaining his border and making sure our young lad knows to stay in our lands."

Belfedrn growled, the guttural sound rattling in his throat.

"This jarl went too far. Having his Serpent warriors bring Deyja to his village without another member of our pack present and trying to entice Deyja or threaten him into joining the Sea Serpent clan should not be tolerated."

"The Serpents are our quiet allies and neighbors. They long have been. Trolls, on the other hand, are our enemies and there's a decimated village we must find justice for."

"Aye, but we don't leave for another couple days. I'm ready now. I wish to run to the Serpent village Deyja was taken to and share a few words with this Vegask."

Vard shook his head, the long hair tied down the middle of his scalp flopping around the stubbled sides of his skull. He rubbed at his shaved cheeks and chin. "We'd depart now, but with the threat of trolls, we're waiting for Athna and Eakthr to return from their hunt in the north."

"I could visit the village and return before the Ulfhednar depart."

"A run to this village and back will leave you exhausted, not to mention pressed for time. We cannot allow another troll attack."

"I want those trolls' heads as much as any, but those beasts should've had their fill for weeks. I'll return before the pack is ready to depart, and if I lag, you can take my house as your own."

Vard pondered his offer. "I don't want your house. I want you alert and ready to hunt."

"I will be."

"And you think to do this alone? Without another pack mate?"

"I'll take Lyrne."

Vard grunted in capitulation. "If my second agrees to it, I'll allow it. And seeing that your mind is set, I have no doubt you'll be able to convince your mate. But neither of you should wear yourselves thin with this. Visit this jarl, speak with him as amiably as you can, but let him know what he did does not sit well with his peaceful neighbors, that we will not tolerate him taking a lone youth again."

"I'll return before anyone notices I'm gone."

8

BELFEDRN

LYRNE STEPPED OFF THE LONGSHIP DOCKED AT THE FAR BANK OF the Scalefanged River. Belfedrn slipped past a few men and women on board, following his mate and stalking into the woods near the Wolf clan's border. Rain drizzled, running off the canopy and dropping in streams.

Lyrne's long pale hair waved around her pelt of Fenrir, which she wore over her shoulders, as she took fast loping strides. She stood a hand taller than Belfedrn and was beautiful, her lupine eyes turning to regard him as they moved through the vegetation. Power seeped from her, hers and Belfedrn's amplified by each other's company.

Convincing his mate to accompany him to this Sea Serpent village had not proved difficult. He had not even needed to beg, not after he shared what Deyja had told him and Lyrne realized the extent of his worries about what could have happened to the boy he vowed to protect. But they had had to sail far and would have to run in order to arrive at the village in a day.

Only Lyrne knew that Belfedrn had stolen scraps of hide from Fenrir, but she believed it had only been once and agreed not to inform Vard if he did not do it again. Unfortunately, he had, which he kept secret from her.

They loped on for hours until weariness fell over them. If Belfedrn had asked his closest comrade, Kesg, to come, he would have joined them as well, but Belfedrn did not want to tire the man out or get him in trouble with his mate. Not again. And Kesg was growing older and more bitter. So was Belfedrn.

"The border runs below our feet." Lyrne paused and grinned.

"These Serpents won't hear two Ulfhednar coming for them." Belfedrn tugged his pelt over his shoulders. The scents of the forest lay thick around him, his enhanced hearing of the Wolf catching sounds of distant prey. "I'm no adolescent trainee, so promise you'll wait outside the village while I speak with the jarl. You can always come running if there's a need."

"There won't be such need. Not from the Sea Serpents. They've been affable with us, if not withdrawn, for decades and most reside on their isles. I think they must realize that if they create any problems, the Wolves could wipe out their few warriors and berserkers on the mainland."

Belfedrn did not allow her distracting words to sway him. "Swear it."

"I swear it." She grinned ruefully and slapped his backside. "Stay safe."

Belfedrn grunted and plowed on ahead, weaving through trees and brush, mindful of the details of Deyja's story and how to get to the village, as the boy's scent was fleeting at best. Lyrne followed but remained behind. In under an hour of travel, a village emerged in the fields beyond, the smell of the sea strong enough for a Wolf nose to detect, even if those waters were still leagues away.

Belfedrn waved for Lyrne to remain hidden as he jogged toward the border of the village and slowed to a walk, spear and shield in hand, longbow slung over his shoulder. Seax and axe at his waist. Twilight was fading, although ebbing sunlight only made his Wolf's vision keener. His ears perked up, catching subtle noises—a man drinking from a horn inside a nearby house, another walking down a muddy street beyond. He veered between huts and approached a longhouse at the center of the village.

"Ah!" a Serpent man in a red tunic shouted, pointing. "A Wolf man." He retreated, yelling gibberish.

Belfedrn stood before the longhouse doors, waiting. Unarmed karls from the village appeared, watching but keeping their distance. The doors before him parted, and a muscular warrior wearing a partial scale of the Serpent stepped out, an axe in his fist. A towering brute of a man followed, two axes at his waist. The second man had a black beard and a braid of hair running down the center of his head, silver bands binding both. Gold bands were clamped around his wrists and upper arms. The Sea Serpent people were wealthy from the sea and trade, and their warriors and berserkers typically wore jewelry, but this man's riches were excessive. Belfedrn did not see the point of any of it.

"Jarl Vegask?" Belfedrn asked.

"Aye, Ulfhednar," the brute of a man said. "Have you come alone? To pay us a visit?"

"I believe you know why I've come."

Vegask stepped past his warrior, a cloying smirk tugging at his lips. "To honor our comradery? Our king recently stationed me here as the new jarl. I'm from the isles, but I've accepted the task and seek to find my way on the mainland beside the Wolf people—neighbors who have been our allies since my father's father was a boy. Since the fall of sly jarl Muthg and the last raids between our clans."

"Then I forgive you for not understanding how things have

been between us." Belfedrn dipped his head in acknowledgment. "But do not *ever* take a young trainee of ours into your lands. Not alone and escorted by your warriors. And you certainly do not invite him into your longhouse to be intimidated by you and your men."

"Oh, the boy." Vegask chuckled and held his midsection. "That's what this is about. I never meant to intimidate him. My warriors found him in our lands and brought him here. It wasn't per my orders or wishes. Those are the laws. The same as with your people, I believe. I simply wanted to make sure he felt safe and that no one was threatening him. I offered him all the food and drink he desired. Then we escorted him back to your lands. No harm done."

"Aye. No harm done. He's a boy and was hunting a great elk. He lost track of his territory. A small slip, but a mistake, nonetheless. I wouldn't fault you or your warriors for questioning him. Even for bringing him to you, although that seems unnecessary for one boy."

"I thought your people always traveled in packs." Vegask raised up on his toes and glanced behind Belfedrn.

"We usually do, but Wolves sometimes grow curious and investigate things alone. And he seems to recall you making him an offer."

"Oh?"

"To leave his people and join yours." Belfedrn tried not to reveal any emotion, his anger simmering.

Vegask laughed, bracing his hands on his knees. "Quite a kick, isn't it? To hear a jarl offer a random Wolf boy a place with his own people? I thought it might make him proud—that we'd want him simply by looking upon him and gauging his worth, that he would one day be able to take up a part of our dead god."

"We do not take one another's people."

"I see. But I wouldn't think it would be such an insult unless you were afraid he might turn against you."

Belfedrn stepped forward and sucked in a deep breath. He could almost hear Lyrne behind him, almost feel her grasping his shoulder, telling him not to kill a jarl of their allies for a mere insult. That would lead to escalating hostilities. He regretted acting wise and cursed under his breath, "Fuck their dead Serpent god, and tear his heart from his chest." Then, louder, he said, "I'm not worried that the boy will join you, but I believe it was meant as a threat for carelessly crossing the boundary without permission. The Wolf warriors and Ulfhednar know not to do this, but we cannot control every trainee and child."

"And yet here you are, standing in our territory without permission, Ulfhednar." The jarl's smirk grew tighter. "I was merely being courteous to an untrained boy who could've been killed, which may've happened if he'd crossed into the territory of another clan who was not so friendly."

The warning made Belfedrn's hackles spike. He took another step forward, considering impaling this berserker.

A hand slapped onto his shoulder from behind. He attempted to wheel about, but Lyrne was there, having made no sound in her approach, her scent still lingering in Belfedrn's nostrils from their travels so that he did not notice her proximity. Not while he was distracted.

"Come, my mate," Lyrne said, probably realizing that Belfedrn had meant to slay the haughty man. "You've had your discussion. I believe both sides are at fault, and now the issue is resolved. We are still on good terms."

Belfedrn resisted her until she tugged harder, her fingers like teeth in his flesh.

"You should listen to your mate, Ulfhednar," Vegask said. "I'm elated that you forgave me—as you said. We don't want any other unfortunate events to occur. Not so soon after my arrival on the mainland."

Belfedrn glared at the Serpent berserker, the threat of death more evident than the sun on a rare clear day of winter. The rules had been set, the consequences for further grievances unambiguous, even if they had not been spoken directly.

"We must return to Nistreel," Lyrne whispered. "We've a long road back."

Belfedrn glared at Vegask for another minute as the jarl held his smirk in place, then Belfedrn turned and strode away with his mate. A quiet conversation between the jarl and his warrior began, and the locals of the village watched them depart, fear and uncertainty seeping from them.

9

CAËTIN

THE TABLES INSIDE THE JARL'S GREAT HALL TEEMED WITH RAVEN warriors and berserkers. So many for such an early hour. Caëtin strode for the raised chair at the end of the central walk, although she searched for her children, worrying they spent too much time around Uktr. Those around eyed her, gulping from horns and slurping up stews brimming with fired meat and dark root vegetables—not atypical for any dagmal meal, the dregs from last night's nattmal served in the morning. It was only the early hour that was off.

Darstrid, the Raven's battle Seidr, sat beside the reedy jarl. Darstrid held magics no one else could wield, magic that came from her Seidr powers and not those tied to the remains of a dead god. The jarl kissed his adopted first daughter on the head, and she stopped slurping from her bowl as Caëtin neared. On the jarl's other side sat his two closest comrades and advisors—Grimmurk and Freydeg, men who had shared most of their lives with the jarl. When Uktr, Freydeg, and Grimmurk were together, all they did was drink and relive old tales of valor and death. Grimmurk's beard and hair had turned gray, his scars numerous across his face and shaved sides of his scalp, his face dark.

Freydeg appeared similar but with silver bands on his arms and more blond in his hair.

"Sister, how did the inquisition fare?" Darstrid asked.

Adopted sister. All of the jarl's surviving children were adopted. Although Darstrid was usually kind, unlike with many true sisters, she liked to remind Caëtin that they had no blood relation. But she had not mentioned that now. "As expected. Once on the Raven's bridge, it didn't take long for Jundr to sign a confession."

The jarl sat with a blank expression, his eyelids drooping above his hooked, beak-like nose as if he had not yet fully woken. He held a horn of mead, its contents reaching the rim but not spilling over. This man always desired his horn to be as full as possible, and although he lacked in many other areas, keeping his drink hand steady was one of his greatest skills.

"You took care of the traitor, then?" Darstrid asked.

"Indeed. Once he signed, I had few options left." She carried her doubts, but she could not have ignored her duty after a confession. Except she had not upheld the jarl's law with that boy who tried to steal one of Muninn's feathers. Violence and punishment were needed in this world, but Uktr was always eager to take them too far.

Darstrid pursed her lips in contemplation, their pinkness striking in the gray light, an apology lingering in her eyes. "Your next task for the failed meet at the Mist Shores has already been set by the jarl."

Caëtin's attention wandered to Uktr, who stared blankly at a torch. Grimmurk whispered some jovial comment and smacked Uktr on the back, and Grimmurk, Freydeg, and Uktr all bellowed with laughter before falling silent as Caëtin waited.

Uktr coughed but did not acknowledge her. Darstrid reached over and brushed the jarl's shoulder with a finger. "Father. Caëtin is here."

"Caëtin?" Uktr blinked several times and glanced around. He squeezed Darstrid's hand like a loving father. "Ah, yes. Darstrid, the dagmal is nearly consumed. Eat your fill. It'll be long before nattmal is served."

"Of course, Father. I always do."

"You sent for me, Jarl?" Caëtin asked. "In the temple?"

The glossiness in Uktr's eyes cleared as he focused on Caëtin. "You can carry more of Muninn than any other, Caëtin, but you fucked us. The Mist Shores? The Sea Serpents?" He shook his head with disappointment. "Not even the mighty Darstrid would meet the Serpent people for trading goods. It could've been a trap, and then you and most of your Knights Black would be no more."

"I take full responsibility," Caëtin said. *His anger seethes and his memory returns.* "There was a small trap, but I avoided it. I believe we spoke of this already. Yesterday."

"Yesterday? You think I should just let such poor decisions lie?"

"Perhaps once?"

His cheeks flared. "No! That's why I called you here. You must renew my respect and belief that you should take this seat after me. A messenger has arrived from Sparsgard, a village in the southern reaches. The people there haven't brought me any taxes or offerings in far too long. None for summer's end. Now they have a problem and came begging. It seems some of their children have gone missing."

"Children?" Caëtin cocked her head in disbelief as she looked around again for her own. None of the berserkers of any god sought out and killed children. "How many?"

"It started a fortnight ago with one, but now only a handful of children remain at the settlement. You'll take a small order of the Knights Black and travel to the village."

"I shall." Caëtin flashed her sternest expression. Uktr was

not kind to anyone but his family, but he would be more worried about children than taxes, no matter what he said. After all, he adopted many Raven children after they lost their parents, even if he only chose those who could bear a remnant of Muninn. "I'll leave as soon as the berserkers have finished eating. They'll need sustenance for the journey."

Uktr grunted and wiped at his beard, his drink hand unwavering. "When I was young, we fought our enemies with axe and spear, and if those failed, we used our fists and teeth. We carved our lands from those around us, raiding and building kingdoms while protecting our people."

What is your point?

"We took what we could and live better for it. We never surrendered or tucked our heads beneath our wings, hiding when we worried another clan was trying to take our lands. We had honor and pride. We accepted the world the gods had fashioned for what it was. We did this, did we not, Grimmurk?" He turned to his comrades. "Freydeg?"

Grimmurk flashed a smile consisting of several broken teeth. "Always, my friend."

Freydeg grunted his agreement.

Uktr faced Caëtin again. "But now my favored child seeks to parley with our adversaries. To make amends and forge friendships with people who've butchered ours."

Caëtin's stomach turned. He was still outraged by her attempt to negotiate with the Serpents. Whenever she failed, it was doubly awful because he tore her a new arsehole in front of everyone while also claiming to love and trust her most of all his children.

"The last time our people died at the hands of the Serpents was decades ago," Caëtin said. "In the mist raids. I was only a child. If any of those who harmed our people are still alive, they must be few and far between."

"But the blood of those bastards flows through the veins of their offspring." Uktr's beaked nose wrinkled. "And you sought to befriend them!"

Caëtin decided it was best not to answer.

Uktr's chest heaved as his fury rolled off him. "Remain strong and fly swiftly for Muninn and the lands where she bled her last and died to end the war of the gods. For she who blessed our people with her final resting place, those she bestowed with her mighty gifts. *Your* people."

Caëtin bowed her head, pivoted about, and strode away, stopping to grab a bowl of stew and a trencher laden with fired oats. She gulped the food down, both dishes hot and savory. Taknhal—a man of five and thirty winters and her adopted brother—cast her a smile from a nearby table. He was tall and handsome, his hair dark and braided. He wobbled in his seat.

Already drunk. Caëtin did not often find him in any other state. He was Uktr's son but further down the line to become the next jarl.

"Mother!" Treln ran from one of the tables and embraced Caëtin around the waist before stepping back. Lythi followed him. "You didn't return last night."

"I had much to do."

"And now the jarl is making you leave again." His eyes blurred with tears.

A Raven warrior strode past, brushing against Treln on his way to the stew. Treln wheeled about and punched him in the back of the leg.

The warrior paused and glanced down, then knelt before Treln and tousled his hair. "He's a feisty one, Caëtin. Will make a good warrior."

Treln balled up his fists and growled, slugging the warrior in the face once and then again and again before the warrior overcame his surprise and shoved the boy. Treln went flying backward, landing on his back with a thump. The warrior wiped at his bleeding lip and eyed Caëtin before turning and striding away.

Treln wailed, tears streaming, and Caëtin loomed over him and said, "You shouldn't have done that."

Treln punched the floor as he scrambled to his feet and ran off toward the stairs, hiding under them. Growing up under Uktr would turn her boy into as violent of a man as the jarl. She needed to find a line that Treln would understand should not be crossed. He had to learn to use his head and wits more than Uktr ever had and to be more understanding.

"Take care of your brother until I return," Caëtin said to Lythi.

The young girl nodded. "I'll try, although he doesn't listen to me."

"I know this. Do the best you can."

Lythi glanced toward the great hall's doors. "I'd rather wander outside the city and listen to the cawing of crows and ravens. To sleep with wolves howling in the forest."

Caëtin hugged her daughter and then cupped her cheek. "My little one, you are like your father. Like Treln is like his. You will be a *gyðja*. I'll take you to the woods soon, but don't leave the city. Not while I'm away."

"Of course, Mother." Lythi stalked toward the stairs.

Uktr's voice rose behind Caëtin as he admonished another. The jarl had wandered over to the closest table and had singled out one of the Raven warriors and a Knight Black, jabbing a finger at their faces. "You damn well should defend your slain comrades and their feathers better than you did at the Mist Shores. If a boy can slip past you and steal a feather of Muninn, only the dead gods know who else can. When I was a berserker, I would've died before allowing a petrified lump of Muninn's shite to fall into the hands of someone who wasn't a Raven warrior."

Caëtin paused from devouring her meal. She could approach the jarl, distract him or take the blame, save her fighters the embarrassment. That was what a true hero of the Raven should do. She hesitated. Uktr would then focus on her again, and the jarl's beratement of her usually lessened her standing in the eyes of the warriors. *Bollocks.* She wolfed downed more of the stew.

"Caëtin." Darstrid tugged on Caëtin's cloak, attempting to guide her outside. Darstrid's voice was a whisper. "The jarl is losing his mind."

Caëtin chewed and swallowed, preferring not to answer as she followed Darstrid outside and into gusting wind and the darkness of morning before dawn.

"Oh, stop fretting over what you say about him," Darstrid said. "You know it. I know it. It's been getting worse. After you left to question Jundr, he ordered the warriors out of the great hall to help the karls refortify the walls of his longhouse while the walls of Aonark crumble. The Knights Black are already tired, and some will have to fly far."

"You mean to challenge him?" Caëtin arched an eyebrow as she scooped oats into her mouth.

"Nay. Don't suggest such things."

"If you don't, someone else could."

"Then I must defend him."

"And let him remain jarl?"

Darstrid sighed as they paced around the perimeter of the longhouse without destination. "I believe you know what we should do."

"I don't. I'd simply like him to keep his mouth shut."

Darstrid glanced over her shoulder, uneasy. "With the recent

Sea Serpent encounter and other unrest, I'm thinking we should allow our people and the outsiders to believe our jarl is strong in both body and mind so trade can grow and flourish without war. So coin can flow through our lands. Uktr must be seen as a man no others would risk doing battle with. The other clans may try to kill you and me, but not Uktr. Not with the reputation he's earned."

"Sounds like your plot to replace him is going well, then, eh?"

Darstrid held up a hand to silence her. "I don't need your endless sarcasm. Before you return, I'll have spoken with the Knights Black who remain behind. Then, both of us shall have a meet beyond the gates with the berserkers and warriors. Uktr could remain jarl in title, but I'm hoping most of the others will understand what must be done. They should all come to you and me for an agreed command before acting on anything the jarl proposes."

Caëtin pondered that. They would be traitors to the jarl, and if he found out, he could demand their heads. But if the berserkers and warriors obeyed Darstrid and Caëtin, Uktr would have no power to enforce such punishment. He would become nothing more than a man on a seat and a threat to outsiders, his waning mind no longer posing a risk for their people. She imagined Uktr wandering around the great hall and surrounding area of Aonark in a daze, issuing commands to the Raven people, the jarl still mighty and a power to behold, if only in his mind. Those he issued orders to would pretend to obey and rush away in response, but nothing would come of it.

"It'll be dangerous," Caëtin finally answered. "For me. He'll forgive you and believe it to be my idea."

"That's why it'll be wiser for me to hold the first meet. Once I have the oaths of the berserkers and warriors who aren't coming with you, Uktr won't be dangerous to anything other than the walls of his loft as he curses at them every morning and evening."

"You believe my errand in the south will be meaningless?"

"Not meaningless. There's probably some issue with Sparsgard and their children—plague, dark elves or dwarves crawling up from the deeper reaches of the world, or another violent madman—but you shouldn't concern yourself with a small village's taxes. Not at this time. We must take charge while we have the chance and not wait until our enemies are at our doorstep. Find what you can but return swiftly."

Darstrid clapped Caëtin on the shoulder and gave her a quick embrace. For all their family dynamics, in the end, they always supported one another.

"He doesn't hate you, you know," Darstrid said.

"He's good at making me believe he does."

"He demands strength and decisions that lead to victories and sees all other happenings and outcomes as weaknesses that should be stamped out."

"A man whose only strength is outrage could hardly recognize anything else."

"It is what it is."

A dozen Knights Black exited the great hall, one after another, hoods pulled over their bowed heads as they formed ranks near the doors and awaited Caëtin's command.

None of the Raven warriors would be able to accompany them. *Not by the means we will use to travel.* She hoped each of the berserkers would be bearing as many feathers as their resilience allowed. The size and number of god parts that an individual could carry all depended on their training and inherent abilities, but it was the *gyðja* and the jarl who decided how many items each person was allotted. Since this venture was not deemed to be too dangerous, Caëtin doubted these people carried more than a berserker's standard wing or tail feather. Yet they were still far more powerful than a Raven warrior, who could only carry a head or breast feather.

Caëtin always carried a second feather in her blade and usually bore more when she traveled—as many as she could manage without the god power dulling her mind and senses too much. What she considered an appropriate amount of feathers was well beyond what any of the other berserkers could handle. She had traveled deeper into Muninn's realm and abode and claimed additional magics no other warrior or Knights Black had, and she had done so before the flaming raven reached her and sent her to Helheim—the potential cost of delving too deep in a quest for power.

A raven sat perched on a crate nearby, eyeing her.

"Oh, fuck, Huginn," she muttered to the bird. "I don't have time for your gifts or to dole out tender touches. Not now." Caëtin faced one of her favored Knights Black. "Sanre. I must ask you to stay here."

Sanre cocked her head, disappointment pulling her lips downward, her red braids dangling.

"I am sorry, but I need someone I can trust to look into why Uktr believed Jundr was a traitor. I need to know if Uktr had a legitimate reason to have him killed."

"There was a traitor at the Mist Shores," Sanre said. "Don't you recall that one of our warriors tried to kill you?"

"Indeed, but we had a trusted berserker as a witness to that man's betrayals, and many at the shores saw him try to kill me. Find what you can."

Sanre dipped her head in acceptance.

"You carry part of Muninn with you?" Caëtin asked the other berserkers to alleviate her fears.

"Indeed," one the berserkers answered.

"Aye," another said.

"Then we fly." Caëtin clutched her pale sword, and she

collapsed, pulled apart into a flurry of wings and beaks and talons. Her unkindness squawked and took to the sky, streaking southward.

The Knights Black burst into similar clusters of birds, soaring after her, leaving Sanre behind.

Below, Huginn watched Caëtin wing away and squawked. Darstrid raised a hand in farewell.

10

BELFEDRN

The longship ran aground on the distant shore of the river, barely more than the scraping of sand sounding beneath them. Belfedrn's back burned with fatigue as he pulled his oar in and stowed it in the hull before opening the trunk he sat on to retrieve his chainmail *brynja* and weapons. Other Ulfhednar furled the ship's dark sail with the wolf head on it, its fabric rippling in the wind.

"You tired already?" Kesg—Belfedrn's closest comrade—asked in a whisper. He was shorter than most of the others but stockier, his hair and beard dark with patches of gray.

"Save your energy for worrying about your own arthritic joints and if you'll be able to keep your head above water." Belfedrn nodded at the river.

"We're in the shallows at..." Kesg scoffed. "Ah, another jest about height." He shook his head and grumbled.

"You two, stop your banter." Lyrne shot them a stern look.

Ylsga, Kesg's mate, seconded the notion as she tightened her braids of silver hair.

Belfedrn leapt over the side of the ship and waded through frigid water that rose to his knees. His oiled boots and leggings allowed only minimal water to seep through. He glanced back at Kesg and was dismayed to find the water only reaching his comrade's upper thighs. The Ulfhednar man was still tall compared to most people.

Belfedrn stepped onto shore and trotted alongside his brethren, shield to shield when the terrain allowed it. Moonlight poured through the clouds, silvering a landscape spotted with snow and rock. Fog sat heavy over everything, mountains jutting up to either side, waterfalls cascading in tiers through mist and trees.

Strength flowed through Belfedrn's arms as he gripped his spear and shield, his *brynja* rolling under his portion of Fenrir's pelt, a longbow slung over his back. He was weary from his recent travels to Sea Serpent territory but hid it well. His armor and footsteps did not create a sound, the power of the dead god suffusing him, the divine parts granting him and his kin peak strength at night.

If only Märren was not alone at night.

Odors ran in rivers, Belfedrn's nostrils picking up the scents of men and creatures who had passed this way within the last few days. He crouched beside a broken blade of grass, sniffing and listening. The score of Ulfhednar, in their wolf pelts and with black paint around their eyes and lines down their cheeks, slowed their pace.

Lyrne knelt beside him, peering into the trees, her lupine eyes bright against the dark markings on her cheeks and her pale hair. "Blood lingers in the air."

"I don't smell it." Kesg sniffed.

"You couldn't smell a pile of dog shite in your own bed," Belfedrn muttered.

"What is it, Belfedrn?" Vard sniffed and cocked his head, his hair short and steel gray. A bearded axe rested over the jarl's shoulder. "Your nose is the keenest."

"Our prey came through here." Belfedrn plucked a blade of grass from the earth and held its broken blade aloft. There was enough moonlight for the Wolf berserkers to see the grass as clearly as any man could on a sunny day. "Though they were moving carefully in an attempt to conceal their trail."

"Into the trees, then?"

"As we expected," Belfedrn answered. "But they hide their passing well. This could be a mistake." He twirled the blade of grass and laid his spear aside before pressing his fingertips into a dark stain hidden beneath a tussock. He did not even have to smell the liquid, its metallic aroma flooding his nose. "There's also blood... I suspect our quarry wants to lead us this way."

"Your instincts have saved us more than once." Vard's shaven face contorted with thought. He glanced at Belfedrn's mate, who was the second of the pack, the berserker ranked above everyone but the jarl. Vard would typically listen to her advice first, but he returned his attention to Belfedrn. "Which direction would you take?"

Belfedrn glanced about, his acute ears picking up a rustle of feet deep in the forest. "We've come across no other trail. To find them, we may have to travel the way they want us to go. But we should be wary."

"This is no witless troll we track." Lyrne stood, her powerful frame looming over Belfedrn. "Something more cunning is at work here."

"Raven or Bear?" Ylsga asked.

"Or Dragon," Vard said.

"Dragons are recluses." Belfedrn stood tall beside his mate, both of them bathed in moonlight. "Deceptive and malevolent certainly, but coming here to set a ruse doesn't smell of their scales."

Vard grunted his capitulation. "Possibly the Spider?"

Kesg scoffed. "The Spider's people would've had to cross

over Raven land and then reach our northern territory without being seen. Not even their people command such stealth."

"Let's hope not," Belfedrn added. "The Raven may have made another furtive allegiance. This time with the Spider."

"Or the Spider could have taken the long way around," Lyrne said.

"Through the territories of the Stag and Boar *and* Bear clans?" Kesg shook his head.

"Or across Sea Serpent domain and the sea and through the Unclaimed Lands." Lyrne met his gaze, defiant. "The Serpent people could've traveled that path as well."

"Enough speculation." Vard pointed at Belfedrn. "You're flank. You asked for the position earlier." He waved them onward. "Into the trees. But not far enough apart that you can't watch each other's backs."

"For the Wolves!" a little more than a score of members shouted in unison.

They fell into formation, side by side, shields pressing together as they loped to the old forest, where the mist hung thickest. Belfedrn separated from Lyrne to pass around a trunk, his keen nose, eyes, and ears working, wary of an attack coming from anywhere, including from the boughs above. He rested his spear's shaft against the edge of his shield, poised for a strike, and advanced. The smell of blood peppered the air here, thicker than where he had found the stain.

"I smell them." Lyrne charged onward, the Ulfhednar second leading the pack.

"I can now as well, and I hear them," Kesg added and ran.

Vard gestured for the others to follow Lyrne and Kesg as he hefted his axe. "I fear what we're about to find."

Belfedrn hurdled a clump of brush, landing and sprinting after his mate and closest comrade, keeping his ears open, Ylsga at his shoulder. The pack pursued their prey now, salivating for battle, which added to their strength but would make them less wary of an ambush. Barren birch and ash and pine branches whipped past Belfedrn as he ran, his blood roiling with the chase, his heart racing, an urge to howl pounding within him.

The crunching of feet grew closer to the pack, then quickened, their prey sensing danger and fleeing. Then the crunching was gone, but something much larger and unafraid lingered. It moved slower. Since it was Belfedrn's turn to take flank, he circled around as the pack approached a dell against a mountainside. Every Wolf detested the two lone positions flanking the pack, but battles had been lost when reserves and flanks had not been kept. It was a necessary evil even for the Ulfhednar.

Belfedrn's brethren plunged into the clearing, shouting and howling as he veered left and scrambled onto a boulder, leaping to another and another, rising higher and higher, each stone more moss-bearded than the last. He stopped on the tallest outcropping, gazing down into the moonlit clearing.

The Ulfhednar snarled as they plowed into the dell, their shields emblazoned with wolf heads locked into a wall, spears and axes jutting from crevices. A pool of blood surrounded a central elm, stains smeared up the trunk. Frayed ropes were scattered across the ground, gathering more blood. Vard lowered his shield and approached, his axe poised for battle as he studied his surroundings. All lay still.

"The smell of troll lingers," their leader said, "but it's not strong enough for one to be nearby."

A few others broke away from the shield wall, fanning out.

"Victims were tied to this tree, and a troll ripped them free to eat them." Lyrne strode toward the elm, stalking about with her spear, sniffing and scrutinizing the scene. She froze, staring at something in the boughs.

A body hung there, partially concealed and impaled on a few high branches that had been shorn off, its head lolled to one side. Belfedrn stalked about on the boulder, his ears straining for the slightest sound, his nose working. Blood dripped from the body's hands and feet into the pool below, its chest and abdomen torn open, bowel hanging like coils of rope.

This was ceremonial, or bait.

One of the boulders on the opposite side of the clearing but close to his comrades shifted, unfolding. Belfedrn bellowed, pointing with his spear. The other flanking Ulfhednar stood upon the shifting rock, peering downward. Draping moss and lichen split apart as a creature rose, grabbing the berserker on its shoulders and breaking his legs with a squeezing fist. Bones crunched.

The rising troll lashed out in an arc, lunging closer but remaining on the opposite side of the pack from Belfedrn. The monster's sweeping blow crashed through three more Ulfhednar as Belfedrn tamped the boulder he stood upon with his spear to be certain it was not alive.

"Shield wall!" Vard roared.

The troll, a massive male in rut—signified by its branching antlers and the tusks protruding from its jaw—lumbered closer, bellowing in the tongue of the dead beast gods, its slow drawl difficult to understand. "Mine!"

The Ulfhednar amassed, taking formation, spears and axes poised for attack. The troll swung its club at the shields, breaking off weapon tips. Belfedrn unshouldered his longbow, drawing and loosing an arrow in one motion. The projectile streaked across the clearing and impaled the troll in the cheek, but the beast merely swatted at it like it was an annoying insect.

Another boulder, this one closer to the mountainside, shifted. Belfedrn's heart dropped.

Lyrne, who was at the side of the shield wall, spun about, but she was too late. A granite club slammed into her shield and then chest, crunching bones and hurling her into the bloody elm.

"My tree!" this troll roared. "My dead!"

Belfedrn nearly fell from his position, his longbow dropping from his grip as his heart clenched and fear and disbelief rode through him on dark hooves. He crouched and regripped his spear, summoning the power and strength of his pelt before leaping, spear held backhand. He flew through air and nearly collided with the second troll before his weapon rammed into its mossy hide, punching deep into its back. This beast also bore a gigantic rack of antlers and tusks. Males of this size never shared company.

The troll roared in pain and reached around for Belfedrn. After hanging by the shaft of his spear, Belfedrn let go of his weapon, having slowed his momentum from the leap. He dropped the height of two men, landing heavily in a squat but drawing his seax at the same time. The beast inside him howled, and its instincts flooded him. He was taking down much larger prey—what the Wolf thirsted for. He swiped at the tendon on the back of the troll's ankle just above its foot. His blade bit deep, hewing through skin and partway through the tendon.

"Break the wall and hunt!" Vard yelled from the other side of the troll, and the clatter of shields and steel followed as many pounding feet sprinted about the clearing.

The troll before Belfedrn bellowed as he wrenched his blade from its flesh. He hacked again, cutting most of the way through the tendon as the troll swung around, its wounded leg buckling. The monster leaned to that side before bracing itself on its empty hand, its club arcing toward Belfedrn. He ducked and darted under its legs, its swollen stones dangling over him as he considered cleaving one of them from the troll's body. But that would only enrage the beast more. Instead, he buried his blade into its inner thigh where the largest vessels ran beneath its skin.

Dark blood erupted, running down his blade and arm and over his pelt as he yanked his weapon free and pulled away.

The creature fell to its knees, wavering.

Growling and howls swooped up behind Belfedrn as the Ulfhednar fell into their berserker attacks without thought, driving spears and seaxes into the flesh of both trolls only to rip them free and impale their adversaries again, the weapons like biting teeth. Axe blades rent muscle and bone on the creatures' legs and arms. Their pack's battle Seidr flung the white fire of the Wolf from her hand. Their thief dived in, striking with furtive attacks in vital areas. The troll before Belfedrn toppled, and he barely rolled out of its path before its body thumped onto the earth. More of his brethren swarmed the monster, driving blades deep into its torso and neck as they yipped and cheered.

By the time Belfedrn clambered to his feet, the troll lay still, its club rolling away from its limp fist. The first troll had also dropped to a knee, spear shafts sticking from its hide like arrows from an archery dummy. Kesg and his mate launched onto its chest, hacking at its throat, Ylsga's silvery hair waving, her long limbs blurring with the enhanced speed and strength from her pelt.

Belfedrn sprinted for Lyrne, dropping his seax and shield and sliding across the ground to reach her. He cradled her head. Her shield lay crushed beside her, the shattered haft of her spear clutched in a tight fist. Her breathing was shallow, her eyes already turning glassy, one side of her chest and ribs concaved.

No! Belfedrn shook his head, biting his lip and holding back a rush of tears. "You'll be fine."

11

MÄRREN

THE DARKNESS FLED, RETREATING TO THE CORNERS OF MÄRREN'S mind, taking the voices and figures with it. She stepped outside the hut near the fjord, sunlight stinging her eyes as she shielded her face from its muted rays.

"This will be good for me," she muttered.

She sauntered down to the stream, her axe at her waist, and followed the current toward the fjord, whose waters were as still as the sky they reflected. Once she reached the fjord, she meandered along its banks, her hand on the skull in her pouch. Eimri's voice played in her head.

"Mother," Eimri called, the ghost of her memory running along the shore, splashing through the water as she laughed, her hands in the air, her bronze hair waving behind her.

"Do you feel better?" Märren had asked.

Eimri ran onward, hollering, acting like a typical child who had completed their tasks for the day. "I feel the sun." She spun a circle. "And the icy water on my feet."

"Then, the voices are gone?"

Eimri sprinted away, flinging water in her wake.

Perhaps I shouldn't mention them when they finally leave her be.

Remembering them only gives them strength. Märren followed Eimri's spirit, Märren's hand still clutching her daughter's skull, recalling the contours when flesh and hair had covered it. Eimri's laughter drove the dragon and wolf in Märren's mind further away.

Märren jogged after her daughter, a bittersweet longing for other children to come and play with Eimri tugging at her heart. Eimri deserved to have friends, but other children would not be available only at times when Eimri was well. They also would not understand why there were so many times when she could not play.

Eimri picked up a length of driftwood and stuck one end against her cheek. "Look, Mother, I'm a Narwhal." She giggled. "The remains of my god are hidden somewhere at sea. I sail with her magics to guide me, and the sea offers me safe passage wherever I go." She leaned over and stirred the water with her narwhal horn. "The water is my guide, my protector. My salvation."

Märren grinned.

Eimri waded deeper into the fjord, smacking one hand against its surface as she tossed her head and horn. "I could swim all the way to the other side of the fjord if I wanted."

Märren's grin became a smile. "Don't attempt it, Narwhal child. No human without water magic can do so. Not even the mighty Eimri."

"I won't go far." Eimri turned, wading parallel to the shore, the water reaching her armpits.

"Aren't you cold?"

"Nay, Mother. I have the blubber of a Narwhal to insulate my bones."

Märren laughed, a strange sound, one that struck her ears as foreign. It had been too long since her laughter had silenced the voices. "You're as scrawny as a sapling. It may be the hot months, but you have no blubber, and you'll get cold soon."

"Not this day, Mother." She giggled again and plowed through the water, her smile broad and infectious.

Märren's heart twinged with bitter joy.

"If you won't become a Wolf warrior or an Ulfhednar, maybe you could join me as a Narwhal," Eimri said.

"Only the Dragon's powers can rid us of... what we carry."

"I'm fine today, and there's no dragon around."

"Aye. These are the days we live for."

Through the ghosts of memories, Märren watched her surroundings as tangible bubbles surfaced on the fjord. A mane of seaweed crested. She drew her seax and slowly carved through a scar rune on her wrist, tracing the same straight lines she had so many times, a line of runes for blood kin and love. She ignored the pain and rolled her forearm over, allowing her blood to drip onto the water, smearing its surface with red. The uisge darted closer, its wake waving behind it as a pale tongue lapped at the red from beneath the surface.

When Marren turned to Eimri again, her daughter was farther away, standing hunched, her toes in the water. Eimri's clothes were soaked and dripping, her hair and face just as wet. Märren's heart clenched.

"There she is," a blond boy a little older than Eimri said, the boy as ethereal as memory. "The cursed little worm." He pointed, and two other boys with him threw rocks at Eimri as Eimri turned and fled, screaming and covering her head.

Märren ran toward her daughter, blood streaming from her rune wound and raining upon the fjord.

"She's why my father hasn't been able to catch many fish this season," the blond boy shouted. "She's cursed by the gods."

Märren yanked her axe from her belt as she sprinted closer,

her feet sinking deeper into the mud with each stride. "Leave her be!"

"She's why my father's crops have all died," a second boy said, hurling a stick at her. It whistled as it twirled end over end. "We've had to replant everything again, and it's late in the season. None of it may grow before the heat leaves Midgard."

A fourth boy in the group, one who had not thrown anything at Eimri, grabbed the arm of the one who had thrown the stick and said, "It's not her fault. She can't do anything to crops or fish."

"Oh, so you love her?" The blond boy clutched his belly as he erupted with laughter. "The cursed one?"

"No," the kinder boy replied. "I just don't think everything bad that happens is her fault, and we're scaring her."

"She won't marry you just because you're nice to her." The blond boy shook his head with disdain. "Father says the stronger you are, the more women respect you." He held out a rock. "If you fancy her, throw it at her. Later, she'll come running to you."

The kinder boy hesitantly reached out and grasped the rock just as Märren arrived, axe in hand, swinging to kill, cursing.

"Mother!"

Märren stopped, breathing heavy as she turned. Eimri sat on the shore, staring across the water at the forest beyond. Märren glanced around at the quiet and stillness. The other spirits had fled. She clamped a hand over her bleeding wrist and tucked her axe into its ring on her belt. She stalked over and sat beside her daughter, watching the uisge, who was not memory, follow the trail of her blood, sopping it up with his tongue as he went.

"Mother?" Eimri asked. "Where do the voices come from?"

Märren exhaled. "We... From the spirits of the gods in Asgard."

Her eyes lit up. "Really?"

Märren bit her lip. "Some have told me that. Others have

told me that they come from the darkest reaches of Nidavellir or Helheim. I don't know what is true."

"Where do you believe they come from?"

Märren sighed. "From doubts and uncertainty. Past traumas and fear."

Eimri plucked a reed from the water and stripped off its outer layer as they sat in silence.

"Why is the world this way?" Eimri eventually asked.

"What way?" Märren stared across the fjord at the cliffs above the forest, where waterfalls flowed through shrouds of mist.

"A place where kindness does not defeat evil." Eimri tossed a stone into the water, its ripples ringing out around where it disappeared. A glow fly hovered over the water, its body lighting up in blue as it drifted toward a clump of reeds. "Why must we rely on violence to save ourselves and take what we need from others?"

"This world left to us by the gods isn't meant for you and me." Märren pulled her daughter close, squeezing her. "We are different. Most don't see things the way we do."

The glow fly buzzed as it flew about and became ensnared in a web between reeds. A black and yellow spider scuttled toward it. Eimri leaned closer, sinking her knees into the water as she reached out and grabbed the fly, breaking the web. She settled onto her backside, opening her palm. The fly lit up as it flew away, buzzing louder.

"You can't fault a spider for acting on its instincts," Märren said. "Like us, spiders also grow hungry and must feed. If they didn't, there would be far too many bugs flying about and no spiders at all." She gently pinched Eimri's shoulder. "And spiders probably get angry when they haven't eaten in a while." She laughed. "Like me. It's time for nattmal."

Eimri turned to study her. "So we're all just animals, acting on instinct and emotion? Trying to protect and provide for our families?"

Already, the spider tightrope-walked across a new thread, reweaving its web.

"Do you think we'll need to weave traps of our own?" Eimri asked. "For our enemies?"

Märren kissed her head. "I'm afraid that's where this world will try to lead us. But I hope that day never comes."

"Maybe that's how you'll finally be able to catch a scale of the Dragon."

Märren froze, brooding as she lovingly placed her hand on Eimri's head, feeling the flesh and hair over her skull. Her life. In reality, Märren's hand rested on the skull she carried, which she had removed from its pouch, and Eimri was suddenly gone, leaving only the shore and uisge's parting wake.

Across the fjord, something moved through the edge of the forest, but whether it was humans, deer, or even trolls, she could not be sure. The shapes vanished under the canopy as quickly as they had appeared. And the boughs waved in the wind.

12

BELFEDRN

"I SEE THE SOUL BRIDGE." LYRNE STARED INTO SOME OTHER world, her voice and breathing faint, her fingers clenching and unclenching. "Give me my seax."

"Stay here." Belfedrn cradled her head but slapped her weapon into her hand, the ravenous appetite of the Wolf making his stomach churn and gurgle so badly with hunger it felt like he had not eaten in a fortnight. It was always this way after using Fenrir's magics in battle. "With me!"

"The Raven isn't at her post, but the Valkyries... Will they take me? Or must I go the other route?"

"You fought bravely." He squeezed his mate tighter. "As one of the Ulfhednar. Nothing could bring you more honor. Nothing could bring me or our warriors more pride. I'm not half the Ulfhednar you are. I'll be lost without you. Stay."

"Don't grieve for me. I walk the path. I'm home."

Her last breath slipped out of her nose, her eyes turning dull, her body falling limp.

Tears rushed from Belfedrn's eyes as he held her head and howled, singing the ancient tune of their people for a pack member's passing, one that instilled honor and pride and longing and heartache. All of his emotions poured through him, calling up the sacred lyrics that he did not fully realize carried past his lips. The rest of the pack, especially Kesg and Ylsga, answered with howling lyrics, for the Wolf people were people of night song, for both celebration and remorse. Memories and heart-wrenching pain hit him like a maul to the chest. He sang on.

Kesg tentatively approached but halted and backed away. Belfedrn's comrade would not know what to say in such a situation, and neither would Belfedrn. It was better to say nothing. They understood each other.

After Belfedrn's and the rest of the pack's howling subsided, the other berserkers addressed their wounds and gathered up the dead. Belfedrn barely noticed.

"I was startled by the trolls, and I made a grave mistake." Vard's voice carried from somewhere. "And I'll be the first to admit it."

"We were taken by surprise," Ylsga replied. "Typical trolls cannot deceive the Ulfhednar by masking their scent. You couldn't have known what deception was awaiting us."

"I won't forgive myself so readily," Vard said. "Curse the bloody dead gods!" The slicing and ripping sound of a blade impaling flesh followed, and Vard cried out in pain, his seax buried deep in his own thigh. "The lives of my warriors lie heavy on me. Shield walls are the first defense with most adversaries, but not with trolls. The hunt is best for weaving around them and bringing them down."

"The others died before you ordered the shield wall," Ylsga said.

Vard ripped his blade from his flesh and pressed a hand to his wound. "Then it was only luck that allowed me not to get any more of the mightiest Ulfhednar killed. And our kind cannot rely on luck."

"These were no ordinary trolls." Kesg paced around the body of the monster Belfedrn had slain, prodding it with his spear. "Two males of this size sharing territory?" He spat on its corpse. "It doesn't happen. And like my mate said, trolls cannot mask their scent from Wolves. These—" His head jerked as he glared at the troll's upper chest, snarling and growling.

"What was that?" Ylsga sniffed the air. An odor like smoke but with a fetid quality floated by, a smell nearly as nauseating as burning hair, only different.

"This beast wore something." Vard scrutinized the troll and ripped a leather cord from its neck. He dangled the plain strap before him and smelled it. "Whatever it was, it's gone now. Burned to ash."

Belfedrn shuddered as a possibility struck him—a god part might have been attached to the strap. But he remained mute, cradling Lyrne's head, staring into her lifeless eyes.

"This one also wore a necklace that smoked," a berserker near the other beast's body said.

"Did these trolls carry scales?" Kesg asked, his voice airy with disbelief. "Or chitin? Did two trolls get a hold of god parts?"

A frightened silence lingered over the dell.

"Could've been Muninn feathers," Ylsga said.

"Or Dragon or Serpent scales," another added. "Or Spider chitin."

"Or pieces of the Narwhal's pelt, or the Stag's, Boar's, Bear's, or—"

"Stop!" Vard silenced them. "Even if they were god parts, untrained trolls couldn't have commanded their magic. We don't know what burned. All we know is that they carried something that's now gone, something that allowed them to conceal their scents from us and strike without warning."

"Made them harder to bring down, too," Kesg added. "These

two were stronger than any trolls the pack has seen in recent years."

Vard huffed as he stalked about, scrutinizing the scene and sniffing.

"The pelts of our dead have been desecrated," Eakthr the Sly —the pack's thief—said, leaving a torn and battered pelt of Fenrir on a comrade's body.

Cut and pierced like Lyrne's pelt. Only *gyðja* and *goði* could perform the proper rites to cut a pelt from the body of their dead god and allow it to retain the Wolf's magics. Like the strip Belfedrn had stolen. Once a pelt was defiled, its magic fled and it became nothing more than fur.

An hour may have passed as Belfedrn held the body of his mate and the pack discussed the matter further, devouring meat to satiate the Wolf's hunger, although it may have only been a few minutes. Lyrne was gone, probably feasting and drinking with the Ulfhednar of old, but nothing in these times was certain. With the gods dead—the humanoid gods Odin, Thor, Frey, Freyja, and all the others having died long before the beast gods—the path to Valhalla was not clear. Lyrne could have gone with Märren's daughter, Eimri, to Helheim. There was nothing Belfedrn could do about it. He closed Lyrne's eyes and kissed each cold lid, attempting to transfer as much of the love that raged inside him as he could.

A bonfire crackled to life nearby and soon blazed. The dead kindred of the Ulfhednar burned in its flames, as well as the body that had been impaled on the elm. Given the symbols woven into the dead man's clothing, he had been a resident from the destroyed village along their borders.

"Take this." Ylsga offered the tip of one of the troll's tusks to Belfedrn. She had already carved a hole into it and run a leather tie through the hole to create a necklace. "The spoils of this hunt are half yours. You landed the first strike on the larger beast and struck the deadliest blow as well. Accept its tusk."

It also killed Lyrne. Belfedrn reached to take the necklace, his arm caked in congealing blood, his pelt in a similar state, his painted face probably no better off. Other berserkers hefted the trolls' tusks and antlers, both of which would fetch good coin, and Belfedrn tied the necklace around his throat as a reminder of this day, for his companions, and most of all, for Lyrne. It would be a memento of her. Always. And he would never make the same mistake again—believing that trolls could not deceive and surprise the pack.

"I vow that to you now, Fenrir." Belfedrn struggled as he carried Lyrne's muscular body toward the bonfire. "I will not be so easily deceived again." Kesg moved to assist him, but Belfedrn drove him away with a growl. "No. This is my task. I'll accept no aid."

Kesg paused before understanding slowly sank in and he stepped away.

If I hadn't taken the flank route to help the pack, Lyrne may still be alive. Even if so many others may have died instead.

Belfedrn hefted his mate onto his shoulder and heaved her into the fire, watching while concealing his emotions. Sorrow and longing burned his heart and rattled the cage he placed them in. His life mate was gone. Lyrne had been his since they had come of age, roughly two and a half decades ago. He should be grateful for so much time together. These days, most people did not have the opportunity to share nearly as many years with their mate. But he was not thankful. Resentment and anger seethed inside him. Now he was alone, granted a flank route from hereon after, the position he had asked for this day—to get his turn over and done with for the season.

The flames chewed and melted Lyrne's flesh, carrying her to the next world. She was a good woman—hunter, lover, companion. Better than he deserved. He could only pray that he had been a good man for her, unlike so many other men in this world. He had treated her with respect and kindness, and he often accepted her advice and direction, and her commands—when he was wrong. Not that he could have bested her in a trial. Most men, especially those in other clans, had not built a relationship nearly so agreeable or satisfying. Not a sliver of what he and Lyrne had shared. Tears rained anew. And she had taken his dark secret of stealing from Fenrir and the pack with her. He did not deserve her, never had. She never made mistakes like that, not like other humans.

Far too many good people died in this world. Too many people died no matter how he looked at it. But that was the way of these lands.

"If it was too sudden for you," Eakthr said, his features sharp, "we can find you a Seidr man or woman upon our return. They may allow you to speak with Lyrne one last time."

"Wolf Seidr magic is rare."

"I'm sure there are still a few about who control such power." Eakthr handed him a hunk of salted meat. "You must eat."

Belfedrn accepted the food, tearing into it to placate his Wolf's hunger as he paced away from everyone and knelt before the elm that had held the dead. He placed a small rune stone at its base and whispered words from the old tongue and the songs of his people, the mournful ones from ages past.

"There's another trail here." One of the berserkers sniffed and cocked his head. "I can smell the musky dung of trolls from a league away. Probably some of these males' mates. We can track them. They're also probably responsible for our dead kindred in the village."

"We shouldn't." Belfedrn turned, standing defiant in the moonlight. "This bait and trap—these trails—and the lack of scent from the trolls in hiding was not a plot that arose in the brain of one of their kind. They are incapable of such involved ploys. A troll trail through the grasses beyond the village and to the forest would've been as obvious as a road to even the most inexperienced of us. Something or someone else took our people and dragged them to the woods, hiding their trail as best as they could so the Ulfhednar would have to come and sniff it out. Whoever did this left their victims bound to a tree and leaking blood to draw the trolls in. To have us believe it was *only* the work of trolls. They also probably gave god parts to these monsters, and that means whoever did this must've made a deal with the trolls and even trained them to be able to wield the power of a dead god." He strained for breath against his burning heart. "But we aren't so easily deceived. Not a second time. Not the children of Fenrir."

Vard wrapped a bandage around his self-inflicted wound as the others waited for their jarl to answer. "I don't deserve to make the next decision, but everything Belfedrn says rings true. Forget the female trolls' trail and scent. We hunt another."

13

CAËTIN

Caëtin's unkindness landed on a lone tree, squawking and squabbling for perches where they could roost. The other unkindnesses made for the sparse trees in the area. Exhaustion weighed heavy on Caëtin, as well as an utter cold that chilled her bones, a hunger in her belly, and a parched throat. The long flight and time as ravens was not easy to bear. She was weak in such a state, a swift traveler but unable to defend herself more than an average unkindness.

Her ravens, the pieces of her body, drank from a pond, then perched on the crooks of boughs, checking for predators and humans before fluffing feathers and shutting her many eyes. Sleep took her, and she drifted off to the bridge realm. Nothing but the loudest sounds would rouse her and return her to her world before she had recovered to some degree.

Hours later, when Caëtin woke, late autumn sunlight filled the sky, the sun hanging low in the south as it always did this time of year. Images from her dreams—of dark creatures pursuing her—quickly faded. Once her unkindness had fed on seeds, they squawked and flapped their wings, taking flight and swooping around the other trees in the area. The other unkindnesses woke and screeched their annoyance before feeding and leaping into the air, following her.

They soared south, landing outside a small village composed mostly of huts. Only a couple longhouses. Ravens whipped about in a tightening spiral and collided with each other, and Caëtin stood, rising from a torrent of feathers. The Knights Black soon joined her. Farmlands surrounded them and the settlement, most of the ground barren or with only brown stems poking from the earth.

Not too abnormal for this time of year. Caëtin continued convincing herself all would be well as she strode toward the outskirts of the village. In the distance, one man working the land gawked in their direction and then hurried for the settlement, toting a hoe and shovel.

"At least there are people here," Halfnr, one of the berserkers behind Caëtin, said, and Thovar, another berserker, grunted his agreement. They too must have been worried about finding a razed village along their borders.

Caëtin pushed her dark hood back in hopes of appearing more friendly and approached the nearest longhouse. A group of four men waited outside its doorway, eyeing them. Several women disappeared into the surrounding huts, ushering two children in with them.

"Hail, visitors," a man in the center of the group said, long white hair hanging around his bald scalp. He held a pickaxe, its head resting on the ground beside him, and he forced an almost toothless smile.

"Good day." Caëtin held up a hand in greeting as she wore her most benevolent expression. "Karls of Sparsgard and the Raven clan, the Knights Black praise you and the vital work you do for our people."

"I'm Othge, the jarl of Sparsgard." The man stepped forward, dragging the pickaxe with him. His hands and arms were dirt-encrusted, as if he had been working the land for days without washing them. "Although I tend to the fields like any other."

Caëtin bowed her head. "Then it's I who serves you, Othge and the rest of you."

Othge's smile fell flat.

Too much politeness? People were often surprised by Caëtin's words, expecting her to be as stern as Uktr. She was never sure if her manner made them warier because they feared she was trying to deceive them or if they were simply surprised by her attempt at kindness.

"What brings you and your warriors to our humble settlement, berserker of the Raven?" Othge asked.

A twinge of surprise struck Caëtin, but she did her best to hide any reaction. He should realize why they were here. "A messenger claimed that many of your village's children have gone missing."

Othge exhaled and relaxed.

He expected something else. "If the same was happening to the children of Aonark, I'd be horrified." Caëtin swallowed a lump of worry, deciding to follow a hunch, not because it was as concerning as the missing children, but rather to determine the man's motives. "Well, we're here to investigate that matter and something else. But it's probably nothing more than a misunderstanding."

"Misunderstanding?" Othge tensed.

Caëtin would not continue using as many gracious words as she had. "Jarl Uktr sent us to look into the children but also to inquire about another issue. You see, he seems to believe that Sparsgard hasn't paid their summer's end taxes."

Othge paled, and his hand trembled on the handle of his tool. "An issue arose in the matter of taxes."

"Pray tell."

"We sent a messenger to Uktr when our children stopped returning from their work. Not because we expect protection for nothing in return, but because they're our children."

"Of course. We'll certainly look into the matter." Caëtin waited.

"The past summer was short on sun and heat." Othge swallowed.

"So no more crops grew than what's needed to feed your people for the winter? And you have no extra coin?" She said it in a placating voice, to ease his apprehension.

"I… wish it were that simple." He furrowed his brow and looked away.

"What else is wrong?"

"There were whispers of a suspicious man wandering the lands around Sparsgard, and over a fortnight ago, he arrived here demanding offerings of coin and food. This was before the issue with the children."

"A collector from Jarl Uktr?"

"We believed so. In the beginning. He wore black, and a group of similar-looking men waited out in the fields." He motioned to the berserkers behind her, who were enshrouded in black cloaks.

"I thought you was them come back," a man with red hair who stood beside the jarl said. "That's why I rushed back here when I saw you."

Caëtin nodded her understanding.

Othge continued, "He told us that if we wanted our village and lands protected, that we must pay homage to the jarl. That's when I asked him who he was."

"And?"

"He wore something emitting power, because my skull was vibrating. Much of his face was concealed behind wraps. Many believed him to be from the Horse or Boar clan, or even a man of the Bear, but he would not say."

"Another clan in our lands?" Caëtin shook her head as outrage and worry worked their way through her. *A man wielding a god part, probably a berserker.* "This man will be hunted down and dealt with. I assume you sent him away?"

Othge's eyes closed. "No. He told us that if we didn't pay him, his people would slaughter our men right then and there, rape our women, and take our children as thralls."

"Bastard," one of the Knights Black said.

"So you gave him what you were going to send to Uktr?" Caëtin asked. "For this man's protection?"

Othge ran a hand across his mustache and beard. "Aye. His wicked calm and threats nearly had me pissing myself. If the Horse people weren't between us and the Spider clan, I'd have thought it was one of the Spider's people. They've decimated two clans already. Or so the rumors claim."

"Minor clans without dead gods. And once any warrior or berserker accepts the substance of one god, they can never control another. In centuries past, tyrants tried to do so. It has never worked. The Spiders are no stronger for what they've done to those clans."

"Doesn't matter. I gave him what we had... I'm sorry. Your kin are too far away. If you must, take me to Uktr, but please, don't punish the families of Sparsgard. And if you and your berserkers could find our children, or what's left of them, we'd be indebted to you. I would've resisted that visitor if I'd known that instead of killing us outright, our children would be taken."

"Don't torture yourself over the matter," Caëtin said. "It's our duty to protect you from outsiders. If we'd known of this, we would've come sooner and killed this man—stuck his horse or boar or bear head on a post to warn off any others who may be tempted to try something similar."

"The man traveled southeast with the rest of those brigands." Othge shuddered. "Toward Horse and Boar lands. It's usually been the children working or playing in those fields who haven't returned."

Caëtin motioned behind her. "I'll station three of my Knights Black here until the matter of the children is resolved."

"He had at least a score of others waiting outside the village, and no one knew they were coming until they were here."

That many outsiders arriving unnoticed? "Three Knights Black will be able to dispose of any berserker and his warriors, even if this man happened to be from the Spider. But if it makes your people feel safer, I'll leave you with six."

"How can you be so certain that with less than half their number you can best these men?"

"Because ravens feast on spiders. No matter how deadly some of those insects become. The Horse and Boar or even Bear are less of a threat." Caëtin bowed her head again. Although she understood the savage strength of the bear and that they had no rival in face-to-face battle, the Bear people were not the most intelligent of warriors. They were easy to understand and predict and thus easily deceived. "Good day. We'll hunt this berserker who uses stealth to slip into our lands and threaten our kin. If he's a Spider, we'll pluck off each of his eight hairy legs and eat them while his warriors watch."

Caëtin strode away, six of the berserkers that she indicated remaining behind, the other six flanking her, their ire palpable and sheeting from them as they walked.

"Be wary," Othge called after them. His lips moved as if he wanted to say more, but instead, he fell quiet.

"Why didn't you send word to the jarl sooner?" Caëtin asked Othge.

"We were afraid that he'd no longer protect us. After not making offerings and paying homage. We've been faithful Raven men and women of Muninn all our lives, but this year we failed you."

"No. This incident occurred in our lands. If anyone failed in dealing with this treachery, it is us. But take heart. The threat will soon be dealt with. As long as you remain people of Muninn, you have nothing to fear."

14

CAËTIN

CAËTIN MARCHED OUT OF SPARSGARD TOWARD ITS SOUTHERN fields, Halfnr and her Knights Black at her heels. In the distance, the River Red and its muddy waters—the border between Horse and Raven territory—wound and rolled across the lands. Long ago, one of the most infamous battles of the region had raged there, filling the waters with blood. No person of the Horse clan had crossed the boundary or made threats against the Ravens in over a decade.

Caëtin's blood roiled with fury. If she found no answers in the vicinity, she would have to cross the boundary and hunt out the nearest settlement. The time may be at hand when the Ravens needed to land on the Horses' muzzles and peck out their eyes.

"Fan out and search for a trail," Caëtin said.

The ground turned softer as she and her berserkers trekked onward, the land beyond the village tilled by oxen and plow. A musky odor rode on the wind. Caëtin gripped her sword's hilt, stemming her wrath as she scanned the landscape for clues of passing warriors, of those from the herd. The other six berserkers spread farther apart.

Perhaps she should not be a fool and rush into Horse territory with only six Knights Black, not after what that berserker had done to Sparsgard. He and his fighters could be waiting, hoping for Raven warriors to show in small enough numbers that they could be ambushed. Some dark elf or troll was probably not responsible for the missing children. Maybe she should first return to Aonark and gather more knights. That would be the prudent thing to do, although Uktr would probably not approve and think her actions were the result of weakness and fear. She groaned in frustration.

First, she would make sure no one of the Horse clan lingered in Raven lands. If they did, she would exact her revenge and return to Uktr and Darstrid with their maned heads.

No footprints or other signs of men passing stood out in the tilled earth. If her knights could not pick up a trail, she would need to fly as ravens and scout around for leagues.

When they neared the banks of the river, Thovar, one of the knights far to Caëtin's right, cried out. He sank into the ground, up to his waist, his arms flailing but finding no purchase.

"What devilry is this?" Thovar glanced around in surprise, his skin paler than typical, his beaked nose wrinkling as he reached out for his closest comrade, Halfnr, who rushed over and grabbed him by the wrist.

Halfnr—a taller berserker with blond hair and no beard—gripped both of his comrade's arms and heaved, but Thovar was barely lifted upward before he slid back down into the dirt. Caëtin and the other knights rushed over to help.

"Don't pull on him," someone said.

Caëtin whipped around to find a boy and girl, neither older than one and ten, standing beside a lone tree and patch of rocks farther to their right. Both had disheveled sandy hair. Caëtin paused before assisting the berserkers with their comrade.

"Why do you say this?" Caëtin asked the children.

"Because he's caught in a trap," the boy replied. "The harder you pull, the more stuck he gets, and then he won't ever break free of the earth. We saw it with Groandr."

"There are traps hidden in the ground?" Caëtin's bemusement rose. "To protect your fields?"

The boy shook his head. The girl gripped his hand, standing a head shorter than the boy and leaning in close to him.

Another knight bellowed and pointed. Nearer to the river, figures slowly rose from the earth—heads, shoulders, torsos—all draped in blood-red cloaks stained with dirt. Initially there were only a few, but then a dozen emerged. More followed. The children darted back toward the village, where the locals stood watching.

Caëtin ripped her blade from its sheath as these red warriors or berserkers rose out of Raven land. The first line of them advanced with steady strides, barbed axes, spears, and crossbows in their hands. A cry of alarm sounded from one of Caëtin's companions, and she glanced in the direction that knight was indicating. More intruders in red rose from the ground between them and the village.

"It's a fucking trap," Caëtin said. These intruders would surround the Knights Black in the open, after having waited until one of her men was stuck. "And we haven't even set foot on Horse land." *Where are the six berserkers I left at the village?* "Flee."

"We can't leave him." Halfnr tugged harder on Thovar, who grimaced.

"My ankles are stuck," Thovar said.

Caëtin judged the distance between her knights and the advancing red warriors on both sides. Several minutes could probably pass before her comrades would be forced to fight more than five times their number of warriors or berserkers. With these odds, it would not matter how strong their adversaries were.

They probably took children to draw us out here. Caëtin glanced back at Thovar. "Dig him up!" She set her sword aside and used both hands to scoop away the dirt around her knight. Others joined in as a couple Raven berserkers stood with their axes poised, positioning themselves between Thovar and the approaching warriors.

Caëtin and those assisting her frantically dug away at the soft soil, exposing Thovar's thighs and then his knees. They tugged on him again, but Thovar would not break free of the earth. They dug deeper still. Below his knees, strands of something bright clung to his boots and cloak. Halfnr used his sword to try to slice through the strands, but the fibers stuck to the tip of his weapon. He tugged on his blade to remove it, but it was also held fast.

"It has my fucking sword," Halfnr said.

Thovar struggled, and more strands wrapped around his knees.

"Stop moving!" Caëtin pulled a knife from her belt and sliced through Thovar's leggings, carefully avoiding the strands. "It's a net of some kind. And sticky..."

For the moment, she ignored the implications as she tried to peel Thovar's leathers downward over his skin, but they were clamped so tightly about his flesh that they barely moved. She sliced through one of his boots, attempting the same strategy for removal, also without success.

"They're almost here!" a Knight Black hollered, her tone piercing. "Two score of these cock suckers are surrounding us. We can't win this."

"Bloody bastards!" A fist of anguish struck Caëtin in the gut. She sheathed her knife and regripped her blade, glancing from Thovar to the line of attackers who were slipping closer to each other and forming ranks as they advanced. Forty enemy axes and spear tips dripped with dark liquid. To Thovar, she said, "Become your unkindness."

He grimaced and shook his head. "I can't leave so many of my ravens—my legs—behind."

"Then you're going to die."

"Better that than be half a man with bleeding stumps below his waist." Thovar swallowed. "Leave me. Fly back to Aonark and bring a legion to wipe out these bastards."

"No." Caëtin struggled with the only other option left to free her knight. "Your legs do not make you a man."

"Go!" Thovar yelled.

"I won't let them poison and devour you from the inside out." Caëtin grabbed his arm. "Halfnr, put a stick in his mouth."

Halfnr shot her a bewildered look.

"Do it," Caëtin said. "The rest of you, hold his arms. I won't leave him."

"I'd rather fight them," Thovar said. "Let them come."

Halfnr shoved a coin purse into Thovar's mouth, stuffing it deep. The others grabbed their flailing comrade. Caëtin glanced at their advancing adversaries. The remainder of her Knights Black rushed out to meet the attackers, the clash of steel on steel ringing across the field.

Caëtin swung her blade, feeling the power of Muninn flowing through its edge. The weapon hewed through Thovar's knee, severing the leg of a Knight Black. Blood gushed. Thovar jerked and then thrashed even more vigorously while two others held him, his muffled shrieks carrying past the coin purse in his mouth. Caëtin sliced through his other leg. Thovar's head cocked to the side, and he turned limp. Halfnr heaved his comrade out of the hole as blood streamed from the stumps of his legs and Caëtin tore sections of cloth from his tunic and cinched them down above his wounds, creating tourniquets.

More steel rang around them, sparks flying as axes and swords clashed.

Caëtin smacked Thovar across his cheeks until one of his eyes cracked open. "We fly! Now!"

She exploded into an unkindness, ravens screeching curses as they hurtled over the heads of the Spider fighters whose faces were wrapped in black linen. The attackers loosed bolts and leapt into the air, jabbing with spears, trying to bring the ravens down. A projectile whizzed toward one of Caëtin's ravens, and the bird tucked a wing and fell to one side to avoid taking the hit. Behind Caëtin, the other berserkers burst into black feathers and beating wings. Halfnr smacked Thovar across the face some more and shouted at him before they too altered and lifted from the ground, the ravens of Thovar's unkindness streaming blood from their legs.

Caëtin soared past the Spiders, streaking toward the village. Once Sparsgard was below her unkindness, she glared down at the locals and cawed with over a dozen ringing voices. Some of the locals screamed and ran while others paled and ducked. Caëtin landed, unfurling and leaving a cloud of feathers spiraling in her wake.

"What've you done?" she asked Othge.

Othge trembled and cowered against the wall of the longhouse. "We didn't have a choice. It was either work with the Spider people or they'd eat us and raze our village to the ground."

"Where are my knights? Those I left to protect you?"

Othge pointed to the other longhouse in the settlement. Caëtin swallowed a lump of fear as she sprinted toward the building. She flung its doors open. Webs spanned the interior, stretching from floor to rafters. Her berserkers hung from the webs in various positions—from their arms, legs, and necks. They were motionless and silent.

"Knights Black, with me!" Caëtin cried into the house.

None of them stirred. The din of yelling attackers drew near. Caëtin darted inside and grabbed her nearest comrade, a woman, and shook her. The berserker was entangled around her chest and legs, facing away. Her head lolled back, her eyes completely white and gaping. Black veins crawled up her neck and across her face, originating from a wound on the back of her shoulder.

Poisoned. Fuck. "Fuck. Fuck." Caëtin screamed, throwing her head back. She would have to return with more knights, and if she must, wait for legions of Raven warriors who did not command the ability to become an unkindness to arrive. Then she would wipe the Spider from the land—return the favor.

Howls of fear carried as marching feet drew nearer to the village. Dark forms descended from the rafters, creeping along the webbing. Caëtin dashed outside, leaping high, the wind shearing her into an unkindness. Ravens circled about the area as the Spider attackers scuttled between buildings and swarmed the longhouse.

Caëtin squawked and hurtled away to the north, the other unkindnesses close behind.

15

BELFEDRN

A CLOUD OF SMOKE HUNG OVER NISTREEL, THE ONLY WOLF settlement large enough to be called a city, obscuring everything but its outskirts. Belfedrn's home. Nistreel's buildings were nothing more than embers and debris. Everything was decimated. Dark clouds hung low, spitting lightning without rain. Thunder boomed.

Belfedrn stepped past Vard, all the members of the pack lost in a world of disbelief.

"By the gods' dead arses, what... happened?" Kesg strode closer to the smoke, shielding his face. Ylsga followed at his heels, snarling and then whimpering.

Shock and fear rode through Belfedrn like warhorses to battle. He gazed over the carnage and smoke, his mouth as dry as sheaves of grass in the hot months. He covered his lips and nose with cloth bandage material and stepped closer. Embers glowed through the haze. Smoke swirled, and flames guttered in the wind. Little else moved. A flash of lightning lit the sky, the answering boom rattling everything around them.

The surviving members of the Ulfhednar marched past Vard, their dark pelts and figures soon disappearing into the haze over Nistreel. Belfedrn's apprehension did not subside, but he strode forward. When the pack members stumbled upon whatever they would find, he should be there to help them bear it.

They had picked up the smell of smoke soon after they began their return journey from the troll hunt. Initially, Vard wanted to believe the smells had been from the bonfire they started to burn their dead, but the reek grew stronger instead of lessening while they loped homeward.

Curtains of haze parted as Belfedrn moved between remnants of torched buildings. Ash drifted lazily like hot black flakes of snow. Bodies lay strewn across the streets, most charred by flame, the remains of shield grips in the hands of warriors, along with scorched weapons.

Belfedrn marched on but halted beside a mound of ash that held the shape of a body. He brushed aside some of the soot. A smoldering skeleton lay beneath, its seared *brynja* not that of a Wolf man or woman. Someone not from Nistreel. He scraped away the ash, exposing more of the corpse. His fingers stopped searching when they fell into the groove of a crest near the body's neck. The flame-tinged armor bore the sigil and runes of the Sea Serpent.

A Serpent warrior? Belfedrn's shock piqued, rage twining with sorrow and burning inside him as he flung a volley of curses at the dead gods.

After stemming some of his overflowing emotions, Belfedrn glanced westward but could not see through the haze. Many Serpent warriors must have sailed from their isles and docked on the spit of land to the west, then snuck into Wolf territory, somehow concealing their scent and silencing their steps so the warriors and berserkers guarding Nistreel could not detect them. These invaders could have even marauded their way across the land to the Wolf city.

Belfedrn kicked aside the charred haft of a Serpent spear, threw his head back, and howled at the sky, unable to contain his misery. After a series of sorrowful cries, he heaved for breath. If any of the Serpent's warriors remained in Nistreel, they would know his whereabouts.

Let them come. Let them ambush him and the pack—what was left of all the berserkers of Fenrir. Some of the mighty Ulfhednar still lived, those who had been tricked into venturing away to troll territory and thus making the razing of Nistreel all the easier. Somehow, the Sea Serpents must have entered the Uncharted Northlands and set up the troll ruse, leaving god parts for those beasts, possibly even training them. The Serpent people must have passed through the Unclaimed Lands.

Let us all die fighting for our slain kin.

But Midgard would not be so obliging as to grant Belfedrn's wish. Great suffering would have to be endured first, as in all of life. He growled in frustration, pain from the loss of his kin making his bones feel like they would splinter and he would shatter to pieces.

A quiet stillness answered his outrage and weighed heavy on the world within the smoke, much of which he now realized was fog—an odorless magical mist shed from Sea Serpent berserkers. That must be how they masked their scents and sounds, similar to what occurred at the village and in the woods he investigated.

Several of the Ulfhednar came running, their dark pelts a blur as if they were wraiths, until they emerged from the haze.

"All of Nistreel is burned," Kesg said. "I found this." He dropped a pocked and burned shield onto the street, issuing a clatter. Once the shield settled, the sea serpent on its face was unmistakable.

"I've found the same," Belfedrn replied.

"Vard!" Their thief—Eakthr the Sly—loped into the area,

saliva stringing from his ash-stained lips, his features as sharp as a blade, soot making his hair blacker than usual. He carried a longbow over his shoulder.

Vard stumbled through the haze, the bandage on his leg dripping blood, his face pale and drawn.

"The cries and smells of women with young ride through this fog, coming from the northern quarter," Eakthr said. "They're locked inside a longhouse. Flames are taking the structure, and a score of Sea Serpent soldiers surround it."

"Run." Vard waved the pack onward but with subdued emotion.

Belfedrn started away before Athna, the Ulfhednar's only battle Seidr, burst through the fog. Her hair was white as snow even though she was still young, not more than thirty winters, her frame slenderer than her kin's.

"To the south!" Athna pointed in the opposite direction from the way they were headed. "The last of the Wolf warriors face off with Serpent berserkers, but our men and women are outnumbered ten to one."

Belfedrn glanced from north to south, his mind churning as the berserkers stared at Vard, awaiting his command. *Rend the flesh from the dead gods! Maybe we should look for Deyja and the other trainees.* His heart clenched with apprehension.

The pack should not turn away from women and children who would be massacred... but those people would not offer them much aid in fighting against the Sea Serpents. The Wolf warriors could join the Ulfhednar and make them stronger, fight back, and maybe one day find revenge. Belfedrn's emotionally weakened bones ached.

"There isn't time to debate the matter," Athna said. "Those I mentioned are probably the last of the survivors of Nistreel."

"Except for another group I caught wind of," Eakthr replied. "Women and children."

"If we divide our numbers, we'll only weaken the pack." Vard spat and cursed. "And there are fewer than a score of us."

Belfedrn was suddenly grateful that decisions for the pack did not lie with him.

"We may be too few to make a difference either way," Vard said, "but we are the Ulfhednar! I'd curse my own blood if we didn't try to defend our weak and innocent. And I'd be a fool to allow the last of our warriors to die. Then these Serpents will kill us anyway." He growled and gestured at the pack. "Northward to the women and children. May our warriors in the south summon what they can of Fenrir and destroy their foes. We hunt Serpents!"

"For the Wolves!" the pack cried and howled, their voices piercing the mist. Belfedrn sprinted away, the pack following and then running alongside him. They veered between the thickest columns of smoke, weaving through the remains of their city while leaping over debris and embers. The din of clashing steel and screams carried, growing closer. Flickers of movement—of warriors in foreign garb—wavered in the mist.

Belfedrn sprang with the might of Fenrir, leaping many horse lengths toward a burning longhouse, his spear poised as he descended, his weapon impaling a Serpent fighter in the back of the neck. Belfedrn landed in a crouch and yanked his weapon out of his enemy's back, letting the soldier topple over as the rest of the Ulfhednar lunged and drove killing blows of their own.

Two score of Sea Serpent warriors surrounding the longhouse yelled in surprise and spun about.

"Shield wall!" Vard cried, and the pack mashed together, shields overlapping, almost intertwining as they advanced on their adversaries.

Belfedrn moved as if controlled by something or someone else, barely registering his actions while he charged and thrust his spear at his enemies. The Sea Serpents frantically formed their own shield wall, although more haphazardly, just as the Ulfhednar shields rammed into theirs with a clash of steel and wood. Men and women shouted. Some of their enemies were launched backward, but many only stumbled before resisting. Spears and axes prodded and swiped, seeking targets.

Belfedrn ducked under an axe that swiped above the rim of his shield. Several people bellowed in pain as the Ulfhednar shoved against the Serpent warriors, but the Serpents pressed back with great strength, maintaining their ground.

"Leap!" Vard hollered and motioned over his shoulder.

Belfedrn retreated a step, allowing Kesg and Ylsga to fill his spot in the wall, and crouched beside Eakthr, who giggled madly and shuffled about. They both leapt, launching over the shield wall and that of the Serpent warriors, spears thrusting and resisting other weapons jabbing at them. One spear whistled as it tore at Belfedrn, who raised his shield and placed it at an angle before his chest. The spear struck with a bang and glanced off, flying away.

Eakthr and Belfedrn landed on the far side of their adversaries' wall. Belfedrn stabbed one warrior in the side as the man turned, the warrior's axe chopping and severing the haft of Belfedrn's spear. Belfedrn drew his axe and lunged at another, cutting him down with a strike to the neck. Eakthr had also lost his spear and drew a seax from his belt, slicing into others.

"Rent!" Vard's voice carried, and the Ulfhednar immediately responded, those in the middle of the wall whisking aside. The Sea Serpent wall gave way, their fighters stumbling and plowing ahead into an intentionally created void.

Some of the Serpent warriors found themselves in the midst of the Ulfhednar, surrounded on both sides as Wolf weapons bit into them. Belfedrn and Eakthr focused on the attackers in the rear, and Belfedrn lashed out with enhanced speed and might, his weapon cleaving armor and hewing flesh in explosive bursts. Blood sprayed. The dying cries of their prey rang in his ears.

The Ulfhednar called upon their skills, fighting as wedges from either side, hacking their way through the ranks of their enemies. Eakthr used furtive attacks with his seax, working around shields and taking the Serpent warriors in weak areas—the tendons on their legs, their backs, their throats.

A spear tip tore over Athna's shoulder, ripping through her *brynja*, and she snarled. She flung white fire from one fist, using a seax in the other to slice into her attacker's shield. The flames took on the shape of a great wolf and barreled at her adversary before she combined the magic with wind. The wind tore the wolf apart, creating a fiery gale that blasted across the Sea Serpent warrior, lighting him up as he screamed. Kesg, Ylsga, and Vard swung axe and spear at their enemies.

When the last Serpent warrior slid off Belfedrn's axe, his vision blurred, fatigue pressing down on him like an anvil. He fell to a knee. Many Sea Serpent warriors and two Ulfhednar lay dead around them, one of the dead Ulfhednar's skin smoking in patches where Serpent venom had been spat on him.

Thankfully, these Serpent warriors had barely had time to summon fog and obscure their ranks, although that ability may only be carried by their berserkers, like calling tentacled monsters and serpents from the deeps. Belfedrn was unsure of their magics.

Kesg and Ylsga removed a beam that had been intentionally placed and flung open the flaming doors of the longhouse. Women and children burst from clouds of roiling black smoke, coughing and gagging. Many of them fell to their knees soon after exiting. Others ran free of the burning structure and huddled together in the distance. No more than a score of them had survived.

"So few," Belfedrn muttered as he bowed his head. Eakthr

watched the flames, the typical madness he portrayed when fire and battle raged gripping him and making him grin.

"Children of Fenrir." Vard approached the survivors. "Flee to the north and east. Avoid Fleecebarrow and the other villages. If they're not already burning, they soon will be. Take refuge in the Moon Woods. These will soon be Sea Serpent lands, but no Serpent knows the forests like we do. You'll be safe there. For a time."

"You're of the Wolf clan." Belfedrn grabbed a bearded axe from one of the slain Ulfhednar and handed it to a woman who had fled the longhouse. "Even if you rear young ones now. You're strong and can defend yourselves, if you're not taken by surprise."

The pack handed out weapons from the dead to the women and two children who were just old enough to carry them. They also replaced their broken spears with intact ones from the dead.

"Avoid the areas of densest smoke and fog in Nistreel," Belfedrn told the survivors. "Serpent berserkers use it to conceal themselves."

"There's no time for rest," Vard said to them. "Go!"

Most of the children wailed as the women nodded their thanks and tugged their little ones along. They weaved their way through the dead and remains of the Wolf clan's only city, the hands of children in one of theirs, spears or axes in the other.

16

MÄRREN

MÄRREN WATCHED COLUMNS OF SMOKE RISE FROM THE countryside, which sprawled away into the distance far beyond her doorway. Three specific rune scars that decorated her body lit up in her mind.

"Everything's burning." The dragon's voice rumbled inside its lair.

"Her house will burn next. Along with her." The wolf in her head stalked about dark woods, snarling.

"We can still flee." The child darted away.

"One of the clans has come pillaging, burning Wolf lands as it goes, Eimri," Märren said to her daughter's memory and scratched at her neck, the thrall collar pinching as she turned her head. "While the Ulfhednar were away. Belfedrn, your uncle... The pack... What has happened to them?"

Märren listened to the silence—the wind off the fjord, the murmur of the stream.

"They're dead."

"She'll die as well."

"The pelt!"

Märren took the wolf's pelt from where it hung on her door,

the pelt her cousin had left when he departed. Rain dripped from its coat, and its power streaked up her arm and rattled her head. She howled and flung it at the door, would not don it and take up the power of the Wolf. Not now. She had already waited too long. She had never desired the pelt, never wished to be part of the pack or linked to the wolf in her mind, and given the amount of smoke, most of the Wolf people were probably as dead as Fenrir.

There would not be much she alone could do by taking up one pelt from their dead god. A Wolf warrior, even an Ulfhednar berserker, needed a pack to harness their greatest might. Two or three Wolves together could wield increasing power, but the more the better. She was alone, had been for a long while, her mate unable to tolerate her episodes, even though he was one of her people and was supposed to mate for life.

She kicked at a patch of dead grass. Even if she somehow managed to remain hidden from the raiders along the outer reaches of Wolf territory, this winter, trolls would venture to her home. Then she would die anyway. She could try to fight them, but if she died, her soul would walk the Raven's bridge, its guardian or the Valkyries forcing her on to Valhalla instead of Helheim. If that happened, Eimri would be remembered by no one and would endure eternity alone, her death and life insignificant.

"She should stay and die where she's comfortable."

"Let them come and burn her without her fighting back. That's what she's best at."

"No. There's still something to live for—another path. And there's never been a better reason to follow it."

Märren cursed as she stepped inside her hut, facing the small skull sitting beside the hearth, flickering candlelight creating pits in its eye sockets and nose. She ran a hand lovingly over its scalp. "I cannot stay here, Eimri. And I cannot leave you. Not ever."

She waited for the skull to reply.

"It doesn't speak."

"It never will."

"Eimri hears her. And she hears Eimri."

"Wake early if you desire another man's life or land," Märren said, recalling the teachings of the divine Hávamál. "No lamb for the lazy wolf. No battle is won in bed." She bit her lip. "We must go now, Eimri. If it comes to it and I'm certain to die, I vow that I'll slit my own throat." She tied a strip of leather around her seax and slipped it over her neck. It rattled against her thrall collar. "Then the Valkyries won't have me. But take heart—I'll carry my axe to protect myself from weaker things, as you demand. Then, one day, we'll return home, even if we aren't true pack members."

Märren picked up the skull, cradling it against her breast before kissing it, slipping it into a pouch, and tying it to her waist. She packed her simple wolf furs, gathered food and supplies and her double-bladed axe that rested beside the doorway, and tromped outside, shielding her face from the sunlight and pressing back the darkness and doubts in her mind.

She cast one last glance over her shoulder, watching the pelt of Fenrir wave in the wind from where it had caught on the handle of her door. If Belfedrn or her past mate ever came, they would realize what the fur was. Others would probably never suspect a pelt so uncared for to be anything other than a fur.

After hiking to the stream, Märren pulled a small faering vessel from its place on the shore and shoved it into the water. Nearby, bubbles rose along the surface and popped. The uisge had taken notice. She hopped into the faering and took up its oars, guiding herself along the narrow and twisting current toward the fjord. She would need to sail across leagues of water and out into the sea if she hoped to reach what she longed for. Passing through the Unclaimed Lands had proven too dangerous.

"I'll find a scale of the Dragon for you, Eimri." She patted the skull in the pouch.

"She's never been out to sea."

"She'll die there in this rotting vessel."

"She can make the crossing to the land of fire and ash. She's sailed the fjord many times."

Märren ignored the voices and rowed on, the turbulent water turning placid after she slid into the fjord. Mountains armored in spruces and pines soared upward around her. Ripples and bubbles followed. A mane packed with seaweed and mud crested above a bowing neck.

"Come with me, if you like." Märren used the seax hanging around her neck to cut a slit through the scars on her wrist, and she dribbled her blood into the water. The uisge rushed forward and thrashed about in a frenzy just below the surface as he lapped up the red stains. "We travel to a land of dragons."

Märren rowed along the fjord, the journey quiet with only her, Eimri, and the uisge, none of whom talked. The voices never stopped, but they faded under the splashing of oars on water. Hours passed.

"I must make one stop before venturing to the land of fire and ash," Märren said to the water and uisge, wherever he had gone. She rowed the faering onto the far northern shore and hopped out into the water. The icy wet pressed against her oiled leggings and boots but barely seeped in. She hauled the faering out of the water. Ahead, a ravine stretched into the mountains, a circle of ancient spruces and elms standing between rock cliffs.

"It's been some time since she risked venturing here."

"And she should not risk it now."

"The old Seidr man. He may not still be alive."

She kept a hand on her axe and stopped before the first tree, kneeling to place a rune stone sacrifice within a tangle of its roots. The feeling of land wights, and of bright or dark elves, and of greedy dwarves from the deep places of the world weighed on the air here. She stepped through the circle.

Within a small clearing, a hut leaned to one side, its thatch roof broken in several places. Firelight shone through the cracks in the hut's walls and doorway. Märren ventured closer, her knees quivering with each step. When she reached the door, she knocked, and the door swung inward with a grating creak.

"Hello?"

"Enter already," a raspy voice said. "It's why you've come. Again."

Märren swallowed and stepped inside, the smell of excrement and rotting food almost making her retch. Ravens leapt about in cages on the walls, squawking in deafening tones. A man so wrinkled he could have been a decaying log sat on a stool, hunched over a fire. A tattered cloak was wrapped around his shoulders and pulled low over his head. Lumps of scarred flesh that may have once been eyelids were in the place where his eyes should be. He had no nose, only widened holes in his face, and no discernible lips, simply a slit of a mouth. Black streaks ran along his face and smeared the area of his mouth and absent eyes and nose.

"You seek to know your fate," the man said more than asked as he threw something into the fire. The flames crackled and flared. "That woven by the gods."

"Aye. I seek the body of the Ormr, the dead Dragon god."

He did not laugh or even study her in bewilderment. "Fate once bound people for all the ages of their lives, but that was before the gods fell in the great war of Ragnarök. However, the worlds did not end as was foretold, and the beast gods took up what they could to control Midgard. Then they too raided each other's lands and realms and waged wars until the last of their kind perished."

He lifted a foot, placing it on a stump between him and Märren, his toes crooked, nails tinged green and extending too far beyond his flesh. He reached out a knotted hand.

"To speak his knowledge, he still expects an offering."

"The vile old bastard."

"Don't."

Märren shut her eyes briefly as she took his gnarled old foot in her hands and massaged his heel, pulling at his toes. Then she took his hand, lifting it to her mouth and licking his cracking palm. She grimaced and stifled a dry heave.

"You know what else," he said.

She released his hand and drew her seax, pulling down her fur and chainmail *brynja*, exposing her upper chest.

"He needs part of her to use his magic."

"He demands her blood. He'll weaken her."

"All of life takes blood, given for oneself and others."

She poked the tip of her seax into her skin and carved specific runes, these symbolizing life. Blood drained down her skin as she leaned over and allowed it to trickle onto the Seidr man's hands.

"Speak of what awaits me in the land of fire and ash," she said.

The Seidr man grunted, catching the blood in his palms and turning his hands over, bathing them in the shower and rubbing the blood into his skin like a balm. Something twitched beneath his scarred eyelids. He leaned his head back, uttering the old tongue as he held his palms upward.

After performing the incantation, he said, "I still see the flames. All that is written in them, the runes they make even though I've not set eyes on Midgard since I was a child several centuries ago."

The fire hummed, its light flickering. Runes engraved into the walls lit up in flashes of orange and red and blue. Märren swallowed her disgust at the Seidr man's body and her fear of the encounter and its outcome as she gripped his other foot, pressing her thumbs into it as he continued his call to the ancient ones.

His neck bent forward, his absent eyes staring through her as he said, "A land wight of old travels with you, and many of the dark elves and dwarves creep out into this world. As do some of the jötunn—the giants. There are no longer gods to hold them back. Do not stay the night here. Press on into the sea."

He fell silent.

"What of the land of fire and ash?" Märren asked.

"There is no more fate, foolish child. The gods are dead, and fate rots in corpses with them. All who've come after are lost."

Märren lurched back, dropping his foot, which hit the stump with a smack. The old Seidr man winced.

"Now, if you wish to see the past again—that which has already transpired—I could aid you. As I've aided you before." His attention settled on the pouch holding Eimri's skull. "But fate decays and festers. There's nothing left of it here in Midgard."

"I don't want any more of the past."

"She runs from it."

"But it chases her. Relentlessly."

"It has broken her."

"Then travel safe." He waved her away. "My powers are fading with the gods. With the lands. I may no longer be here when you seek me again."

Märren stood and exited the hut, a knot of unease and apprehension brewing in her gut. She returned to her faering and set it into the water, leaping inside and rowing on. By the time she passed beyond the mouth of the fjord, darkness had nearly fallen. The breakers of the sea rammed against her small craft, flinging up its bow and slamming it back down, shoving her back toward the fjord again and again. But she could not rest in the ravine or along the banks of the fjord here, not after what the Seidr man had told her.

"This'll be a struggle, Eimri, but we can do it." Märren dug deep into the water with her oars and heaved, pulling as hard as she could as she strained and grunted. The uisge surfaced and swam back and forth behind her, his neck dipping into the water and emerging again farther away. This creature would not follow her into the open sea.

It took Märren eight attempts and timing the swells to pass beyond the crashing waves and out into the sea beyond. Once she made it past the breakers, sweat dripped from her forehead and down her back, her breath rasping in her throat. Waves rocked the faering side to side, threatening to pitch icy water over its side and into the hull.

"You'll never cross the straight in that small of a vessel," a quiet and strained voice said, one Märren was unfamiliar with among those in her head.

Her blood chilled as she glanced down toward Eimri's skull in its pouch, afraid the darkness was taking her and she was hearing her daughter's voice again, only different.

"Her mind is lost."

"She hasn't even yet made it to the open sea."

"She has. The sea is around her. And she's closer to Midgard than so many others will ever be."

Märren glanced about the waves as they tumbled around her vessel. The uisge's head surfaced, resembling a horse's but with a shorter muzzle and the sharp teeth of a predator, seaweed covering much of his hide.

"Was that you speaking, Uisge?" She shuddered, realizing

she must be losing her mind. No one she knew had ever heard an uisge speak.

"If that's how you wish to refer to me." The creature's mouth moved as it spoke, but the action did not make Märren feel any surer that she was not turning to madness. "I have no other name from your kind."

"I didn't think you would follow me out to sea."

"I can travel through seawater as easily as I can travel through a fjord." The creature swam closer. "I heard you speak to yourself so many times when you fed me. I know you long for the Dragon's breath. To feel fire and scale. To ride a beast of wisdom and malice and terrible power. I know what it is you seek."

"Then you understand me better than most—if you're truly speaking to me and this isn't the darkness that's been growing stronger since Eimri's death. You know the fjords and the lochs and even the stream, but do you know the sea and how to cross a strait?"

"Well enough to realize that the people of the Dragon only make the crossing in longships or larger vessels."

"Then I'll drown?"

"I can show you a path, in return for saving my life from that troll who stalked me at the fjord."

"I can feed you as well."

"Your blood soothes me, but at times, I require full meals."

"Human bodies. That's what uisge feed on."

"If he grows hungry enough and cannot find another, he'll eat her."

"He won't. He owes her a life debt, and uisge can feed on creatures other than humans."

"I'll do what I can to keep you content," Märren said.

"Then follow." Uisge plunged into the water, bubbles surfacing before his trail formed a wake. He swam northwest.

17

MÄRREN

MÄRREN ROWED AFTER UISGE. SHEETS OF RAIN ROLLED IN FROM the north, dumping over the sea and darkening everything before night fell. As the tempest neared, rain roared as it struck the sea and hit the faering, the tumult drowning out all other noises. Märren cursed under her furs, facing forward and keeping an eye on Uisge's mane as it bobbed in water that rose higher and higher with each swell. The waves lifted the faering before dropping it back down with a jolt and thud. Choppy waters in the trough between swells then crashed into the boat's side and over Märren and her supplies.

"Steer northward!" Uisge's voice barely carried over the din. "A serpent hunts these waters."

Märren lurched, her eyes darting around, trying to pierce the gray wet as it plummeted around her and stirred the sea. After all these years, it had taken Eimri's death to make her seek the lands she had dreamed of since she was a child. She had already failed once in reaching the mystical Dragon, and her current path seemed even more difficult than crossing the Unclaimed Lands.

She clenched her teeth as she hefted her axe and swung it

downward, burying its blade deep into the wood on the side of the faering. This would hopefully stop a wave from washing her weapon out of its strap on her waist and into the sea, as well as position the axe so she could grasp it in a hurry. Her pack floated in the hull. She scanned surging waves for the spines of a serpent as she angled her faering north and rowed hard. The wind gusted, throwing rain sideways.

"These conditions are those favored by sea serpents."

"Serpents prefer their prey not to see them coming. Then they wrap up a vessel and devour those on board."

"If it comes near, she'll spot it."

A scar rune on Märren's hip lit up in her mind as a warning. She regripped her oars and pulled, following the seaweed mane that emerged and disappeared in the rolling swells, the land behind her growing more distant.

The massive arch of a serpent rose from the sea to her left. She rowed harder, but the serpent glided through the turbulent waters as easily as a leech through the fjord while her faering floundered. She gripped her axe, wrenching it from the wood and standing in the surging rain and rocking waves, staring at the humps of the beast, daring it to come.

"Maybe I'll take part of a serpent before I take a piece of the Dragon," she yelled into the storm.

Her faering bucked, something having smacked into it from beneath. She tumbled forward, nearly pitching over into the sea, but dropped onto her knees and face to stop herself from flying overboard. She smacked her chin against the frame, rattling her head, her knees thumping with pain after they struck the hull. While struggling to regain her footing amidst the rocking, with a bright sphere in her vision and the sea spinning around her, she used one hand to grasp the side of her vessel. Her axe remained in her grip.

A wave surged and smashed over the bow, blasting against

her and nearly washing her out. A spiked hump rose from the water, plowing toward her craft, and Märren stood, rearing back to swing. A harder hit came from below and behind her. Märren catapulted out of the faering, the sea rushing up to meet her. Her head plunged below the frigid wet.

She rolled about, spewing bubbles, her gaze darting here and there through thick foam and whitewater below the surface, expecting the face of a beast to emerge. A length of scales and muscle wrapped around her legs and torso. Her neck. The serpent's fanged head broke through the foam and sneered at her as its coils clenched and squeezed, its head as large as her body. She tried to hack at its scales with her axe, but under water, she could not gain enough momentum to cut into its hide. She had to end it... end her life, somehow. And quickly. Before this monster killed her.

Märren's legs cramped with pain, and her chest could not expand for air. Her lungs burned, demanding her mouth to open. The beast's tongue flicked out, but the coil around her neck did not choke her. The serpent tried, its muscles tensing around the thrall collar, but was unable to crush the steel.

Märren gripped the seax attached to the strap around her neck, imagining freeing herself of this life before being killed in battle. She would join Eimri. She plunged the blade at her throat, but it sank into the coil around her neck. Blood rushed out into the sea, turning everything dark. A hollow bellow rang in the deeps. She yanked the blade free and drove it into the beast again and again.

The coils relaxed and slid away. Märren broke through the surface, waves rolling around her as she gasped and sputtered for air, struggling to tread water and maintain her grip on her axe. Uisge floated in the trough below the wave she rode on.

Bloodied coils slipped out of the water and wrapped around Uisge's neck. Uisge wailed and thrashed about.

Märren plunged down the wave, kicking herself toward the pair. When she reached them, she reared back and swung, burying the blade of her axe into the serpent's hide. Steel bit deep. Another bellow sounded in the sea, and black blood erupted from the beast's wound. Märren gripped onto Uisge's tail and yanked her axe back, hacking the serpent again.

The coils unraveled and slipped below the surface, leaving a trail of blood. Märren heaved for breath, the black paint she wore on her cheeks smearing across her furs as she glanced around for the faering while holding on to Uisge's tail to help keep her afloat and anchored to something. Uisge rode the waves with ease.

Märren's boat was nowhere around. She frantically felt for Eimri's skull in the pouch at her waist, patting about.

Still there.

Uisge's face lifted from the water, watching her. "Climb onto my back."

Märren hesitated. That was the classic trick all uisges used to ensnare their victims. "I hear things others don't, but I'm no fool. You'll bind me to you and take me down into the deeps. Drown me. Then eat all of me but my liver."

"I won't bind you or do any of that," Uisge replied.

She scoffed. "You already promised to take me on a safe path across this strait."

"What you believed was happening when we met isn't true. You didn't save me from the troll. I was trying to lure the creature into the water to devour it, but you thought you saved me by deceiving it in that ridiculous manner. It gave me laughter. Then you fed me, and I stayed for your blood." He tossed his head and mane. "You may ride me, and I will not eat you. I swear it upon the serpent you saved me from and the sacred waters."

"You expect me to believe that after what you just admitted?"

"The storm is too much, and there's no safe path. You won't

make the crossing even if you find the faering. I'll take you to the land of fire and ash."

Märren considered it, slowly pulling herself closer to Uisge's back and the seaweed there while gripping her axe tighter.

"I won't betray a life debt," Uisge said. "Not to you. You're unlike the others of your kind, and I'm in your service now. If I'm ever tempted and start to dive, take your axe to my skull. Kill me first."

"If I kill you, I'll die out here. A Valkyrie could consider that an honorable death."

"I'll take you on a ride I never would've allowed you or any human to experience before."

Märren glanced around at the raging sea they floated upon without effort, white water rolling around her, waves cresting. They rolled down one swell, riding it to a trough. The crest of the next wave loomed far overhead.

"Damn the dead gods," Märren cursed, kicking and pulling herself onto Uisge's back and lying across him. She swung her leg over, straddling him bareback, and patted Eimri's skull to make sure her daughter was still with her.

Uisge rose from the sea until he nearly stood on its surface, riding the trough, his hoofs and lower limbs blending into the waves, the margins between creature and water indistinct. He snorted at the incoming wave and galloped sideways along the swell as it rose, the foaming white water cresting far above them. Märren watched the towering wave with dread, unable to believe it would not smash into them and drive them to the deeps.

"She wants to die now. To fall prey to treachery."

"She has no hope and will allow the creature to devour her."

"Uisge runs on water, and she rides him as comfortably as any steed."

Hoofbeats pounded on the sea, flinging spray into the air,

Uisge charging along the rolling wet faster than a palfrey across a field. The threatening wave crashed behind them, and Uisge galloped up the incline of another that was not as steep, rising to the summit and pausing.

At the pinnacle of the sea, Märren took in the rain and the raging water around them that looked akin to a kingdom of mountainous dark peaks. Tumultuous peaks.

"Thankfully for both of us, that was a very small serpent," Uisge said.

They rode the wave, rolling over other peaks before Uisge lunged forward and barreled on.

18

BELFEDRN

"We should venture to the jarl's longhouse," Athna said, not meeting Vard's gaze, the implications of his family's fate hanging in the smoke-ridden air. The bodies of the Sea Serpents burned in their fires as the pack feasted to quell the Wolf's hunger after utilizing their magics in battle. "It's not far."

"I won't place my own above those who may still be alive." Vard faltered. "First we travel south to see if we can aid the warriors we disregarded earlier."

"Or perhaps we should look for the trainees," Belfedrn said as thoughts of Deyja, the boy he had sworn to protect, tormented him.

"South first," Vard commanded.

The pack gathered, their loyalty and strength pulsing when they pressed together. Some of Belfedrn's exhaustion washed away.

"For the Wolves," they cried and loped off, the streets and razed huts and market houses passing too slowly for Belfedrn's liking.

Soon, a scent of fresher blood and burned flesh carried across the distance, although there was no clashing steel or shouting. Thunder rang overhead. The pack ran faster, following their noses, entering a denser fog than that which they had already passed through.

Belfedrn burst into a square, shoulder to shoulder with Kesg and Ylsga, apprehension seeping from them and overpowering optimism. They slowed their pace, the smoke and lighter Serpent mist churning, the scents they were tracking directly ahead. Belfedrn waved to dispel the haze.

The seared shoulder and arm of a Sea Serpent warrior poked through a layer of ash, stiff as a beam. More corpses lay twisted around the perimeter of the square, most of these Serpent warriors. Belfedrn stepped past the bodies. Beyond lay dead Wolf warriors who grasped charred axes and spears, their faces blackened by fire, although Belfedrn preferred to think of them as painted in the manner of the Ulfhednar.

"All dead." Eakthr swept low over the ground, sniffing as he pranced about, his eyes wild. "All of this warrior pack."

"They fought courageously," Athna said, rage and a need for vengeance causing her voice to crack. "So many Serpents are dead as well."

Vard whimpered as he stalked about the area. "We couldn't have saved the young and these warriors. So I won't curse myself for this outcome, but I am a fool. These people could have aided us more than those we saved."

"What do we do now?" Kesg knelt over a fallen warrior and grasped the body's charred hand. "With their bodies already burned, the Valkyries will have taken them to Valhalla."

"We stop by each of our homes," Vard said. "My longhouse, our great hall, comes last. We pay our respects and go from there."

The pack limped toward Vard, gathering, pressing in against each other as tightly as when in the shield wall. Arms and shoulders of comrades shoved into Belfedrn, and yet the sensation brought a sense of stability and comfort. This reassurance by the pack, through its members, eased his immense pain. He no longer felt like he would shatter to pieces.

Something rustled to Belfedrn's right. He crouched and snarled, raising the spear he had acquired and his shield. Ash shifted then fell still. The collapsed beams of a longhouse jutted out from its charred foundation, all of it creating a heap.

"What is it?" Ylsga paused, sensing his alarm.

"There's movement." Belfedrn approached the beams, jabbing the butt of his spear into the debris.

The ashes shifted again.

"I heard it this time." Ylsga knelt and began digging through the remains of the structure as Belfedrn and Kesg together hefted a beam and tossed it aside. "Although it may only be settling embers."

"If a Serpent head pops up, I'll skewer it." Eakthr watched with wild eyes as he stalked about the area and giggled. He pulled his longbow from his shoulder and nocked an arrow, drawing until the string was taut against his cheek.

Belfedrn heaved another beam aside, revealing the pale skin of an arm. He fell to his knees and dug, flinging debris away until Kesg assisted him and they uncovered the chest and face of a young Wolf warrior. Belfedrn grabbed the man under his shoulders and tried to heave him out as Kesg and Ylsga hefted another beam. The warrior's waist was stuck for a heartbeat before the beam was moved and he slid free from the wreckage. Belfedrn dragged him out of the heap and laid him down.

The warrior gasped, his head lolling, eyes fluttering.

"Warrior of Fenrir." Vard knelt beside the man. "I'll warn you that when you wake, it'll be to a nightmare, but wake you must." The jarl of the Ulfhednar shook the warrior and dumped his waterskin over the man's face. Water splashed across his cheeks, sweeping soot away and exposing pale skin.

The warrior's eyes slowly opened as he glanced around and lurched. "Where?"

Belfedrn grasped him tightly, holding him still as Vard said, "We retrieved you from the remains of a longhouse. You and your pack were fighting those who ambushed Nistreel."

The man's darting eyes settled, and he slowly nodded, his furs torn, his small piece of Fenrir's pelt filthy with soot. He was barely a man, with only a hint of stubble on his chin. "My sister!"

The warrior rolled toward Belfedrn, thrashing against his restraint, reaching for the wreckage.

"She's gone," Belfedrn said.

"She can't be," the young warrior replied. "I was protecting her. Whatever fell would've hit me first."

"Buried deeper than you, it seems." Eakthr kicked at the smoking beams. "She wouldn't have been able to breathe. And the longer we linger, the more likely we are to die as well."

"Dig her out!" The warrior struggled against Belfedrn, but his feeble attempts to break free were futile. "You don't know how long we were under that. Not long—not long at all." Desperation laced his tone.

Vard grunted, studying their surroundings, probably pondering the chance of more Sea Serpents returning versus if anyone could still be alive in the remains of that structure.

Belfedrn released the warrior, pessimism latching its claws into him as he shook his head but dug deeper into the debris. Kesg, Ylsga, Eakthr, and Athna joined him, flinging aside cinders, releasing more ash and smoke. A body lay beneath where the young man had been trapped, hands covering a face. Belfedrn grasped its wrists and dragged it out—a young woman probably a couple winters younger than the boy of a man they freed. Pale golden hair and wan skin, most of her stained with soot. She also wore a *brynja* and leathers.

Kesg aided Belfedrn, and they laid her beside her brother, who clung to her and shook her. The woman also wore a patch of Fenrir's dark pelt.

Another Wolf warrior.

"Wake, Thelira," the man said. "Wake!"

Belfedrn dumped his waterskin onto the woman's face. She gasped and lurched away, covering herself, dark water streaming away in runnels from her hair and cheeks.

"Thelira!" The young man rolled closer and threw his arms around her as she coughed.

"I-I saw the beams coming," she said in a quiet voice hoarse from smoke. "I covered myself..."

"And bought yourself a bit of air," Belfedrn said. "You're both alive." He glanced around. "Better off than the others here. Do you remember what happened?"

"They came out of nowhere," the man replied, his eyes turning distant. "Fog rolled in from the sea, sweeping across the plains and highlands. It covered the city. We couldn't see or even smell or hear what was hiding in its gray arms."

"The Sea Serpents," Vard said in disgust.

"I believe so. All I remember are the death cries and my pack racing for the fog. We faced off with it and whatever it held but were driven back by their sheer numbers. The warriors compressed around me." He trembled. "I couldn't see. Couldn't move. Felt like I couldn't breathe. I pushed Thelira behind me. I can't recall much more. Only the clash of steel. The flash of flame. Warriors striking the pack out of nowhere."

Belfedrn looked the two warriors over. None of their limbs jutted out at strange angles or were twisted around the middle of their bones. "Can you stand?"

"Aye." The young man grimaced as he shifted his weight. "I think so." He steadied himself by gripping Belfedrn's arm and slowly rose. Thelira followed, moving even slower.

"Good," Belfedrn replied. "Resting will get you killed."

"I'm Dradn." The boy of a man nodded to Belfedrn.

"We're what is left of the Ulfhednar." Belfedrn spread his arms to indicate his pack.

Dradn's eyes widened with awe as he and Thelira shared a glance. Dradn said, "I... thought it was ash and not paint smeared down your cheeks. Word was the Ulfhednar left Nistreel to look into an issue with trolls."

Belfedrn squeezed Dradn's shoulder. "We did. And I'll curse myself the rest of my days for falling for that ruse. No matter how short those days may be."

Vard motioned for the pack to move on, but Belfedrn grabbed the jarl and eased him away from the others.

"They should come with us," Belfedrn said.

"They'll slow the pack. None but the Ulfhednar can travel with us. By the looks of them, those two are barely warriors."

"Then make them Ulfhednar. They have nothing. Look around us. Give them hope."

Vard cocked his head, studying Belfedrn as if he had lost his mind before staring off into the distance. "Ulfhednar without the required training and accomplishments? Next, we'll be taking on simple mercenaries for hire, diminishing the ability of our warriors and the pack as a whole. The pack is only as strong as its weakest member."

Belfedrn summoned as much empathy as he could muster in hopes of persuading his jarl. "If they don't come with us, they'll die here. Their pack is gone, and our clan has lost everything."

Vard grunted as he turned away from Belfedrn. A few breaths later, he said, "Come, Dradn and Thelira. You're no longer warriors."

The siblings' heads slumped in shame.

"You'll now consider yourself members of our pack," Vard added.

Dradn's head jerked up, and he studied the jarl in disbelief. "Us? Ulfhednar? But we cannot command the magics that you berserkers do."

Vard stalked close to Belfedrn. "They're your problem now, Belfedrn. You'll have to protect them. And train them. Even though they'll probably end up getting us killed."

Kesg chuckled and clapped Belfedrn on the back, as if in support, but stronger in mockery.

Belfedrn nodded, and a sinking feeling pulled at his guts.

19

CAËTIN

THE UNKINDNESS DESCENDED BEFORE A BARE ROWAN TREE INSIDE Aonark, squawking, merging into Caëtin before they touched the ground. Caëtin landed softly, sheathing her pale blade while striding toward the jarl's great hall, the cold aftereffects of flying as ravens making her tremble, her mind bleary with exhaustion. Her stomach squeezed with hunger, and her throat burned with thirst. Sanre, the knight Caëtin had left behind to determine Jundr's guilt, waited nearby.

The other unkindnesses alighted or flew around Caëtin, spiraling about and forming into berserkers. Sanre rushed forward and assisted Halfnr with carrying Thovar, the stumps of Thovar's legs dangling over the street, his leggings soaked with blood where they were knotted below the amputation sites.

"Hurry." Caëtin waved Halfnr on as she shoved the great doors inward. "Bring him inside. We'll call for a healer."

The few surviving Knights Black who had accompanied Caëtin to Sparsgard rushed past her as Halfnr and Sanre carried their comrade to the closest table. With a sweep of his arm, Halfnr knocked the trenchers and horns from the table and laid

Thovar on its surface. Thovar was paler than a typical Raven berserker, almost like snow, his breathing faint, eyes cloudy.

"Sister!" Darstrid hurried away from the throne and many others who were downing drink and bellowing with laughter. A man slapped her on the arse as she marched toward them, and she did not seem to notice. "What did you find?"

"We need a healer," Caëtin said. "Now."

Treln and Lythi emerged from somewhere and ran toward Caëtin, but when they saw Thovar, the children stopped and gawked. Lythi wrapped her arms around her brother, keeping him at a distance.

Darstrid reached the table where Thovar lay, studying him. "It's too late. Can you not see that?"

"Of course I see," Caëtin snapped. "But we can't stand here and watch him die without trying to save him! He's a Knight Black."

"You're right. Forgive me." Darstrid motioned toward the throne, but Uktr was not seated upon it. "Bring the Seidr woman."

"She's not allowed—" A voice came from the loft where the jarl slept, but it was not Uktr's.

"Bring her, now!" Darstrid said. "And quickly."

Footsteps thumped on the stairs as several feet hurried down. From behind the throne, a Knight Black and a woman emerged in the torchlight, the woman young and scantily clad beneath a cloak of ordinary raven feathers.

Why's there a Seidr woman here? She looks like a typical gyðja. Caëtin waved her toward Thovar, hoping her magic of the other worlds and spirits was strong.

Three men descending from the loft followed this woman and the berserker. The Seidr woman looked Thovar over, inspecting his injuries. He barely winced. She opened his eyelids, the whites laced with red vessels, and his eyes shut as soon as she released them. She waved a hand over him, brushing his legs with a feather as she muttered something in the tongue of the dead gods, most of which Caëtin could not understand.

Thovar gasped, and his eyes opened, unblinking while he stared past them as if seeing another world.

"You look upon the Raven's bridge," the Seidr woman said. "And a shieldmaiden comes for you. Let Muninn take you, my brother. Feel her wing and rest beneath it."

Thovar's head lolled to the side, his gaze turning dull as he expelled his last breath. A few heartbeats of silence passed.

"There was nothing more that could have been done," the Seidr woman said. "He'd lost too much blood already."

"Damn this cursed day," Caëtin muttered.

Halfnr clasped her shoulder. "He would've died if you'd have left him to the Spider people."

"He died anyway," she snapped. "After suffering the loss of his legs at my hand and making a long flight in anguish. The Spider laughs at me now." She steadied herself, weakness, guilt, and worry rising within her, the desire to fall into the unkindness and flap away nearly overcoming her.

Halfnr squeezed and then released her shoulder. Treln ran up and wrapped his arms around her waist. Lythi waited patiently behind her brother.

"Then you found people of the Spider clan at Sparsgard?" Darstrid's tone carried only a wisp of surprise, as if she had already suspected it.

"Aye." Caëtin placed her hand on Thovar's chest and spoke to him as she patted Treln's head. "Find the Ravens who've already crossed the bridge, berserker of Muninn, and hold your weapon close while you make the crossing." She folded his fingers around his axe. "Do not hold a grudge against me for my decision and your pain."

"Did you kill him?" Treln asked.

Caëtin winced. "I tried to save him."

"He's hearing the ravens sing now," Lythi whispered, sounding as if she were seeing the bridge world as well.

"What happened?" Darstrid asked.

"The Spiders set an ambush for us. The children who'd gone missing had been caught in web traps hidden in the fields between the village and the River Red."

"Then these invading Spiders are still alive?"

"We were forced to flee like winged rats. They surrounded us. Outnumbered us. Half of my berserkers were trapped in webs in the village. I think the locals knew what was coming, but they didn't warn us."

"The gods shite on such traitors." Darstrid paced in the central walk, and she flung a horn aside, its contents spraying over several men. "You and your berserkers rest here. I'll take a legion and wipe this enemy from our lands." She paused. "However, I'm curious as to how the Spiders managed to pass through Horse territory without word of their raids spreading."

"Maybe the Horse clan made some deal with them. The Horse people could have avoided battle and death by allowing the Spiders to reach the Ravens instead."

"Are we greater enemies of the Spider than the Horse is?"

Caëtin pondered that but did not know why the Raven would be. Another boy ran up and stood beside Treln, staring at Thovar's body. The boy chewed on a slab of meat, its juices dripping from his hand.

"Trade with the Horse people will be disrupted either way," Darstrid said. "The flow of silver and goods will dwindle, and our people's wealth will ebb. But addressing this attack takes precedence." Darstrid gestured at the Seidr woman behind them as she continued to speak to Caëtin, although quieter. "Before you rest, Sister, you have more work to do. Uktr has found another traitor in our midst."

"The Seidr woman? Is that why she's here?"

"She had one last chance to prove her innocence by healing Thovar. She didn't, and Uktr suspects someone has been passing Muninn parts to our enemies."

Caëtin faltered. "Feathers? They're our greatest treasure but would be of little use to any who are untrained in our ways."

"Uktr thinks some of the small feathers are being passed along our trade routes to another clan."

Caëtin's breath caught in her throat. "No. No member of our clan would do that. And there's no reason another clan would desire them more than silver or gold. Not enough for someone to risk torture and death or worse for whatever another clan could offer in coin."

"He wants you to interrogate her."

"No. Not again. I'm a terrible inquisitor."

Darstrid strode on, nearing the throne as Caëtin followed. "I know. But *she* asked that you do it."

Caëtin glanced over her shoulder at the Seidr woman. "Why would she choose me?"

"Because our inquisitors always get their confessions."

"And I got Jundr's, even though I still have doubts about its validity." Caëtin looked about for Sanre, wondering what the knight had found out.

"The Seidr woman asked for you, and I do not command that tier of magics. We waited for your return before dealing with her."

"Has Uktr fully lost his mind?"

Darstrid bobbed her head in a noncommittal manner.

Caëtin sidled over to Sanre and whispered, "What did you find out?"

"That Uktr had no evidence." Sanre spoke quietly. "The jarl believed there was another traitor and assumed it was Jundr because he was originally from another clan."

Bloody fuck... Uktr is mad and eager for violence.

Treln stepped closer, and the other boy followed, still chewing. Treln spun on the boy and punched him in the nose. Blood spewed as the boy fell back, and Treln jumped on him. Caëtin cursed under her breath and hauled Treln off the boy, his fists still swinging.

"Stop!" Caëtin said, hurling her son away. "He is not attacking you. He's not your enemy. Violence should not be your first reaction!"

Treln sprawled across the walk. When he slid to a stop, he slammed his fists against the floor and wailed before scrambling to his feet and rushing off into the commotion of those feasting.

Caëtin inhaled slowly to control her need to find and reprimand her son further. "Lythi?"

Her daughter stared up at the rafters, holding a horn of drink and smiling. She glanced at her mother.

"Can you look after Treln until I deal with whatever I'm supposed to address now?"

Lythi nodded, weaving away through the crowds around the tables.

Caëtin turned to Darstrid and lowered her voice. She suddenly trusted her sister and Darstrid's latest plan all the more, since Uktr was no longer levelheaded. "And what has come of the shite-brained idea we discussed before I left?"

"I'm working on convincing the knights and rangers to pledge their swords to us, but it's a delicate conversation to have." Darstrid glanced away. "I can only speak with one of them at a time for fear of what could happen if two or more were outraged by the idea and turned on me. I'm one of Uktr's daughters, but usurping his authority would still mean death for me. It'll take more time."

"I'll be able to help. If Father stops giving me errands." Caëtin faced her knights, who lingered around the table Thovar lay on.

One of the three men who had come down from the loft approached her. Taknhal. Uktr held this son in high regard, and Taknhal would be first in line to the throne, even before Caëtin and Darstrid, if he were able to command half the power of Muninn that either of them could. And if Taknhal were not so often drowning in drink.

"Caëtin." Taknhal smiled warmly at her, his balance wavering as he wiped at his mouth. "My favorite sister."

"I believe that as much as I believe you wouldn't hump me if I passed out from drink," Caëtin said.

Darstrid chuckled.

Taknhal's smile grew broader as he glanced at Darstrid, his gaze taking longer than normal to focus on her. "My two favorite sisters is what I meant. And we've no blood relation, so the offer of humping is always there. Even if you're awake."

Caëtin cringed. Taknhal was an attractive and powerful man, but sex with him seemed somehow unnatural. He also took every woman he could get his hands on, although he may prefer drink over women.

"I'm glad you've returned." Taknhal stepped aside to make way for the other two men who had followed him from the loft —Grimmurk and Freydeg. "And I'm sorry you have to do this so soon upon your return, but it must be done."

"What must be done?"

Taknhal indicated Grimmurk and Freydeg, Uktr's closest comrades who had fought alongside him in the battles that shaped the Raven clan's territory. Scars and wrinkles riddled Grimmurk's and Freydeg's faces and arms, and they were taller than any other Raven in the room. Grimmurk's long gray hair swung about his chest and the golden clasps holding his cloak around his shoulders. Freydeg bore more silver and still had some blond in his hair. Both were powerful but aging men. Like Caëtin's father.

Grimmurk strode past them and grabbed the Seidr woman by the neck, shoving her toward Caëtin. The Seidr woman stumbled but regained her balance and walked on, pausing before Caëtin. She held two horns full of drink.

Grimmurk lumbered up behind the Seidr woman, speaking to Caëtin, "You've heard?"

"About the inquisition?" Caëtin asked.

"Aye."

"I'll take her to the temple once I've rested and recovered from my flight." Caëtin grabbed the Seidr woman by her wrist.

"No." Grimmurk dug his fingers into the back of the Seidr woman's neck. "We do this inquisition here."

"Why?"

"Uktr, Freydeg, and I want to watch. To see what happens on the Raven's bridge with this one."

Caëtin bit her lip. "I don't want to question her there. I'm not an inquisitor."

"But you are." The voice came from the loft. Uktr's sunken face peered down at her, his eyes shadowed and bloodshot behind his beaked nose. "You got Jundr's confession and didn't let him get away with betraying us. I'm coming to trust you more and hoping that the Raven's throne will be safe with your arse in it."

He's been drinking with Taknhal, Freydeg, and Grimmurk but seems alert and aware. He must be angry. "I barely know how to pry into a traitor's mind."

Uktr clumped down the stairs. "I trust you more than any of the other inquisitors."

"I want you to do it." The Seidr woman's eyes filled with entreaty as she held the horns out to Caëtin. "It must be you."

"This woman told us that she'd admit to everything if you were the one to take her to the bridge," Uktr said. "Eat and drink quickly. Recover. Your skills are needed once again." Then he addressed Darstrid. "Take your berserkers south and clear the fields your sister mentioned. Pluck any spiders you find from their webs and devour them. The way a raven would do with their kind. Make it clear to the people of Sparsgard that they reside in our lands and are Raven people. Leave a warning, but don't kill them. We'll deal with them after we know what's occurring and why we still have a traitor or two in our midst."

Darstrid dipped her head and clasped Caëtin's arm. "I'll return soon, Sister, and I'll restore what relations and trade routes we have with the Horse clan."

"Take many more knights than you think you'll need," Caëtin replied. "Those Spiders crawl out of the buggering earth."

"I will, and I'll send a legion of our swiftest warrior riders to meet us. Just in case."

"Be smarter than I was." Caëtin patted her back.

"So I don't have to cut off the legs of one of my knights?"

A blade of guilt twisted in Caëtin's heart. "That's not what I meant. Don't get taken by surprise."

"I was only mocking." Darstrid grinned, something Caëtin had seen many times before—the subtle quirk of her lips revealing she had drunk too much as well. Darstrid usually turned boisterous and bawdy with drink, probably why men were slapping her backside and she did not mind. "To ease your pain with a laugh. I thought it was what your smart arse would say in this situation."

Darstrid stalked away, headed toward the entrance of the longhouse. Caëtin's mirth at her sister's sarcasm was short-lived.

Uktr stepped onto the ground level and said, “Come.” He waved Caëtin closer, walking behind the throne.

She followed Taknhal, Freydeg, and Grimmurk around the dais. At the rear of the great hall, an empty table and chairs waited. Horns filled with dark liquid sat before each chair.

Uktr leaned over the table. “Shall we get to it, then?”

20

BELFEDRN

Flames roared, consuming the jarl's longhouse, all of the structure ablaze and cracking. Lightning flashed overhead, and thunder shook the air—a lingering storm that could not have been coincidental this time of year and must have been summoned by a powerful Sea Serpent berserker.

Vard barreled through the flaming entryway, the doors hanging open.

"Don't go in!" Belfedrn rushed after him.

Inside, fire feasted upon the walls, and heat hit Belfedrn like a wave, almost knocking him over. Dense smoke clung to the loft and rafters, lesser amounts whirling about the lower areas. No one had been left alive. Bodies burned. So did the throne and its fur lining, forming a mass of towering flames, the wolf head crowning its chairback blazing and staring back at them with empty eyes.

Vard rushed deeper into the interior. Belfedrn tried to stop him, but the jarl was too quick. Belfedrn and Kesg followed, the heat singeing their skin. Belfedrn coughed even though he was covering his mouth and nose with a damp fur. Ahead, Vard knelt beside a smoldering body, caressing it.

His mate's. Her hair smoked, a blade clutched in a blackened hand. Behind her, another body was bent over backward at the waist, draped over the steps leading up to the throne. *By the Wolf's mercy.*

The heat sweltered, and pillars and beams cracked. Cinders dropped around them.

Belfedrn jerked on Vard's arm. "We must go!"

Vard allowed his mate's body to fall back to the floor. The flames would take her and aid her in her passage to the next world. She had died fighting. Died with valor. Unlike Belfedrn and Vard, who lingered on. Belfedrn pulled Vard out of the collapsing longhouse and into the wreckage of Nistreel. Kesg followed.

Tears rained down Vard's cheeks. He dropped to one knee and lowered his head, whimpering and sputtering in the smoke as he hacked and covered his face with his hands. The rest of the pack formed a circle around their jarl, heads bowed in remorse and reverence for the dead.

The situation had been the same with every pack member's house thus far, only the larger structures had taken longer to burn and had not already been embers when they arrived.

Enormous beams cracked and fell in the great hall, its walls folding inward as the structure collapsed. Smoke billowed from its open roof and plumed into the sky.

A sickening feeling of loss tugged at Belfedrn's core as memories of his people and mate tormented him. *Lyrne.* At least she had found glory and now resided in Valhalla. He should not be disheartened, but he was. They had never had children. Probably his fault. Not that magnificent woman's. Since her death, whenever she had been mentioned, he had tried to display pride as he was supposed to, but the sorrow that came crashing upon him with the sound of her name was suffocating.

He was alone in this world. No, not alone. He had the pack,

just no one bound to him by blood... except for Märren. Märren did not often come to mind, not with her residing so far away, but she could still be alive, could have avoided the Sea Serpent onslaught.

Belfedrn stared northeasterly through the haze. No matter what the pack was to do after this, he would encourage them to visit Märren, or he would take his leave and do so alone.

"Eakthr." Vard stood, tear tracks running in pale lines through the black paint and ash on his cheeks. "We must visit your home before the pack moves on."

Eakthr trembled. "No. I cannot do it." He cowered and whimpered.

"If you never know—if you do not have closure—you'll regret not going to look." Vard shook his head.

"I understand." Eakthr swallowed. "But we all already know what's happened. It's been the same with everyone."

"This is your last chance." Vard snarled. "If you're too weak and frightened to face reality, it'll haunt you the rest of your life."

Eakthr's eyes fell shut, and his head and shoulders sagged as he shuffled about whimpering. "The pack moves on."

Vard grunted in frustration. "I cannot force you to face such pain." He pointed into the distance. "Then we make for the sacred ground."

"Would these bastards defile even that?" Dradn asked, his face drawn as he looked to his sister and new pack members for reassurance. "But they'd have no reason. They couldn't..."

Deyja...

"Come." Vard loped westward toward the old quarters.

"For the Wolves," the members said, their voices subdued and mournful.

Belfedrn joined the pack and followed Vard through the fog, traveling across streets once familiar but which now appeared as foreign as those of another clan's city. After a short run, walls of stone emerged like dark giants in the haze. These walls did not burn, but fires speckled the area before them.

Vard led the pack between pillars and under towering archways, into the sanctuary, and a sense that something was missing hovered in the air. Dread pressed a heavy fist against Belfedrn's chest and caused him to struggle for breath. The trees around the periphery of the interior resembled flaming torches. Bodies had been staked to the upper boughs—like the body in the woods that had lured the trolls in—flesh melting and dripping. Belfedrn cringed, his stomach churning with bile, nausea rising, its sour vapors haunting the back of his tongue as he searched the faces of the bodies. They were too burned and disfigured to identify.

"Blood shall not be spilled on holy ground," Athna muttered, rage sharpening her words. White fire jutted from her fingers and dripped flames that hissed as they fell to the ground. "Do the people of the Serpent not know the common laws?"

Dradn gagged and retched, his long brown hair draping over his face as vomit spewed from his lips and struck the ground. He groaned and straightened, wiping at the soiled fluff of a beard around his nose and mouth. Thelira rubbed his back, her expression taut, the naïve look of an adolescent girl having fled her.

"Most are the *gyðja* and *goði*." Ylsga gestured upward, indicating the burning bodies and the remnants of furs that had been cloaking them.

"Have these Serpents no decency?" Athna growled. More flames dripped from her hand.

The pups, the trainees, would've been slaughtered as well. The pack members understood this, but no one uttered the fact, fearing to release it into the world. Belfedrn had failed Deyja and failed the boy's father, who had been one of his two closest friends and an Ulfhednar before he died honorably in battle.

His hand slipped to a pouch at his waist where he still carried the strip of pelt he had blackmailed a *goði* into stealing for him, a memento he could not seem to part with, although it could cost him his comrades' trust.

He had blackmailed the *goði* for Deyja, back when Belfedrn first became beholden to the boy. Belfedrn had considered passing the scrap to Deyja many times so the boy could accept the power of the god part into his body, to help make up for the lack of a father and a father's training and love, and now Belfedrn wished he would have given the scrap to him. That last time he spoke with Deyja, he had almost offered it to the boy. The only thing that had stayed his hand—the issue that always made him reconsider—was Deyja mentioning how he was advancing faster than the other trainees. Belfedrn thought it unwise to offer the boy more power, but it could have saved his life here, could have given him some advantage over the Serpent warriors.

Belfedrn cursed himself and his weaknesses. This strip was not the only piece of Fenrir's remains that he had smuggled out from the sanctuary over the years. He had passed other scraps along to different trainees he had known, those who had been disadvantaged for one reason or another, to aid them in their struggles, struggles Belfedrn remembered all too vividly from when he was their age. He had never had a son or daughter, although he desired both, and for some reason he felt obligated to help other children. Lyrne had told him his meddling would only weaken those he tried to help by giving them an unfair advantage in training and thus would make them less careful in battle. He believed life routinely offered advantages and disadvantages, and he could not sit idly by, watching while some received all the benefits this world handed out. That was why he stopped admitting his indiscretions to his mate.

Now she was dead, too.

"There aren't enough bodies here for all the trainees to have been killed," Ylsga said as she passed Belfedrn, probably hoping to ease his pain. She and Kesg knew of his oath to their deceased friend.

Belfedrn surveyed the area, clinging to a flicker of hope.

"It's true." Kesg pointed around them. "Some were killed, there's no doubt of that, but the Sea Serpents may have taken many."

"It's no time for speculation," Vard said. "We keep moving!"

The pack darted between the flaming trees and into the clearing beyond. Belfedrn forced himself after them. A gargantuan stake stood in the middle of the area, and a chain with links as big around as a hefty man lay in a heap beside it. The sacred grounds. The skeleton of Fenrir rested on its side, sprawling across much of the area. The god's neck was still bound by the chain, his remains as large as a dozen warhorses combined, although the Wolf was much taller and lankier than any steed.

Belfedrn shuddered as fear, awe, and love embraced him in a strong grip. Then dread and wrath slipped in. Fenrir instilled these emotions whenever Belfedrn looked upon the god's remains. Time crawled by before he realized what had been missing when he entered the sanctuary—the sensation of his skull rattling.

"It's gone." Athna cautiously approached the god's remains, as if afraid Fenrir might rise from the dead and swallow her. "All of it."

Eakthr crept closer, quieter than the others, taking mincing steps, his shoulders and back hunched even more so than typical.

"Damn these bloody serpents." Vard spat as he followed their battle Seidr and thief, marching closer.

Belfedrn joined them along with Kesg and Ylsga, all striding toward the twisted bones and yellowed fangs. Much of Fenrir's skeleton bore the marks of fresh blade attacks. Belfedrn's rage intensified. No flesh had remained on the Wolf's skeleton for longer than Belfedrn had been alive, but now, the god's entire pelt was gone.

"They took every last piece of his fur," Athna said. "And defiled his bones. Slaughtered all the *gyðja* and *goði*. As well as the Ulfhednar masters and some trainees."

Another blade of pain pierced Belfedrn's heart. He winced but suppressed his agony. Such deep emotion would have to be faced later. Like with Lyrne's death, he could not fully take it in or face it, could not grieve and mourn appropriately until vengeance had been dealt. It would break him. He prayed that Deyja and some of the trainees were still alive. He knelt and placed a rune stone near the stake and chain, the ancient words he uttered barely loud enough for him to hear them.

"Why take the rest of Fenrir's pelt?" Dradn reached out to touch the snout of the god beast but paused. "Everyone knows that trained berserkers who have wielded the parts of one god cannot take up those from a second and survive. It's been tried."

"The reason is simple," Kesg said. "The Sea Serpents didn't want to leave anything for Wolf survivors."

"Then why not burn the remains of his pelt here?" Belfedrn stalked around the skull of the god. "Our Wolf warriors were already carrying as much of his pelt as they had earned."

"But not all were carrying as much as they could tolerate," Vard added. "Segments of pelt would have made some of our fighters stronger."

Belfedrn shook his head. He did not wholly accept Kesg's theory. "The Sea Serpent jarl I met—Vegask—would find pleasure in insulting our people, but the Serpents must desire pelts for another reason. Fragments of Fenrir are valuable. Maybe they hope to trade them or simply want to keep them with their Serpent god's remains. Like hoarded treasure."

Athna paced, her long white hair flowing around her shoulders as sparks snapped on her fingers. "Men will always covet items linked with power and will wage war to keep such treasures out of the hands of others. Especially the hands of their enemies."

"It doesn't matter why the Serpent people did what they did," Vard said. "Not now. And it won't affect what we must do. Nothing remains of Nistreel. There's only one way the sorry lot of us survivors may find peace—by unleashing revenge upon the Sea Serpent clan and freeing any captives they took. In doing so, we'll likely die, but then we may join our loved ones in the house of the dead gods."

"For revenge," Belfedrn muttered, turning the word over in his mind, his wrath burning. "It'll be a long road if we hope to deliver much vengeance. There are so few of us left. And so many of them."

"We could attack them now." Eakthr flashed a rueful grin, hopping from one foot to the other, lifting his knees in some bizarre dance only the dead gods would understand. "We'll die all the quicker and join our families."

Vard grumbled to himself. "If we, the last of the Ulfhednar, are slain, the Sea Serpent will prevail and rule their lands and ours. We shall find our revenge, but first, we travel to the Moon Woods. We'll see the last of Nistreel's women and young ones to safety and possibly find more survivors along the way."

"For the Wolves," the pack members minus Dradn and Thelira said, their words solemn and nearly lost amidst the crackle of flaming trees.

21

MÄRREN

MÄRREN SHIVERED WITH COLD AS SHE TRUDGED THROUGH shallow water and stepped onto shore—a land covered in snow, her boots sinking into a wet top layer and crunching through ice beneath. She gazed into the distance. There was nothing but hills of white and distant mountains jutting into the sky, tattered lengths of fog clinging to the landscape.

"Uisge lied to her." The dragon reared its head back in the darkness, smoke rising in wisps from its nostrils.

"He'll leave her to die in these lands." The wolf stalked around a lake, its eyes glowing red.

"She's closer now than she's ever been." The silhouette of the child darted through the darkness.

"This cannot be the land of fire and ash," Märren said. A scar rune on her neck shone in her mind.

"It is." Uisge's footsteps slid along the ice behind her as he neared. The sound of his movements changed from slogging wet beats of four to a slower crunching pace, and then something more familiar. Beats of two.

Märren glanced back. A man with a long mane of wet hair and who wore a sodden cloak strode toward her, thick stubble across his cheeks. He was strikingly handsome, in a dangerous and threatening sort of way.

"She's lost her mind."

"She'll never again know what is reality and what isn't."

"There are tales of Uisge taking on human form."

"Don't fret," the man said in Uisge's voice. "My kind have been able to appear this way since before the beast gods died."

Märren lowered her axe, unaware she had raised it for a strike. "I've heard the old tales. Uisge sometimes appear like men to entice women into the water. So they can devour them."

"That was what I was doing with the troll, remember? When you 'saved' me?"

Märren scoffed. "You were trying to seduce the beast?"

"Hardly." He chuckled. "I cannot take on the appearance of something much larger or smaller than I am. I'm still the creature you've seen, only veiled by a cloud of magic for any eyes that fall upon me." Uisge strode through the snow, heading north, his feet sinking deeper as he went.

"Where are you off to?"

"You seek the Dragon's scale, no? This is the land of fire and ash. The land of the Dragon people. Just because everything is covered in snow doesn't change what it is." He pointed to a mass of fog in the distance. "The earth still smokes beneath the white." He trudged on. "I'll be your guide."

A harsher chill slid under Märren's furs and across her skin as she looked toward the mountains. She cupped the top of Eimri's skull.

"I lost my pack at sea," she said. "I've nothing to eat or drink. No shelter."

"I can find more water than you'll ever need." He paused and tapped the ground with his foot.

The snow there sank inward, and water pooled around the toe of his boot, whether by magic or knowledge of its whereabouts, Märren could only guess. She knelt, cupped her hands, and drank—clean fresh water, if not icy cold. "And food?"

"We'll have to make do with what we can gather." He paced north. "If we're not careful, some of the Dragon people will spot us. We must travel swiftly."

"I am sorry to delay my endeavor, but I'm still human and will die from the elements soon." Märren stood her ground, shivering in the icy wet of her clothing. "I need fire."

"Hm. Indeed. But only until your clothing dries." Uisge dug through the snow, pulling up dead wood. "Then we hurry on."

Märren assisted him, and soon, they had a small fire burning between rocks under an overhang. Märren stripped off her outer garments and laid them out to dry, trembling from the cold and sitting so close to the flames that areas of her skin were uncomfortably hot while others were freezing. She rotated around, allowing the heat to work its way into her undergarments and flesh.

Eventually Märren asked, "Could you really eat a troll?"

"Not all at once, but aye, in the span of a fortnight. I have many times. Over the centuries anyway. A single troll can sustain me for months. I take them down into the deeps and anchor their body there, drown them. Then I feed, stuffing myself as much as I can before fish and other less savory creatures pick away too much of my victuals. I leave only the liver. Such a disgusting organ. Nothing more than a filter for all the toxins a creature ingests."

Uisge placed his palm against one of her furs. "Your garments are dry enough to be uncomfortable for me. We must move on. Before we're seen." He threw the fur at her, dowsed the fire, and strode away.

Märren dressed and followed Uisge's broken trail, which made travel easier. They hiked over hillocks and down into ravines, headed toward the mountains. Uisge started chuckling, which quickly transformed into stilted laughter.

"What's so amusing?" Märren glanced around.

"You." He laughed again. "When you came toward us—that troll and me—approaching the creature from the other side of a spit of water. Wise move, by the way."

"That is not so funny. More dark in my mind."

"If you saw it from my perspective, you'd have a different opinion."

"I thought the troll had you trapped in the shallow water near shore and was about to devour you."

"That's what I wanted him to believe. Trolls are as witless as children of your kind. I should know." He bellowed with laughter. "I'd already chewed off three of his fingers, one each time he tried to grab me and pull me from the water. On land, I'm much weaker, and he would've been able to kill me, but you know trolls—they're capable of regenerating limbs and appendages over some days, so his missing fingers didn't deter him."

"It looked like you two had been struggling for hours and that you were about to be caught."

"That's when you plucked the troll's fingers from where they were floating on the water."

"I wouldn't have been able to stop the beast from harming you or kill it by myself."

Uisge shook his head as he grinned, his brown locks swinging around his shoulders. "So you said, 'Hey, troll.' And the beast lurched and studied you. He thought you must be a völva—a witch—since you took him by surprise, even though he had been distracted."

"When he said 'völva,' the idea came to me."

"So you raised your axe and took it to your other hand, chopping and pulling your fingers back behind your palm as you did so. You made it seem like you chopped each finger off but without any spray of blood. At that point, I didn't know what to make of you. You pretended to lose three fingers as the troll watched from across the cove, perplexed." Uisge snorted with laughter. "You told him you were a Seidr woman and that you'd taken his power of regeneration. After you dropped your axe, it looked like a troll finger was growing out of your hand. But I'm not as cretinous as a troll. I knew you'd placed the fingers inside your cloak and advanced them from there."

"I didn't know if the brute would buy it, but I was too far away from both of you to do much else. And I wasn't going to swim over to him."

"His eyes grew to the size of melons, and he kept looking at his hand and then to yours. That's when you surprised me—when you told him the only way he could get his power of regeneration back was to cut off one of his feet. The monster grunted in outrage, but when your second troll finger started growing, he grabbed his rock axe. Then off came one foot. When you told him to cut off his other foot to ensure that he could maintain his regenerative power and not lose it to a völva, he almost hurled his axe at you."

Hearing all this through the mouth of another allowed Märren to see the event recur as if she were there watching herself. Uisge's tone carried praise and mirth, but the ruse had been so foolish she could hardly believe she had done it.

"The troll watched as his third finger grew out of your hand, each finger nearly the size of your arm," Uisge continued. "You said you were turning into a troll and would become him if he didn't remove his other foot." He bellowed with laughter and clutched his stomach. "So off came his other foot, and he collapsed on the shore with only one working hand. You should have seen the look on his face when you let his fingers fall and said, 'Uisge, swim away now. The troll cannot catch you.' The troll dropped his axe in disbelief, and it took him a good span of time to think it over and realize the fool he'd been. By then you were gone."

"And you were safe."

"And fed."

Märren studied Uisge closer. "What do you mean? A troll would've regrown his feet and left in shame."

"If he'd lived long enough. After you departed, he crawled to the water to wash his wounds. From there, I was able to convince him that in return for letting me live, I'd give him a ride to the other shore so he could chase you down and seek his revenge. He came into the water, and I pulled him down. Supper for days."

22

BELFEDRN

A WOLF PELT WAVED IN THE WIND, HANGING FROM THE DOORWAY of the small house in the highlands, the fjord and stream in the distance. Snow fell in light flakes, patches of it accumulating across the terrain. A hint of smoke hung in the air, but no fires burned here, only in the lands behind Belfedrn and the pack.

Belfedrn wiped the grime of soot and blood away from his face as he braced himself for what he must do. If Märren were still alive, she would not take what he was about to share with her well. However, she should no longer be able to turn away from the pack. Not now. She was needed, and there were so few of their people left.

He ran a hand along the pelt, its power lashing out at him like many tails of a whip. How could anyone, much less someone who carried his blood, disregard such a holy artifact? Fenrir's remains were now gone, taken somewhere by those Serpent bastards. To not take up a pelt was one thing, but to leave it out here in the rain like a superfluous fur was abominable.

After rolling up the pelt, Belfedrn stuffed it into his pack. "Märren." He pounded on the door. No one answered. "Märren!

It's Belfedrn. If you're in there, we must speak. The Sea Serpents have invaded our lands. Nistreel burns." He pounded again. "No matter what ails you, open this door. Most of our people have been slaughtered."

He pounded again before summoning the might of his pelt, although its powers were much weaker without the pack. He lunge-kicked forward into the door, his foot landing hard and breaking a latch. The door flung inward.

The interior was dark, but that did not mean Märren was not here. She lived in such a state most of the time. Maybe he should have seen her potential as a Seidr woman rather than as a Wolf warrior or Ulfhednar. But she had so much skill with the axe.

Belfedrn stalked inside the house. "Märren?" It took less than a heartbeat for his wolf-enhanced eyes to adjust to the lighting. The place was empty, most of the food and supplies gone. His cousin could have seen the destruction from afar and fled. If so, it was probably best she had never joined the Ulfhednar. For a decade, Belfedrn had been convinced that Märren would have made a great asset to the pack, but every pack member had to place loyalty to one another above all else. In that, she would have failed, making the pack weaker. Perhaps it was best she never took up the pelt.

He stepped outside, throwing back his head and howling into the sky, passing along the tone that all was well here along with a feeling that his blood relative was no longer around. His call echoed. Answering howls rose in the distance, in the direction of the forest, carrying feelings of comfort while urging Belfedrn to return to the pack.

Belfedrn paused, focused on the hut nestled between two rock mounds, which obscured the structure from casual eyes. Memories ran rampant. The house had been his uncle's, and his family frequented it during the summers when Belfedrn was a child. They would come up here and hunt and fish and romp around the fjord. He had grown closer to Märren than any of his other cousins. He swallowed his recollections and the burning sting they brought and loped away from the house, headed for the Moon Woods. Snow fell around him, painting the hills in white.

Later that evening, before twilight settled and firelight would be easy for their enemies to see, he joined the Ulfhednar. They cooked an early nattmal meal over a flame that would be veiled by the forest. The smell of roasting rabbit and venison filled the air, drawing saliva out of Belfedrn's mouth.

"It isn't much." Eakthr turned a spit, pulling at his patchy beard, roasting three conies and one small deer. The women and children who had survived the attack on Nistreel and fled surrounded the fire, watching with hungry eyes.

Belfedrn's stomach grumbled, and he cursed his weakness. "Can't the mighty Ulfhednar do better than this?"

"We didn't have much time to hunt," Eakthr said. "You weren't gone visiting your uncle's hut for very long. And we've been fleeing for days. All the game seems to have sensed the danger and fires and fled to other lands. Other forests."

"I'm famished," Athna said with a low growl. "We've been running for far too long—the troll hunting errand and then... Nistreel. Now to the Moon Woods."

Vard sat near the small cooking fire, staring into the flames. "The pack will eat whatever we can scrape up. It'll be meager for a while. We tighten our belts. We live here and forage for what's available. With winter coming, this is the worst time this could've happened, but it wasn't our choice. Our dead suffered much more than we will, and once this becomes routine and we've settled, it'll be easier."

"And what happens when the Sea Serpents come looking for the last of the Wolves?" Ylsga combed out her silver hair.

"We ambush and kill whatever Sea Serpent bastards enter our forest," Vard replied. "The Moon Woods are the last place a Serpent from the sea will find an advantage. We use our lands against them. In doing so, we can keep them at bay... for a time."

A stilted silence fell over the pack and the Wolf women and their young. The crackle of the flames and searing meat were all that broke the quiet.

Eakthr pulled a spit from the fire and used a knife to slide the cooked conies onto a rock. "How do we divide our meager rations amongst us?" He glanced around at the scores of hungry onlookers.

Vard grunted. Belfedrn imagined wolves tearing into their prey, snapping and snarling at each other, eating in order of pack status. He winced and shook his head. There were women and children here.

"We feed our warriors to keep them strong," one of the women said. "Otherwise, if the Serpent people come, we'll fall. I'll skip this meal, and my share can go to my son."

"The children should be fed first," another woman added. "Then their mothers and the warriors. We've been running for days and must care for our young."

Agitated mutters rumbled around the pack as Eakthr giggled with anxiety and rubbed his head. He sliced up the conies while Ylsga and Kesg worked at the deer. They filleted off chunks of meat. There were no vegetables. No belly-filling grains. No stew.

"Since Lyrne has passed," Vard said, "and has done so as honorably as any Ulfhednar, I must name a new second."

Belfedrn's stomach clenched into a tight ball, the Wolf's hunger burning him and almost turning him mad with a need to fill it.

Vard glanced around, rubbing at the stubble growing across his typically shaven cheeks. He studied Eakthr but quickly passed over him, looking at Ylsga and Kesg, then Athna. He should choose Athna. She was formidable and not to be reckoned with. Vard studied Belfedrn, who looked away, his stomach tightening further. He could not fill his mate's position, or the pack would be lacking. Lyrne had been good at issuing orders when Vard could not, thus keeping the pack in line and on objective, making the hard decisions.

"Belfedrn will be my second," Vard said.

Belfedrn's breath hissed as he exhaled and worry sank sharp teeth into him. He took a moment before attempting to meet his jarl's gaze. This was not right.

"And as my second, Belfedrn,"—Vard watched him with regretful eyes—"your first task shall be to distribute the rations."

The clenching in Belfedrn's stomach jerked with what felt like a kick to his gut. *Damn the dead gods. Especially the Sea Serpent.* His agitation spiked, and he clenched his fists. Vard did not want to make this difficult decision and take blame for not putting children first, nor for his warriors becoming weak or ill when they were needed most. As a jarl, it was a wise move. Place a choice with no right answer upon another. Vard had already been forced to make an impossible choice in Nistreel.

Belfedrn's head drooped while he accepted the first cuts from Eakthr—a cony leg and section of ribs. Eakthr winced but chuckled. The smell of the meat in Belfedrn's hands hit him, and his mouth watered, making him realize how famished he and the pack had become. They had not expected to be gone long hunting trolls and had not carried enough rations, believing their errand would be short and that they would eat well after their return. Days had passed running for the Moon Woods with only strips of salted meat and breadcrumbs in the bottoms of their packs to tide them over.

Belfedrn's muscles ached, and he was weak with hunger. He bit his lip and paced over to the children, who crowded around him, drooling like hungry dogs. After considering halving the portions even further, he decided against it and gave the leg to one child and the ribs to another before returning for more cuts.

Once the children were all offered a meager nattmal meal, which they swallowed in a few gulps and then gnawed and sucked on the bones, Belfedrn cursed again. He cursed during every trip he made around the warriors and women who watched him eagerly, hoping he would choose to feed them. If the pack's second offered, they could not be blamed for accepting.

After the children, he fed the women who had traveled so far and done so much to save their young. Without them, the pack would die, no matter how many years the Ulfhednar could protect themselves. The women ate quickly and sat with their children, humming songs of the Wolf and the night, reminding everyone of days when they had wandered as packs and these wild lands were all they had.

Eakthr tore at his beard as he watched Belfedrn make his rounds, the thief growling under his breath as Belfedrn handed out more food. After the women, Belfedrn offered a cut of venison to Vard and said, "In the wild, the alpha eats first. If he doesn't, he weakens and can no longer lead the pack."

"You mean the alpha pair." Vard's eyes closed in regret, but he nodded, accepting the stringy meat and shoving it into his mouth, guilt riding his hunched shoulders. "In the wild, a mated pair usually lead the pack. Not just one."

Belfedrn handed Athna the following cut, and she accepted it with a hand laced in flame, a dangerous look in her eye. In a fight, the battle Seidr could save more of the Ulfhednar than any other pack member. Then Belfedrn walked toward Ylsga and Kesg, the portions growing smaller and smaller, and he was unable to decide whom to give it to. After this, there was little if any meat left. He hesitated, his stomach burning with hunger, the smell of the food he carried tormenting him more than having to make these decisions. Maybe that was the real reason Vard had passed the duty off to another.

"Give it to her." Kesg nodded to his mate.

Ylsga shook her head and replied to her mate, "You've always needed to eat more than I do."

Belfedrn growled and slapped the chunk onto Ylsga's hand. "Each of you take a bite, then. There's no more." He turned away before they could protest.

Eakthr held out the last strip.

"Tomorrow, the Ulfhednar will have to be better hunters," Belfedrn said as Eakthr snarled, the thief's eyes wild with hunger.

"There are still eleven of us who haven't eaten," Eakthr said, desperation and outrage sheeting off him.

"And I wish I could feed you." Belfedrn grabbed the meat and turned away.

"You fed Vard first." Eakthr's voice turned harsh and confrontational, and Belfedrn feared if he did not turn around, he might be pounced on. "So you could make sure that as the second you should also eat before the meat is gone."

Belfedrn paced toward Dradn and Thelira and offered the young woman the last bone with small bits of meat clinging to it. "These two have seen worse than the rest of us, and yet they pressed on. They refused to die." He addressed Thelira. "You two have at it."

Thelira hesitated before accepting the bone and gnawing on it like an animal before forcing herself to hand it to Dradn, who licked the shaft until it was clean.

The rest of the pack slowly sank into the grass around the fire, staring with dead eyes. Dradn yawned and sat, smoothing out a spot for Thelira.

"You two do not get to rest," Belfedrn said. "Not yet."

Dradn paused, glancing up in surprise.

“Both of you need to follow me into the woods,” Belfedrn said. “It’s the only reason I gave you the last piece.”

“Why?” Dradn asked. “We’re famished and exhausted.”

“Do you think the Sea Serpents will give two shites about how you feel? They’ll storm through these woods soon, and they’ll pray that we’re starving and weary.”

“Where are we going?” Thelira asked, gripping her spear.

“To train like an Ulfhednar.” Belfedrn stalked away, his stomach releasing growls of protest.

23

CAËTIN

THE WAVERING BROWN AND GRAY WORLD OF THE RAVEN'S BRIDGE surrounded Caëtin. Dark souls floated past in greater numbers than when she had last visited, all gliding along in silence, faces concealed by cloaks. They diverged, taking one of two paths in the distance. Wraiths in black tormented the dead who did not bear a weapon by obstructing their path and prodding and shrieking at them.

The Raven Seidr woman suspected of being a traitor knelt before Caëtin, the woman's head bowed.

"What is your name?" Caëtin asked.

"It'll be easier if you don't know."

Caëtin's forehead wrinkled in confusion. "Easier how?"

"You'll see. Ask me to confess."

Caëtin glanced around. "Where's Uktr? And Grimmurk, Freydeg, and Taknhal? They were to join us here."

"They're not here." The Seidr woman looked up at Caëtin, and her face was as clear as it was in Midgard, her skin and eyes and hair just as tangible. Her locks were as bright as gold, her eyes black, pupil and all. "I'm one of Muninn's most powerful *gyðja*, although I'm known as a lowly follower to all but a few. I banished the others from our proximity. They reside here, but in the distance. Unseeing. They search for us and will come soon."

"So you're a traitor?"

"Of course." She flashed a wicked grin. "But allow me to tell you what I must before I sign my confession."

Somewhere far away, Caëtin's heart beat faster. The *gyðja*'s words landed on her as true and yet not, something akin to Jundr's.

"Tell me," Caëtin said.

"Muninn is dead, but her power has not fled the land." She grasped at Caëtin's ethereal leg, her bony fingers digging deep, inciting pain. "Her dreams can still be seen by some."

"But portents in dreams are so often misleading."

"Not this one." She pointed to the ice-haloed sun and then the mountains of snow that were ravaged by fire. "Darkness spreads across the land, snuffing out lights and lives. Whole villages. Cities. After waiting until they harnessed the power they required, they're now coming."

"Who?"

"You know."

"The Spider?"

"Those who come seek to wield what you control."

"But Spider berserkers, their so-called widows, can't harness feather *and* chitin. They'll die."

The *gyðja*'s eyes widened as she looked at something behind Caëtin. There, four wandering souls not cloaked in black stood across the bridge, watching. These figures were ethereal, but their faces were recognizable as Uktr, Freydeg, Grimmurk, and Taknhal.

"Come." The *gyðja* snatched Caëtin's hand, tugging her along. "They've found us already, must have sought aid from another. I couldn't speak with you alone in Midgard, but I was hoping to do so here. Now I won't be able to show you how to look at the past."

Caëtin allowed herself to be guided farther along the path of the dead, toward the diverging stone of the bridge as wraiths whipped past. A steady humming rose in Caëtin's head suggesting there were god remnants nearby. The four men pursued them, but the bridge ran for several leagues.

"The jarl is no longer trustworthy." The *gyðja* paced along even faster.

"That's no secret to anyone but him."

"But he's also growing paranoid of everyone around him. All but Grimmurk and Freydeg, his last companions from childhood."

"There has been at least one true traitor. One of our warriors. At the Mist Shores, Ningor attempted to kill me. Darstrid and I suspected he had betrayed us for the promise of some mighty gift from the Serpents. Another berserker witnessed him meeting with them."

"Are you certain he was a traitor to the Raven? Or acting on someone's orders?"

Caëtin's thoughts whirled with confusion.

The *gyðja* ducked under a group of dark souls floating over the bridge. "Perhaps he was simply following the orders of another who wanted to turn against the senile jarl and obtain the power of the Raven."

Thoughts of Darstrid sprang into Caëtin's mind. Caëtin should be warier around her sister.

"Take this." The *gyðja* spun about and knelt before her, holding a feather as black as shadow but shimmery like polished steel. It was longer than the feather in the hilt of Caëtin's sword and twice as broad. The largest flight feather. One of a pair from Muninn's remains.

"I can't bear more parts of Muninn without consequence."

"Are you certain?" She shook it before Caëtin's face. "Accept it!"

Caëtin grasped the feather and another item hidden behind it that was cylindrical, and power plunged into her like an axe to the chest. She slowly rotated the feather around to see what else she held.

"When taking up the power of Muninn, only you delved into the deepest reaches of the Raven's upside-down temple, traveling through all the tiers while the flaming raven—the god-killer—hunted you. Only you did not flee the temple when that creature came so close to taking your life, the potential price for your ambitions of power."

The feather blurred between Caëtin's fingers as it spun in her grip. Hidden alongside the back of the feather was a curved black talon from Muninn's foot, its tip as sharp as a blade.

"That's why *you* must bear these gifts." The *gyðja* kissed the back of Caëtin's hands. "There hasn't been a paladin of Muninn since before the great Raven fell in the war of the gods and giants."

Paladin... It was not a familiar term, foreign or ancient even, but when Caëtin had been a child, she had heard it used in a legend about a Raven berserker—more recently termed a Knight Black. This berserker became a paladin and carried more god parts than any other, wielding that power for their people.

"There's been no one more fitting to take up her cause," the *gyðja* continued. "There's still no one worthy, but out of all who remain, you're my choice. It isn't only those who are living who call for this. You'll have to do."

"I'll do for... a paladin?"

"In the shadow of Muninn and her holy wings, in death and dreams, she sees you. In memories that have not yet come to pass, she beholds you. You alight on her wing and carry her voice. As her high *gyðja*, I name you her paladin. The last paladin of the Raven. You are *not* a chosen one. You're all there is."

"I… what do I do?"

"You'll do your duty, as you did when you were one of her knights. Uktr's will drives our people." She stood and spread her arms. "Now, my time is done. I've served Muninn as best I could in Midgard. I confess to everything."

The *gyðja* reached and tore a parchment from Caëtin's cloak, one Caëtin did not even know she carried. The *gyðja* bit into her own wrist, and blood spouted, draining across her hand. She scrawled a finger across the parchment.

"It's done," the *gyðja* said. "I'm a traitor to the jarl. I must be slain."

Caëtin's hand found her sword's hilt and squeezed. "No. I cannot kill you. Not a *gyðja* of Muninn."

"But I'm a traitor to my god and her people. You must! I've admitted it." She shook the parchment and flung it at Caëtin's face, splattering her with blood. "Strike me down, or Uktr will. And if you don't, you'll be seen as weak and unable to lead the Raven clan when the time comes. These things are law."

Caëtin's hand trembled, her blade suddenly unsheathed, its tip pointed at the *gyðja*.

"He comes." The *gyðja* pointed over her shoulder. Uktr strode closer, Taknhal, Freydeg, and Grimmurk flanking him. "Hurry! You know what the cost is if you don't dole out your punishment. You'll lose everything you've gained since being adopted by the jarl. And if you fail and are stripped of power, he'll send me to a true inquisitor." She smirked. "That's why I chose *you*. You already killed another who was not a traitor, and you knew it. You can do the same to me."

A stab of apprehension and surprise struck Caëtin. She cursed under her breath. Violence was not always the answer.

"Do it, or I'll be tortured," the *gyðja* continued. "Then those working against Muninn will learn everything—what I've given you without their consent. What I've told only to you."

Caëtin cried out, wanting to believe that the wraiths flew at her and confused her, spinning the ethereal world around and around. She imagined she was defending herself from them. But deep down, she knew that was a lie. Violence won again, although this time, it may have been justified. This *gyðja* had truly betrayed the clan, had taken parts of Muninn... to pass them along to Caëtin.

I am also a traitor.

The *gyðja* slid off her blade, leaving a path of blood as she fell backward and hit the bridge of stone with a thud, her body limp and lifeless, a look of pain and anguish written across her face.

24

CAËTIN

CAËTIN WOKE WITH A START, SITTING UP, HER MOUTH PARCHED. She was no longer at the table behind the throne but on a heather bed beneath a blanket. On a loft. Hearth fires crackled somewhere below. She rubbed at her eyes, her head aching as she glanced about.

The power of Muninn coursed through her in waves like she had never experienced before, throbbing in her head. Recollections of all that had transpired on the Raven's bridge came back to her in a flood as she rubbed at the bridge of her nose, her skull pounding like a hammer on an anvil. A sickening wave of guilt and anger rose. She had killed a Seidr woman or a *gyðja* so she could keep her good standing with the jarl.

Caëtin hissed. She was done with Uktr's laws and the inquisitions where no one could escape confessing, but she had little choice in the latest matter. She ran her hand along her waist and chest before it settled on the stiff fibers of a feather and a talon between her breasts. At least no one but Igendrn the *goði* would find them there.

The gifts have returned with me to Midgard. Her skull thrummed with their power.

"Then we pounced on those Bear bastards from the lip of the ravine." Uktr's voice carried up from the ground floor, followed by his bellowing laughter and the slamming of a horn against a table.

Grimmurk's and Freydeg's hearty guffawing followed, along with laughter from another.

Lamplight flickered below, but the interior was otherwise dim. It was always dark inside a longhouse, but no sunlight filtered through the smoke opening in the center of the roof.

"We decimated them and their mighty Bear," Grimmurk said with the smack of a palm against wood, followed by giggling from several women.

"I can only hope to retell tales of such glory," Taknhal replied in a slurred voice. He was usually drunker than Uktr and the jarl's comrades at any hour, another reason why he would never rise above Caëtin's position as next in line to be jarl.

Caëtin stood, the pounding in her head amplifying before slowly fading. She was dressed in her full garb of tunic, leggings, and brigandine, as if she had walked up from the table below and taken her bed. She also still wore her boots and cloak. Her stomach rumbled with hunger. She tromped down the stairs, the great hall empty save for the voices coming from the area behind the throne.

Taknhal leaned back in his chair to get a better look at her. Two women sat on his lap, the one with long brown braids running her fingers over his chest, the other giggling. Nothing unusual for her brother—drunk and whoring. Three other women sat draped over Uktr, Freydeg, and Grimmurk, all three men holding horns.

"You've been out for two days," Taknhal said to Caëtin as he tore his attention from the women.

"Two days?" Caëtin asked. "You have to be fucking with me."

He shook his head. "It's true."

Caëtin ran her hands along her torso and arms in disbelief, as if that would confirm if any of this was real. She approached her father and his company, wondering what could have caused her not to return to Midgard for two days. She had never experienced that before nor heard of any Seidr magic affecting someone in such a way. Maybe it had only been her exhaustion after her flight home, but she had never slept for two days after utilizing Raven magic either.

"Who prepared the Seidr draught for visiting the Raven's bridge?" Caëtin asked.

"Disldryn?" Uktr studied her with blurred eyes. "Is that you?"

"It's Caëtin," she replied. *Not one of your dead wives.*

"Caëtin?" His forehead furrowed in confusion, and the woman focusing on him cupped his cheek.

"Your daughter, Jarl." Grimmurk jostled his arm, and Uktr blinked several times. "Not Disldryn."

"Adopted daughter," Caëtin said. When Uktr still did not seem to recognize her, she added, "The one who tried to negotiate a truce with the Sea Serpent clan."

"Those bloody Serpent swine." A snarl lifted Uktr's upper lip, and he shoved the whore away. "Never negotiate with our enemies. It's a sign of weakness and makes it seem like we need aid. The other clans will see it as an opportunity."

"We've had fun going over this already," Caëtin said. "I've been admonished multiple times."

Uktr's fist nearly crushed his drinking horn. "Aye. But never enough times if you thought it was a good idea." He exhaled. "That reminds me—why did you and the Seidr woman run from us during her inquisition?"

"She... convinced me she would only confess if we were alone," Caëtin lied. "Again, who prepared the draught?"

"One of the *gyðja*," Taknhal replied.

"At least you killed her," Uktr said. "Another cunning traitor lurking within our people. This one was even posing as a Seidr woman. Disgraceful. But we witnessed you run her through. Her blood was still fresh when I came to." He motioned across the table to an empty chair. "You're getting stronger, Daughter. Maybe not yet strong enough to lead, but stronger than when I took you in as my own."

Footsteps sounded behind Caëtin, and she glanced back. Darstrid approached. Her sister had also been inside the hall. Two of the women entertaining the men at the table grumbled their displeasure at the interruption. The whore with braids stood to leave, but Taknhal grabbed her by the wrist, stopping her.

"Darstrid?" Caëtin asked. "Why aren't you at Sparsgard dealing with the Spider?"

"I've already returned." She smiled.

"And where are my children?"

"Sleeping in the nest hall. Under the care of the servants."

Caëtin's unease settled a little. All their extended family's children were often cared for by the servants in that hall.

"We searched the entire settlement at Sparsgard and its fields," Darstrid said. "There were no Spiders about, and no sign of them anywhere in the area. We also made sure that the trade routes to Horse territory are not being watched."

"The Spider people killed my knights and strung them up in a longhouse in the middle of the village."

"Then that must've been cleaned up. The people of Sparsgard were nervous but begged for forgiveness. They told me the same story they told you—about a man arriving and threatening them if they didn't give him what they had saved for taxes at summer's end. The people handed their goods over to him. Then their children started disappearing, but since your visit, no more have gone missing. I re-instilled their trust in our power and reminded them that for any land to remain prosperous, trade and coin must flow."

"You left the village unprotected? After all that happened?"

"No, Sister." Darstrid clapped a hand on her shoulder. "I left a score of Raven warriors to guard the settlement and our borders, along with six Knights Black. At the first sign of any Spider attack, or anything else suspicious, one of the berserkers is to fly here and issue a warning."

Caëtin's mind spiraled with bewilderment, given her sister's lack of findings. "Their supposed absence is some kind of trap. They mean to deceive us. Again."

"Or they initially wanted to draw us out there and kill a few of our knights," Uktr said. "To test us. Then, after Caëtin survived their ambush and returned to Aonark, they knew we'd return and wipe them out, plant their chitinous heads and bloated bellies on stakes. So they fled."

"Maybe." Caëtin was not convinced, and the others seemed too calm for what they should be preparing for. They knew what she had encountered in Sparsgard. She faced Darstrid. "Did you cross the river to investigate further?"

"No." Her sister frowned. "We didn't see any sign of trouble in Horse territory, and we didn't want to be led into a trap in another clan's lands."

"The Raven lands belong to us," Uktr said. "We protect them alone. We do not protect any other clan's territory. Not even if we believe one clan is more dangerous than all the others."

Caëtin could not hold back a retort, not with how fed up she was with the jarl's laws and the inquisitions she had been forced to undertake. She would no longer abide by his rule. She would follow what she believed to be best at the time. "If the Spiders were allowed passage through Horse territory—or if a more unfortunate situation allowed them to make the crossing—it would behoove us to know." She paused. "And if no one else will, I'll investigate the matter."

"We shall stay inside our lands." Uktr glared at her.

"Then sit on your throne, Jarl." Caëtin pivoted about and strode for the exit, her mind turning over the events of the bridge and Darstrid having returned so soon. Had two days truly passed already? "I'm taking my knights and having another look in the south."

"You'll remain here." Uktr's chair skidded across stone as he rose.

Caëtin heaved the doors of the great hall open and strode out into the night.

25

BELFEDRN

DRADN'S AXE CLASHED WITH BELFEDRN'S, SENDING SPARKS INTO the night, and the warrior grunted as he tried to match the might of a Wolf berserker. At first, Belfedrn resisted, using his superior strength and the power of his full pelt. Dradn needed to learn that he was not as strong as everyone he fought—a common problem with young warriors. The boy also needed to learn to use his head.

"Keep him locked up," Thelira said to her brother. She had been quiet and reserved since she had been pulled from the collapsed building, but during their training, she turned energetic and outspoken. Snow drifted through the canopy, most of its flakes shielded by the trees. "I'll circle around him." She advanced, trying to move to Dradn's left, her spear held high.

"Your trainer's a weak and scrawny old bitch of a Wolf," Kesg hollered to the youngsters from nearby. "Keep at it, and you'll tire him out."

"I thought my body was the only reason you've ever liked me," Belfedrn retorted.

"I don't think anyone has ever liked you for that sweaty old flea house of yours."

"That stings."

Belfedrn pressed against Dradn with greater force, shoving the warrior at an angle to block Thelira's path. Dradn's eyes bulged as he realized he was overpowered, and instead of trying another tactic, the younger man dug his heels into the ground and struggled, fighting to resist Belfedrn even more. Belfedrn pulled back and stepped to the side, letting Dradn sprawl forward, his legs churning to keep himself from falling onto his face.

As Dradn stumbled past, Belfedrn smacked the warrior on the head with the flat of his axe, creating a dull thump. Dradn cried out and dropped like a stone. He would have a nice lump to remember his mistake.

Thelira snarled, jabbing with her spear but side-stepping and circling around Belfedrn. She fought differently than her brother, but if these two could not use their alternating styles in tandem, they would never benefit from their training.

"You're part of the Ulfhednar pack now," Belfedrn said. "Your place is not always at Dradn's flank."

Thelira growled and leapt closer, feinting with her spear but quickly landing, springing to the side and lunging forward again in a true attack—the same as she had done several times now. With enhanced swiftness, Belfedrn twisted to avoid her blow as he closed the gap between them, slapping her on her leading knee with the side of his weapon. Steel smacked against bone, and Thelira shouted in pain before snarling again.

"Your leg is useless." Belfedrn slid up to her, placing his blade against her throat. "As is your head."

"Fuck," Thelira yelled.

Dradn groaned and rolled over, sitting up and grasping his head.

"We cannot compete with you like this." Thelira stormed

away, her cheeks flushed with wrath, her spear arm lowering. "You wear a full pelt."

"Aye." Belfedrn recalled the other pelt in his pack, the one Märren had left behind. He could only gift it to one of these two, and only after they had earned that right. Hopefully one of them would be able to control its power. "Sea Serpent berserkers wear a full scale, and they won't hold back their acid spittle or storms or strikes of the Serpent from within the mist when they cut you down like untrained children."

"Children?" Thelira threw her spear down. "We are—were—Wolf warriors."

Dradn struggled to find his feet as he winced.

"You are warriors who use the same methods of fighting over and over again," Belfedrn replied. "You must learn several new tactics or you'll be dead soon after any battle begins. You can't rely on the pelt segments you wear to save you from what is coming." He turned to Dradn. "You're not a Bear warrior, much less a berserker. You can't expect to overpower your enemies. You two must fight together. As a pack. Not you first and then your sister taking up the rear."

Dradn paled as he felt along his scalp and winced while prodding a lump there.

Thelira grumbled. "When we finished our training at the sanctuary and began sparring with the Wolf warriors, they also used to beat us down, to show us we knew nothing. I believed you Ulfhednar would be different, more confident with less need to assert your dominance. I never would've thought your kind would need to lord your abilities over us just to feel superior."

Belfedrn folded his arms across his chest, studying her. She carried the Wolf's fire inside her and would not back down to her enemies. That was good. "I'll never beat you down for the sake of belittling you and draining your confidence, nor to remind you to keep to the lowliest positions in the pack. I do it so you'll understand that if I was your enemy—a Sea Serpent berserker—you would've died. I want you to realize what you do wrong and to stop following the same attack patterns over and over again. Those techniques may've worked well when sparring amongst trainees in the sanctuary, but a seasoned warrior will quickly find your weaknesses. Then they'll kill you both. Strengthen what you lack. Hone what you're best at, but do not solely rely on it. And hide whatever you cannot improve."

Thelira retrieved her spear and faced Belfedrn, preparing for another round.

"Find your rest," Belfedrn said. "Both of you."

"So soon?" Thelira shot him a teasing grin.

"You'll be sore tomorrow, and tomorrow could be our last day in Midgard. The pack may need all your strength."

Thelira paced over to Dradn and assisted him by wrapping his arm over her shoulder, taking some of his weight as he stumbled along and she limped away.

"You really know how to handle the young and their training." Kesg grinned with mockery as he stood.

"It's not me who likes to handle the young. And unless you want me to inform Ylsga of your doings, I'd keep quiet."

Kesg's mouth gaped in feigned shock as Belfedrn stalked away.

"You two are ridiculous," Ylsga said from across the way.

Once Belfedrn was alone, he sighed, pressing his back against an elm trunk and sliding down it until he sat at its base. Soon, thoughts of Lyrne and the city of Nistreel, of Deyja and the boy's father, started to creep into his mind. His stomach rumbled with hunger, and he groaned, leaned his head back, and stared skyward.

His hand passed over something firm but moist. Between two roots punching through the earth and grass, a few mushrooms grew. They were conical with spongy pores. He recognized this variety—Seidr man's fungus. It was worth a bit of nutrition but had the side effect of altering one's thoughts for a time, making it easier for a Seidr man or woman to work seer magic or whatever else they did.

Belfedrn plucked the largest mushroom from the grass. His stomach gurgled and ached, and saliva wetted his tongue. Without another thought, he shoved the fungus into his mouth, swallowing it whole. Its bulk would help tide his hunger over until tomorrow when the pack could hunt, and he had suffered the effects of the mushroom on prior hunting ventures. It should not affect him as much as heavy drink.

He wiped sweat from his brow and closed his eyes, pulling his warm pelt tight about him as wind soughed through the boughs and snow flurries danced in the night. In the distance, the sounds of singing and conversing, of women and children, mingled with that of a dying fire.

Sleep would not take him, not now, but he breathed deeply, his body relaxing, hunger abating. Belfedrn was no Seidr man, would never be, but he knew some of the things he could see in the coming stages. It did not take long for one something to reveal itself.

A lighted spirit within the elm at his back crawled out of the trunk and sat beside him, a humanoid with boughs and a few leaves jutting from its body. It was feminine with long shimmery hair. She sat beside him, saying nothing before leaning her head on his shoulder.

Belfedrn's pains lessened, and he forgot his hunger. A water spirit from the nearest stream stalked about in liquid humanoid form, approaching and sitting before him. Another spirit made of swirling snow joined them as well.

"Even if your kind all die, the killing won't stop," the water said.

Belfedrn grunted noncommittally. Previously, when he had described to a Seidr man and woman what he had seen in a similar situation, the Seidr people affirmed the existence of specific spirits, but they warned him never to trust such land wights. These creatures were capricious, their words irrelevant to anything that would occur in Midgard, and they could be deceitful, and at times, dangerous.

"Night comes and so do the Wolves," the snow added.

The tree wight hummed a melancholy but soothing tune that put Belfedrn at ease.

"We should retire from this world for good," the water said. "Slip away across Alfheim and make music and art and magic with the bright elves."

"Or venture to Nidavellir and visit the dark elves," the snow added. "Or the dwarves. These lands are fading. So few hear our call, and even fewer leave rune stone sacrifices. I've found more of those who will listen in the other realms."

Belfedrn sat in a daze as they spoke more nonsense until a lithe dark figure slipped out from behind a tree, its ears pointed.

An elf... or a dark elf. Belfedrn's limbs trembled as he reached for a weapon, his movements sluggish.

"The elves call to me." Whipping flakes spiraled around the snow spirit's body. "They offer me all the runes I could ever desire. And more."

"The dwarves of the deeps craft jewels and arms unfathomable in Midgard," the water said. "And when they do, I often visit."

The tree spirit tittered and ululated, her tongue rolling over other sounds. Then she lurched and straightened. The silhouette of the elf jerked back behind a trunk.

"Another comes." The snow spirit stood, glancing around before stepping away and fading into flakes.

The water had already vanished along with the tree woman.

Trepidation lanced through Belfedrn. His wolf mind locked in on the sounds, the scents. In the distance, twigs cracked under a boot. The smell of a human not cloaked in Wolf drew near, a human tainted with something else, another creature.

Belfedrn crouched, slowly rising, his hackles spiking as he sniffed. *Danger.* He stalked toward the sounds and scents, gripping his axe and seax. He moved no more than a dozen strides before two other pack members came tearing up behind him, growling.

"Someone comes," Thelira whispered in a hoarse tone. "Someone smelling like those who came to Nistreel."

Belfedrn reached out to hold her back, but she and Dradn raced past him. Belfedrn cursed and loped after them. Only the smell of one outsider was near, perhaps a scout... unless their berserkers were hiding their scents like they had with the trolls. He quickened his pace, following as best he could while the siblings crashed through the brush and pounced.

A bellow from someone not of the pack rang out, the woods deadening the sound. Clashing steel answered, and Belfedrn sprinted faster, landing in a dell between scattered spruces. The cries of Ulfhednar carried in the distance. The pack was coming.

Thelira and Dradn circled around someone who was smaller and younger than they were. This boy wielded a spear and a shield with a Serpent symbol emblazoned on its face. Fury climbed its way up Belfedrn's neck and smeared its heat across his painted cheeks. The boy faked a lunging attack and spun about, tearing away into the woods, yelling.

A Sea Serpent scout.

Belfedrn raced after him, Thelira and Dradn already in pursuit and moving faster. They hurdled a downed tree and then thickets of brush, weaving between trunks, their urge to howl almost palpable.

"Stay silent and return to the pack!" Belfedrn said in a such commanding tone that the two young warriors slowed and glanced back at him.

"He's one of *them*." Dradn kept running. "One of those who slaughtered our pack. You won't steal my vengeance. Nor my glory."

"He's nothing more than a boy," Belfedrn barked. "Stop! Soon enough, there'll be greater vengeance to be had. There's no glory to be obtained here."

Thelira did not slow her pace. "We can't let him return to whoever else is out here, or more will know where we're hiding."

"He won't," Belfedrn snapped. "Don't allow guilt to haunt you for all the years you may live."

Thelira and Dradn slowed to a loping pursuit.

"You won't realize it until his body slides off your spear," Belfedrn continued, "his blood soaking your hands. But you will. Now stop!" He grabbed Dradn and threw him down into the snow and wet foliage.

Thelira paused in surprise as Belfedrn barreled past them.

26

CAËTIN

THE DARKENED STAIRWELL LED CAËTIN DOWN INTO THE HEART OF Muninn's temple, through violet and emerald light emitted by hundreds of candles. On her way here, she had stopped to check on her children and moved them and her personal servants to her house so she would not have to worry about them as much.

A *gyðja* stepped aside without a word, withdrawing into the shadows and allowing her to pass. Caëtin grabbed the *gyðja* by her feathered cloak and pulled her back into the light. Her face was taut with disbelief.

"Find the Knights Black who are loyal to me," Caëtin said. "Those who last flew with me as well as any others who are worried about the Spider. Have them meet me outside the temple, ready to fly."

The woman stared at her, unblinking.

"I am a fucking knight of Muninn." Caëtin shook her and shoved her toward the entrance. "Do it."

"Of course." The *gyðja* rushed away.

Caëtin continued her descent. When she reached the lowest, dimmest floor and the stench of death rose, someone grabbed her by the elbow, leaning in close. Too close.

"What're you doing here?" It was Igendrn, her *goði* lover, although his body was veiled by darkness.

"Coming to find you." Caëtin shoved off his grip, facing him. "I need to speak with you."

"Again so soon?" He straightened, his cloak thrown back over his shoulders, revealing his striated chest and stomach.

"This visit's probably not what you're hoping it to be."

Igendrn checked their surroundings and motioned for her to follow him as he stepped toward the pedestal holding the dead god's remains. Caëtin's head vibrated but not with the same severity as when she last visited. After she woke bearing another feather and a talon, the effects of the god parts had diminished, either that or she was becoming less aware of the sensation. Strange.

Caëtin said, "I cannot bear any more—"

Igendrn held up a hand to silence her. "I wouldn't dare take anything from Muninn without the authority of the *gyðja* and the jarl." He led her to a darkened corner and through a curtain of common raven feathers, into a cramped chamber barely large enough for one person to stand in its center and have three or four others crammed in around them.

"An inquisition chamber of the *gyðja* and *goði*?" Caëtin asked.

"In this instance, it won't be used as such." Igendrn's lips thinned. He appeared concerned, and rightly so given that Caëtin had never sought him out like this before. "Tell me why you're here."

"The jarl believed a Seidr woman to be a traitor to the Raven, but she was more than a Seidr woman. She was a *gyðja* as well."

Igendrn cocked his head in confusion.

"She was being held in the great hall," Caëtin continued, "and I was asked to perform an inquisition there."

"Asked by whom?"

"Primarily by her. Or so it seemed. But also by the jarl."

"Who was she?"

"She wouldn't tell me her name, but she was young and claimed to be the high *gyðja* of Muninn. Her hair was golden, her eyes entirely black, although that could have been the Raven's bridge affecting her."

"Fihre?" He brooded on it, rubbing at his chin. "She hasn't been around of late. It could be true."

"Is there a high *gyðja* who is so young?"

"Yes, but we of the temple wish to keep the distinction unknown to those outside."

"Why?"

He glanced away, holding something back. The walls seemed to close in around them.

"Why?" She drew a knife at her waist and pressed it to his side.

"Would you really kill me?"

"I don't want to, but I seem able to kill anyone for anything. Or you could just tell me. I am your lover." When he hesitated, she pushed the tip of her blade into his cloak and positioned her lips closer to his face. "Violence is in my blood, and if I'm pressured or angry, I always seem to resort to the blade."

He swallowed with apprehension. "Temple dynamics work best when the high *gyðja* is veiled. This has been true since the gods passed. We give the people a face for authority, someone to bathe in power and respect, but we have another who is most adept at interpreting the dreams Muninn left us. The latter is our true high *gyðja*."

Power without seeking admiration and respect? That was a new take. "Why would Fihre betray the Raven people by giving away her god's remnants?"

Igendrn shrugged. "I can't know what the high *gyðja* foresaw, but Muninn's will and the will of the clan don't always coincide."

"So you're saying Fihre could've been a traitor?"

"I don't know."

"Well, we are Muninn's people now, because the Raven chose to die in our lands. If she had a choice in that matter. Before that, our ancestors were no more bound to Muninn than any other god. But if for some reason the Raven grew angry with our people and wanted others to live here, then I would betray her as well."

Igendrn pursed his lips. "I cannot say if Muninn would've preferred other people over us as her worshippers, but since she died here, I don't think so. I hope not. To be forsaken by your god and discover that they favored another clan would be... disheartening at the least."

"Indeed." Caëtin moved to exit the chamber but paused. "Thank you for confirming who the high *gyðja* was. Beyond that, you haven't been very helpful, but your ability to obtain secrets isn't why I fancy you." She leaned back and kissed him hard on the lips. "Till next time."

Igendrn's reply was muffled. Caëtin quickly exited the chamber, pausing before Muninn's remains and scrutinizing them. The rear talon on one of the Raven's feet was missing. Shame spiked through Caëtin as the missing part grew heavy between her breasts. She raced upward through the temple, retracing her prior route. At the ground level, she did not wait for a *gyðja* to part the entrance doors but shoved them open and stepped outside.

Five Knights Black, including Halfnr and Sanre, awaited her, their heads bowed. A twinge of fear arched through Caëtin as she glanced around, worried that Uktr might be waiting nearby, ready to punish her for her betrayal. Or the berserkers could be here to escort her to the great hall—and to use force if necessary. There was only one way to find out.

"We fly south," Caëtin said. "To Horse territory."

No one responded.

"Do you have your feathers?"

"Aye," they all intoned.

"Then follow me." Caëtin let herself drift apart, her unkindness rising on determined wings.

After a brief rest from flight, the unkindnesses flew toward Sparsgard. The area around the village was unchanged from Caëtin's prior visit. Men, women, and a few children milled about in the fields and around the central longhouse. The ravens shrieked and soared past, and the people cowered, glancing upward as the birds darkened the sky.

All appeared as Darstrid had described—normal. Except for the knowledge that children had been taken by webs in the fields, there did not seem to be anything wrong. Caëtin cawed and flew onward, across the south fields toward the River Red. Its waters sparkled under winter sunlight although clouds were matted up against the horizon, the blur of rain hanging beneath them.

The river came and went, and the unkindnesses soared over Horse territory, swooping upward to take in as much of the area as possible. They flew for leagues, scouring the lands for any sign of the Horse people while praying to Muninn that those people would not unleash a volley of arrows upon them. A village neared, and the ravens passed overhead. No people walked between its huts or longhouse. No one worked the fields. No smoke rose from the opening in the longhouse's roof.

Caëtin spiraled lower, not quite landing before she strode forward in human form from a mass of feathers, drawing her blade of Muninn. She glanced about as her knights landed behind her and rose as cloaked men and women wielding axes and swords.

"Where are the people?" Halfnr asked.

"That's what I'd like to know." Caëtin approached the longhouse's entryway. "As well as why there are no archers about trying to shoot down so many ominous ravens."

"Be wary." Sanre, who wore her cowl hanging over her face, only her red hair visible, took a position on the far side of the doorway. "No matter who or what we find, they won't be pleased by our visit."

Caëtin shoved on one of two massive doors. It creaked and slid inward.

"Hello?" Caëtin peered inside. Dark as night. No torches on the walls, not even a hearth fire.

"Be ready to fly." Halfnr pushed on the other door, swinging it inward so he could step inside, his bearded axe held high.

One pale sunbeam slipped through the hole in the roof, lighting up a circle on the floor. Dust motes floated about in the light, but nothing else stirred.

"I don't see any webs suspending bodies from the rafters," Caëtin said over her shoulder. "Bring torches."

Within minutes, the knights had pulled a few torches from the outside of the structure and lit them with flint. Caëtin reached for one of the torches, but Sanre pulled hers away so Caëtin could not take it.

"I'll go in first," Sanre said.

"No." Caëtin snatched the torch from her. "We're here because of one of my only faults—curiosity. If anyone is to die, it should be me."

Caëtin stepped inside, holding the torch high, her blade poised in her other hand. Firelight danced about tables strewn with horns, plates of half-eaten food, and drying pools of drink.

She strode farther in. Three rats squeaked and leapt off a table, knocking over horns. Caëtin lurched, her heart racing.

After a few breaths, she settled and crept along the central walk, looking in both directions, Halfnr and Sanre at her heels. There were no bodies and no people. They neared the jarl's chair—simple wood with engravings but no silver or gold embellishments. A hide of horsehair covered the throne's back and seat, red stains splattered across it. Caëtin circled the chair, glancing toward the loft. Nothing moved.

"Search the huts." Caëtin pointed toward the entrance, and the berserkers exited the longhouse as she climbed the stairs. The beds on the upper level were empty, blankets and clothing in disarray. There were still no people nor bodies. No webs.

Caëtin descended from the loft and headed outside. Soon, the knights she had sent away returned.

"The huts are all empty," Halfnr said. "The entire village is abandoned."

Caëtin glanced about, the scent of fear thicker than a conjuring of her imagination.

"Where are the Horse people who live here?" Sanre asked.

"Dead or dying somewhere else," Caëtin guessed. "We fly onward."

27

MÄRREN

Concerns about Uisge's intentions when Märren had resided at the hut near the stream rolled through her mind as they both continued their trek northward. Would Uisge eventually see her as he had seen the troll and trick her into becoming his next meal? Maybe Uisge had only allowed her to live this long because she had bled herself to feed him—what at the time appeared to be an injured and helpless creature. A scar rune on her stomach surfaced in her thoughts, glowing and spinning around.

"He will still try to eat her."

"When she's injured or asleep. He hungers for flesh, and nothing can change that."

"He's become her friend, and she saved his life at least once, with the sea serpent."

Not far ahead, smoke rose from a few huts clustered atop a hill, which overlooked the area. Uisge veered up the incline, traversing snow-covered terrain. Other plumes of smoke dotted the lands around them, rising from the ground beneath the white. Their strange appearance had been everywhere during their journey through the land of fire and ash, making it impossible to identify any human-made fires, at least before these huts came into view.

Uisge gnawed on the bones of a perch, one he had managed to pull from a frozen pond with no more effort than dipping in through a hole in the ice and popping back out. He was soaked but apparently unaffected by the cold. He handed the uneaten half of the fish, which included its head, to Märren. She studied the pale and squishy meat bulging from where he had chewed into it, and a pang of hunger landed in her stomach. She accepted his offer and bit into its scaly skin, unconcerned that it carried almost no flavor other than leaving behind a fishy aftertaste. If she had not been so famished, its uncooked texture might have otherwise made her vomit. She wolfed down the rest, and Uisge smiled, watching her.

"You would've made a good uisge," he said.

She ignored him and marched on. When they reached the hilltop, they found a man crouched over a smoldering fire between three huts, stoking the embers. He glanced up at them, his face drawn and haggard with graying stubble and oily hair.

"We've no extra food here," the man said.

"He would as soon kill her as tell her where she can find a Dragon's scale."

"He and his people will kill her, and then they'll smash Eimri's skull to pieces."

"She realizes the risks."

"We aren't looking for food," Märren replied with the best smile she could manage.

The man studied her before pivoting and addressing Uisge. "You and your thrall woman are a long way from whatever village you come from. And she speaks before you. It'd be best to address that insult."

Märren's hand crept up to her neck and the iron collar there. *Anyone who sees the collar will believe me to be a thrall.*

"Indeed." Uisge cast Märren a stern look before speaking to the man again. "My friend, I am Uisge. This is my thrall."

Several faces peeked out from the huts—a couple men, women, and a few children, each dirtier than the man before them.

"Uisge?" The man's forehead furrowed. "As in the water wight who feeds on people? That's a curse of a name for your parents to have given you."

Uisge scowled. "I was birthed into a pool, and I swam before I could walk."

"Ah, a fitting title, then. It's intimidating and has likely scared away some adversaries."

"Aye."

"I'm Midr. And which village did you say you were from?"

"I didn't say, but you see, we got a bit lost during the last snowfall. We were on our way to the sacred lands where the Dragon fell."

Midr's wrinkled face lifted in bewilderment.

"Of course we know the general direction in which those lands lie," Uisge continued casually, "but we don't know exactly where we wound up."

Midr chuckled. "You ended up in the outer reaches. Only the strong survive here."

"It looks that way."

"All we need is a map or directions," Märren said, hoping to push the conversation along.

Midr glared at her. "Your thrall has no manners and surely doesn't know her place. She also carries a battle axe even though you do not."

Uisge tilted his head and grinned. "She'll be reprimanded, but not here. And she's quite a warrior. She's saved me more than once. I trust her."

"You shouldn't trust a thrall. Especially not a warrior thrall."

"I'll take your words to heart, brother, but for now..." Uisge gestured northward.

Midr stood over the smoking fire. "Which village did you say you came from?"

Uisge waved a hand to the east and mumbled something incomprehensible.

"You arrived from the south," Midr said. "I saw you coming. You best be on your way. Dragon berserkers still roam this territory, even the godforsaken hills way out here. If they find you, they'll tear you up and spit out your bones."

Uisge grumbled something else under his breath but did not make any indication of departing.

"If you leave in peace, I'll let you in on something else," Midr continued. "But don't get any ideas. We have more people here than you, and if we must, we will kill you."

Uisge shrugged and waited.

"I see the way you look at your thrall." Midr snickered. "She's obviously your whore thrall. We can't have those in these parts—not enough food to go around to care for an extra bed woman, but it'd be best not let her stray. It'll take less than a berserker to steal her from you and feed her to the giant."

Märren flinched more from surprise than offense.

"A giant haunts these lands."

"A giant and the people of the Dragon. She'll never succeed. She's never succeeded at anything."

"We don't even know if this man is lying."

"What sort of jötunn do you refer to?" Uisge asked. "A fiery one or one made of frost?"

Midr glowered and shook his head as he looked at Märren's axe, which she held tightly in her grip. His tone was less confident than his words. "Be off, outsider. Before we slaughter you and take your thrall."

Uisge lunged forward and grabbed Midr by his stained tunic,

shaking him and forcing him back at the waist, bending him over the embers. The people inside the huts gasped, but only two men older than Midr stepped outside. They did not advance on Uisge. Uisge pressed his face close to Midr's, and Uisge's visage contorted, whatever he revealed hidden enough by his hair so that Märren could not see it.

Midr screamed. "Who are you?"

Uisge leaned in closer. "The stuff of nightmares."

"What do you want? We have no silver and little food. Not enough to last us through winter."

Märren edged closer, placing a hand on Uisge's shoulder. "Do not eat him. Not yet." She faced Midr. "We already told you what we're after. All we want to know is where the Dragon's remains are. Not where she fell, but where her parts were taken."

Midr swallowed. "You're hunters, then. But you're sorely unprepared for what lurks within our lands."

Uisge shook him again. "Then it's time you enlighten us."

Midr held up a hand in placation. "I will. But you'll never reach her scales. The Dragon died in the battle of the gods and giants, falling there." He pointed to the mountains.

"She resides in the mountains?" Märren asked.

Midr shook his head. "She is the mountains. Her spine creates the peaks. Her skeleton was buried deep over the centuries, as no man could carry her bones, only her scales. Long ago, the berserkers gathered what had not rotted and stowed those remains in their temple, but after centuries of slumber, the giant who warred with the Dragon awoke. This jötunn was only resting, healing. He destroyed their temple and took all of the Dragon's remains."

"Then where are your berserkers' dragons?" Märren asked. "Surely they could defeat this giant and reclaim their scales."

Midr paled. "The jötunn took their dragons. He imprisoned

them in mountain holds, and he feasts on human flesh and dragon eggs. He resides north of those peaks, in the frigid regions, awaiting sacrifices—feedings. The ill and old volunteer to be offerings, but times often come when the berserkers must draw straws and take people from villages so the giant will not destroy everything and eat us all."

Questions ran rampant in Märren's mind, and the voices spewed many more. "Is it a fire or a frost giant that plagues the Dragon people?"

"He's not a simple fire giant. It is Surtr himself—the jötunn of fire and ash. The flaming one with blackened flesh. He came from Muspelheim to fight the gods, and after their deaths, he remained in Midgard."

The wind whipped past them, flinging snow around the hilltop as Uisge tensed.

"Where you recognize evil, speak against it, and give no truces to your enemies," Märren muttered.

"The words of the sacred Hávamál?" Midr studied her anew. "From the mouth of a thrall?"

"You shouldn't try to keep Surtr's presence a secret."

"We must, or the berserkers will take us as the next sacrifices. They worry that if any of the other clans learn of our weakness, they will invade our lands and we will fall."

"It seems your people have already fallen." Märren stood straighter, sighting northward. "And your berserkers won't free their dragons and kill this giant?"

"Surtr cannot be slain. *He* felled the Dragon herself. No man or dragon could ever overcome him."

"Come, Uisge." Märren waved her companion on, and Uisge dropped Midr onto his backside. Midr hollered in pain and rolled out of the embers. "To find our scale, we must pass through the mountains."

28

CAËTIN

THE UNKINDNESSES HURTLED OVER THE COUNTRYSIDE AS THE SKY spat rain. These more southern lands held on to less snow than most, although drifts from early winter had accumulated against rocks and hillsides. Horse land and streams passed beneath them, the grasses and brush brown and dead.

They flew for hours, continuing southward toward the Horse people's largest city while sweeping west and east to get a better look around. However, even when flying as ravens, they could not hope to search more than a fraction of these sprawling lands.

As Caëtin soared, thoughts about her children weighed on her. Perhaps she should be around them more often, but if the Ravens could not protect their lands, the lives of all the clan members were at stake.

A memory of Treln running through a field similar to one below surfaced. He had been foraging with the other boys when a fight broke out, as it often did. Caëtin had not been there. She should have been. Treln shoved another boy, and the boy tumbled down a cliff, which ended up breaking one of his arms and legs. Treln swore he did not know the cliff was there, but

Caëtin was never convinced that her son spoke the truth about the matter. Other people's recollections of the event made her worries linger.

When the sunlight faded, exhaustion and cold battered Caëtin's unkindness, and they veered toward a copse of birches, hoping to land and find undisturbed rest. Voices carried from the far side of the copse, and Caëtin squawked, soaring onward and circling around.

On the other side, people poured out of a massive hole in the ground, pursuing a woman dressed in a horse skin. She sprinted away from the masses at full tilt, across uneven terrain. Caëtin pulled up short, silencing her unkindness's cries.

At least two score of people chased the woman, all of them carrying weapons and shouting obscenities. They were dressed in black and brown cloaks and armor. Some of the men threatened that when they caught her, they would slit her throat. Others would rape her in groups.

Caëtin swooped past the pursuers and woman, landing in a clump of rowan well ahead of them and taking her true form. Her knights joined her.

"We can't save that woman," Halfnr said. "There are too many hounding her. And they're gaining on her." He pointed into the twilight at the approaching silhouette and the horde coming closer.

Caëtin cursed. "She runs like a horse, but she's tired. Very tired."

"Same as us."

They watched as the woman neared, but the fastest men overtook her. One shoved her from behind, and she sprawled forward, crashing and tumbling into the grass. The two score of others fanned out and surrounded her as she struggled to find her feet. One man loomed over her and grabbed her tunic, yanking her to her knees before shoving her backward, causing her to fall again. The man said something, but his words were lost to the distance.

"Are you carrying a crossbow?" Caëtin asked Halfnr as she led the Knights Black closer, creeping through evenfall and staying low in the brush.

"Aye." Halfnr unslung the weapon from his back, cocked the windlass, and loaded a bolt.

Caëtin took it from him. "I can't demand that you do what must be done." *Violence is needed once again.*

Halfnr cleared his throat, probably chewing over how to best phrase his concerns. "As mighty of a knight as you are, you're not the best shot with the crossbow. If you hope to kill the most aggressive of those men, you might end up hitting her."

"That insult pains me." Caëtin rushed closer to the scene but remained hidden as the men tightened a circle around the woman, who stood as they tore at her horsehair tunic, ripping it until she was half naked. They shoved her around between them, grabbing and slapping her. The tallest man wrapped her in a bearhug and squeezed. Another came up behind her wielding a dagger dripping liquid. He sliced the woman's back and she screamed.

"These are no Horse warriors turned against a traitor," Caëtin said.

"No," Sanre replied. "They are not."

Caëtin dived into the grass and took aim, angling her bolt so it would hopefully pass through the outer circle of attackers.

"If you kill any of them, we'll all be in danger," Halfnr said. "They'll know in which direction the shot came from."

Sanre grunted her agreement.

Caëtin squeezed the tiller toward the handle, and the rope snapped forward. The bolt whizzed toward its target, tearing past the men composing the periphery of the group, buzzing over a shoulder and between faces. The projectile lodged into the woman's neck with a thud that silenced its whistling. The woman did not even shriek. She simply fell limp.

The attackers hollered in surprise and outrage, whirling about.

"You hit the woman," Halfnr said in disbelief.

"Of course I did." Caëtin slunk backward through the grass. *Violence can sometimes be wielded for compassion.* "We can't kill them all. And I don't want them to see us become ravens."

The circle of attackers cried out and came barreling in the knights' direction.

"Too late for that," Sanre said.

Arrows whizzed around them, thudding in the earth. Caëtin turned and sprinted for cover, but as they ran, their pursuers gained on them, moving faster and faster as night fell.

They're more powerful in the darkness.

Several projectiles streaked around them.

"Take flight." Caëtin lifted into ravens and soared upward.

Her knights followed her lead, and their pursuers bellowed their fury, pointing at the birds and loosing bolts and arrows. Caëtin's unkindness wheeled about as they ascended the currents, squawking her victory. She soared back over to where the woman's body remained. Caëtin's victim lay on the ground, lifeless, her face in the grass, a bolt protruding from the back of her neck. Branching black vines had wormed their way under her skin.

Caëtin circled once to get a better look. Those black markings arose from the area where her attacker had sliced her. Caëtin cawed in outrage and soared away into the night, the cries of her pursuers carrying after her. She did not stop until she could no longer hear their shouting. Then she found water and a hazel thicket to roost in, her body so drained she could barely keep flapping, her limbs so cold they would not move.

She landed, her wings folding and her eyes closing immediately as she drifted off.

When the sun rose the following day, Caëtin woke and glided away from the hazels to land on the ground beyond the thicket. Her unkindness swarmed together until she sat there. The Knights Black soon joined her and chewed on clumps of oats.

"Those were not men of the Horse clan," Caëtin said. "Not in that garb."

Halfnr crunched a mouthful of seeds. "Spider would be my guess."

"Given the weapon they used on the woman and the black consumption or creeping vine look we saw on her, I'd agree," Sanre added.

Caëtin exhaled slowly. "Aye. They came bubbling out of a hole in the ground, and when night fell, their powers amplified."

Sanre spat. "Spider indeed."

"I fear they were Spider berserkers," Halfnr said. "Widows."

Caëtin grumbled, praying it was not true. "Spider recluses, their warriors, are more accustomed to the light, even if they don't become half as powerful as widow berserkers in the darkness. We shouldn't jump to conclusions. Not yet."

"Jump to conclusions?" Sanre's tone was incredulous as she gulped down a fistful of her dagmal. "We found two score of Spider people in our lands, then more in Horse lands, and only one Horse person, who is now dead, and you think we're jumping to conclusions about Envikia's widow berserkers being here?"

Caëtin swallowed the last of her meager meal, brooding on what they had seen. "We need to be certain of what's happening beyond our borders before we return to Aonark. Darstrid seemed convinced that all is well and that our people have nothing pressing to worry about."

Sanre shielded her eyes from the muted sunlight as rain drizzled between them. "And how do we become more certain?"

"I'm afraid of the answer," Halfnr muttered.

Caëtin stared at the ground, her thoughts and concerns sparring with each other. "We fly deep into that hole we saw the Spider people rise out of, and we find out where they sleep."

29

BELFEDRN

BELFEDRN TRUDGED BACK TO CAMP, BLOOD ON HIS AXE, HIS SHIELD strapped to his back, not a single new scratch on himself. The skirmish with the Sea Serpent scout had not been half as difficult as sparring with Thelira and Dradn. It had only been a boy, but a boy with a secret to pass along. A boy who belonged to the wrong clan. At least Belfedrn had left the boy's body with an axe in hand, unlike with the other Sea Serpents they had slain. There had been no honor in the fight, only guilt.

Belfedrn's eyes remained downcast as he strode past Thelira and Dradn, who watched him. Thelira stepped forward and opened her mouth, but Dradn pulled her back before she could speak. Belfedrn was in no mood to discuss anything. To forget and never think of the encounter again and never see its haunting images in his mind—the ability to accomplish that would be magic he would truly envy.

Vard awaited him, but the jarl made it appear as if he were unconcerned, sitting and staring into the fire. Belfedrn stopped and said, "The scout won't be able to pass word along of what he saw, but when he fails to return, the Sea Serpents will come looking."

"We're safe in the Moon Woods," Vard replied. "For now."

Belfedrn walked to the edge of the pack and sat with his back against a spruce trunk, allowing the effects of the mushroom to rewrap his brain in fog. No more spirits came to visit, but his eyes slowly closed to the crackle of the fire and the humming song of Wolf mothers. Sleep took him, filled with memories of Deyja and then Lyrne—lying together, hunting, training, her love. Even though Belfedrn was a lesser Ulfhednar, she had taken him as her mate and accepted him and his flaws for what they were. Flaws he still carried, like the scrap of divine pelt he stole.

He awoke to the sounds of people whispering in the first light of dawn, the fire being stoked, and the smell of roots charring over flame. Children hunched over the fire, their breaths steaming, mist floating through the woods like wraiths.

"Ulfhednar." Vard paced around the camp. "We hunt this day. The children and women will dig. Athna"—he gestured at the pack's battle Seidr—"pick two others and travel to the western border of the woods. Watch for enemies coming our way."

"Why me?" Athna brushed off her pelt and used a bone comb to tame her hair.

"Because you're the strongest fighter," Vard replied, "and the worst hunter. We don't need our meat burned to a crisp just to catch it."

"For the Wolves." The Ulfhednar's words barely carried enthusiasm.

Athna grunted and chose two members, who prepared and headed west while the rest of the pack ventured east, deeper into the woods. Belfedrn kept his ears keen and his nose working as he walked near the head of the pack, searching for signs of prey passing through. He hoped for more than deer, perhaps reindeer or elk or even larger creatures, and to pick up a herd's trail. And he remained wary for any odor of troll.

Dradn and Thelira followed in his steps, hopefully watching and learning how Ulfhednar moved during a hunt, but Belfedrn was not naïve. He and Lyrne could never have children, but he had been around many of them. Most young folk believed they already knew everything their elders did.

Eakthr ducked behind a trunk, motioning with a tilt of his head. Belfedrn froze. Beyond the tree, a hart grazed on brush, jerking its head up and glancing about, its ears flicking back and forth. Belfedrn drew an arrow and sighted as the creature chewed. He loosed, bringing the animal down with a clean shot to its heart.

"The first time I've ever seen him do that in one try," Kesg said.

Ylsga smacked her mate on the back of the head. Dradn and Thelira rushed forward and cleaned and dressed the carcass, and an Ulfhednar dragged it back toward camp on a sledge. The rest of the pack trekked through the woods for hours, scenting every bush and gust of wind while a rain and snow mix fell through the canopy, dampening everything.

"Will you teach me how to use the longbow?" Thelira asked from behind Belfedrn. "During my initial training, I wasn't good with the weapon and so I was given the spear, but I've always wanted to master the bow."

Worries about how much training it would take for her to become proficient with the weapon, as well as at stealth and hand-to-hand combat, surfaced. If she were capable, she would need to eventually raise her skills to the level of other Ulfhednar. "Maybe soon. But not while we're in dire need of food."

Thelira fell silent as they stalked onward, passing down a ravine and up a mountainside, creating a switchback path on the ascent. Dense pines and birches pressed in around them while streams gurgled down the slopes.

"The herds have moved on," Eakthr the Sly said, kneeling to inspect the banks of the stream for prints. "The few tracks here are at least a week old. There's been too much smoke and destruction too close to the woods, and the herds have ventured east toward Boar and Bear territory."

"We won't survive the winter without meat." Kesg rubbed his belly. "Not in the Moon Woods. And the Wolf farms and fields have probably been destroyed or taken."

"The foraging magics of the Boar people would aid us right about now," Ylsga added.

"Keep hunting." Vard trudged onward, up the incline until they crested the mountain and climbed over its ridge.

Midday passed, and evenfall crept closer. After a day's hunt, the mighty pack had only managed to bring down two deer and a few rabbits and squirrels. One badger they crossed paths with, they left alone. They had enough to feed their survivors nattmal but not enough to sustain them for more than a few days.

"We press on," Vard said. "We cannot return with so little. We need food so we can spend time attending to more important tasks such as planning and preparing for what may come."

"These woods come alive at night," Ylsga said. "And Fenrir has blessed me with his eyes."

"The pack will divide in two." Vard waved Eakthr and Belfedrn and a few others northward as he took a more southerly route with the remainder of the Ulfhednar. Thelira and Dradn had not been directed one way or the other, and without hesitation, they followed Belfedrn.

As they stalked on, night fell with a sheet of darkness, the moon and stars veiled by clouds dropping snow. Something rustled in the brush before Belfedrn. He drew his bowstring to his ear and edged forward. Eakthr nocked an arrow.

Something large burst from the vegetation, charging straight at them. Eakthr screamed and leapt aside, and this squat creature with tusks came barreling at them, snorting. Belfedrn elbowed Thelira aside to get her out of its way and flung himself from its path. One large tusk still managed to graze his pelt as the creature tore past. He rolled through the foliage and came up ready to loose, but the boar was gone. Only the shaking branches it left in its wake showed where it had run. Kesg bellowed with deriding laughter.

Dradn stood nearby, shaking, grasping his side.

"Did it hit you?" Belfedrn raced toward Dradn and removed Dradn's hands from the area in question, then lifted the warrior's cloak, *brynja*, and tunic out of the way. Dradn's ribs were already bruising, but there was no gash. No flayed flesh. "You'll be fine. And you'll now know to get out of the way of a charging boar."

Dradn was pale, but he nodded.

"That beast will feed us well." Eakthr giggled and raced after it.

Belfedrn sprinted off, following the boar's trail, his night vision revealing the details of the forest as well as if it were in direct sunlight. He leapt a stump and caught up to Eakthr, the others charging after him.

A howl rang out, carrying from somewhere far away. Belfedrn stumbled to a halt, and Eakthr crashed into him.

"Did you hear that?" Belfedrn cocked his head to listen.

Eakthr did likewise, and the pack held their panting breaths. An answering howl replied, and the first repeated.

"Danger approaches the woods." The sensation of the communicated emotion rolled through Belfedrn. "Athna and the others call us home."

Thelira and Dradn whispered to each other, their voices haunted with fear.

Belfedrn summoned the magic of his pelt and howled his reply to let the others know their calls had been heard. Then he took off at a dead sprint, away from the fleeing boar. The others followed, weaving through the forest behind him, the Ulfhednar not silent in their haste but only rustling the brush. They ran like wolves, their breaths rasping, tongues panting, lungs burning, and they did not stop. Not when hunting as a pack.

Sometime after midnight, they passed through the Wolf camp, where the children wore looks of terror and pointed west to the open lands. Belfedrn raced on, the howls of the others having fallen quiet. When he finally neared the edge of the woods, firelight shone between trunks.

"Our enemies camp just beyond," a voice said from the trees. Athna knelt in a leafless bush between trunks, her eyes shining with moonlight.

Belfedrn slowed so the half of the pack who had hunted with him could catch up. "Then we kill them."

"Not when they're in the open." Athna stood. "There are probably more than two score warriors and berserkers."

Belfedrn heaved for breath, hoping that any Wolf trainee captives would be with them, although he knew that would not be likely. Captives would have been taken back to a more secure location. "If thirteen Ulfhednar take them by surprise, we can kill them all."

Thelira and Dradn crashed through the brush, followed by Eakthr and the others.

"But you only have half the pack with you." Athna folded her arms across her chest. "And two of them are children. With all that's left of the Ulfhednar, I agree we may be victorious, but we'd suffer losses. Too many for how few members we have."

"Then we allow the murderers of our people to sleep within our lands? Just outside our woods?"

"For now. When they venture into our terrain, which they

soon will, we slay them. But you're the second now. If Vard doesn't arrive soon, it's your decision."

"Where's the jarl?"

She shrugged. "He should've answered my calls and returned with the others."

Given the proximity of the Sea Serpents, Belfedrn's need for vengeance flared brighter, but he choked the sensation down. Vard would probably agree with Athna's reasoning, but the thought of waiting to find revenge did not settle his emotions. He stalked about until he found a patch of mostly dry ground at the base of a spruce and sat, watching the firelight beyond the woods. A moment later, he stood, swallowing his exhaustion but not his emotions. Kesg came over and patted his head in an attempt to calm him.

Belfedrn said, "When they step foot into the forest, we slay them all. Come. We have work to do."

30

CAËTIN

CAËTIN'S UNKINDNESS FLEW THROUGH SPEWING RAIN AND MUTED sunlight, the ravens staying low to the ground, skimming over brush without cawing. Her knights trailed her, keeping an eye on their surroundings. What they were about to do could get them killed, but this errand should not lead to a trap set up by the Spider.

The gaping hole in the earth lay ahead. Caëtin's birds winged toward it, and when it came rushing up to them, the ravens swung upward before plunging down into its darkness. Some of the ravens clutched torches in their talons, and her guess had been correct—there were no torches burning down here. The Spiders needed no light to see, not even their warrior recluses who could command the power of their god in daylight, although their magics were nothing compared to the rumored might of their widow berserkers.

Caëtin's ravens soared into the depths, most of her knights trailing her, although one unkindness would remain outside, keeping watch on the opening. Shouts carried from behind her, near the lip of the entrance, as the unkindnesses hurtled past.

Guards. They're watching. Caëtin's unkindness found a wider area in the hole, and they swarmed about, cawing until her knights joined her.

"Damn bloody birds flying into our tunnels." A voice carried from the darkness, the light at the entrance already a distant blur.

"Crows looking to feast?" another asked.

"Or do you think it's them Raven folk?"

"They're carrying torches. It can't be hungry crows coming for the dead."

The first soldier appeared in the torchlight, shielding his eyes. He carried a barbed axe and was armored in a steel helm and chainmail. A diamond of black chitin was fastened to the breast of his *brynja*.

Caëtin dived at the recluse, turning human, her blade pointed downward as she plummeted the final horse length, impaling him. She held several small torches in her other hand and yanked her sword out of the warrior's chest, letting him topple over as more recluses bellowed and charged them. The four Knights Black with her drove killing blows, using sword and axe.

More Spider warriors charged into the firelight. Caëtin drew upon the feather of Muninn in her blade, as well as the new feather and talon she bore, calling upon the higher magics she had sought in the deepest tiers of the temple in the bridge world. She lashed out with enhanced quickness and agility, her blade carving through armor and shields and flesh in explosive bursts. Black blood sprayed the cavern walls. Dying cries rang in her ears.

When she was done, her knights watched in awe as her limbs trembled with power, but soon, her energy drained. She wobbled, bracing herself against a wall.

"How deep do we risk delving here?" Sanre asked.

Caëtin wiped her blade clean. "As deep as it takes to find

their nests... or spider houses, or whatever the fuck resides down here."

"Just keep your eyes out for webbing," Halfnr said. "We don't want a repeat of what happened at Sparsgard."

"And try to create a map of these caverns in your little raven minds." Caëtin pointed at three branches in the tunnel behind them. "I've a feeling this won't be as simple as I was hoping."

Halfnr grimaced. "No bird is meant to fly below the earth."

"Then we make this quick." Caëtin fell into an unkindness that shrieked and flapped away, some of her ravens still clutching their torches.

She picked one route and flew along twisting and winding passageways, banking and veering to keep from hitting the walls. She raced toward a net of webbing, and the ravens squawked and separated, slowing as best they could while twisting and dipping to avoid the strands before flapping onward.

A deep rumble carried through the earth, echoing along the cavern. Caëtin's unkindness angled into a passage where the sound was loudest. The others followed. They continued their winding flight, avoiding more webs and making sharp turns until they entered an area where the din arose. The air was different here—less dense and stale, which created a sense that a chamber sprawled on for a league, and burning torchlight shone faintly along the walls ahead, enough to see into a vastness.

There are more here than widows and recluses who wouldn't need light. There must be other fighters as well. Many of them.

Caëtin's unkindness dropped their torches outside the entrance to the chamber and glided in. From there, they flew toward the ceiling and clutched onto rock ledges near the top while the din rattled their heads. At least ravens should not be heard over the noise. The knights soon joined her, all watching silently in bird form.

Below, masses of people sprawled across an expansive chamber. They were gathered in ranks with lines of men and women facing a dais where a few others in full armor stood. A woman paced about on the dais, her movements too quick and fluid to be unenhanced. Her armor was black and barbed, her hair resembling red flame. She towered over those around her, her skin as white as snow.

"Bring on the next aspirants," she said, her voice carrying to the ceiling like a blast from a horn.

The ranks below her stepped forward, probably a score of men and women—no, they were young. These were adolescent men and women at best, but they wore chainmail and carried axes, marching in unison.

A man in violet armor who bore a massive sword led the first line forth. The aspirants stopped before a row of widow berserkers who loomed over them from the dais, each widow holding something in their fists, their skin as ghostly as their leader's.

The aspirants climbed the steps to the dais and knelt, their hands held outward.

"Deliver the gifts," the leader said.

The berserkers leaned over and placed what looked to be diamond-shaped cuts of parchment in the youths' hands before stepping back. Nothing happened. The offerings might not be simple parchment, but they were not black like the Spider's chitin, rather brown. The aspirants remained kneeling as the chamber fell silent, many hundreds or thousands of spectators unable to look away.

The leader paced before them, scrutinizing each aspirant in turn. "Accept the gifts of the god into your hearts. The part of you that is Spider can never be taken from you, but what is given to aid our people is a blessing, a sacrifice each of you must make."

One boy cried out in pain before screaming and then falling onto his side, writhing in agony. Two more joined him. Then the rest. They thrashed about, some rolling down the steps until they all lay still. Recluse warriors in patterned yellow and brown armor hurried up to them and ripped the parchment from their hands, returning it to the Spider widows above. Then they dragged the dead away to a pile of many others that had been there since before Caëtin arrived.

Another line of aspirants was called forth, and they undertook the same ceremony. They also died.

They're not afraid of killing so many of their own. But that should only be true if...

The eyes of Caëtin's unkindness were drawn to an area directly below, where webbing wrapped around massive egg sacks. Her ravens fought off caws of protest and shudders of revulsion. Thralls wearing iron collars moved around the webs, pulling newborns from individual eggs, infants who appeared like any child born to a human woman. The thralls carried the infants away into the tunnels.

Impossible. So many are being born in such a short time. The power of the Spider god and the magics she bestowed upon those who bore her chitin had been underestimated by everyone.

The aspirants continued to be tried, leaving only one boy standing after at least three score had died. The adolescent joined another young man and woman near the far side of the dais. This ceremony had likely been going on for some time before Caëtin arrived, and there were only three survivors.

"I'm beginning to question your ability to train our young," the leader—who, if the rumors were true, was probably Envinkia—said to the recluse in violet.

The recluse dipped his head. "They were pressed hard. Possibly too hard, but you'll find more than you need in this crop."

"I hope so."

Several more waves of aspirants were tested before six held their parchments. Most of these six were shaking, but they stood proud. Then a recluse man in red armor led his ranks forward, and they followed the same ceremony, yielding a few more survivors. By the end, well over a hundred young had been carried off and piled on the heap.

Envinkia held her arms wide as she faced the surviving aspirants. "From here, you will be thoroughly trained, and you'll carry great power that will aid the nest and the Spider clan. This may not have been the god you desired to carry, but it's what has been given. Nothing is without cost or sacrifice. Yours will add another layer of armor to us all."

Cheers resounded throughout the cavern, deafening tones that surprised the unkindnesses. Caëtin barely suppressed her urge to shriek and fly away.

"The last coat of the Horse has been handed out," Envinkia said, and Caëtin's stomach felt like a weight of lead that would pull her birds off their perches.

The remains of the Horse... But a berserker cannot wield the parts of more than one god. Any such person would immediately die. The fact was well understood.

Caëtin's mind churned. These adolescents must have been trained in the handling of god parts, but they were not Spider berserkers. They did not bear the chitin.

Bugger the jötunn. These aspirants had been saved in reserve to bear something different, something other than chitin. They were meant to wield a different power that would aid the Spider, shield their people's weaknesses and hone their strengths. The powers of the Horse now lay in the hands of the Spider people.

Their warriors and berserkers wielding Spider and Horse magics would fight side by side for the same end.

"It could be days or a month until our Spider warriors find their next meal," Envinkia said, "but it matters not. Our people are strong and need little to sustain them. The weaknesses of our human bodies are lessening, and we're becoming more like the great Spider. Any march north will be long and full of confrontations, so let us eat our fill this day."

The chamber fell silent.

"Now feast!" She pointed to the piled dead, and the warriors and berserkers and the others inside the chamber swarmed the heap of bodies, pulling the dead away and cutting into them with knives. They carved into their own as emotionlessly as a butcher would take a cleaver to a swine carcass, and they feasted. Newly hatched babies were offered hunks of flesh, which they gummed and swallowed whole.

Caëtin's unkindness retched, and a caw of fear and outrage and revulsion rang through the chamber. When her cry fell silent, her ravens lifted from their perches and flapped away, her knights barreling after her as they headed toward the chamber's exit.

"What was that?" the Spider captain in red shouted.

"Ravens." Envinkia's word followed the unkindnesses like a predator weaving after them.

The clamor of running feet and the cries of hundreds or thousands roared through the hall as steel was unsheathed. Caëtin's unkindness swooped for the torches she had left behind, and talons wrapped around wood. More than a few of the unkindnesses' torches had died out in the dirt and stone, but they needed all that were lit. The branching tunnels would be difficult if not impossible to recall while fleeing as fast as they could, and if they added darkness to that crucible, they would never escape.

The ravens soared on, squawking and flapping as fast as they could. Caëtin led the others, and a triple branch in the tunnel swiftly approached. She slowed as she tried to recall the way to go, but she had not seen all these routes because some of the tunnels were hidden when traveling downward. The din of weapons and armor rang behind them. Sounds of scuttling feet rushed along the walls. Some of the unkindnesses' torches snuffed out, and bird-cries of terror and death answered.

The widows had arrived.

An unkindness swooped past Caëtin, barreling on into the right passageway.

That is the way... but there was something we're supposed to remember when—

Shrieking erupted ahead, causing fear to surge through Caëtin. Her unkindness followed the one that took the lead, the rest of the ravens picking up speed behind her. They swung around a bend and found the source of the commotion. Two ravens from the unkindness in the lead were trapped in glistening strands, flapping and attempting to break free but only entangling themselves further as they screeched. The ruckus from their pursuers grew closer.

Caëtin's ravens veered and angled between strands of web, the others following her route. Most of the unkindness in the lead had made it through. The knight should survive.

They continued weaving through the passageways, no longer slowing their pace, dipping and rising to avoid walls and webs until faint light rose in the distance. Then they flew faster, taking the last few ascents over mounds in the cavern and bursting out of the hole in a dark cloud, cawing in rage and terror.

The unkindness that had been watching the entrance shrieked in reply and soared after them. Together, they winged onward through rain and over rolling hills where the Horse people used to run wild, but soon, one of the unkindnesses started shrieking and would not stop. Blood streamed from these ravens' left wings. The birds from that unkindness circled lower and landed on the summit of a rock mound.

Caëtin wheeled about and joined them, landing and merging into herself. The unkindness that was screeching became Sanre, who clutched at her arm that now ended in a bleeding stump at her elbow.

The ravens caught in the web were her forearm and hand.

One last raven streaked from the hole, bobbing in flight, one wing struggling to flap. It barreled at Sanre and flew into her arm, releasing a plume of feathers.

Sanre hollered in pain as Caëtin climbed over to her and took a closer look. Sanre now had more of her arm, which ended in a bleeding stump at her wrist, but black vines crawled up her forearm. At first, these tendrils writhed across her skin before gradually creeping upward, although the latter movements were so slow that they could almost not be perceived unless Caëtin looked away and then back again.

"Widow venom must've been used on one of her ravens," Halfnr said, his voice airy in shock. "The last arrival. And now poison courses through Sanre's blood."

The Spiders had probably cut and poisoned one of the two birds that had been caught, then released it to infect its knight. The other raven was likely dead.

"Cut it off!" Sanre said. "It burns. Once it reaches my heart or head, I'll die. I know it to be true."

Caëtin ripped her blade from its sheath and raised it to strike but hesitated. "I can't. I've done so before. Thovar died anyway."

Sanre screamed, raised her axe, and brought the weapon down, cleaving through her flesh and bone above the creeping tendrils, severing her forearm against a chopping block of rock.

31

MÄRREN

The bulk of the mountain range lay around Märren, peaks soaring into the sky, most of them draped in white. She and Uisge hiked the lowest pass they had been able to find—a ravine winding between two cliffs. A river flowed between icy banks in the ravine, mounds of snow piled around it. Märren would have left a rune stone sacrifice at the base of the mountain they trekked past, but she had lost most of her belongings to the sea.

Her axe hung from her waist, and her fingers were pulled inside the palms of her gloves and creating fists to keep the cold from turning them numb. Her bronze locks were caked with frost. "I wish there was a way for us to have gone through the mountains instead of over them."

"There is, but none would advise taking it." Uisge walked on the ice over the river's edge without creating any cracks, his hair wet and dangling over his face, having never dried.

Märren avoided stepping on the ice over the water, afraid it would break and she would fall in. "And why is that?"

"Dwarves and dark elves and even darker things lurk in the deeps. We'd not be welcome there."

Images of such creatures, which Märren had only heard

described by bards and storytellers or had seen in a couple old books, floated through her thoughts. A line of scar runes on her lower back glowed in her mind.

"She'll freeze in these mountains."

"Or become trapped between the cliffs in this ravine by trolls or worse."

"She must sacrifice to find the Dragon's scales."

Märren squeezed Eimri's skull for comfort and followed Uisge higher into the pass. Her inhuman companion had continued to provide them with enough food from ponds and rivers to keep them alive, and they had passed the nights in the best sheltered areas they could find with whatever fire they could build, although Märren had not been warm since leaving Wolf land.

Uisge is saving me now.

She pulled her furs tighter about herself and trudged onward, stepping carefully, moving too slowly for her liking. She had never taken up the pelt, but she would not forget her people or what had happened to them. She did not blame and despise all of them. Nor did she love them. If she could acquire a scale by any means—including stealing one or joining the Dragon clan by offering her trained person to their cause and earning it—and cure herself of her illness, she might eventually find a way to return to Wolf territory. From there, she would assess what was left of her lands and people and could act against the enemies who had raided them.

"How did she die?" Uisge asked.

Märren flinched.

"She hates to talk of it."

"Remembering the event will cause her to spiral down into her darkness."

"It is always painful."

Uisge paused and glanced back at her. "The skull you still cling to. She was your daughter."

Märren swallowed and nodded. "I found her in the fjord."

"Eaten?" Uisge tensed.

"No. Floating. Facedown. Peacefully on a cold spring morning."

"I am sorry. What happened?"

"I don't know. She carried the same darkness I do. I tried to keep her away from the villagers and those who looked upon her with disdain as much as I could, but the other children harried her. Relentlessly. Especially when I was not around. Eimri didn't want me to protect her. She thought she was strong, that she could fight her own battles."

"You believe some of the Wolf children drowned her because they were afraid of her? Because they thought they might catch her illness or their lives would be affected by her curse?"

Märren's stomach heaved, and she nearly vomited. "I don't know what to believe, if it was the children or if the children only strengthened the darkness enough that it took her. I found no evidence of a scuffle and had heard nothing that night. No one would admit to harming her." Guilt stabbed at her heart and stomach like a thousand blades, causing her to grimace. "When I woke, she was not there. She would not answer my calls..."

"That's why you never took up the pelt. You blame your people and their children for what happened to Eimri."

Märren swallowed a wave of bile. "That's partly true." She hid some of her wariness of the Wolf people. She was fond of her cousin, Belfedrn, but there were not many still alive whom she felt a kinship with. She distrusted and feared far more of them, all those who blamed her and her daughter and mother for any unfavorable events that occurred. "But I've also always desired to wield the scale. It is said a part of the Dragon can cure the mind."

"Who has said that?"

"Father... myths and legends." Her mind swirled with confusion as the voices raged. "It's all Mother ever wanted for me. It's all I've ever desired. Father told me the old Seidr man said it was so, and the Seidr man would know more than any Wolf person could ever hope to about matters of the Dragon clan and their scales."

Uisge waited for her to say more.

"And there has been no other cure mentioned for the voices, the darkness," she said. "A scale is my only salvation."

Uisge eyed the sack where she kept Eimri and slowly turned away, seeming satisfied as he fell quiet and thoughtful. They trekked through winds that skirled off the mountains, bringing the frigid cold of the ice above. Farther in, the ravine walls narrowed until the river filled the flat portion of ground between them. Uisge did not seem to mind but took note of Märren attempting to avoid the water and trudged up to a footpath along the slopes. On this path, they had to avoid snowdrifts, but the trail was primarily composed of compact snow and ice.

"Don't you ever get cold?" Märren asked, the darkness not ebbing after their discussion. She wanted other voices to muffle those inside her.

Uisge cast her a bemused look. "It's colder out here than in the water, but I don't worry too much about temperature."

Märren scoffed. "And do you know these lands? It seems like you have some idea of where we're going."

"I've traveled many waterways over the centuries, but here, I'm simply moving in the direction you wish to go."

A distant rumble echoed off the mountains. Märren crouched, glancing up. High overhead, on the cliff on the opposite side of the river, snow avalanched from an outcropping and tumbled through a gulley, flinging up powder and clouds of white.

Märren stood straighter as Uisge kept up his pace, and she asked, "Do you think the avalanche could fill the entire area and bury us up here?"

Uisge studied the falling snow as its rumble grew deeper. "If we don't hurry, it may." He squinted. "But I get a sense that it's not natural, rather more of a warning. Or a signal."

The hair on the back of Märren's neck spiked. "A warning or signal for what?"

He shrugged, a rueful smirk tugging at his lips. "I don't understand the drylands all that well. Do you want to turn around?"

Märren glanced behind them at the gorge they had traveled through and to the white lands beyond. Many days had already passed on this venture, and she could not return to her homeland. Not now. Not when she had come so far after waiting for so many years. She could not return to people she feared and distrusted, as well as invaders.

"She will die in battle. It cannot be avoided. Not for a Wolf warrior."

"Eimri is already lost to her, and soon, she'll be lost to Eimri."

"The Dragon awaits."

"We press on." Märren hurried along as snow plunged across the river, piling higher as it fell, its rumble deafening. At least if she were crushed or suffocated by an avalanche, she would not have died fighting.

Once they passed beyond the area where the avalanche reached the lower ravine, they slowed their pace but continued hiking for hours. The sun quickly passed over the slit of sky visible to them, and something to Märren's left moved. She lurched, her curled and frozen fingers reaching for her axe.

"What is it?" Uisge paused.

Märren glanced around, searching for what had caught her eye. "I'm not sure. Does it smell like troll?"

Uisge sniffed. "I only smell snow and ice, and the fresh water below."

Märren let her axe slide back into its loop. "I thought there was another—"

What looked like arms reached out of the snow wall beside Uisge, wrapping him up as he jerked and fought against whatever it was. Before Märren could shout or draw her axe, similar-appearing arms reached for her. She dropped and rolled aside, ripping her axe free and swinging it, cleaving through a white hand that came at her.

A bellow sounded, rising from the snow itself, before the outline of a creature camouflaged with the white opened its eyes and stepped forward, one of its arms now a bleeding mess. Märren swung her axe again as Uisge yelled, but his cry was swiftly muffled.

The snow beast before Märren resembled a troll, but it was covered in thick fur billowing with hoarfrost. It yanked its wounded hand to its torso while advancing, towering over her. Another beast slid out from the snow beside the first, and Märren growled, raising her weapon.

Ice trolls. Although she had never seen such beasts before, she was certain what they were, and she realized she could not defeat them. She stepped back, returning her axe to her belt like a desperate coward, unlike any Wolf person she had known, while feeling for Eimri's skull.

More ice-cold arms ensnared her from behind, squeezing until her breath rushed from her mouth. The creature before her that she wounded lumbered up to her, snarling in her face, drool stringing from its lips and tusks.

Kill me. She clutched Eimri's skull tighter. *My daughter, I can almost see you...*

"Ah, good work," a voice called from within the ravine ahead. A man in a white cloak strode around a bend using a staff to assist him. He was young, younger than Märren. Five and twenty winters at most, with curly dark hair and a haughty look. He marched up to the troll that restrained Uisge and tapped his staff of gnarled wood to Uisge's hands while muttering something.

Uisge struggled, attempting to speak, but one of the troll's hands covered his mouth.

"It's too fucking cold here for even the greatest mage's magic to work properly," the man swore. He tapped Uisge's hands again and said something. Nothing happened. He hurled his staff against the ground. "Damn the bloody buggering dead Dragon and her babies."

The man dug into a pouch at his waist, his garb beneath the white cloak a brilliant blue and adorned with golden stars. He removed a few strips of leather and wrapped them around Uisge's wrists, cinching the bonds tight. The man approached Märren and did the same, the cords biting into her flesh.

"You must walk," the man said to Märren and motioned to the beast holding her. The troll set her down as the man turned to the three other beasts.

"Hurt," the injured troll said as he clutched his wrist. Blood covered his other hand.

"Stuff some ice on it," the man replied. "It'll heal." He retrieved his staff and started off in the direction Märren and Uisge had been headed. "We caught these two just in time. If they had made it to the village, we wouldn't be getting any coin. No coin, no food." He shook his staff in the air as if to remind the trolls of the phrase and marched off.

32

BELFEDRN

THE SEA SERPENT WARRIORS AT THE CAMP BEYOND THE WOODS waited for full sunlight before breaking down their shelters and tramping toward the forest.

Belfedrn rubbed his aching, bleeding hands. Weariness hung heavy on him after a long night of preparations, but since his enemy started later than anticipated, he had found time to eat some of the spoils from their hunt. He had also been able to catch a couple hours of rest. Dradn and Thelira crouched beside him, and Dradn favored his ribs where the boar had struck him. Both of their hands were just as torn and blistered as Belfedrn's.

"It's time," Belfedrn said. "Wake the pack."

Dradn clenched his shield without the wolf head markings of the Ulfhednar, as well as his spear, and darted off through the woods in stooped fashion, making little sound.

"Stay safe." Thelira crept off in the opposite direction.

Stay safe, young Wolf. Belfedrn snuck through the foliage, watching as ranks of Serpent warriors approached the tree line. He maneuvered to the north and did not stop until he passed beyond the row of their warriors. The Serpents paused just beyond the forest, more than two score of them. This was probably one of their smaller legions.

"Damn spooky woods," a warrior with a piece of the Serpent's scale on his breastplate said to another beside him. "No wonder that scout never returned."

"I bet Wolf ghosts roam about in there," the other replied.

"Probably trolls, too."

A towering brute of a man with an axe shoved through the ranks, two full scales stacked on his *brynja*. A berserker. "You craven warriors. Nearly all the Wolves have been slaughtered and now you're afraid of their ghosts?"

"We don't—aren't accustomed to forests," the warrior who had mentioned the ghosts replied. "Give me the sea and an island any day. Or at the least, open land."

"Get in there." The berserker's breath steamed through a beard bound with gold and silver rings.

A rush of power vibrated the air, rattling Belfedrn's ears. Fog rolled in from the plains. Storm clouds gathered, streaking toward the Moon Woods and darkening the sunlight. Sheets of rain blurred the sky, and in the distance, thunder cracked. The Serpent army waited until rain washed over the area, roaring as it struck fields and trees, the mist billowing into the woods. Lightning flashed across the sky.

The enemy berserker looked upward with arms spread, basking in the deluge of rain. "I'll send any Wolf ghosts or survivors awaiting us a message from the Serpent—rain and water." He smacked the warrior on the back and guffawed. "All of your pitiful magics will now be enhanced."

"I was hoping you could summon a kraken to tear through these woods," another warrior muttered.

"March!" the berserker said, pointing at the forest.

Their ranks stepped into the trees, the berserker following, and the army fanned out to search. Every Serpent was drenched and calling upon the power of the sea to aid them.

Let us slaughter these heartless bastards. Belfedrn waited until the closest warriors passed then moved in behind them. Rain streamed through the canopy, soaking his furs, and streams quickly formed on the ground. *They don't know what's coming.*

The Sea Serpents marched on, creating a tumult when passing between branches and over dead leaves and brush. A cry of alarm rang in the distance, and the Serpent warriors ahead of Belfedrn lurched, glancing around.

"What was that?" one warrior with a broad back asked another with lanky arms.

"Ghosts?"

More screams rang out, these carrying but quickly diminishing in volume before terminating. A dark smile lifted Belfedrn's lips as he stalked the warriors, his wrath seeping from his pores.

"What is it?" The berserker's booming voice carried from not far away.

Shouts were relayed from warrior to warrior before the berserker could hear what they said, although Belfedrn—with his enhanced ears—caught the word long before. "Pits."

"Our fog will only help hide any traps waiting for us," lanky arms said, and broad back took slower, more careful strides while scrutinizing the ground.

Vegask was not here, but these men would have to do. For now. Belfedrn kept his distance, waiting for their ranks to travel deeper into the forest before making his call—a low howl.

Cries of alarm erupted in the woods ahead. The Sea Serpents probably feared that they were surrounded by Wolves, but their fear was misplaced. A few breaths later, the rumble of boulders tumbling down an incline echoed in the forest, the screams of the enemy warriors not loud enough to drown out the din.

Belfedrn crouched in the safe area at the backside of a trunk, waiting for the boulders to stop. One rock rolled past him and hit a stump, bouncing away. This trap would have divided the Serpent army into halves, hopefully killing many in the middle. He followed the warriors closest to him, moving northward as firelight flared through the trees.

The flaming arrows. Balls of pitch would have tumbled down with the boulders and were now lit. More death cries answered, but the flames quickly dwindled under the rain. Lightning struck a spruce nearby, igniting its top and exploding. Chunks of wood and branches flew in all directions as the answering boom of thunder blasted Belfedrn's ears with its fury.

Belfedrn ignored the ringing in his head as he rushed after his quarry, but his Wolf instincts and magic detected a trap. He slowed before approaching a pit he had dug the night before, one whose cover had been broken through. At the pit's bottom, four Serpent warriors lay still, each of them impaled by stakes, their blood coloring water that quickly grew deeper as streams drained into the hole.

One warrior down below raised a trembling hand, reaching for Belfedrn and saying, "Please." The man could not rise because a boulder that stuck out above the water had crushed his leg and pinned him there. "Help."

Belfedrn glared down at him. "Help you in the same way you aided my kin at Nistreel? When your flames burned so many innocents in their homes?"

The warrior whimpered, scrabbling around in the mud and water. The rain continued funneling down, and the water level rose past his neck.

Belfedrn howled, releasing a call of rage and vengeance, which the Ulfhednar would feel in their bones. The Serpent warrior's mouth and then nose disappeared beneath the water, and Belfedrn strode on.

He crept through a tangle of ash branches, stepping closer to his prey. Ahead, the hulking Sea Serpent berserker knelt over one of his warriors who had fallen. Belfedrn raised his spear, advancing. The berserker's back was turned. A surprise attack from this angle would not be an honorable strike. Belfedrn paused, weighing if he should call out and face this man who could be his equal or better in a duel, as an Ulfhednar should. He did not ponder the decision long. He was alone, weaker without his pack, and this berserker was mighty by himself. Why should he allow this Serpent bastard the chance to injure or kill him? This man did not deserve his honor.

Belfedrn stepped closer, rearing back and ramming his spear through the aventail chainmail armor on the back of the berserker's helm. The spear's tip plunged through the links and buried into flesh as Belfedrn's adversary roared in surprise and pain. The berserker rolled away, bringing up his axe as fog engulfed him. Belfedrn lunged forward and drove his spear down again as the berserker began to blur and initiate an attack. Belfedrn's spear bit into the Serpent man's arm, skewering his bicep and punching through the other side.

The berserker vanished into the fog, appearing several strides away, although he remained on his side, his axe falling from his grip, Belfedrn's spear sticking through his arm. The berserker snarled, his teeth caked in red as he spat blood.

"You cannot run." Belfedrn advanced with his axe in hand. "Not anymore. Where did your people take the Wolf trainees?"

"Trainees? Any captives would've been taken back to the isles. To become thralls, or sacrifices. Or to be turned into soldiers."

"You cannot turn a Wolf into a Serpent soldier."

"You'd be surprised what the right kind of initiation and training can do to anyone."

Belfedrn kicked him in the ribs, cracking a few of his bones. "What you did to my people will *not* go unpunished. You distracted the Ulfhednar with trolls that you lured in with gutted bodies, and you offered the monsters Serpent scales so we could not detect them. But you did not kill all the Wolves. You should have."

"We had no choice." The berserker rolled onto his back and stared skyward, clutching his side.

"You always have a choice."

"Our king's family was taken. His first wife, and their children."

Belfedrn paused. "By whom?"

"The Spider. If he didn't order that raid, they would've killed his family."

Belfedrn crouched over his enemy, staring into his eyes while remaining aware of the man's good hand. Although he appeared weak and on the verge of death, Belfedrn would not fall for any more ruses. Not from the Sea Serpents. Not after what happened to Lyrne.

"The Spider demanded the Sea Serpent to invade Wolf territory?" Belfedrn asked, his tone as sharp as his axe. "Without the Spider offering the Serpent anything in return?"

"The Spider is crawling its way north across Horse and Raven lands. They will meet us here soon."

A slippery chill slid down Belfedrn's spine. He had had enough. He buried his axe into the berserker's throat. The berserker's head fell back, blood draining, his eyes dull. Belfedrn's chest heaved with the pangs of wrath and revenge, but fear also swung in and joined them. His mind jostled with questions, the most important ones—what had happened and why—having no clear answers. He would discuss what he had learned with Vard and the pack. But another question lingered. Was he losing the last of his Wolf's honor by attacking his enemies in the same fashion the Serpents had used against his people?

He growled and sprinted through the trees until he came upon the ranks of the remaining Serpent army. He unslung his longbow and began loosing arrow after arrow into the warriors' vital areas, the might of his bow singing with the power of Fenrir.

He should have made the call to the others already, but he wanted the confrontation to be... safer, although he was not sure why. After he had slain many of their warriors with arrows, he finally howled.

Answering calls rang out, and soon, half of the Ulfhednar poured from the woods and fell upon their adversaries with axe and spear. Among them, Dradn and Thelira hacked and swung their weapons. For those two, it was warrior matched against warrior instead of Ulfhednar against Serpent warrior.

Only then did Belfedrn realize why he had waited to kill the berserker and many others before calling for aid. Dradn and Thelira were part of the Ulfhednar pack, but they were not as skilled as the others, not nearly as well trained. For them, the young, it was far more dangerous.

Belfedrn watched as the Ulfhednar hewed through ranks of terrified Sea Serpent warriors, and his arrows followed the path Dradn and Thelira took, offering them cover assistance.

Was he keeping those two weaker by helping them more than the others?

33

CAËTIN

CAËTIN ENTERED UKTR'S GREAT HALL, HER SHOULDERS HEAVY, her mind dense with fog after the long flight and no rest. Her limbs shook with cold, her stomach painful with hunger, her throat parched and burning. She looked for her children but did not see them. Her surviving knights trailed her, their feet scuffing stone. They had lost one comrade. Sanre's stump of a forearm was bleeding through its bandage, but she was alive. Thankfully, the hand she lost was not from her axe-bearing arm.

Raven men and women crowded the great hall, laughter punctuating boisterous conversations, horns of drink in every hand.

Darstrid was chugging mead, telling a story to two male berserkers who were eyeing her body. One grabbed her arse, but she caught sight of Caëtin, pushed them away, and rushed to her.

"What's happened?" Darstrid asked.

"The Spiders are coming," Caëtin said.

The great hall fell silent. Flickering torchlight danced across the many runes running along its walls. Uktr slowly rose from his seat, Taknhal, Freydeg, and Grimmurk following suit. The women who had been sitting on their laps slipped aside.

"The Spider?" The emptiness in Uktr's eyes was replaced with fire. He spoke with his old steely demeanor. "Then we go to battle. We haven't had war in decades, and my heart longs for it. Grimmurk?"

"I'm here, Jarl." Grimmurk stood rigid behind him.

"Freydeg?"

"I'm here as well."

"Wouldn't it be nice to taste the thrill of battle once more?" the jarl asked them.

"Aye," Grimmurk said. "And if you command it, I'll follow you into the pits of Helheim."

Uktr bellowed with laughter, and many others in the hall released awkward chuckles. Caëtin's anger flared. She did not want to carry out Uktr's commands, not anymore, and she had renounced the jarl's authority by disobeying him and departing for Horse lands with her knights. However, she should not turn her back on her people. She had to stay to help them prepare.

"I would strongly advise against marching south to meet them," Caëtin said. "That's probably what those bastards want. To draw us into an unfamiliar land riddled with traps and webs. They could flank us, surround us, crawl out of the earth, and eat us alive."

"No Raven should be frightened by the Spider!" Uktr's cheeks reddened. "Ravens eat spiders like children pick berries from bushes."

"These Spiders should frighten you," Caëtin said. "I've seen inside their caverns. We couldn't find more than a single surviving person of the Horse clan, and she didn't live for long. Envinkia births offspring like insects—in droves. They carry the power of the Spider and have berserkers in reserve who are trained and ready to wield the god parts of any clan they conquer. And they don't need the amount of food we do to survive. The Spiders could outlast us in any war, and they certainly scared the shite out of me and my knights."

"Then you suggest we remain here and wait for them to besiege us?" Uktr strode toward her. "A terrible idea if they need little food. You're as unwise in these matters as you are in believing negotiations with other clans will benefit our people."

Caëtin ground her teeth. She had had enough of this man. Her words became venom. "The Spiders will overrun our southlands before the deep of winter, if they haven't already. There are traps waiting for us to spring them. The Spiders hope we'll be fools enough to come to them. I'm certain of it. That's why they took the taxes from Sparsgard and lured us there in the first place. I've seen what happens when their poisoned weapons cut flesh. A blackening sickness spreads like vines across its victim. I doubt there is any escape from a mere flesh wound."

Darstrid grabbed Caëtin's arm, and Darstrid tilted her head twice to suggest they step outside. Caëtin shook off her sister.

"Come, my favored daughters," Uktr continued as he spread his arms in an accepting manner. "This night we feast together with all the Ravens, and we shall discuss what is to come. We've already made the sacrifices to Muninn." He indicated a half-eaten boar and giant bear carcass, both roasting on spits over the central hearth. A bucket of their blood had been dumped on the stones around the fire. "We've offered the damn Boar's and Bear's creatures to the Raven. I loathe those bastards, but perhaps we should've sacrificed the Spider's creature instead." He turned to those in the hall. "Has anyone seen a spider about?"

Drunken laughter burst forth, shaking the hall, and someone shouted, "I see a few up in the rafters."

Once the laughter died, Caëtin asked, "What's the point of sacrificing anything to Muninn if she's dead? Unlike with our ancestors, sacrifices to the gods are now pointless, no matter if the ceremonies reassure you and your men."

Uktr shook his head and paced about, limping on his bad leg. "Could you just take up a horn and join the feast, Daughter? We're here to discuss many important matters. You'll have your chance to say all you want and try to convince everyone with your opinions."

Servants approached, bearing horns and platters for Caëtin and her knights. Others cleared away food and spilled drink from a nearby table.

"Are you well enough to enjoy a celebration?" Caëtin asked Sanre, who was pale.

Sanre nodded through her weariness. "I'm exhausted, but I'm also famished and thirsty. I don't know about enjoyment, but I'd prefer to take my food and drink first and then find a bed."

Caëtin cast a questioning eye to her other knights, who gestured their agreement, and she led them to the table. She took up a horn and sipped its sweet contents while Sanre downed hers. The others tore into roasted pork and seeds. Halfnr closed his eyes, savoring a rank cheese over dark bread. Caëtin gnawed on a hunk of tough bear meat.

Uktr limped about the hall, drinking and clapping berserkers and warriors on the back while he and Grimmurk and Freydeg were quick to praise and encourage merriment. Taknhal wobbled as he paced behind the trio of old warriors, sharing slurred words with their people.

Treln and Lythi raced over to Caëtin's table, and Treln hugged his mother. "You've returned again, Mother."

Caëtin ruffled his hair, not surprised that her children and servants had been invited to a feast. Few would turn down such an offer. "I told you I would." She scooted aside, making room for her children.

Treln sat beside her, and Lythi took a seat on her other side.

Caëtin ran her hand over her daughter's hair and kissed her forehead.

"How has the feast been?" Caëtin asked them.

"Great," Treln said.

Lythi groaned. "Loud."

Caëtin handed each of them a hunk of bread and hugged them tighter to her sides.

"Thank you all for coming to the great hall this night." Uktr raised his arms high as he stood before the hearth and the roasting carcasses.

"Skål!" The people cheered and drank.

"I wish to commend you all, brave knights and warriors."

The people pounded their horns on the tables.

After the commotion subsided, Uktr said, "None of us would be in this hall feasting and drinking as our people have done for centuries if not for the continued sacrifice of all those present."

More pounding.

Uktr stalked in a slow circle around the hearth, his cloudy eye darting about faster than his other. "My daughters." He lifted a hand, indicating Caëtin and Darstrid as he walked behind Caëtin and paused, making her blood rush with unease. She tried to keep an eye on him, but he shifted and remained directly behind her. "And my son, Taknhal. Their bravery and the courage of you knights and warriors is all that has maintained our borders and stopped other clans from raiding us over this past year as I've grown older."

"Nah!" some cried. "Not true."

"Oh, but it is. I am hale now, but I won't live forever. One day I will travel to the great halls of the gods and feast with my ancestors and yours, even if the gods are no longer there to take part."

Someone bellowed something about saying hello to their father and brothers.

"I will," Uktr said. "I'll take all your greetings to them, if I'm to visit them before you! But some of those here have less time in Midgard than even I. Not much longer than this night." He stalked about behind people as more turned to watch him with increasing apprehension. "I was going to speak to you of next summer's raids to Boar and Bear territory, or of sailing to the isles and raiding the Sea Serpents for their riches."

The Raven people stomped and cheered.

Uktr continued, "But within this hall, another important meet must be held, as meets have been so many times in centuries past." He paused. "The Raven people now stand upon the blade of an axe. If we do not keep our balance, we fall. And times are shifting. The blade we walk upon is swinging." He grinned and drank. "Most of those here are to be celebrated. That's why I feed you from my tables and allow you to drink from my barrels." He glanced around. "But there's a traitor in our midst."

Everyone fell silent, and only the tap of a boot and clink of a horn was audible over the roaring fire.

By Muninn's fucking beaked arse. Not this again.

The great doors parted, and a few warriors strode into the hall bearing axes stained with blood. Uktr did not pay them any mind, but those who had been feasting gawked. Caëtin tensed.

Uktr paced behind Taknhal and patted his son's shoulder. "My adopted son, who replaced the one of my blood after Juktr died in a raid. I could not be prouder of the man you've become."

People hollered, but Taknhal suddenly sobered, turning rigid. Uktr drank and paced on. The jarl stopped behind Darstrid and ran a hand over the back of her head, smoothing her hair.

"My adopted daughter who has replaced my blood daughters," Uktr continued. "She's a feared battle Seidr none would want to stand against."

Many of the knights and warriors applauded and hooted.

Uktr strode over behind Caëtin again. "And my other adopted daughter, whose ability to command Muninn's power is unmatched by any in this hall."

More cheering. Caëtin's fear amplified as she tried to keep a furtive eye on her father's hands, hoping her distrust of him was not too obvious. Uktr sidled just out of her sight. He could have learned of Darstrid's plot to usurp his power and control the Raven knights and warriors. Was he going to take his revenge on one or both of them?

"But Caëtin shall no longer be next in line to follow me as jarl of the Raven clan," Uktr said from behind her, the rattle of an axe leaving his belt sounding simultaneously. "Her choices of late have instilled weakness in our people." He leaned over, his hot breath whispering in her ear. "And you disobeyed me when I ordered you to stay at the great hall."

Caëtin wheeled about, but Uktr stood upright and paced on to the next table, patting his palm with his axe. He strode up behind one of the warriors who was drinking.

"And this bloody traitor seeks to undermine my authority." Uktr swung his axe, his blade hewing into the warrior's neck. Blood spurted. Uktr tore his weapon out of the man's flesh and reared back again, his second blow decapitating the warrior, whose head flew across the floor and rolled about as his body slumped against the table.

Caëtin leapt to her feet, staring in bewilderment for several breaths before she could find any words. "Buggering gods. Were you certain this time? Certain that this warrior was a traitor?"

Uktr swung his axe wildly, his weapon coming close enough to the warriors seated near the man who had been beheaded that blood sprayed their faces. Freydeg wrapped the jarl up from behind, hauling him back. Uktr kicked at Freydeg's shin, issuing a crack. Freydeg cried out and released the jarl, who spun about, swinging. His axe cleaved into his comrade's face, directly between his eyes. Freydeg jerked and toppled, smacking against the floor, lying face up, Uktr's axe buried into his skull.

The hall fell silent as Uktr wrenched his axe free and wiped it clean on the decapitated warrior's cloak. "Another bloody traitor. Right beside me. And for so long." The jarl spat on Freydeg's corpse.

"You're growing paranoid of everyone," Caëtin snapped, pointing at her father, who turned his cloudy eye toward her. "Including your loyal warriors."

"Loyal?" He chuckled. "Is that what you call this? What some of you are trying to do? It's why you're no longer to be jarl, Daughter. I love you as my own, but my love only goes so far."

"I don't want that damn chair anyway." Caëtin flung her horn down and stormed toward the hall's doors, dragging her children with her.

Darstrid hurried after her, and Caëtin's knights followed.

"Every knight, ranger, and Raven warrior, prepare to march upon the invading Spiders." Uktr bellowed as if tasting victory. "We shall not have to wait for summer to raid."

Caëtin exited the great hall, and its doors slammed closed behind those following her. She released her children, and Darstrid grabbed her and shoved her against the longhouse's wall as she said, "Listen to me."

Caëtin shoved her sister back, and somewhere nearby, Huginn shrieked, always protective of Caëtin. Lythi wrapped her arms around Treln, keeping him away. The knights maintained their distance, but their tension and readiness to leap to Caëtin's aid showed in bent knees and hands upon hilts. Caëtin raised a hand to stop them. Huginn flew overhead.

Caëtin said, "He's mad, and he'll get all of our people killed.

If we follow his orders, the Ravens will soon be as dead as the Horse people. Do you realize what he just did? He murdered two of our own and probably had no evidence of wrongdoing whatsoever, just his damn gut feeling that he trusts so much."

"It's done," Darstrid whispered.

"What is?"

"Uktr is no longer our jarl, other than in title."

Caëtin raised an eyebrow. "The fighters won't follow his commands?"

"No more than a handful of those in the great hall will, and once they realize that their comrades aren't joining them, they'd be fools to march to war. And after that display, I think any doubts they had will be erased."

"Unless it makes them fear him and his wrath all the more." Caëtin considered it. "What order shall we give our people?"

Darstrid stepped back and lowered her head as Taknhal exited the great hall and joined them.

"It's not as simple as I'd hoped," Darstrid said. "About six in every ten of all the knights, rangers, and warriors have pledged themselves to me."

A sinking feeling pulled at Caëtin's stomach. "And the others?"

"Most of the rest, Taknhal has convinced to follow his lead. They've pledged their swords and axes to him."

Taknhal bowed his head. "But I do not carry their respect like Uktr did."

Darstrid grabbed their brother by the arm and squeezed, shaking him. "You can, if you stop the incessant drinking and self-pity. You can lead them. Show them how mighty a berserker you are."

"It's not that easy," he said.

"Oh, but it is," Darstrid added, "and I can help you." She rubbed his arm affectionately. "You just need to believe in something or someone else and give up the drink. For them." She jerked her head at the longhouse.

They all looked at each other for a second too long, and disbelief and resentment twined in Caëtin. She said, "I thought it would be you and me leading our people, Sister. I'm about ready to renounce the ways of this clan and leave for good. You're doing little to keep me."

"We need you, Caëtin." Taknhal placed a hand on her shoulder. "You're the most powerful of the Knights Black."

I'm a paladin now. Whatever good that title is.

"It's not like we planned it this way," Darstrid said. "I wanted the warriors split equally between us. You offered to help me convince them, but then you left when we asked you not to."

"I was a little preoccupied trying to save our lands and people," Caëtin snapped.

Darstrid frowned. "It was much easier to convince the warriors to pledge themselves to my sword and magic and even to Taknhal's over someone who wasn't here and was falling out of favor."

"I bet it was so much harder," Caëtin replied. "Then I command only the five knights who came with me?"

"And a few more," Taknhal said. "There are a handful of rangers and knights who still believe you should lead the clan."

"Not enough to put a whore into a dress. But I still won't march to war with those loyal to me. Not for either or both of you. That would be certain death."

"That's why the three of us need to talk." Darstrid tugged at her ear. "It's no use arguing with Uktr. The jarl just does what he always has—yells louder and louder and then threatens to punish anyone he wants. I'll make sure the clan doesn't march."

"What will Uktr do when he finds out you're a traitor?"

"He doesn't leave the great hall anymore. I swore to the fighters that I would act as the liaison between them and him.

They won't have to suffer his wrath other than when eating in the great hall."

"You didn't protect the warrior tonight."

"I didn't know that was coming. But I'll warn everyone and have them prepare to stand against the few still loyal to Uktr, in case anything like this should happen again."

Caëtin grunted in frustration. "So what do we do?"

"We prepare and wait." Darstrid smiled with relief. "I agree with your instincts—the Spiders are coming."

"Can you imagine the Spider people also wielding Boar or Horse magics?" Caëtin addressed Darstrid and Taknhal, trying to determine if they understood all she had suggested. "That may not be too terrible. The Spiders wouldn't be carrying anything more deadly than what they already possess. However, they will have strengthened their weakness. Now some of the Spider warriors and berserkers harness Horse magic and can move with great speed across any terrain, without tiring. They can also deliver more powerful strikes."

"Aye," Taknhal said. "Not good, but not too terrible."

"Now picture the Spiders turning into ravens and flying as far as they desire," Caëtin continued. "Their warriors moving with speed and stealth above and below ground while carrying poisoned blades, attacking with the swiftness of Muninn's beaked strike. They'll have dreams and portents. They will control the Raven's bridge."

Taknhal and Darstrid stared at her, realization seeping into their pained frowns.

"Now you understand," Caëtin said. "If the Spiders come to possess Raven feathers, they'll command more power than simply adding a Wolf pelt or the strength of the Bear to their masses. The magics of Muninn are surely the god parts they most desire, the most powerful complement to what they already possess. The Raven's feathers will imbue them with more magic than any other clan could hope to control."

A long spell of silence followed as the potential repercussions settled on Caëtin's siblings.

"If they take our temple and Muninn, we'll have no chance of defeating them." Darstrid paled. "The idea of bringing trade to all the clans now seems insignificant compared with the news you carry."

"We cannot let this happen." Taknhal wheeled about and marched back into the great hall, his hand on his axe.

34

MÄRREN

Two ice trolls marched before Märren and Uisge and two marched behind them, including the beast Märren had injured, who snarled at her whenever she caught the creature's eye. Thus far, the troll had only managed to regenerate a hand the size of a human child's.

After having traveled for a few days, they emerged from the mountain pass and stood upon an icy tundra to its north. Pockets of smoke rose from the snow, and light glimmered beneath the accumulation in these areas. To the northwest, an orange glow hung along the horizon, blurred by clouds of smoke.

The heart of the land of fire and ash... Only it's veiled by winter. Märren paced on.

"She's arrived, but it has all been for naught."

"For her, death is imminent. For this foolish venture. For turning away from the Wolf and her people."

"She's a prisoner, but nothing is over and she hasn't died in battle. She hasn't lost Eimri."

Eimri's skull bounced against Märren's thigh where her axe should have been, but her weapon had been confiscated by the injured troll. Strong hands shoved her from behind, causing her to stumble and almost trip and sprawl out on the frozen path. When her knee hit the ice with a thud, she grunted in pain but caught herself, cursing under her breath. She paused for a respite, her wrists still bound, and she wiggled her fingers as best she could, trying to keep them from losing all feeling.

When Uisge walked up alongside her, she managed to whisper, "I'm sorry to have brought you into this."

Uisge shrugged, licked his lips, and then mouthed, "It's the price I pay for your blood."

The injured troll smacked Märren on the head, which almost dropped her flat. Her neck popped a few times, and pain shot down into her right leg. She shook her head to clear the bright flash caused by the blow and struggled to her feet before shuffling on.

"No talking," the man in the lead of the group reminded them. "We're only taking you to the village, and you've almost completed the journey. There's no need to grow desperate."

They slogged on, and soon the gleam of firelight emerged in the tundra. A towering gated archway awaited them, torches flickering along its face. Log walls ran in either direction, and beyond the walls, firelight shone from houses perched on a tiered rock hill. A longhouse squatted atop its summit, overlooking the surrounding territory.

The man led the trolls to the archway, where two guards in furs and *brynja,* who also wore helms and held spears and shields, stepped forth. The sigil of a dragon in flight was emblazoned on their shields. The sight of this made Märren's heart beat faster, releasing a warmth that clawed its way from her core and into her limbs, thawing her frozen extremities.

"It is I—the venerable Jestorg, the white mage." The man leading them raised his staff and spread his arms as if he was going to command the gates to open. "Take me to your jarl."

"You also brought your pet trolls along," one of the guards said. "What filth are you trying to sell us this time?"

"A strong woman who is only thirty winters, and her man who may be older but is no more than five and forty."

"Strong?" The guard stepped forward. "These aren't emaciated runaway thralls like the ones you usually bring us?"

"This supposed mage also claimed that those thralls were strong," the other guard added.

The first soldier hmphed his agreement and motioned for Jestorg to bring Märren and Uisge forward.

"Step aside!" Jestorg bellowed at the trolls. "Or I'll launch a blast of flame from my staff that's so hot each of you will be nothing but puddles."

The lead trolls shuffled aside, and the guard approached Märren, scrutinizing her as he asked, "Where are you from?"

Märren did not answer and simply stared at the ground.

"Does she speak?" the guard asked.

"Not that I've heard," Jestorg lied as he crossed his arms over his puffed chest. "A great candidate, and a fine, fine woman to offer."

The guard reached under Märren's furs to feel her neck, and he paused when he found the iron collar there. "Another fucking thrall. Who did you steal this one from?"

"I didn't steal her from anyone," the white mage said. "These two came from the south and trespassed into our lands. They're outsiders."

The guard looked Uisge over and said, "He's as oily and wet as an otter. How's he still warm enough to be alive?" He prodded Uisge with the butt of his spear.

Uisge flashed the guard a smirk that was partially concealed behind his dangling locks, and the guard grunted and turned away.

"I'll give you a piece of silver for both of them," the guard said.

Jestorg laughed. "Take me to your jarl. I only deal with him."

The guard cursed under his breath and returned to the gates. "Let them in!" he shouted, and the creaking of bracing beams being removed followed. The guard faced Jestorg. "Your trolls stay here."

Jestorg beamed. "Of course."

The gates parted. Beyond, waited a score of guards carrying torches. Once Jestorg led Märren and Uisge past the gates, the guards surrounded them and escorted them along a main thoroughfare that wound up the hill. They passed huts and then single-room stone and wood houses, snowdrifts piled against their sides. Curious faces peeked out from doorways as Märren walked up the tiers of rock and dirt, the ground within the village a muddy mess. The smell of piss and hogs clung to the air, burning Märren's nostrils.

When they reached the village's summit and the longhouse there, more guards parted the longhouse's doors and allowed their escort to march inside.

"What scum enters my hall?" A booming voice carried from a throne down the walk.

"Far from scum," Jestorg said. "It is I, the venerable Jestorg, the white mage."

A massive man with a bulging belly stood, his beard hanging to his waist, firelight silhouetting his figure. A few warriors with axes stood below him.

The jarl said, "I should've smelled you coming, although my runners already informed me you'd be here. What do you want, *mage*?" He spat the last word like an insult.

"The turning of the moon approaches. The giant grows hungry."

"More thralls?"

"At this stage, I thought you'd be willing to take anyone I brought. So you don't have to send your own people or make them choose their weakest as sacrifices."

"Two silvers."

Jestorg chuckled. "That's funny, Jarl Breagr, because your guard at the gates offered me nearly the same. But you see, I've had to travel through the ravines again, contend with trolls, and overcome them with my powerful magic—which is always taxing—just so I can again save your good people." He planted his staff on the ground, creating a dull thud against stone.

"The thralls you bring are starved and don't appease Surtr." Breagr cracked his knuckles as he eyed Jestorg. "Lately, the other villages have thought of us as unobliging, and they've threatened war if we continue to send only meager offerings."

"These two are in fine health." Jestorg stepped aside to better display Märren and Uisge. "You'll run into no issues with them."

Breagr stalked closer, his boots thumping and punishing the stones beneath his feet as he moved, his eyes locked on Märren. He circled them.

"I've come so that I may bear a scale," Märren said. "To join the people of the Dragon and fight alongside them. I am trained."

Breagr's brow lifted with surprise as he scrutinized her before bellowing with laughter. His warriors joined in with his guffawing. Märren did not lower her gaze.

After a few breaths, Breagr regained his composure and shook his head in disbelief. "Four silvers for them both. And not a trinket more."

"Jarl, you understand that these two will save two of your people from becoming sacrifices, and if I cannot make any profit, I'll be forced to stop bringing anyone to your village." Jestorg frowned. "Then, well, since I'd still have to make coin to survive, I'd probably have to visit Jarl Grinth instead."

Breagr snarled. "Damn you, you piss of a wizard. If you weren't able to somehow convince ice trolls to aid you, you'd be nothing." He paused. "Eight silvers. And get out."

"Ten, or I'll go elsewhere with my future spoils."

Breagr roared and turned back to his throne, yelling, "Get him his coin before I chop his bloody head off."

A man with an axe approached, a scowl on his face as he dropped silver arm rings into Jestorg's hands. The mage spun about and marched away, casually lifting his staff in farewell. "Until next time, Jarl."

Breagr spat and punched a massive pole supporting the roof as a guard grabbed the bonds around Märren's wrists and shoved her toward the entrance.

"Take them to the caravan."

35

CAËTIN

"We must fly." Taknhal marched through the muddy streets of Aonark, the morning sunlight still pink and red. He showed no signs of intoxication. "As quickly as we're able."

Caëtin trailed behind him, hesitant. Huginn was perched on her arm, her latest gift—the rotting tail of a fish—in her hand while she stroked the raven's neck. Caëtin had been avoiding Ukir the last few days while she and her knights recovered from their ordeal with the Spiders and the long flights. "Back to Sparsgard?"

"Aye."

"If the Spiders arrive in masses, it'd be best to stay here and defend the city and our temple. We should also send a warning to the towns and villages and have their people come to Aonark for safety, unless you're about to suggest that you're flying south to offer yourself to the Spider as a sacrifice."

"We need to travel to Sparsgard because there are a few enemies there. We can fly down and dispatch them straight away."

"I thought Darstrid left six of her knights and a score of warriors there. They should be able to deal with a few Spiders."

Caëtin was not sure she should believe the claims coming from Darstrid and Taknhal, but she preferred their presence over Uktr's.

"There isn't time to discuss every detail." Taknhal faced her, his tone imploring. "We must arrive as soon as possible. Many lives are at stake. As well as our lands."

"And Darstrid?"

"She isn't coming. She has other matters to attend to here. But please, I beg you, follow me." His cloak collapsed around him as he became an unkindness, shrieking and flapping away to the south.

Caëtin groaned in frustration, glancing around. Halfnr, Sanre, and the rest of her loyal knights were not around. *This had better be quick.* Caëtin divided into her unkindness and streaked after her brother, leaving Huginn flapping and squawking in protest.

Their pair of unkindnesses soared for hours and did not stop to rest, finally arriving at Sparsgard during twilight. When Caëtin landed outside the village and drew her sword, her arm was leaden, her eyelids sagging. She stumbled. Taknhal paced on ahead of her, an axe in his fist.

Caëtin rushed after him, fighting off exhaustion and the cold that settled within her as she rubbed her eyes, trying to remain alert and ready for combat while ignoring her thirst and hunger. Taknhal had to be as weary and affected as she was. They entered the village. No one was about.

"Are the warriors and knights who were stationed here passed out drunk in the longhouse?" Caëtin asked.

"One of the knights flew to Aonark yesterday to pass along the message that a few widow berserkers showed up without warning." Taknhal faced her, his tone somber. "Our warriors used torches and as much light as they could get to keep the Spider berserkers at bay and from growing too powerful. The

Ravens drove the Spiders back, but these widows didn't flee south into Horse territory. They fled west."

"Across our lands?" The thought struck Caëtin like a fist.

Taknhal scratched his beard. "Our knights and warriors chased after them."

"Leaving no guardians here?"

He shrugged. "That's when Uktr came up with an idea."

An icy snare encircled Caëtin's throat. "What idea?"

He glanced away. "A lot happened while you were visiting Horse territory and when you were recovering. Uktr had already sent messengers, calling for the Raven towns and villages to send their warriors to Aonark. He wanted everyone to amass there and for the warriors to prepare to move south. To war. He doesn't believe it's wise to wait for our enemy to come to us."

"But Muninn's temple is in Aonark. We'd have the advantage—"

"Any war there would destroy our city and the surrounding lands."

Caëtin looked southward toward the River Red and the fading sunlight. Thoughts of widows coming for them caused her to shudder. "Then what are we doing here?"

"What has to be done so our people can survive."

She whipped her head around to study him. "The two of us are going to try to hold off our enemies here?"

"No." He swallowed. "You see, the village and city jarls are delaying, waiting to decide how they want to deal with this threat."

"I can understand their hesitation."

"They no longer fear or trust Uktr! They're openly defying our clan's jarl. I told Father what you said—about what would happen if the Spiders claim Muninn's remains. That all would be lost."

"Then we've flown all the way here to scare the bloody shite out of a few old men and women? And what's left of their children?"

"The people of Sparsgard were the first to give in to the Spider. They gave their taxes to our enemy."

Caëtin's stomach turned. She did not like where this conversation was headed.

"They housed some of the Spiders and allowed those chitinous fucks to ambush you inside our own lands," Taknhal continued. "That alone is punishable by death."

"We're not here to scare the locals, are we?" She made fists to stop her hands from shaking. "We're here to kill them. We're supposed to act as Uktr's assassins, and we're to do this while the other Raven warriors and knights are away chasing widows."

"We have to make it look like the Spiders did it, that the Spider people wiped out an entire Raven village. Only a few people closest to Uktr will ever know the truth. So word will never get out. Then all our towns and villages will unite against our common enemy."

A wave of nausea swam in Caëtin's throat. "I should've known that Uktr would come up with such a plan and want to go through with it, but you?"

"At first I didn't, but after thinking over the options, it seemed like the best way to unify our people. So a few die here, and in return, we save hundreds or thousands of Raven lives."

Caëtin sheathed her sword. "Then why isn't Darstrid here?"

"She had matters she needed to address in Aonark."

"That's why you wouldn't explain this errand to me before we left. And you hoped that once I was already here, you'd be able to convince me to follow through with this heinous deed." Her voice turned steely. "This degree of violence is too much. Against our own people..."

Taknhal hefted his axe and rested it against his shoulder. "There aren't many still alive in this village anyway, and we could allow the few children to escape, as long as they don't see us."

"*You*—as long as they don't see *you*." Caëtin clenched her jaw. "I won't fight you to the death over this, but I implore you not to do it. Do *not* kill our own. I'm returning to Uktr now, to discuss the situation before any other abominable deeds are committed by Raven fighters. It's time the senile old bastard is confined to his loft. I'll no longer kill innocents for him. Neither will you." She glared at her brother until he looked away in submission.

Caëtin drifted apart into her unkindness and circled the village. Smoke rose from the hole in the longhouse's roof and from a few of the surrounding huts. She squawked at Taknhal to reprimand him and then winged her way northward.

The great hall waited as dawn rose red on the horizon. Caëtin stormed toward the longhouse and flung its doors inward, entering, her weariness so thick it fogged her mind, her bones aching with cold. The jarl's table was set before the throne and beside the central hearth, and Darstrid and Grimmurk sat at it, huddled together, whispering. They glanced up, their conversation halting.

"Where is he?" Caëtin asked.

"Sleeping," Darstrid said. "After raging about the city."

"And my children?"

"With your servants at your house. As you ordered."

Some of Caëtin's fears ebbed, although the thrumming sensation of many god parts in close proximity struck her, which was troubling. "You wouldn't believe where I just came from and what I was expected to do."

"I have an idea. Uktr wanted to send me with Taknhal

because he was worried you wouldn't be strong enough to carry out his wishes."

"Strong enough? Of course that's how the old bastard sees it. Someone's strong if they can slaughter people, even their own kin, without guilt. If they don't have a conscience. I'm done with him and his ailing mind and his ability to influence others—even Taknhal, who was on our side. Uktr only seems to find reason when he stops speaking of battles long past and wants to remind me how I've failed him."

"I refused to obey his order."

Caëtin edged closer, watching Grimmurk out of the corner of her eye. "Did Taknhal know that you refused?"

She nodded.

Questions about Darstrid's and Taknhal's trustworthiness circled in Caëtin's mind. "Our brother claimed that he came to me instead of you only because you had other matters to attend to." She glared at Grimmurk, Uktr's last comrade from his younger years. Where did he fit into this?

Darstrid stood and hurried toward Caëtin, moving faster than she should be able to, although her knees wavered. She guided Caëtin toward the doorway, and said, "Let's talk." But Darstrid did not exit the great hall. She stopped beside the first table near the doors and sat beneath a flickering torch. She poured two horns of mead and passed one to Caëtin. "I sent messengers to all the clans, including the Spider."

Caëtin wanted to ignore her sister's offering, her mind already riddled with exhaustion, but her thirst was too great. She grabbed the horn and drank, not stopping until the mead was gone. "To what end?"

"To make alliances. To see if we could find peace with the other clans before these events turn to all-out war. Most reasonable jarls should see the benefit of peace and trade rather than pillaging and death and poverty."

"I'm sure Uktr loved you for doing that." Caëtin paused. "You didn't tell him, did you?"

"I did." Darstrid took a swig.

Caëtin released a half chuckle, half scoff. "Did you also send messengers to the Sea Serpents?"

"Aye."

"I bet Father pissed himself."

Darstrid laughed. "He may have. He threatened to lower my standing below Taknhal's and yours. I believe your reasoning of making allies instead of enemies is sound, and I think trade is our future."

"And where is our dear father?" Caëtin looked past Darstrid. Grimmurk had wandered closer, straining to listen to their conversation while making a poor attempt of acting like he was uninterested and cleaning up a table.

"Still asleep in the loft." Darstrid refilled her horn and another, her hands shaking but not with fear. With power, maybe? "When the messenger knight from Sparsgard arrived and told us what'd happened at the village, it didn't take long for Uktr to come up with the idea of killing Sparsgard's survivors in hopes of bringing our people together."

Caëtin winced.

"Taknhal and I argued with Father, but Uktr somehow managed to convince Taknhal that his plan had to be carried out if we were to save the Raven people and Muninn's remains. Uktr told Taknhal he needed to be strong if he wanted to lead our people after his father was gone. Taknhal took the bait. Above all else, I think he wants to impress Father."

"Or be jarl."

"And this happened just as I was helping Taknhal avoid drink and focus on other, more important matters."

"What did you have to do to draw our brother away from his temptations? Offer yourself to him?"

Darstrid's eyes clouded over as she stared into the nothingness, unblinking. "I... shouldn't have hoped that I could help him and also have him on my side."

A spell of silence followed as Caëtin considered the implications of what her sister had said and what she did not mention.

"There's something else." Darstrid opened her cloak to expose her chest. Six Raven feathers hung from a chain.

"By Muninn's blood." Caëtin gawked at the number of god parts. No wonder her sister trembled and was acting strange. Darstrid carried enough magic to shatter her own bones, and it was affecting her too much. "The *gyðja* granted you that many?"

Darstrid yanked her cloak back around her torso. "I'm afraid each of us will have to carry all the power we could ever hope to bear and more if we're to stand against what's coming."

The weight of the flight feather and talon between Caëtin's breasts seemed to grow, although she did not notice any ill effects from them. Maybe it was the same with Darstrid—one could not see or sense their own altered behavior or impending downfall.

Darstrid leaned closer and whispered, "There is a smuggler amongst us. Both of Muninn's largest flight feathers, and one of her talons, are missing."

"*Both* flight feathers?" Caëtin caught herself, realizing she should not admit to what the high *gyðja* had bestowed upon her. The *gyðja* had been trying to keep it secret. She also should not give her sister any reason to be suspicious.

Darstrid did not look distrustful. "None of the *gyðja* or *goði* can account for where they've gone."

"If there truly is a traitor, we'll find them. As long as we stop killing anyone who's a suspect while hoping it's them."

Darstrid drained another horn. "Do you think Taknhal will go through with it?"

"Will he kill the people of Sparsgard?" Caëtin bit her lip. She had assumed he would not. Not by himself and not after she berated him for his cowardice. "I don't know, but other than crossing blades with him, I did what I could to dissuade him."

"The great Caëtin has returned." Uktr stood atop the stairs near the loft, peering down at Caëtin, his steel-gray hair oily and covering much of his face, only his beaked nose protruding beyond his locks.

"He won't admonish you in front of everyone," Darstrid said to Caëtin. "I won't let him."

"It's not like you can stop him from ranting once he starts," Caëtin replied. "No one can."

"My favored daughter," the jarl said. He held a palm against the loft's floor to steady himself as he descended one step at a time.

"Am *I* his favorite again?" Caëtin whispered to Darstrid, trying to determine if the jarl mistook her for someone else or if he had forgotten her recent transgressions. "I thought he demoted me."

"His rule is over, and he finally understands that," Darstrid said. "After he issued several orders that no one followed, he and Grimmurk discovered that most of the knights and warriors are now loyal to me. Uktr berated me for it and made it known that he'd seek to put Taknhal on the throne. Then you. In that order."

"And how did Grimmurk take it? Is he waiting for you to turn your back?"

Darstrid tapped her chin with a finger. "He offered to provide me with his council. I suspect he wants to remain aware of all the happenings and to keep Uktr informed. Either that or he simply enjoys being in the jarl's confidence."

Caëtin rubbed at her scratchy eyes.

"I've commanded the knights and warriors to ready themselves for the coming of the Spider," Darstrid continued. "All of

Aonark is preparing. I've also sent messengers to the Raven cities and villages, as you suggested, in hopes of convincing them of the truth—that if they come to Aonark, we'll all be safer and stronger."

"Uktr couldn't have taken that well. The villages defied his messengers' offers. Father probably wants them all to die."

Darstrid chuckled. "Uktr's finally realized that the Raven people will no longer bow to his every desire."

Caëtin sighed with relief as she watched their father descend the stairs. "Well, it's good to know that you're in control of the situation, Sister, and that you're not charging south to die alongside our warriors."

"Things will be better." Darstrid gripped Caëtin's wrist and squeezed. "Once this is over, trade will flourish. Then so will our wealth. Go get some sleep. You need it. And you should be well rested when our enemies arrive at our gates."

Caëtin stood and nodded a greeting to their father before marching for the doorway.

"You can take a bed in the loft," Darstrid said.

"If I'm sleeping, some in this house may not resist the temptation to shove a dagger into my back."

Caëtin strode out into Aonark, and Huginn flapped overhead, following her.

36

BELFEDRN

"We keep to the plan," Vard said as he wolfed down strips of smoked venison while sitting near a fire, the spoils from the Sea Serpent army piled high behind him. "We brought down more than two score of their warriors with one swift blow."

"But we lost two Ulfhednar," Belfedrn said. After the falling boulders had split the Sea Serpent ranks, the other half of the pack—those who had been with Vard—attacked. They faced off with more than a dozen Serpent warriors and another berserker, and the berserker managed to kill one Ulfhednar using veiled strikes of the Serpent and acid spittle. Another member of the pack had been gravely wounded during the skirmish and died soon afterward. Three nights had passed since then, and the Ulfhednar had used this time to recover while Belfedrn continued to train Dradn and Thelira multiple times each day. "We won't be able to keep using this method against the Sea Serpents for long. Not if we lose a couple of our own with every legion they send against us."

"Then you'd have us flee our lands like whipped dogs?" Vard shook his head. "I made you the pack's second for a reason, but I'd like more opinions on this matter."

"I can slip out and raid any who come near." Eakthr the Sly snickered. "To keep us fed even if the herds have moved on." He wore several new bands of silver around his arms and in his braided hair, his plunder from the battle. He chewed on bread and a round of cheese, its reek turning Belfedrn's stomach.

"Until you're caught," Belfedrn said. "When any of us hunt alone, we're not at our best. No matter what we want to believe. Someone would have to come with you on your raids, and that someone would probably have to be me. I want to reclaim our lands and pillage the Serpent Isles to free any captives they took, but we cannot accomplish that with so few of us and while hiding in the woods."

"Most of us already know what you believe we should do, Belfedrn." Athna devoured a stew, dunking bread into it until the bread was dripping and then wolfing it down in a couple snarling bites. "I believe Belfedrn may be right, but I can't see us leaving our lands to these bloody bastards. No matter how ruthless they are, they wouldn't have killed every person in every village. We could sneak around the countryside and gather some of our people while learning where the Sea Serpents are and how to best retaliate against them."

"And if we're caught out in the open, we'll be butchered." Dradn's cheeks burned with ire. "I saw how many warriors they brought with them. The two berserkers and forty warriors we slayed aren't a tenth of them."

"Only pack members will speak on this matter," Vard said.

"We are pack members," Thelira replied. "You said so yourself."

Vard scowled and glanced at Belfedrn, probably reminded of how Belfedrn had convinced him to allow this. "But you're not true Ulfhednar."

Thelira spoke again. "By killing off a few Serpent warriors at a time, it'd take us years to drive them all out."

"And leaving the Moon Woods in pursuit of the herds won't help us reclaim our homelands," Vard said, "unless we plan on waiting generations until our numbers swell and then returning. Unfortunately, that day would come long after we're dead and our sons' sons no longer remember our lands, their people, or the grievances the Sea Serpents have caused us."

"I wouldn't plan on leaving for generations." Belfedrn chewed on a Serpent's salted fish. "I simply suggest that we seek out the Bear's and the Boar's people. We could parley with them and hope that one or both are reasonable and willing to aid us before the Spiders sweep north and unite with the Sea Serpents, crushing all in their path."

A few heartbeats of quiet passed.

"If we stay and the Serpent jarls send more of their warriors to the woods, we can deal with them then." Ylsga tossed her silver hair, brushing it out. "We've already taken many of their scales."

"We should burn the remnants of their god," Belfedrn said. "Serpent scales are of no use to us."

"They could fetch good coin." Fakthr studied the pile of spoils, sniffing about and craning his neck.

"As long as they remain, the Serpents could reclaim them." Belfedrn snarled. "Remember what their kind did to our sanctuary?"

"Burn the scales," Vard ordered and turned to Ylsga's mate, who sat beside her. "And what say you about staying or leaving?"

Kesg ripped off a piece of salted pork with his teeth. He spoke through a mouthful. "I'm in no hurry to leave the lands our fathers left us."

Belfedrn stalked low through the grasses under moonlight, following Eakthr, the stealthiest of the pack. The night invigorated Belfedrn as they slipped across the countryside well beyond the Moon Woods, having traveled for hours in search of Wolf survivors. Dradn and Thelira crept behind them. Belfedrn had argued for them to remain behind and hunt and prepare for the coming of more Sea Serpent warriors, but Vard had reminded him that they were his responsibility. He was to mold them into Ulfhednar. And traveling in a small pack would make them all more powerful compared to venturing out alone or as a pair.

A village lay ahead, and firelight shone from within a few houses there. Any Serpent warriors and berserkers would not be able to see well at night, not nearly as well as those endowed with the magics of Fenrir. As long as Belfedrn and his small pack stayed together and avoided water, he and Eakthr should hold an advantage over a Sea Serpent berserker. Hopefully in this situation, Dradn and Thelira would also be more powerful than a typical Serpent warrior. Thankfully, the sea and any fjords and lakes were not close.

“Step where Eakthr steps,” Belfedrn said over his shoulder to the young pack members. “He’s a master at this, even compared to other Ulfhednar. Move like a wolf. Let whoever is the most adept at whatever skill you’re trying to master teach you. Don’t try to learn everything from me.” He waved the siblings forward and took up the rear, keeping watch behind them as they approached the village.

“Some of it’s burned, but not all,” Dradn whispered before Eakthr silenced him with a crazed glare over his shoulder.

Eakthr hurried onward without creating a sound. Thelira and Dradn attempted to keep up with him but rustled through the brush and then slowed their pace. Belfedrn caught up to them.

"Avoid brushing against those blades of grass." Belfedrn pointed to the dead grasses that were sheltered from the rain, those that were not as wet as the rest.

"I can't move quickly and watch out for every weed." Dradn's tone was bitter.

Eventually, they neared a few of the houses. Eakthr was nowhere in sight. The smell of people hung around this place, and they carried the scent of the sea.

They aren't masking their odors. "The Serpent's people are here. They don't expect us, but we can't know how many there are. Be wary."

Dradn crouched lower in the grass and watched the area while Thelira slunk around the perimeter. Belfedrn followed her. A nearby pen held hogs, the animals still alive and sleeping. If the Sea Serpents meant to raid and pillage and then return to their isles, they would have burned everything they could not carry with them. Invaders who did not destroy excess food sources planned on staying... at least until the Spider arrived. Perhaps longer.

In the distance, two Serpent warriors stood beside a doorway, staring blankly into the night. Belfedrn nocked an arrow and drew his bowstring while sighting one of them. He released a low howl, sending his feelings to Eakthr. The warriors stepped away from the house, glancing around before losing interest in whatever animal was about and shuffling back toward their posts.

A few breaths later, Eakthr darted from the darkness around the house, approaching the warriors in their blind spot. He grabbed one warrior from behind, yanking him off-balance and slitting his throat. Belfedrn's arrow flew and impaled the other warrior in the neck, nailing him to the house with a thud. The man went limp but hung from the arrow.

Damn weak aventail behind his head. Belfedrn waited, his

tension mounting, but no door flew open. At least the house could not hold many people. He jogged toward the structure as Eakthr dragged off one victim.

Then the door creaked open. Belfedrn dived behind a well and peeked around it, nocking an arrow. Two naked people, a woman with small breasts and a muscular man, who were probably both Serpent warriors, exited.

"Did you two hear—you fool!" The man shook Belfedrn's victim. "You can't fall asleep or—"

An arrow plunged through his open mouth, silencing him. Belfedrn loosed, and his arrow buried into one of the woman's eyes. They both fell with thumps. Belfedrn raced from cover, reaching the dead guard he had shot first and tugging, ripping the arrow loose from the wall behind him. He used his enhanced strength to heft the man onto his shoulder as Dradn arrived, grabbed one of the dead naked warrior's feet, and dragged him off. Thelira crouched before them, watching the other two structures in the village that had firelight burning inside.

After removing the dead and hiding them in the vegetation, they waited, watching. An hour or so later, another door opened, and a woman with graying hair and a tunic stole outside. She headed out from the village and squatted in the grass. When she was finished and walked back toward the house, Eakthr sprang from the foliage and grabbed her, wrapping a hand over her mouth.

Belfedrn hurried to join his comrade, and the young members followed.

"... like an Ulfhednar," the woman said, her eyes wild as she trembled but stared at Eakthr's black-painted eyelids and cheeks, as well as his pelt. "But it can't be. The Serpent people said you fell for a ploy when you left us. That you're all dead."

"Not all of the pack." Eakthr giggled. "Fenrir hasn't departed these lands forever. Not yet anyway. But tell me—how many of these Serpent swine are about?"

"There's one in my house, and if you killed four as you said, then there are still two others in that house." She pointed to the last structure with firelight. "There's also another family member in my house."

"Man or woman?" Belfedrn asked.

"Woman."

"Is the Serpent in your house sleeping?" Eakthr asked.

"Aye. Bastard." Her eyes turned distant as she relived some memory.

Eakthr nodded at Belfedrn, and Belfedrn drew an arrow as Eakthr crept to the doorway.

"You two wait on either side of the doorway of the last house," Belfedrn said to Dradn and Thelira. "If anyone resembling a Serpent exits, kill them."

Dradn and Thelira rushed away. Eakthr slowly pushed the door inward. It creaked on rusty hinges, and a muffled voice sounded inside. Soon, a face appeared in the doorway, that of an older woman, who squinted as she glanced around and said someone's name. Belfedrn stayed his hand as a deeper voice carried out. Eakthr pulled the woman aside and rushed in. A shout sounded before ending in a gurgle.

Someone in the distance hollered. Steel clashed with steel, and a grunt followed. Belfedrn spun about and raced for the last house.

There, Dradn swung his seax at a nearly naked man with a shield. With her spear, Thelira skewered a second man who emerged and jerked her weapon out of him. Her adversary grabbed at his wounded shoulder but still wielded an axe. He lunged at her.

Belfedrn aimed, but the Serpent warriors were so close to the young, all of them striking and blocking and circling. His bracing arm shook. He could not be certain of his target. The bow fell from his hand as he drew his axe and sprinted toward them.

Dradn parried a blow and then sliced his enemy's thigh before darting in and finishing him with a cut across the chest and one to the throat. By this time, Thelira had already impaled her adversary a couple more times, and he slumped to his knees, pitching forward onto his face.

When Belfedrn arrived, Dradn and Thelira faced him, preparing for more.

"Are there any others?" Thelira's gaze darted around.

"No." Belfedrn sighed with relief, his worry ebbing as he fought off tears that stung his eyes.

37

MÄRREN

THE LINE OF THRALLS AND OTHER CAPTIVES, WHO WERE BOUND IN iron links, marched northward. Armored warriors of the Dragon —the Ormr—surrounded them, the orange glow on the horizon growing brighter as they walked toward it even though the night was growing later.

"She's a thrall again."

"It's all she'll ever be. It is her fate whenever she leaves Wolf land, and it cannot be changed."

"She can't fight back now, and she won't be tempted to. She'll see Eimri soon enough."

At least no one had seen the point of taking Eimri's skull from Märren, although no warriors would listen to her when she mentioned her training and ability to wield a scale or when she offered to join their people. The iron collar aggravated and blistered her neck, its movement more pronounced when linked to others. Her hands were still gloved but bound and numb, and a scar rune on her inner thigh shimmered in her mind. Uisge marched behind her. It was her fault that a centuries-old creature was going to die.

Eimri. I'm coming.

They had already slogged along for days with little rest, warmth, or food, and now they trekked through the middle of the night. Hundreds or thousands of torches burning in a city larger than any in Wolf territory passed on their left. That must be where the Dragon people's jarl or king—not a simple village jarl like the one who had purchased them—resided. Where their temple and the scales were kept. If she were to be brought there, she could attempt to steal a god part, but they trudged past.

Before the early hours of the morning, the orange light on the horizon grew more intense, and hotter. Ahead, a mountain towering into the sky spewed smoke and fire. Ash drifted around them like blackened snowflakes. *This* was the land of fire and ash.

A massive bonfire burned at the base of the mountain, its flames reaching as high as the tallest spruces in the old woods. As they plodded on, heat returned to Märren's cheeks, then to her body and finally to her hands and feet. The warriors lashed at the captives when anyone stumbled or stalled, and sweat began to bead on Märren's forehead as they ventured closer to the mountain.

The snow on the ground became less deep, much of it melting, although more flakes plummeted in sheets from the sky, mixing with the ash. Ahead, other people waited, surrounding the inferno at the mountain's base.

"We're late," a Dragon warrior said. "There's already a circle of human sacrifices."

A Dragon berserker with an entire red scale upon his breastplate grunted as he studied the scene. "We should still offer our captives. In case they're needed. If not... there's always next time."

The Dragon people urged Märren and the caravan on. Once

they came within several hundred strides of the fire, a Dragon warrior shouted, "Spread out and approach the fire."

The woman in front of Märren covered her face with her hands and sobbed, her chain links rattling with each shudder.

"Accept your fate with courage," the warrior added. "Then maybe the Valkyries will take pity on you sorry lot and will carry you off to the great halls of the afterlife." He cracked a whip.

Märren sidled aside, helping to create a ring of captives as they approached the inferno and at least twice as many thralls who were already staked out around it. She had been expecting a jötunn, not this mountain and its conflagration. Heat billowed across the gap between them and pounded against her, the fire not appearing to be fueled by wood or anything else. Perhaps it was a vent for the mountain's heat and flame.

Uisge trailed her as the captives with them fanned out more, and she cast him a side glance, wondering if he was desperate to remain in this world and if he had some plan for escape. His eyes were completely black, and his typically sodden hair no longer dripped water. His tongue hung past his lips as if he were parched or could not catch his breath.

He's suffering already. A rush of guilt flooded Märren again, although she was not worried about herself. Where she was headed would be more enjoyable than Midgard had become, unless a Valkyrie thought she was being courageous for not being frightened of death and took her somewhere other than Helheim.

"The Valkyries won't save her."

"But one never knows. If they do, she'll never see Eimri again."

"Eimri will always be with her."

Some of the Dragon people shoved Märren and the captives with her into a semicircle and toward the sacrifices who had already been staked out around the fire. Warriors hauled more iron stakes from a cart and slid these through the chain links running between Märren and those she was bound to. Other Dragon people approached, wielding massive hammers meant to pound the stakes deep into the icy melt and earth beneath.

"Stop!" the Dragon berserker said. "Move back, now! Everyone back! Get the carts moving."

The woman to Märren's right wailed, and the fire roared on, its flames dancing higher. Märren tugged on the chains running to either side of her collar. None in her caravan had been staked to the ground before the warriors hurried off. Only those in the circle of prisoners closer to the blaze were held fast. It did not seem like any giant had awoken, and unless this jötunn lived in the mountain itself, he was not around. Even then, it would take hours for him to climb out of the smoking crater above and walk down—

The inferno blazed higher still, its crackles snapping in Märren's ears, almost deafening her. Some of the captives screamed, and the horses pulling the carts stamped and snorted before galloping away. Many of the thralls with Märren also screamed, pulling against the weight of the chains and the others who were frozen with terror, allowing none to move. Märren slowly walked backward, unable to take her attention from the sacrifices before her.

The flames elongated, and parts of a charred humanoid appeared within them. Fire danced upon this creature's blackened head, face, and across its shoulders, erupting through areas of its chest and limbs. Märren's heart clenched, missing several beats. The burning monster stood, rising as tall as a giant spruce and stretching broader than many trolls. It faced the ring of captives and lumbered forward, the earth shaking with each footfall. A flaming sword almost as tall as this jötunn was clenched in its fist.

Surtr... The greatest of all the fire giants had come to Midgard. Märren trembled with terror and nearly fell to her knees. She could not avoid that emotion before death. Not here. Not with Surtr looming before her.

"By the great dead gods."

"There is no escape for anyone. This jötunn is a god slayer."

"She shouldn't look at it. Instead, remember home. Remember Eimri."

She glanced at Uisge, who was not retreating, as she squeezed Eimri's skull. Half of the thralls bound to her were trying to scramble away, but the other half had fallen to their knees, resisting those who wanted to flee. Uisge stood with his head bowed, his drying locks covering his face, his appearance wavering in the heat. For an instant, his hands resembled hoofs, seaweed above them. The ice beneath his feet melted faster than that which was around him, like when he had created water for them to drink by summoning a pool from the earth and snow. He yearned for life. Even now.

Märren grabbed his shoulder and shook him. "We're not staked to the ground. We can run. If we can get the others to come to their senses."

"Fear and noise will ensure that you're one of the first to be taken," he said. "Move slowly and quietly."

"Do you think we can escape?"

Uisge shrugged, his tone shakier than the calm confidence he was attempting to exude. "The thought crossed my mind, although I'm not sure how we can accomplish it. Even if we somehow break free of our chains"—he glanced behind them—"there are many Dragon warriors watching. They'll ruin any chance we have of fleeing from this jötunn."

The captives who were closer to the giant shrieked and cowered, most of them huddled and covering their heads. Märren followed Uisge's lead as he took a small step away, her breath rasping in her throat.

When Surtr neared and towered over the first ring of

captives, he snatched up the loudest, a woman who was screaming and flailing about. The flames on Surtr's fingers engulfed her, and she shrieked one last time before her body blackened and shriveled like wood turning to ash. Surtr lifted her searing corpse, her chains turning red and then orange and yellow, the stakes around her tearing from the ground.

Surtr raised the victim to his mouth and bit her in half. Märren's blood ran with ice. The giant finished the rest of his meal and turned for the next cowering sacrifice. The jötunn used his sword to cleave through the chains before dropping his weapon and plucking up two more people, one in each hand. They burst into flames. The Dragon people's resulting cheers were reminiscent of spectators at a duel.

"Run," Märren said.

Uisge grabbed her arm, holding her in place just as she took her first stride, and he said, "I realize you may want to die, but being killed by Dragon warriors is hardly better than burning in Surtr's fire."

"I cannot display fearlessness or bravery." She shook her head. "Or I may be taken to Valhalla."

"So you're wanting to die quickly?"

"No. And I don't want you to die while aiding me on this mad venture."

Surtr finished devouring the captives to Märren's right and turned back for the rest. Intense heat passed by, scalding her, and Uisge's chain jerked, pulling them both along with the other fleeing thralls. Surtr glanced in their direction before a man below the jötunn screamed in horror. Surtr looked down at the sacrifice.

"Run." Uisge was the first to turn and try to barrel away, although his chain quickly pulled taut, jerking him by the neck and throwing him onto his back.

Märren grabbed the woman on the other end of her chain,

who had fallen onto her knees and was wailing, and dragged her along as Märren scrambled away at an angle, toward Uisge.

"Drag the person next to you!" Märren shouted to those she was bound to, and she jerked her head toward a man on Uisge's far side, who was sobbing and hiding his face with his hands.

Uisge shook his head, dazed before reality dawned on him and he found his feet. Märren's movement had given him enough slack so he could step close to the man beside him. He wrapped his chain around the captive's waist and pulled the man along. A couple of the others had done something similar, and now, with most of the thralls rushing off and their strength combined, their line dragged away the last few who were immobilized by fear.

Shouts of outrage rose in the distance, erupting from the Dragon warriors they were headed toward. The ground boomed and shook as Surtr turned. The giant roared.

Märren glanced back as Surtr looked about in confusion. She hurtled along even faster, the melting snow making for treacherous footing. Märren and Uisge raced on as fast as they could while hauling their burdens, and Uisge helped steady Märren while they fled across the terrain. The last cries of the sacrifices faded as the Dragon warriors fanned out around the fleeing captives.

The berserker of the group rode his horse closer, holding up a hand and pointing behind them. "Stop your flight! It looks like Surtr has gotten his fill. For now. Enough so that he isn't wanting to chase a bunch of cowards across the tundra."

Behind them, the giant's movements slowed as he sauntered about, chewing on the last of the sacrifices who had been staked before him. As time crawled by, he became more fire than jötunn.

"Unfortunately, he did not receive a full feast, and so his hunger will come sooner the next time." The berserker grinned as he spoke to his warriors. "At least we know which thralls will be sent to him then."

The warriors dismounted, and along with many others, began to force the captives back into a line.

"Do we march for Torank?" a warrior asked the berserker.

"No. Not yet. I have another use for these cowards."

38

CAËTIN

WARRIORS STOOD WATCH ATOP THE WALLS OF AONARK, MOST OF them facing southward. Caëtin ascended the stairs toward the walk along the wooden battlements, searching for Darstrid or Taknhal. Both of them were supposed to be around. Caëtin had slept for over half a day and then ate well with her Knights Black before she left them. Her weariness had not completely departed her, but the sensation was only a mild annoyance.

Huginn alighted on a pole nearby, watching. Raven people ran about the area, stacking supplies along the base of the walls or carrying arrows and spears up to the walk, filling vats with pitch, and making torches. The Spiders were coming, although no one knew when.

Better to be prepared and waiting for nothing rather than have our city taken while our knights have their leggings around their ankles. Once she reached the top of the stairs, she tapped a Raven warrior who paced along the walk on the shoulder and said, "Have you seen Darstrid?"

The man faced her, his nose flat from being crushed in the past, and he pointed away from them. "Last I saw her on my rounds, she was near the southwest corner."

Caëtin marched on. Much of the city extended beyond the walls, having grown over the decades. During times of peace, there were far too many karls to house within the walled portion of Aonark, but these workers would be brought inside when the first messenger arrived carrying word of an approaching army.

After traversing most of the southern wall's walkway, Caëtin spotted Darstrid, her back turned. Caëtin paced faster as Darstrid barked orders to the knights, warriors, and unenhanced soldiers all around. Darstrid limped about, shouting as she gestured south, the sensation of too much power still sheeting off her.

"Most of you haven't seen what those of the Spider can do," Darstrid said. "If we don't prepare, we're as good as dead."

"Darstrid." Caëtin waited until her sister turned before indicating Darstrid's lame leg. "What happened?"

Darstrid stiffened, attempting to hide her pain. "It's nothing."

Caëtin strode closer, lowering her voice. "It is something. You're not easily injured, and all the feathers you're carrying are weighing heavy on you."

Darstrid glanced at the fighters around her and addressed them. "Keep up the preparations and watch in shifts. I'll return soon." She stepped past Caëtin, pulling Caëtin along. "Walk with me."

They headed toward the nearest stairs leading down into the inner city, not speaking until they reached the bottom. Once they put some distance between themselves and the walls and karls and soldiers, Darstrid lowered her head, her limp becoming more pronounced as she moved.

Caëtin grabbed her sister by the arm. "We don't need to return to the great hall to discuss this. Just tell me what happened."

Darstrid shrugged off Caëtin's grip but grimaced and

clutched her side. "Keep walking. Something happened not far from Sparsgard."

A chill slipped down Caëtin's back. "While I was sleeping?"

"Aye. I traveled with a small group of knights. It wasn't supposed to be much of a concern. We were only meant to assist those I'd left at the village with the cleanup of the Spiders they'd hunted down."

"You should know by now that the Spiders are trying to deceive us," Caëtin snapped. "Don't be a fool and travel lightly."

"The messenger who informed me of the need for assistance was a knight, and his unkindness escorted us to the site in the countryside. Nothing there was out of sorts or troubling. It wasn't a trap. Until it was."

Images of Spiders boiling out of the ground filled Caëtin's head.

"There were three dead enemies when I arrived," Darstrid said. "All were recluse warriors, although the Knights Black believed they had been pursuing widow berserkers."

"And these widows then ambushed you?"

"No." She pursed her lips, her eyes falling shut as they headed toward the great hall. Huginn's shadow passed on the ground beneath them. "But one of the knights had been cut by a poisoned widow's blade. Perhaps one of the recluses carried the weapon."

"I saw the results of that with Sanre. The black seeped up her veins. She wanted me to cut off her limb, but I wouldn't."

"Is she still alive?" Darstrid's eyes gaped as she grabbed Caëtin by the front of her cloak, shaking her.

"Aye. She cut off her wrist herself."

Darstrid sighed and released her. "Then she's all right?"

"She was when I last saw her."

"Then there's a way to stop the poison from spreading. This

knight was cut on his side. He hid whatever pain he was in until it was too late."

"Then he died?"

"No. We were searching the ruins of a settlement in our territory, a place that nobody has inhabited in a century. He collapsed. I ran to him, but he started seizing. Violently. I held him down, and that's when I saw the black tendrils running up his neck and face. His eyes bulged, and foam spewed from his mouth."

"Muninn have mercy."

"Muninn could no longer save him. He lashed out at me." She spat as they neared the jarl's longhouse. "His axe bit into my thigh and stomach before I even realized he was coherent. He'd become something else. Something dark. The blackness engulfed him, and he climbed to his feet as I backed away trying to stem my bleeding. He came at me, swiping, mad and raving. It took two knights to cut him down."

"Piss on the dead gods." The implications settled on Caëtin like a boulder.

"The knights found a black spider under his hair, at the nape of his neck. Its head was implanted into his skin like a tick's. They think it was controlling him. Either the spider or the poison. Or both."

Caëtin shuddered. "Bloody disgusting." A memory of when she shot down that lone Horse woman who had been running from the Spiders resurfaced. She had saved the woman twice. Once from rape and torture, and a second time by not allowing her to turn into whatever it was a stricken person became. Violence was beneficial in some, if not many, instances. "These Spiders have more tricks than a seventy-year-old whore. And all of them more treacherous than the last."

"I'm afraid we don't understand what powers the Spider has

bestowed upon those who carry her chitin, but we need to before her warriors and berserkers arrive."

"We should not venture out and confront them. Not again. Not even in hopes of learning more. Too many will die."

Darstrid paused outside the great hall, her face wan and tense. "I believe you're right, but Taknhal is starting to see things the way Uktr does. Our brother wants to send a dozen of his loyal knights to do battle with the Spiders. To find their weaknesses."

"We'll hardly learn anything if none return."

"He wants to put three others in the distance to watch. They're to flee before joining in any fight."

"What do the knights think of this?"

"Most won't speak out against Taknhal, but some think it's folly and a waste of lives for little or no gain."

"That's probably true." Caëtin took Darstrid's hand, less suspicious of her sister's intentions. She pushed Darstrid's cloak from her shoulders. Dark stains seeped through her sister's brigandine and leggings, and she still bore six Muninn feathers. "You should relieve yourself of such a heavy burden. It's granting you power but draining your stamina. It'll take longer to heal properly."

Darstrid yanked her cloak closed. "The feathers are giving me the strength to stay on my feet and walk about. I cannot show weakness. Not before battle. It's not only the karls of the city who are frightened. Terror seeps from the warriors, rangers, and even the Knights Black. Our people need their jarl to be hale and ready, or the coming storm and the horror it'll bring with it may prove too much."

"You should rest. Regain your health. Our enemies probably won't show themselves in the next few days. I believe they're preparing their entire legions to storm our lands. The Ravens who are watching will send word long before the Spider armies arrive."

Darstrid turned and winced. "If anything, I'll need to convince the *gyðja* and *goði* to allow me to carry a full talon before the Spiders show their faces. You and Taknhal may need to bear one as well. The Muninn paladins in the old legends were said to have carried talons in times of the great wars following the deaths of the gods, and their power was unrivaled among all the Ravens."

Caëtin held her tongue, still unsure what she should share with whom.

"Did Taknhal spare the poor people of Sparsgard?" Caëtin's insides clenched. She assumed her brother would not commit such a horrible deed alone, the reason why he needed her there—to help him along.

"I don't know," Darstrid said. "He returned somber and distant and has spent much of his time at the temple. If you want to ask him, he's probably still there."

"I'll find him. You should rest and unburden yourself of Muninn so you can recover. Dreaming without using the Raven's powers for portents won't hurt you."

"Unless the traitorous smuggler of god parts comes for me while I sleep. At this time, I don't think it's wise to relieve myself of Muninn."

Caëtin cocked her head as she considered the potential outcomes of her sister either wearing or relieving herself of the divine parts. The power granted by such items was addicting to all berserkers and warriors but was something they had to endure for the good of the clan. Caëtin realized how clear her mind was while bearing the extra feather *and* a talon. It seemed likely that she too was not aware of what the magics of a god were doing to her, and her body could be growing dependent on that power and craving it. Perhaps she would never be able to bring herself to part with her pieces of Muninn.

"Please, Sister, take my advice and let yourself heal," Caëtin urged. "The desire we have for god parts is no different from Taknhal's need for drink. If you see it that way, you may be able to resist its temptation. After you've recovered, you can don all you're able and prepare for battle."

Darstrid forced a smile, and Caëtin departed for Muninn's temple. Huginn flew on ahead, cawing and watching over her.

39

MÄRREN

MÄRREN AND UISGE WERE SHOVED TOWARD THE MOUNTAIN OF fire by a Dragon warrior. The two of them were separated from the other captives but still chained together, similar to the other thralls who remained in pairs but were forced in different directions.

The slopes of the mountain neared, the orange light in the sky coming from its summit and casting shadows all around. A flicker of firelight shone in the mountain's base—an opening.

"Don't go too far inside," the warrior said to them. "Only through the portcullis to gather what's waiting in the outer chamber."

Märren trudged closer, the voices in her head raging.

"I say this for your own good," the warrior added. "Because your lives are still worth something to us. And to Surtr. You cannot escape into the mountain. You'll be consumed by fire."

A yawning cave sealed off by a portcullis awaited them, but the gaps between this portcullis's iron rods were large enough for a man wearing armor to pass through without difficulty. Heat radiated from the cavern, but not to the degree that had wafted from Surtr.

Märren strode onward past Uisge as he paused. She slipped through a gap in the gate, entering the mountain, the chain between her and her companion pulling taut before he slowly followed. The cavern was bathed in firelight but had no open flame. Along the far wall, a massive tunnel veiled by shadow burrowed deeper into the mountain. Beside the opening, what looked like two barrels lay on their sides in the shadows.

Märren strode toward them but continued past, heading into the tunnel.

Uisge tugged on their chain, slowing her down. "In case you didn't hear, we're supposed to take these out to the warrior. That's all. Even if you want to, you can't flee deeper into this place. You'll burn."

"We keep going. A little farther." Märren tugged at their chain, using its links to guide Uisge into the tunnel, his feet dragging. "We may burn yet, but I don't think it will be from the mountain's fire."

Uisge hesitated before his resistance eased. "What else do you believe is being kept in here?"

"A dragon. And I've come for one of the Dragon's scales."

Märren marched ahead, dragging Uisge with her. They followed a broad passageway with a soaring ceiling that wound through rock, headed toward the heart of the mountain, the temperature rising steadily. Eventually, the tunnel opened into a second chamber filled with firelight.

Flames danced in alcoves, appearing to be fueled by stone and dirt. At the far end of the chamber, a scaled beast as massive as the Wolf people's great hall lay curled around itself, its chest rising and falling with breaths, steam pluming from its nostrils. Spikes protruded from its topline, head, folded wings, and limbs. Horns curled and bent upward from its skull, its scales as red as blood.

Märren stood frozen in awe, the events with Surtr a distant

memory. The slumbering beast snorted and shifted. A line of scar runes on Märren's side that meant dragon throbbed.

"We should return to the outer chamber," Uisge said, his voice a whisper as it cracked with fear.

"She's stumbled upon a dragon."

"It will devour her."

"It's what she's always dreamed of finding!"

"Märren!" Uisge tugged on their chain.

The beast snorted a blast of air and shifted again, lifting its neck and turning a head larger than a warhorse, the scales on its underside a deep yellow. Uisge retreated as far into the tunnel as the chain between his and Märren's collars would allow, pulling against her. The dragon's eyes popped open, its pupils narrowing and focusing on them. It released a low growl as it stretched out of its curled position and rose, stalking toward them, tail flicking.

Only Märren's neck seemed able to move, and her head tilted upward to look the dragon in the eye as it towered over her. Her mind was barren of thought, her mouth bereft of words.

"You do not flee in terror," the beast said, its voice grating inside its throat and creating a deep rumble that echoed through the vault of its maw and around the chamber. "You should. You are unwise."

Märren reached out as if to touch the dragon's snout, but it was too far above her.

"Märren!" Uisge said. "Get back!"

The beast's neck snaked out, its head darting closer, jaws gaping. Fire brewed in its throat, and light spilled out between the scales of its neck, wafting heat. The dragon snarled.

"Death has come for her."

"She'll roast in fire hotter than Surtr's."

"She stands her ground before the beast."

The dragon cocked its head. "You do not fear death?" Its

voice boomed in the cavern and blasted over Märren like a gale, blowing her hair back and causing her to squint.

Märren's lips worked a few times before her shock subsided and words came to her. "Only death in battle."

It sniffed her. "You were in the presence of Surtr, and you carry death with you." It turned its head and scrutinized her, its attention settling on her waist and the pouch there. "You are unlike others of your kind."

Eimri. Märren patted the skull and stepped closer to the creature, placing her palm against the spikes jutting from its lower jaw. The dragon hissed, the firelight in its throat blazing, smoke billowing from its nostrils.

"You are a fool," it bellowed, the blast of air leaving its jaws sweltering and so forceful that it shoved Märren back. "Or you are mad."

"I may be both." She pulled Eimri's skull from its pouch and held it out to the beast, who recoiled.

"Your young has perished and yet you keep hold of... her." The creature whipped around, shaking the cavern as it moved, its wrath seething.

"I am angry, too."

"And yet you do nothing to the one who murdered your offspring?"

"How do you know I've done nothing?"

"Because if you had, you would lay your offspring to rest."

"Maybe I'm mad."

"Even the mad will do this once vengeance has been served."

"And how would you know?"

The dragon shrieked, its cry ringing against the walls as it faced Märren again. "Because I've lost *many*. More than you ever will."

Märren's head quaked from the outburst, but she stretched

upward and touched the underside of the dragon's neck. "I feel your pain."

"You know nothing of it!" The beast pulled away. "You cannot understand a dragon's pain. And for that, you will die." It reared and parted its jaws again.

"She doesn't realize how it's suffered."

"She'll never know."

"The dragon has been hurt like she has. It wants to be understood."

"You've lost your young," Märren said. "That much is clear. I've walked the path to this cavern. The Dragon people's thralls are made to deliver your offspring to the jötunn."

The beast clamped her mouth shut and snarled. "It's not that simple."

"They're your young. I understand that. When you birth an egg, is it not the same as me birthing a child?"

The dragon released a high-pitched whine and pulled away, regarding Märren with renewed interest. "How could you possibly feel empathy for me?"

"Because we're both living creatures. We've both suffered the same."

The dragon faced the far wall and stared into a corner. "Surtr slayed our god—the Dragon herself. *The* Ormr. His flaming sword severed her head from her body, and she crashed into the earth, creating a swath of destruction. Over time, her spine petrified, forming the mountain range to the south. Her head rolled into the sea. Humans harvested her scales for power, becoming the Dragon people. And yet those people who worshipped her and whom her offspring once bonded with—those *we* allowed to ride us—ended up using her power to save their own kind!"

"I am not surprised by this."

"But you do *not* understand everything!" The beast paused,

smoke curling from her nostrils, although she still faced the wall. "After the Dragon's death, Surtr fell asleep, becoming the fire outside the mountain, burning for centuries, recovering from the wounds the Dragon dealt him. When he woke from his long respite, he arose famished. Those who worshipped the Dragon tried to stop him, but the jötunn from Muspelheim cannot be killed. Not even by a god. Surtr took me and my kin from the Dragon people and threatened to destroy all their cities and villages if they did not feed him. So the people appeased him with sacrifices while allowing the Dragon's offspring to remain imprisoned. To this day, they appeal to his needs, in more ways than sacrificing their own kind."

"They offer your eggs to the giant," Märren said.

"Aye." The creature paused as her wrath burgeoned. "Surtr prefers dragon eggs and young hatchlings over humans. Our kind do not burn like the people he touches. For him, dragon eggs and dragonets are a delicacy. So Surtr allows people to enter these caverns. At times, I devour them, especially if they are the craven warriors or berserkers of the Dragon, but these few men provide me with little nourishment, and after I eat them, their people stop delivering me any meals. And so Surtr continues to starve my kind inside this mountain unless we provide him with our clutches."

"I do not judge you."

The dragon's head drooped in shame.

"Either you starve," Märren continued, "or you do what you must to feed yourself and survive while hoping to one day escape and seek vengeance for all you've suffered. To one day birth more offspring who may live."

The beast groaned. "There are some of my kind who have died inside this mountain. Because they would not sacrifice their offspring for their own needs. But most of my kin are not generous or kind. Neither am I. It is the way of the dragon. We cherish and protect our offspring, but malevolence runs through our veins as strongly as wisdom. We are greedy, selfish creatures who live only for ourselves."

"Then we have more in common than you believe."

The dragon whipped her head around, baring her teeth. "What do you want, outsider? To escape my wrath? To appease Surtr?"

Märren stepped closer, pulling Uisge along with her until she stood before the creature's fangs. "I was once told that the only way to stop the voices that plague my thoughts is to take up a scale of the Dragon. I want to free you and your kind. To ride on the wind. To find all the vengeance you have ever sought, and to do this from a place where I won't easily die in battle. If I may be granted such a position, then with your aid, I would seek to destroy the god slayer. I desire to kill Surtr."

40

BELFEDRN

Nearly a fortnight had passed without more Serpent fighters venturing to the Moon Woods.

"But the Sea Serpents will visit us again," Belfedrn said. "And next time, they'll be better prepared. The survivors from the village we visited saw hundreds of their warriors sweep through our lands before returning to wherever they're making their central camp."

"We'll deal with them when they're brave enough to show their faces here," Athna said. "They're probably afraid, after two score of their warriors did not return from this forest."

The few people Belfedrn and Eakthr had found living in the village traveled back with them to the woods. Each of these Wolf karls had hauled as much barley and oats as they could and led their surviving livestock away, although their food stores would not feed all the people residing in the Moon Woods for more than a fortnight, especially not with the Wolf's hunger affecting the Ulfhednar after each confrontation. Each berserker would then eat a couple stones' worth of food.

"How many of the Serpent people did our karls claim they saw?" Kesg asked.

"Several hundred warriors and scores of berserkers." Ylsga slapped her mate on the back of the head. "Don't you listen?"

Kesg grumbled something under his breath.

Similar to the numbers Dradn and Thelira saw storming through Nistreel as it burned.

"The Sea Serpents are probably preparing to pay us a second visit." Vard stalked off. "I'll take watch for a while."

Belfedrn motioned to Dradn and Thelira. "We train."

"Again?" Dradn licked porridge from a flat of wood. "We just—"

"Again." Belfedrn kicked at the boy's backside as he strode past. "It's been quiet for too long, far too long for enemies who outnumber us and should be enraged by their losses."

Thelira paced after Belfedrn before Dradn sluggishly climbed to his feet and joined them. Belfedrn unslung his longbow from his shoulder and offered it to Thelira.

Her eyes widened. "This is the day?"

"Today is as good as any we may live to see." Belfedrn showed her how to best draw for ease and stability and how to hold the bowstring with the arrow's fletching brushing against her cheek. "Sight along the arrow's shaft and envision what you want its broadhead to streak toward."

"If Belfedrn's ever craving praise," Kesg said, taking a seat on a downed log, "and needs to hear kind words so he doesn't feel too terrible about what the dead gods gave him in life, I'd say he is decent with the longbow. I wouldn't destroy my honor and lie and claim he's good with it, but he's not as terrible as some. You should listen to his instruction with this weapon."

"Thank you for the heartfelt words, my brother," Belfedrn replied. "In such times of darkness, they lift my spirits."

They targeted stumps and trunks, and over the course of a couple hours, Thelira's ability to aim and hold an arrow nocked and drawn improved dramatically. During this time, Belfedrn sparred with Dradn, Belfedrn wielding a hefty stick so he could attack in his most aggressive manner while Dradn defended himself with spear, axe, and shield.

"Seeing you train others is as invigorating as watching the harvest fields during winter." Kesg stalked off.

Belfedrn hammered a blow down against Dradn's shield, the power behind it knocking Dradn onto his backside. Dradn raised his axe, but Belfedrn batted his shield aside and swatted him on the arm. Dradn cursed and dropped the shield, grimacing and rubbing his shoulder. Thelira stepped up to him and offered him the bow.

"You could use a break while you practice archery," she said.

"Nah," Dradn grumbled. "That's your wish, not mine. You should keep at it."

Thelira shrugged and walked toward the stumps.

"It's past your turn, Dradn," Belfedrn said. "Take the bow."

Dradn muttered something under his breath.

"Now," Belfedrn said more sternly.

Dradn sheathed his weapon and hesitantly accepted the bow from his sister. He nocked an arrow and looked at Belfedrn, who impatiently waited for him to begin. Dradn drew the bowstring and loosed without taking time to aim, as if he were already resigned to whatever the outcome may be. His arrow sailed wide of a stump and skittered off into the brush.

Dradn groaned. "I've never been good with this weapon."

"Then you should train twice as long as Thelira. Until you're a decent shot." Belfedrn patted him on the back. "And loose like you intend to hit something. Your survival may one day depend on your skill with the bow."

"I prefer to stand before my enemies when I kill them."

"In these times, our people will need to hunt to survive. It's not about—"

Howls erupted in the woods, their urgency resonating in

Belfedrn's blood. He dropped his training stick as his hackles pricked up.

"Stay here, and don't disobey me." Belfedrn loped away, heading for the western borders of the woods. The Ulfhednar in camp moved along their own paths but in the same general direction.

When Belfedrn neared the boundary of the forest, he crouched in the brush and stalked to its edge. Nearby, Eakthr lay on his stomach, staring beyond the boughs, and he whistled like a songbird. Ranks of Sea Serpent warriors sprawled across the hills beyond, at least a score of powerful berserkers leading them, their silver scales shimmering on their chests. One of these berserkers had to be Vegask.

The berserkers blew horns, and the warriors rolled balls of straw that had probably been soaked in oil toward the woods.

"They're going to try to drive us out with fire and smoke," Belfedrn said. *But I will kill them all.*

"They'll find that a wet forest doesn't burn very well," Eakthr replied and giggled.

"Unless they have oil and get a fire burning so hot that the dampness cannot contain it."

"But for that, they'd need wind to fan—"

In the distance, dark clouds rolled in over the fields, a gale shoving them along. These clouds did not suspend sheets of rain, and in fact, they did not drop any rain at all. But lightning flared and crackled in their midst. Soon, keening winds reached the Sea Serpents, who had to lean into their force to avoid being blown over. Then the gale smacked into the woods, bowing trunks and snapping branches. The last of summer's dead leaves still clinging to the boughs took flight, and debris rained from the canopy. Belfedrn covered his head with his hands before realizing his helm would offer superior protection.

A howl rang out, the command of fleeing and returning to

camp carrying in its call. Eakthr rose and slipped into the woods, moving quickly. In his need for revenge, Belfedrn resisted the call until it came again, more earnestly this time. He slowly backed away from the forest's edge.

The clouds rolled in, and lightning arced down in jagged spears, hammering into the trees and igniting them in blue fire that winked out and then raged red in the canopy. The Serpent warriors shoved their balls of straw and pitch to get them rolling toward the forest and then shot them with flaming arrows. These balls burst into fire, and black smoke plumed in thick, rank clouds.

They stole that tactic from us.

The balls collided with brush and trunks, burning, their flames leaping higher and melding with the lightning-induced fire above and roaring as the gale swept this inferno farther into the forest. Belfedrn sprinted toward camp. When he arrived, the women and children and Ulfhednar were packing their supplies. Dradn and Thelira raced up to him.

"What did you see?" Dradn asked.

"A powerful Sea Serpent berserker and his tempest blowing a wall of flames into the Moon Woods," Belfedrn said. "With lightning to help feed his fires."

"Pack whatever you can carry." Vard paced about, motioning to people and barking orders. "We cannot stay here."

"Then we move east, deeper into the woods?" A nimbus of white flames surrounded Athna's fingers, her tone full of malice. "Their fires could still find us, and if they don't, their warriors will."

Vard glanced at Belfedrn, his tone somber as he said, "We retrieve our longboat from the river and sail east. Into Boar territory. Let us pray that we find welcome there."

41

MÄRREN

"IT'S TIME FOR YOU TO LEAVE," ORSTENSHARD—THE DRAGON WHO had identified herself and who Märren had continued to speak to—said as she curled up and lay down against the far wall of the chamber. "Surtr has returned to rest in the great flames, and I grow tired of your presence."

Märren glanced at the tunnel behind them. Uisge continued to remain as far away from the dragon as the chain between him and Märren would allow.

"I will not hold you bound to your brave talk and any desires of freeing me and my kind," Orstenshard said.

"I hold myself bound." Märren's chain jingled as she turned away. "I will return, and if I manage to free you, I hope to be bestowed with a scale of the Dragon."

"I don't possess any of her scales. You'll need to take one from a warrior or berserker."

Märren pondered that and did not depart, instead holding up the chains on either side of her thrall collar. "Can you help us with our inconvenience?"

Orstenshard eyed her. "My fire could burn through those chains, as well as through your flesh and bones."

Uisge cowered, covering his head.

"You have claws that are stronger than steel blades," Märren said to the dragon. "You could sever the links as easily as a blade could slice through flesh."

Orstenshard grumbled and shifted her massive weight. "Come closer. Both of you. This will be the last I speak unless you return to free me and my kin. I grow hungry and irritable." She snarled, waiting for Uisge to shuffle forward. "But if you are truly considering attempting such a feat, you should know the Dragon's tale. About when she attempted to drive Surtr from this world. She blew her mighty breath upon the jötunn over and over again, hoping to consume the giant with her fire, the most formidable of flames. But even the breath of a god didn't seem to affect him. The giant ran through her flames and used his fiery sword against her. His blade sheared through her scales, rending the muscles and flesh beneath. He nearly severed one of her legs from her body, but she managed to land on him and begin tearing into him with teeth and claws. Surtr was gravely wounded, but the Dragon's effective attacks came too late. For she initially believed that her fiery breath was her greatest power and that it was superior to what any other could possess. It was her undoing. The god and jötunn were locked in battle, struggling, strength against strength, blade against claw. In the Dragon's weakened state, Surtr broke free of her grasp. With one mighty swing, the jötunn cleaved the Dragon's head from her body, and the last of the gods fell in Midgard."

Märren stood rigid, entranced.

"That was when Surtr claimed these lands but retired into the great fire, where he slept for centuries," Orstenshard continued. "Unfortunately, you are now living in the time when he has awoken. With each passing moon, he grows hungrier and more demanding."

Orstenshard used the tip of her claw to grasp Märren's chain.

The dragon pulled her closer, which also tugged Uisge along with her. Orstenshard ran a long finger up the chain, creeping closer to Märren's neck. Märren swallowed but met the dragon's gaze as the creature sneered at her. Orstenshard's claw swiped toward her head.

Märren's heart beat wildly as Orstenshard's claw sliced through a link beside her neck. After a few breaths, Märren recovered her senses and lifted the chain hanging from the other side of her collar. Orstenshard cut through it and then Uisge's chains with the precision of a legendary smith. Only their collars remained.

"Now leave me to my slumber," Orstenshard said.

"I hope no more of your offspring will be taken before I return to free you." Märren wrapped her chain over her shoulder and handed the other end to Uisge so they could pretend they were still bound.

The dragon huffed and turned away, unimpressed.

"She shall never return."

"If she does, the jötunn will devour her."

"A scale is nearly in her grasp!"

Uisge hurried back through the passageway toward the portcullis gate, and Märren trailed him. When they arrived at the opening, a Dragon warrior pressed his long face between the bars.

"What's taking you so long?" the warrior asked. "We thought the dragon decided to eat you. Get the eggs and get out here. And hurry, or I'll kill you myself!" He pointed behind them.

Uisge retraced his steps and picked up one of the barrel-shaped structures at the rear of the chamber, although it was only about half the size of a barrel. He slipped out of the shadows toting an egg with a shell as red as blood and composed of overlapping scales. Märren swallowed her defiance and retrieved the other, whose scales were rough against her hand. She rolled it along the ground and out between the bars of the portcullis, into the tundra beyond.

"Take them over there." The warrior indicated a few carts that were already laden with eggs. In the darkness, he did not seem to notice that Märren's chain was not linked to her or Uisge's collars.

A skirling wind raged, throwing about sheets of snow, the cold overpowering the heat of the mountain. The great fire that had risen and become Surtr blazed in the darkness to the north.

"We cannot make the return journey until daybreak," the Dragon berserker of the group shouted from nearby. He stood with his back to a fire that burned outside a portcullis gate, many Dragon people crammed into a half circle around him and the flames. Their horses were packed in tight nearby. "Or we'll lose too many. Make whatever fires you can and try to keep them lit."

The captives and thralls who were still chained to each other set to work striking flint, attempting to light whatever wood was in the carts.

Märren turned and trudged northward, into the storm.

"Where do you think you're going?" the warrior watching her and Uisge asked as he paused on his way to the Dragon people's fire.

"To a place where I can keep myself alive despite this cold," Märren said.

"Don't go far," the warrior replied, his words muffled by the wind. "The farther you get from the mountain, the more frigid it becomes. And if you stay on the wrong side of one of those portcullis gates for too long, you'll be devoured. We may not have been kind to you, but we still don't want you to throw your life away. Try starting a fire just outside one of the cavern openings where there's shelter from the wind. There, the mountain's heat may help keep you alive." He lobbed his flint at her, and she caught it. "And don't try to run. You'll freeze to death in a matter of minutes, and if somehow you don't, your chains will burden you and we will track you down long before you make it far in this tundra."

Märren edged onward as the soldier joined his comrades at their fire.

Uisge hurried after her. "Now what?"

"I have to find a Dragon scale. To free my mind and the dragons inside this mountain."

"I don't think any of these warriors or berserkers are going to give you theirs. We should concentrate on finding a way to survive this storm."

"Then we'll have to convince them to do so. And I am finding a way to survive."

Märren no longer carried a blade, not even the seax she had tied around her neck in case she needed to end her life. She grimaced and bit into the softer flesh above the scars on her wrist. Blood swelled and drained, dripping onto fresh snow. Uisge fell onto his knees and lapped at the red, then turned and opened his mouth to catch her runnel of blood as flakes whipped about in the wind, its icy fingers biting through Märren's pelt.

"Now you've been fed a bit." Märren glanced to the north where the blaze of the great fire raged. "If we sit beside that fire, we'll have no trouble keeping warm. We may even be comfortable enough to find sleep."

"Next to that fire?" Uisge wiped blood from his lips with the back of his hand and licked his skin clean, looking a little less dehydrated and exhausted. "That would be utter madness."

"I know nothing else. You don't have to come with me, if the cold isn't too much for you."

Märren let her chain fall, and she clamped a hand over her wound, marching north, tugging her pelt over her frosted hair and face, her extremities turning numb. When the wind gusted, it nearly knocked her over, but she reached her destination before collapsing. She sat as close to the blaze as she dared, facing it, rubbing at her hands and feet. Warmth returned to her body, and soon after that, weariness pulled at her, causing her head to droop.

"She will sleep."

"If she does, she'll never wake. The jötunn will feast on her charred bones."

"She'll find warmth, and tomorrow she will rejoin the people who carry the scales of the Dragon."

Uisge emerged from the night and sat beside Märren, his side touching hers, his face shadowed by his hair, which was again wet. His body heat comforted her, and her eyelids grew heavier.

The fire cracked and popped.

"Fuck." Uisge leapt back and scrambled away, cursing before the flames settled and turned quieter. No giant rose from them. After a time, he returned and sat beside Märren again. "I certainly hope we don't wake Surtr, or I'll regret coming with you on this venture."

"I don't believe we will. Not after he has feasted."

Uisge studied her. "Why do you seek the Dragon's remains with such tenacity?"

Märren wanted to ignore him, to rest. Her words came out choked with sleep. "My father and the Seidr man both said it's the only antidote for my madness, which wears on me every day."

"You hear voices?"

"Aye. They make me weaker—grind me down so that I often can do nothing more than try to ignore them and accomplish what I need to survive. A scale will free me of the darkness. It's what I wanted for Eimri."

"She heard voices as well?"

"Indeed."

"Then why not take up the pelt of Fenrir? Surely its magics could also drive your madness away."

"A pelt didn't help my mother."

"I am sorry. There's no need to speak more of it." Uisge leaned against her, wrapping her in a comforting embrace.

Märren did not know why, but discussing the voices sometimes muted them. "The darkness and the figures the voices stem from haunted my mother as well. Like her mother before her, but it's gotten worse with every generation. My mother was not only a Wolf warrior. She took up a full pelt and became an Ulfhednar. Like Belfedrn. Like I could've been. But a pack is only as strong as its weakest member. And that was my mother. At times, she couldn't hold formation, and when she faltered, the rest of the pack was at risk. When I was a child, several trolls killed many Ulfhednar because of her and her weakness. I won't lead my kin to their deaths. And dragons do not roam or fight in packs."

Snow dropped in sheets, most of the flakes gusting around the fire and flashing in yellows or oranges before disappearing, and the blaze shoved back the cold like a shield wall against enemies.

"That's the other part of why I did not take up the pelt," Märren said. "That and my distrust of the Wolf people because of how they treated us. How they behaved toward Eimri. After my mother died, I only had Father, and I was a burden to him until he passed. He was probably grateful to be gone from this world and me."

"I'm sure he didn't feel that way about you or his home."

Märren did not respond. She pulled the skull from the pouch at her waist and stared into its eyes, the firelight casting its face in shadows. "If only I could've saved Eimri by finding a scale and giving it to her. Now I must either die a coward or find a remnant of the Dragon and cure this madness for me and her. For all we've endured."

"She cannot be rid of us."

"She'll die before I leave her to her thoughts."

"I won't ever leave her side."

Uisge unwrapped her furs from her arms and legs and removed her gloves and boots. He rubbed life and warmth into her hands with both of his, then worked on her feet. When he finished, and feeling had returned to each finger and toe, he turned Märren's face toward his and kissed her.

Märren gasped and pulled back, staring past his wet hair and chiseled cheekbones, into his dark eyes. The voices cried out—one with disgust, another with outrage, and the third with excitement—shredding any feeling of self-consciousness.

She hesitated but leaned forward and kissed him back, and he gently pulled her furs from her body, running his hands across her neck as the fire warmed them both. She raised her arms, and Uisge lifted her tunic over her head. When she was naked, she pulled his head against her breasts as she lay back on a pile of their clothing. His hands searched her skin, feeling, wrapping around her, squeezing, and he mounted her.

42

CAËTIN

Many Raven warriors stood guard around the heart of Aonark—Muninn's temple, the hold the Spider would be seeking more than any other. Caëtin's unkindness swooped past them, through the open doors of the temple, and spiraled downward over its stairways while the *gyðja* and *goði* stepped aside and bowed to her.

The unkindness flew to the deepest level. Muninn's altar and the pedestal for her remains waited ahead, and a man in a cloak was kneeling before them. Caëtin dropped into her true form and approached the pedestal and the man.

"Taknhal?" she asked. "What happened in Sparsgard?"

Taknhal slowly stood and faced her, his cheeks pale, eyes downcast. "I..."

"You didn't slaughter those people, did you?"

Something inside his cloak fell, and a metallic clatter sounded. When it settled, an axe covered in blood stains lay on the stone at his feet. "I... did what was necessary."

"You killed innocents? Our own people?" Caëtin grabbed him by the throat and shook him. He teetered, the smoldering reek of drink heavy on his breath. "If I'd become jarl, I would've forbidden you from leaving Aonark!" She spat on his blade. "I should have killed you instead of leaving you there."

"Uktr's methods will best aid the Raven clan. I see that now. Only I have to find his strength."

"Being able to murder your own without guilt or remorse isn't strength. It's always harder to care for and love others. To worry about what may befall them and struggle day after day to prevent any hardship you can. That is where true strength lies."

Taknhal shook off her grip and stepped back, wobbling. "Warriors from our other cities and villages now march to Aonark. Our numbers will swell, and our resistance will be fortified."

"At what price?"

"The cost of not allowing the Spider to massacre us!" he screamed in her face as he staggered. "The cost of not letting another clan overrun the lands of our fathers!"

Caëtin shoved him, and he tripped over the lip of the pedestal and fell back, smacking his head against its stone. He groaned and rolled onto his side, clutching his temple.

"Darstrid nearly helped you pull yourself together," Caëtin said, "but you faltered anyway." *Or she turned her back on you once she realized you were gaining control of the knights.*

"Tell me you're not the smuggler of Muninn's parts, Caëtin," he finally said, wincing as he turned and scrutinized her. "Her two largest flight feathers and a talon? Those haven't been bestowed on anyone since the great wars after the fall of the gods, and only then to the paladins of Muninn."

She glared at him and kicked over a tankard of drink sitting beside him. Its froth washed across the stones.

"You're strong with Muninn's will," Taknhal added. "The *gyðja* and the jarl would've convened and given you and me and Darstrid all we could bear. They would've given the same to every Knight Black and warrior who defends this city."

"The time for such things will come soon enough, but before the Spiders arrive, none should carry what will only tax them more. Bearing too many god parts for too long will weaken and tire our warriors." Caëtin glared at him and shook her head before storming away. She had gotten her answer—the one she feared would be true.

"What if I were to marry another of Uktr's heirs?" Taknhal called after her.

Caëtin paused and slowly turned about. "Even if you married Darstrid, one of you would have to be the acting jarl."

"Not Darstrid. You." One of his eyebrows arched. "We're not truly brother and sister. Only in title. If we were to wed and we worked together, our loyal knights could match the numbers loyal to Darstrid."

"Why are you saying this?"

"Because I'm afraid that if you aren't the smuggler, then our sister is. Maybe that's why she drew me in only to let me go at the edge of a cliff. And if Darstrid works against the will of the *gyðja*, then she cannot become jarl."

"You butchered innocents in Sparsgard. Looking upon you makes my stomach froth with disgust."

"I was afraid you'd say something like that." He nodded solemnly. "Did our sister tell you that her knights brought back a handful of Spider captives? Including a recluse warrior?"

"And Darstrid knows this?"

"Aye. The recluse is being kept in the dungeon near the great hall. Her knights injured the man and removed his chitin. She hopes to interrogate him. To learn the Spider's secrets."

"Has she sent an inquisitor to the recluse?"

"I believe so, but she won't speak with me about it."

"Neither would I." Caëtin hurried away. At the foot of the stairway ahead, Igendrn stood with his arms folded across his chest, awaiting her.

"Please, stay a while, Caëtin," the *goði* said. "Take your rest. Recover. I'll tend to you and any injuries you carry. I'll wash away your weariness with my hands and body."

Temptation tugged at her almost as strongly as the need for rest, but she quickly stamped down her desire. For now. Soon she would probably need a distraction from the long wait for the Spider. "I fear I already don't have enough time to accomplish all that's needed."

"What is there to do?"

"Everything I can. Prepare two draughts and meet me outside the great hall's dungeon before the sun sets."

She burst into her unkindness and flew past Igendrn, up the stairs to the entryway. The *gyðja* there parted the doors, allowing her to pass outside into dumping rain. The unkindness flew over Aonark, taking in the inner city, its walls, its people. Huginn flew with her, cawing and weaving in and out of her birds. Once she spotted the areas where groups of Knights Black were clustered, she veered for one of them, and her ravens whirled about in a tightening cloud, colliding atop the battlements. The warriors there turned in surprise. The knights stood rigid.

In human form, Caëtin stood in the midst of more than three score of knights and rangers who were spread out along the upper walk. She said, "Jarl Darstrid orders your ranks to the great hall. You are to convene with her."

The knight who stood before their ranks dipped his head but did not move. He held his hands out to either side of his body to stay the rest of his comrades. Others cursed or muttered under their breaths, their discontent wafting from them.

"Then you and your lot obey Taknhal." Caëtin shook her head. "When war rages, divided fighters will weaken the Raven people. Do not harbor hate against your own. Not now."

"I respect your authority, Caëtin of Muninn," the lead knight said, "but we're to remain here until Taknhal tells us otherwise."

He could not meet her gaze. "Or perhaps you and your brother and sister should appoint an acting council until the next jarl is chosen."

"Bah." Caëtin exploded into her unkindness, squawking in fury as the ravens flapped about, circling higher until she located another cluster of knights.

There were probably a hundred men and women in this group, and they assisted the karls of Aonark with stacking weapons and buckets of water and shoring up the walls, replacing aged stakes with others that had freshly sharpened tips. Caëtin landed behind them in a flurry of cawing and drifting feathers. Several of the knights faced her.

"Taknhal demands that you gather at the southern gates," she said. "With your feathers. You are to march out of Aonark."

"We do not follow the first son's commands," the knight closest to her said, anger lacing his words.

Caëtin nodded. "Then I order you to gather at the great hall. All the Knights Black must unite before the first Spiders arrive."

Several of the knights stepped away from the others, but those who moved made up less than a score. Their comrades muttered to them and held them back.

I've impressed fewer of them than the traveling bards manage to. These were Darstrid's loyal lot. "Then remain here and continue preparing the city until Darstrid addresses you directly."

"It's not anything you've done, Caëtin," the knight before her said. "We respect you as a leader of the Knights Black and all you stand for, but we've pledged our blades to your sister, the battle Seidr. Darstrid is jarl now. Not you."

Caëtin smirked. "Indeed she is. And this division has driven a wedge between her fighters and Taknhal's. On the eve of battle. Let go of your anger for those who chose Taknhal over Darstrid. For now. Your feelings are justified, but they will not help the Raven people." She looked over the knights behind him. “Animosity will only make a Spider victory all the more likely.”

The man bowed his head in subservience as others grumbled.

“There’s a prisoner who needs to be questioned,” Caëtin said. “Good day, and be ready for anything.” She hesitated. “Has Darstrid been acting like she’s injured?”

The knight pondered her question. “In the south, she took a blow, but she recovered quickly. Muninn blesses her with immense power.”

“May Muninn bless us all.”

43

CAËTIN

Caëtin wound through the inner city, her pace faltering, her feet dragging in the mud as twilight fell across the land and she approached the dungeon. Rain spewed around her. Huginn flew near her shoulder, dipping and rising as they traveled. Seven warriors stood guard before the entrance to the dungeon, which led down into the earth.

Not a wise place to imprison a Spider recluse. He could escape... but hopefully he would not be able to burrow out if he was not bearing his chitin.

"Caëtin." One of the warriors nodded as she approached. He wore a helm, his eyes silvery, his jaw slender. "An inquisitor of Muninn has already come and interrogated the prisoner."

"Did this inquisitor learn what was needed?"

The warrior shrugged. "I overheard most of it, but the recluse didn't mention anything more than what rumors have already passed around Aonark—rumors of what you and your knights witnessed the Spider doing beneath the surface of Midgard."

"You overheard them speaking?"

"Aye. Four of us were stationed outside the cell while the inquisition occurred."

"You shouldn't have been able to hear anything beyond the initial introduction. Not if the questioning took place on the Raven's bridge."

"No?" The color drained from the warrior's cheeks. "Of course not. I didn't realize... The inquisitor carried the usual draughts inside with him, and he was accompanied by four others."

"Then they should've had no issues administering the draught to the prisoner."

"Maybe they didn't believe the Spider was fit for the Raven's bridge."

"Perhaps. Or perhaps it was something else. I shall interrogate the captive as well." The idea caused apprehension to rush through Caëtin. She had grown to hate that place—the bridge. As of late, she despised every visit she had been coerced into, and now she wanted to take a recluse there with her.

"Of course." The warrior bowed his head. "We are only stationed here to make sure the recluse doesn't escape, and to keep him alive. The inquisitor believed he would return soon and continue questioning the prisoner. It was Jarl Darstrid's orders to allow for whatever would best assist our people, as long as no one killed the recluse. He's someone important to the Spider, and we could use him for bargaining. If it comes to that."

"Then I'll spare him. I do not murder those who can't defend themselves and have not confessed." *Violence when necessary. Otherwise, a calm mind and steady hand.*

"There's already a *goði* waiting for you down below." The warriors stepped aside.

Igendrn. Caëtin descended the stairs, and four of the warriors followed her. The acidic reek of piss and feces hung in the air, mixed with molding straw. Torches clung to the walls, their light dim, which threw shadows about the walls. At the foot of the stairs, Igendrn waited, holding two horns filled with dark liquid.

"Your draught won't cause me to sleep for two days, will it?" Caëtin asked.

"Not unless you're entirely drained by your magics and your body requires the rest."

Caëtin glanced back at the warriors. "Which cell?"

"Allow me." The man she had spoken with stepped past her and led her to a door. He removed a key from around his neck and unlocked the cell, shoving the door inward. Rusty hinges squealed like wraiths.

Caëtin strode inside. A man with no hair and skin as pale as snow kneeled in the straw, his hands in fetters with chains running from them to the walls, his body skeletal. He hung limp against the tension on the chains, his head drooped over his chest and ragged tunic. Three torches had been placed along each wall of the cell, all of them burning brightly.

"Because their kind are weaker in the light," the warrior said when Caëtin noticed the number of torches.

"That's mostly, or only, true for widows," she replied, suddenly unsure about much of the magics of these Spider people.

The prisoner groaned and shifted. He looked up, his eyes white and without pupils, one swollen. He had no beard nor any hair on his body. Dark bruises covered his skin, his nose bent and a trail of dried blood crusting beneath each nostril. Caëtin hid a shudder.

The prisoner smiled. "Another berserker who's come to see a poor recluse of the great Spider?"

Caëtin hid her revulsion and more than a little fear. "We're going on a journey."

"Ah. I do enjoy traveling. Although I prefer crawling underground to flying."

"Your body will remain here, in irons. It's only your soul that I want."

He cocked his head, studying her. "Death, then?"

She shook her head and took the two horns from Igendrn. "You'll join me at the Raven's bridge."

The prisoner's jaw dropped, and he trembled. "No. The last inquisitor vowed that you wouldn't take me there if I told you all I knew. I'll speak again, retell everything, answer each question you have. Just don't take me to Muninn's world. I've climbed high up the metaphorical web of the recluses. I could be traded for coin or held as a hostage to deter any attacks on this city. But only if I'm alive."

"I won't believe what you tell me unless we're on the bridge." Caëtin motioned to the Raven warriors behind her. "Grab him."

The warriors strode forward and grasped the prisoner by his jaw and temples, tilting his head back and forcing his mouth open. Caëtin dumped the contents of one horn into his mouth, and a warrior clamped a hand over the recluse's lips and slammed his jaw shut while pinching his nose.

"Swallow it," the warrior said

The prisoner thrashed about, sputtering drink, attempting to spew it out and fight. Another warrior rammed the back of the recluse's neck with the butt of an axe. The captive went limp, and the first warrior kept his hand over the recluse's nose and mouth until he swallowed. The warrior released him, and the prisoner sucked in a ragged breath.

Caëtin downed her draught and sat with her back against the far corner, speaking to the Raven warriors. "Do not leave us. I'm no inquisitor, and I know little of the Spider. Thus far, everything I've learned about them is more frightening than expected."

"We'll stay until you can walk out of here," the slender-jawed warrior replied.

Caëtin's eyes grew heavy.

She woke with a start in a land of drifting wraiths, although she did not stand on the bridge. The prisoner was bowed before her, the sky and surroundings only as solid as mountain mist but in shades of brown and yellow. The ice encircling the setting sun appeared more solid and blue than usual, and the fire halo on the mountains raged higher. Massive humanoid silhouettes stalked about in the haze around them, neither coming closer nor passing farther away.

Caëtin shivered. She had never seen this place nor heard it described by any of Muninn's *gyðja* or *goði.*

Is this one of Muninn's visions of the past? She had never experienced such a thing, but the idea of standing in the bridge world and looking into Midgard's past had always intrigued her. A raven flew overhead, and she had the notion that the creature had to be Huginn.

"Who are you?" she asked the prisoner.

The recluse looked up at her with eyes as red as blood, although his skin was just as pale as it was in Midgard. "Nethrmon. I'm a recluse, a warrior, of the great Spider."

The ground shuddered, a mound forming, dirt falling away to reveal the top of a tree, which thrust upward from the earth. The tree rose to the height of many men, its trunk made of bone, dirty white and cracking, its boughs bare. A murder of crows squawked and flew closer, landing and hopping about for space. Caëtin stared.

What the fuck are these portents supposed to mean?

The tree burst into flames, which roared, igniting the birds as Caëtin flinched and shielded herself with her cloak. Crows shrieked and took flight, departing as balls of fire in every direction. Then, suddenly, ice covered the bone tree and its limbs, smothering the flames. The fireballs of flying birds snuffed out, falling as chunks of ice.

Caëtin gawked for a minute before the tree exploded into a thousand fragments, which rained around them. She shielded herself until the fragments stopped falling, then looked again. The fragments and the tree and birds had vanished. She stood straighter before her prisoner, trying to ignore the portent and the bewilderment running through her. "You are my captive, brought to the Raven's bridge by—"

Nethrmon cackled.

"You will truthfully answer any question I ask," Caëtin commanded, "and feigning madness will not save you. Not here."

"But it's you who are mad. We aren't on the Raven's bridge."

"We *are* in Muninn's world."

"And you can clearly see that the jötunn are crossing through." He motioned at the enormous silhouettes around them. "From Jötunheim and Muspelheim. There are elves from Alfheim and dark elves passing as well. Dwarves from Nidavellir. So many are coming."

Caëtin grabbed him by the back of the neck, drawing her pale blade. "How is this possible?"

"The gods are dead. Everything they held control over is crumbling. Seeking power for oneself and for one's people is the only answer. It's the lone path to survival."

"How do you know this?"

"Envinkia told me."

"And how does she know?"

Nethrmon shrugged.

Caëtin's apprehension spiked. There were probably a few reasons why someone with magics could know this, but only one option sprang to mind—that Uktr's suspicions were sound and a Raven traitor had passed off a part of Muninn and their draught to the Spiders. That could have led to someone with enough knowledge and power to initiate the realm crossings.

"Do you know if these giants can be stopped before they enter Midgard?" Caëtin asked.

"If you were a god, you could try to stop them." He laughed maniacally.

"Then the Spider, along with all the other clans, will be slain by the jötunn."

"Not if we harness the power of the mighty Raven. If some of our people control the magics of each god, we can defeat anything. Anyone. And Muninn's powers best complement our own."

Caëtin released him. "I've already realized what your kind is after. Now, you will tell me about all the magics the Spiders possess."

Nethrmon grinned, his gums bloody, teeth broken. "We possess the Horse magics, and the Sea Serpents serve our cause."

Dread rushed through her.

"The Wolf clan has fallen, and the Dragon, Bear, and Boar are plagued by giants who have already made the crossing. Soon, the Spider will rule, and there'll be no berserker or warrior alive who is not of Spider blood, no matter if he or she carries pelt or scale or feather."

Caëtin clenched her jaw to control her outrage. "You will describe what magics the chitin grants your recluses and widows."

"You've seen our power, haven't you? Or at least you experienced what you cannot see—widows moving swifter than horses through the darkness. They are more deadly than any Bear. More venomous than the Serpents. Only light weakens them. And light is the only reason the Spider god was slain. But we've discovered ways to extinguish lights, to snuff out torches. To be patient until the sun falls. There is no safe harbor for you. Run! Run now!" He cackled again.

Caëtin reared back and used the hilt of her sword to punch Nethrmon in the face over and over again until his laughter ceased. "Those who your widows poison with their blades rise again as fighters for the Spider. That is true, isn't it?"

"Aye. Mindless beasts who rush into battle without fear or remorse. Their numbers swell, and they will be the first legions we send against our enemies. Our offspring have long hatched at unprecedented rates, and we've swiftly trained them to wield the magics of a god. We lose many by this method, but no matter how many die, there are always more. You cannot oppose us."

"We are safe behind high walls with many Knights Black and Raven warriors protecting our city. We will not be conquered easily."

Nethrmon shook his head. "Do you believe that walls will save you? When our widow berserkers become spiders? Some of your ravens have seen where we reside, just as I've now seen the inner city of Aonark."

Caëtin's mind spun. This warrior had wanted to be captured. To be brought into Aonark. *He's seen the temple.*

The recluse smirked, a wretched gleam in his eye. "When the Spiders arrive, I'll point them to the gates of your sacred building. Then Muninn's feathers and talons will join the chitin."

Caëtin bit her lip. The best way to protect the temple would be to hide it from the world, but if this recluse already knew where it was, erecting a cover around it might not matter. Nor could the temple be moved.

Her wrath blazed as she lifted her blade but was reminded that this man was defenseless and had not confessed to any heinous acts, had only made threats about what his people could accomplish. Nethrmon was also someone important to the Spider clan, someone who could be used for bargaining. Perhaps Darstrid was saving him for that reason. Caëtin had vowed against killing more people on the bridge. At least those who were not guilty. Uktr and now Taknhal were tyrannic and brutal leaders. She did not want to become like them. There had to be another way—Muninn's justice, perhaps? But if Nethrmon were to be rescued, he would certainly tell his people of all he had seen.

"The Spider will take the Raven's bridge and pass a web over it," Nethrmon said, "creating a trap for souls who are crossing. Once they're ensnared, Envinkia will decide where to send them —Niflheim, Jötunheim, Helheim. Or to no place at all. When the karls and thralls realize this and understand our true power, we'll control all of Midgard."

Caëtin's rage amplified, and she did not think before swinging her blade, hewing through the recluse's neck with a ringing of steel. Blood streamed skyward as the silhouettes in the haze roared.

Her chest heaved, expelling fury with each breath. Brutality had taken her... again. There was no escaping it now. Not if she wanted to save her people. The line between her morals and Uktr's methods blurred. She would have to try to find it again sometime, but this would not be the day.

The wraiths kept passing, and another rose from the Spider's body and hovered before Caëtin, neither following the road to the bridge nor fleeing from it.

Huginn dived at the wraith, shrieking.

44

BELFEDRN

The pack rowed along the river, their oars dipping into the water with little more than a whisper. As far as Belfedrn knew, this Ulfhednar longship could be the last of the Wolf fleet. They sailed south and east into the lands of the Hildisvini—the Boar people and their dead god. Wind gusted, billowing their wolf sail, and they glided along as silently as raiders.

It would be better to remain unseen and choose when they wanted to reveal themselves. If the Boar people spotted them and assumed the worst, it would ignite old tensions and bring about a battle that would not end until one side was killed.

Belfedrn dipped his oar into the water, timing his strokes with the other Ulfhednar, the might of the pack flowing through them. Firelight shone through the night and the branches on the far side of the river, and music loud enough that a Sea Serpent warrior could hear it a league away carried. Eakthr high-stepped one leg at a time—perhaps with agitation or impatience—as he shifted the rudder and guided them downriver and onto the bank.

Belfedrn leapt out, slipping into icy water that rose up to his knees. Thankfully, his oiled leggings and furs repelled most of the water. He and Kesg helped drag the longship onto shore to hide and stow it. Once their vessel was secure and covered with branches and the pack was ready, they stole into the woods toward the firelight and music.

"These people must not be afraid of anything or of anyone hearing them," Thelira said. Because of the din, she and Dradn followed Belfedrn, passing on another stealth lesson from Eakthr the Sly.

"The Boar is mighty when defending its territory but weak on offensive tactics," Belfedrn said. "The Boar people don't often seek out battle, and most clans avoid raiding their lands."

"It seems these people enjoy a celebration as well," Dradn said.

"That they do." Belfedrn ducked beneath a mass of spruce boughs as he stalked along. "And drink."

"But be wary," Kesg added. "Their warriors and berserkers may act like drunken fools, but their ability to process and detoxify poisons, including alcohol, is unmatched. If warranted, they can sober up in an instant."

The pack stepped out from the trees. A village was nestled into a clearing, firelight burning bright around its perimeter. People stumbled about or danced around huts and a few longhouses. There did not appear to be any guards about.

A stout man composed of muscle and a hefty layer of fat tottered toward them but stopped near the edge of the firelight. He stared at Belfedrn and then Vard and took a long drink from a horn.

"Them are Wolf fighters," he said, gawking at the pack members.

Another man a bit taller than the first but similarly built staggered up beside him and scratched his head as the music played on. "Nah. Those are Ulfhednar. Look how they paint their faces black." He took a swig from his horn.

Belfedrn attempted to display his best amicable expression with a forced grin and relaxed posture. His spear was set in a non-threatening position straight up and down at his side, but the awkwardness of the situation caused him to squeeze its shaft. He had no idea what would happen here in Boar territory. "We're—"

"Huh." The first man shrugged and stumbled away, sipping from his horn.

"You care to join the festivities?" the taller man asked them.

"We bring grave news," Vard said. "I'm Vard, jarl of the Wolf clan, and these here with me are the last of the Ulfhednar. Not long ago, the rest of the Ulfhednar, our warriors, and many of our people were butchered by Sea Serpent raiders."

The man stared as if dumbfounded, and he took another drink.

"We've come looking for aid from those who would like to ally themselves with us," Vard added. "We seek revenge and to reclaim our lands from the Serpent people."

"I'm Cherd," the local said without any shift of emotion. "Given the state of the music, our jarl's probably in the central longhouse. You probably want to speak with her."

"Are you a Boar warrior, Cherd?" Belfedrn asked.

"Nah." He turned away and followed his comrade's trail.

Athna chuckled. Belfedrn shared a bemused glance with Vard and said, "They don't seem too concerned about anything."

"Not even when the Ulfhednar arrive at their village." Vard waved the pack on.

"Those two are about as bright as Belfedrn and Keeg when they're sparring with words," Ylsga said. Several snickers followed.

Belfedrn kept his spear in the least threatening position he could as he strode toward the longhouse, his bow slung across his shoulder, his shield strapped to his back, his axe and seax at his waist. Music from pipes and lutes flitted around them like song from morning birds, and a rich voice belted out a ballad.

Ere the day best to pull the cart
Ere the night ought to dance and wink
For the toil brings calm to the heart
But I prefer it with lover and drink

Locals all around joined in the singing as the song grew bawdier, their lyrics becoming distorted with out-of-time voices and slurred words.

"Would you warriors like a drink?" A woman with mousy-brown hair, who wore a stained tunic, approached, holding two horns in each hand and proffering them to the pack members.

Dradn reached to accept a horn, but Belfedrn knocked his arm aside and said, "We cannot. We've come from a dire situation and must speak with your jarl."

"Ah, well, she's in there." The woman nodded over her shoulder. "And she should be finishing up soon, but you can go inside and wait for her."

"Thank you for your hospitality," Belfedrn said.

The woman wandered off, and Belfedrn led the pack to the longhouse and knocked on its doors. Louder music carried out from inside, probably making it difficult for anyone in there to hear him. He shoved the doors open and stepped into the interior and its firelight, his comrades following.

Music carried from a lute player who danced off to the side. Belfedrn halted in shock, staring at the table before the typical throne at the end of the walk. Atop the table, a woman with muscular limbs and a broad back bobbed up and down atop a man who lay beneath her, her bare breasts bouncing, her side turned to the Ulfhednar.

Belfedrn's mouth worked a few times, but no sounds came out. He glanced around as Vard tensed. The man playing the lute took no interest in the events on the table but gamboled to his own melody, a pile of empty horns lying around his feet.

"Go back outside." Belfedrn waved for the others to exit as Dradn and Thelira peeked around him.

"What is—" Dradn tried to say, but Belfedrn shoved him away.

Thelira retreated. "She's humping him right on the table."

"My bloody eyes," Kesg muttered.

They all exited, but as they were shutting the doors, a muffled groan sounded and the rhythmic thumping of the table halted.

"Stay where you are." The thick woman climbed off the man and the table, pulling her tunic back up over her neck and donning a boar pelt. She ran her fingers through her hair and paced toward them. "Welcome to my great hall."

Belfedrn said, "I'm sorry to disturb—"

The woman dismissed his concerns with a flick of her hand. "Come inside." She studied their faces and shields. "You are Ulfhednar?"

Belfedrn hesitantly sidled past the doors he had almost closed. "We were told we could find you here but didn't know..." He glanced into the distance.

The woman bellowed with laughter. "I always forget that you Wolves are such bashful prudes. I don't give two boar shites what you saw. Long as you don't try to join in." She eyed Belfedrn, smiled, and winked. "Unless I invite you."

A rush of heat climbed Belfedrn's neck. For all he had seen —many battles and so much death—nothing had prepared him for this woman. He cleared his throat, meaning to meet her gaze, although her bulging breasts caught his attention before he could look her in the eye.

"It's been some years since I've had any Ulfhednar in my longhouse." She approached Belfedrn and Vard, her breath rank with drink. "I'm Onunith, a Boar berserker and jarl of Matterdreg." She tugged on her boar pelt with its sparse but spiky hair.

A berserker. "We've come from our lands in search of allies and aid," Belfedrn said. "The Sea Serpents deceived us by drawing us into the forests to hunt trolls while their warriors and berserkers raided and pillaged our lands. Many were slain."

Onunith ran her fingers through her brown hair, working out several tangles. "Then it's time for you to drink and forget. Dwell no more on this tonight. In the morning, we shall discuss it further."

She strode past them and exited the longhouse, spreading her arms wide and belting out a song. Her lyrics told a story of drinking and fornicating and feasting, and the man playing the lute hurried after her. The man whom she had been straddling on the table had fallen asleep, his snores punctuating the music.

Belfedrn sat beside Dradn and Thelira at a table in Onunith's great hall, slurping up hot oats. His impatience ate at him. Onunith finally woke and stumbled down the steps from the loft, although it was late into the morning. She looked at Belfedrn but served herself dagmal and ate alone on her throne. After finishing her meal, she went back for second and third helpings and downed several horns of mead.

"I cannot wait any longer." Athna rose from her seat beside Vard and approached the throne.

Onunith turned, her layers of muscle and fat making her as thick as an ox. "I'll have another bowl. Then I'll speak with the Ulfhednar." After she paced to the table crowded with breads and a vat of oats, scooped out another bowl, and filled another horn with mead, she wandered over and plopped down on a seat across from Vard. "Now tell me again why you've come."

Vard summarized the Wolves' situation, and Onunith leaned forward as if intrigued and hearing it for the first time.

"And what do you hope the Boar clan will do to aid you?" She continued eating, her question sounding rhetorical.

Vard shifted in his seat. "If the Sea Serpent and the Spider are not stopped, they'll eventually come for your lands. After they've solidified control over ours."

"I cannot send my warriors and berserkers off to aid other clans with their troubles."

"I understand that your berserkers are most comfortable with defensive tactics," Vard added, "and venturing into another clan's territory won't be without risk. But the option would have its advantages over waiting until all the other clans are wiped out and yours are the last people for the Sea Serpent to conquer."

The Boar jarl tilted her bowl against her lips and slurped the last of its contents before speaking through a mouthful. "And you believe the few of you along with a legion of my warriors can reclaim your lands?"

"I do."

"And how would the Boar clan benefit from so generously offering our aid?"

"You would find peace with your neighbor. No more raids. Not that we often entered your lands, but the Wolves will swear to be your ally for all the days to come, and when you ask it of us, we shall rush to your aid."

"Ah, is that all?" She eyed Belfedrn. "I was hoping I could hump your second."

All eyes turned to regard Belfedrn as he considered whether Onunith was jesting or not.

Kesg bellowed with laughter. "He needs it."

Belfedrn grimaced, but he would do whatever was needed to save his people, especially if that deed was all it would really take. *If* he could physically manage to get aroused, which he had his doubts. The act would disgrace Lyrne, his life mate, whom he had vowed to cherish in the way of the Wolf, which was a commitment even after her death. But such oaths were not as sacred as they used to be, especially not when one's home was lost.

Onunith guffawed. "Don't look so grief-stricken, berserker. I wouldn't break your cock, but if I did, that would only be the start of it." She faced Vard. "If only it were so easy. We've got problems of our own."

"Such as?" Vard asked.

"Jötunn."

"There's a giant in your lands?"

"Aye. It moves like snow, unseen even though it is as tall as the hills. It decimates villages and kills everything, devouring its victims." She studied the Ulfhednar's taut faces. "Sea Serpent raiders don't sound so bad now, do they?"

"How long has this jötunn been plaguing your people?"

"Not a year ago, he awoke, but his visits are growing more frequent. He crossed over from Jötunheim—the king of the frost giants himself."

Vard arched back from the table in disbelief. "What does this king want with Midgard?"

"Have you not heard? Or have your Wolf ears been buried in the snow these past centuries?" She drank from her horn. "In the war of the gods, the jötunn were victorious. This is obvious. The Bear and Boar battled in these lands, and both were injured. The Bear threw down the Boar, and our god crawled her way back here to die. The giants took this as their cue. They traveled from their worlds and struck down whatever wounded gods still lived. The weakened Bear was killed by the frost giant king who now haunts us. The jötunn yearn to be the gods of Midgard." She shrugged. "And there are no other gods to oppose them."

"Have you fought this frost king?"

"Ah, it all sounds bad, but the situation isn't so much worse than it's been with some of the battle-crazed jarls we've had within and outside our lands. Each of their raids killed many a villager, and those occurred frequently enough, if not as often as the giant's visits. The frost king roams our lands and those of the Bear, taking victims from both sides."

"We're seeking the aid of the Bear clan as well," Belfedrn interrupted. "If we can unify the Ulfhednar, Boar, and Bear people, we could crush the ranks of the Serpent for good. Then we can establish peace."

"Peace between clans won't last longer than a good piss."

"Have you confronted this frost giant?" Belfedrn stood, his patience dwindling.

Onunith furrowed her forehead and brushed greasy hair from her cheeks. "We can't find him. He moves like a storm and is just as invisible. Until he isn't. At least that's what the survivors who've seen him claim."

"We shall locate this jötunn's den and hunt him while he rests. Take him by surprise instead of waiting for him to show up at a time and place of his choosing."

"How?"

Belfedrn's thoughts whirled. "We'll figure it out."

Vard held out his hand to calm Belfedrn and said, "If we help your berserkers kill the giant, will you aid us in our cause?"

Onunith picked at something in her mouth, her jaw gaping and revealing crooked teeth, some of which jutted like tiny tusks. "I'll tell you this—if you can convince the Bear to assist you and we remove the frost king from Midgard, I'll follow you back to your lands with all the Boar warriors in Matterdreg. I'll help you slay the Serpent people. But I doubt any will survive a battle with our jötunn. He finished off the Bear god himself."

Vard glanced around at the Ulfhednar. "To Bear territory, then?"

"For the Wolves," Belfedrn said, and the others echoed him.

"And I won't even make you loan out your second to me as my whore." Onunith put on a sultry grin for Belfedrn.

45

CAËTIN

CAËTIN WOKE WITH A START. THE PRISONER IN CHAINS HUNG suspended, his head rolling across the floor and coming to rest, staring up at her with white eyes.

"His head just came off," the slender-jawed Raven warrior said in disbelief.

"I cut it off," Caëtin replied, her remorse subdued.

"Well, there's not much I can do to keep him alive now." The warrior bit his lip and grunted.

"We must conceal Muninn's temple. Now. Aonark's fortifications may not be able to stop the Spiders, but our enemies won't be able to burrow through the temple's stone walls. Hiding the temple could buy us time. At least that's something."

"How do we conceal a stone temple?" Igendrn knelt beside Caëtin and assisted her to her feet.

"We build what looks to be a few average longhouses over and around it." She staggered out of the cell as feeling came back into her legs, Igendrn and the Raven warriors following her. "And position the walls of the longhouses so that the temple is hidden between them with no doorways to access it, sealing it off. For the time being. The Spiders won't find it unless they realize there's too much space missing from the interior of a couple houses and start chopping through walls. We also decorate some of the other longhouses in Aonark. To make them look more splendid than the temple's guise."

"Perhaps we should take Muninn's remains and flee the city," Igendrn said. "Hide them somewhere else."

Caëtin halted so fast that the *goði* crashed into her. Move their god from where she had died? Caëtin contemplated the strategy. "We'd be vulnerable while roaming open lands, and our treasures would be exposed. Wherever we decided to hide them wouldn't be as well fortified as Aonark. The only advantage I see by doing so would be that our enemies shouldn't expect the move. But they also shouldn't expect us to hide Muninn's temple. We're not supposed to know what they're after." Her eyes closed in thought. "I'll discuss the idea with Darstrid and perhaps Taknhal. Maybe even Uktr. We should talk it over before anyone makes a rash decision."

They passed a cell door, and sobbing carried out from inside. Caëtin glanced about at the other cells.

"Who's in there?" Caëtin asked the warriors.

"A Spider captive," the slender-jawed warrior answered.

"Does she cry often?"

The warriors shared a confused glance. None of them could commit to an answer.

Caëtin stepped up before the door in question. "How many Spider captives are down here?"

"Eight, but Darstrid and her knights believe that only the one you interrogated was of value to us or them. The rest are neither berserkers nor warriors."

"Karls, then? Or healers?"

"Maybe even thralls, but no one of significance. The inquisitors spoke with each of them."

"Open this door." Caëtin pressed a palm against its steel as the sobs turned to a whimper.

There was a long pause.

"Are you certain?" The slender-jawed warrior approached and withdrew his keys, hesitating for a moment, as if hoping Caëtin would stop him. He unlocked the door and shoved it open.

The whimpering stopped as Caëtin strode inside. An adolescent girl of maybe six and ten winters crouched in the straw, her hands in fetters, and she could have been praying. She glanced up and cowered, tear tracks running through black paint around her eyes and mouth, and she scooted farther into a corner. She wore a dark tunic that was torn and hung off one shoulder. Sympathy tugged at a cord in Caëtin's heart as she imagined what it would be like if her daughter were taken and put in a similar situation.

"Who are you?" Caëtin asked, and the girl lurched with fright.

She did not answer. Caëtin stepped closer and squatted so she could look the girl in the eye at her level.

"You do not have to be frightened of me," Caëtin said, "unless you refuse to answer my questions."

The girl's eyes vibrated with fear. "I-I am Hildm."

"You are a Spider?"

She nodded.

"You're a young warrior in training?" Caëtin asked. "Meant to bear the remains of another god?"

Hildm's jaw dropped open.

Caëtin leaned closer. "Answer me."

"Aye."

"Then the Raven berserkers saved your life by bringing you here. I've seen what happens to the Spider's trainees. They die. In droves."

Hildm swallowed and studied her hands.

"Were you specifically trained in hopes of bearing Muninn's feathers?" Caëtin asked.

The girl remained silent, picking at something on her fingernails.

"Answer me!"

She lurched. "The Spider is my god. You cannot take her from me. She's in here." She tapped her chest.

"It's not my intention to make you renounce your god who demands that you kill yourself by attempting to carry the powers of another, although that sounds like a wise choice."

"It won't happen. Not ever."

Caëtin smirked but studied Hildm intently while asking her next question. "Have you seen Muninn's temple?"

Hildm's eyes narrowed with bewilderment, and her lips pursed.

Her confusion is true.

"No," the girl said.

Caëtin stood and faced the warriors. "Are there more like her here—young trainees?"

"No," the slender-jawed warrior replied. "The others are men and women. Some are middle-aged."

"Why had the recluse seen the temple and not her?"

The warrior bit his lip again. "I... the knights didn't think to hide it from them when they were led to the dungeons. They didn't walk right past it, but if someone was searching for it, they would have seen it in the distance."

"Release her," Caëtin said.

"Sorry?"

"I said, release her." Caëtin gestured at the adolescent. "But keep her in fetters. She will accompany me wherever I go. As my servant."

"If you need a thrall, we can find you another who is—"

"No. She will do. She's not even a warrior, and she carries no god parts. She won't pose any danger."

The Raven men hesitated before Caëtin cocked her head and they capitulated, stepping past her and heaving Hildm to her feet. They released her fetters from a chain anchored to the wall.

"You are my thrall," Caëtin said to Hildm. "You will stay close to me, which is an order and will be for your own good. If any Ravens spot you wandering about alone, they will kill you. If you try to aid your people in any way, I will kill you. Do not doubt that."

Hildm swallowed, her eyes downcast.

"Come." Caëtin exited the cell and marched up the dungeon's steps, out into the night, the warriors and Spider girl following. Huginn winged past overhead. Torchlight burned brighter than ever before in Aonark. The Raven people feared what was coming, and they believed their enemies may only have one weakness.

Caëtin stomped her foot on the muddy street as a rain and snow mix plummeted around them. "We need to shore up what we never thought to shore up before. The ground."

The warriors eyed the mud. "To prevent spiders from entering the city through the earth?" the slender-jawed warrior asked.

Caëtin nodded.

"How can we possibly accomplish such a feat?" He shook his head as he glanced around.

"Carry as many flat stones as you can find anywhere in the city and beyond," Caëtin replied. "And logs. The one advantage we already have is that the Spider won't be able to dig through the stone of Muninn's temple. Lay everything you can gather across as much ground in the inner city as possible."

The warriors stared at her in disbelief.

"Find others to watch the dungeons," she said. "Begin shoring up the city, now!"

The warriors rushed off in different directions, hollering for karls and their comrades. Frightened faces emerged from doorways all around, people who were afraid the Spiders had arrived in their streets.

Let them be frightened. At least until the city was prepared and formidable against an enemy unlike any the Raven had encountered.

"You should find rest," Igendrn said to Caëtin before casting a wary eye on Hildm. "I'll watch over you in the temple."

Caëtin squeezed his arm. "I can't. Not now. There's too much to do. I must find Darstrid. If I need you, I'll find you when I'm alone." She jerked her head toward her new thrall.

Igendrn dipped his chin in acknowledgment, and Caëtin hurried away, angling for the great hall. As she passed, people emerged from houses, whispering, trying to understand what was happening. Some pointed at Hildm, who trailed behind Caëtin. A few shouted curses at the thrall, and Hildm ducked her head and rushed along faster, catching up to Caëtin and staying close. Huginn landed on Caëtin's shoulder and preened herself as Caëtin stroked the raven's neck.

They passed what resembled a gibbet, but the bodies there were not hanging by their necks. They had been flayed open, and blood and entrails hung around them.

All Spiders. Captives the knights must have returned with. Caëtin inspected the dead—none were dressed as warriors or berserkers. Probably more servants and karls Darstrid or the knights let the Raven people get a hold of.

Hildm cringed and trembled, backing away.

"Come." Caëtin waved her on, and the girl rushed past her dead kin.

46

CAËTIN

CAËTIN NEARED THE GREAT HALL. THERE WERE SO MANY TORCHES burning along its walls that it looked like a beacon. She paused, leaning over. Dark stains splotched the stones around the doorway, and a trail of them led away from the longhouse. She knelt and ran her fingers over the splotches. Still wet and sticky.

Blood.

She heaved the doors inward, sending Huginn flapping away, and called, "Darstrid? Are you here?"

A moment of silence passed.

"No," Grimmurk's voice answered from the loft, grumbly with sleep. "She hasn't returned this night. Not for nattmal or sleep or anything else. What's happened?"

"The people are strengthening the city against the magics of the widows and recluses. No messengers have arrived with news of the Spider people's coming. You and Uktr can rest. Is all well in the great hall?"

"As far as I know."

A half-asleep grunt from Uktr seconded Grimmurk.

Caëtin shut the doors and picked up the blood trail, which quickly disappeared into the mud and rain in the street. Hildm hunched over in her tattered tunic, her black hair drenched, her fetters clinking as she stuck to Caëtin's backside. Caëtin halted, searching for any more of the trail.

Huginn cawed and landed on a pole. A red handprint was smeared across the wall of a house beside the raven. Caëtin hurried over, and when she arrived, Huginn flew off to another area where there was a bloody print on a wall. Together, Caëtin and Huginn tracked the blood to a darkened region between a longhouse and a cluster of huts.

Animosity between the splitting factions of knights and warriors may have spilled over to bloodshed. She needed to quell their fighters' ire... after she found out what had happened.

A cold wind gusted through the gap, rippling Caëtin's raven cloak and spiking the hair on the back of her neck. She covered her pale skin as much as she could with her cloak to keep from standing out in the shadows and drew her sword. Steel rang against wood. She edged forward, the smell of blood and death thick. Something fetid hovered amongst other odors.

Hildm waited in the distance as Caëtin quickened her pace, glancing behind piled crates as she moved. In the shadows ahead, a dark heap stood out, unmoving.

A body. "Darstrid?" she whispered.

The heap did not move or respond. Caëtin scanned the area to make sure no one was close enough to jump out of hiding and attack her. She knelt before the heap, which was a body lying beneath a cloak. Black-streaked pale hair covered its face.

"Darstrid." Caëtin suppressed her dread and felt for a pulse on Darstrid's neck. It was faint but present. Caëtin tore her waterskin from her belt and splashed some of its contents onto her sister's face.

Darstrid wheezed and stirred.

"What happened?" Caëtin asked as she lifted Darstrid's arm

in hopes of assisting her to a standing position. At Darstrid's waist and leg, her brigandine and leathers were soaked in blood —in the same area where her wound had been—and a pool had formed on the ground around her. *So much blood.* Caëtin tried to heave her up, but Darstrid shoved her away.

"Leave me," Darstrid croaked, her voice weak. "The boy. He came for me."

"What boy?"

"The one we gave a beating to."

Caëtin's mind reeled. They had killed so many, but a boy... "The one at the Mist Shores who stole a knight's feather?"

"Aye. Halvi. He knew. Somehow he knew I was weak and carried too much."

In the darkness, Caëtin was unable to see well enough to determine if her sister still wore all the feathers she had been carrying. Caëtin felt around Darstrid's chest. "Your feathers are gone. All of them."

"Halvi took them." Darstrid grimaced and shifted. "I didn't expect anything when another boy led me here to show me something suspicious, but Halvi was waiting. He carried another feather. I didn't even get to use my magic against him. He was agitated but powerful. Maniacal."

"Someone must've given him what he's been craving since the Mist Shores... and maybe a bit of training as well."

"They used him to get to me. Find him." Darstrid lifted a shaky hand and pointed into the darkness.

"Someone!" Caëtin shouted back toward the entrance to the alley. "We need help!"

"You have one of them with you—a Spider captive." Darstrid raised her head enough to look toward Hildm. "I let our people kill most of those we brought back."

"She may know something that could help Aonark," Caëtin whispered so Hildm would not hear. "Something we see or hear could give her some indication of our enemy's intent. She'd be of no use locked away in the dark."

"Get my feathers back."

"I'm not leaving you like this."

"I'm already dead. You don't see the Raven's bridge, but I do."

Darstrid had been mortally wounded, and only her extra feathers had kept her alive and given her enough strength so she could pretend to be hale. Now that they were gone, she would not survive. Unless Caëtin could get them back quickly. She placed Darstrid's hands over the bleeding wound on her side and had her apply pressure.

"Hold on, Sister." Caëtin darted off into the darkness, weaving around corners of buildings and through narrow streets as Hildm shuffled after her and Huginn occasionally passed overhead. No torches burned here. She tripped over strewn remnants of a crate but caught herself and crouched. She could become an unkindness, but that would not help her see any better. If she ran into a major street and found nothing, then she could become the ravens and circle the city in widening arcs.

She rushed on, stumbling, probably unaware of many hiding spots in the darkness, but her blade was ready for the slightest movement. Ahead, firelight from a street carried into the alleyway, and another body lay slumped at the margin where torchlight and darkness met. It twitched erratically. She sprinted closer until she stood within striking distance.

The figure trembled but did not attempt to stand. Light flickered across his face—a boy with his eyes closed. *Halvi.*

Caëtin grabbed his tunic in a fist, and he barely groaned. His limbs shook violently, drool trickling from his lips. She had been the one who had spared the boy's life. Only for this end. Only for him to kill Darstrid, who had wanted the jarl's laws carried out on him. Caëtin's guilt exploded before she could shove it back down.

Whoever gave the boy a part of Muninn is to blame. Not me or Halvi alone. "Where are the feathers?"

Halvi did not answer, and she shook him again.

"You're feeling the aftereffects of losing Muninn's touch, you fool," she said. "My sister and I weren't jesting when we said wielding its power would kill anyone who hadn't received proper training."

"B-but I… I needed it." He coughed up blood, spraying Caëtin's face with a thick mist of it.

She wiped some of the wetness away. "That's the addiction. Mortals aren't supposed to command the power of a god. I do so only after decades of training, and even I could not give it up. I *warned* you. Where are Darstrid's feathers?"

He coughed again. "I could almost fly. Fly! But I crashed and then couldn't move. I won't move again."

"Where are they?" She slapped him across the face.

"He took them." Halvi hacked and rolled onto his side, sputtering up blood, quivering, his face turning blue. "The Axe." He vomited yellow foam, and his eyes stared blankly into the torchlight of the street beyond as he went still.

Fuck. Caëtin stepped out into the street, glancing about, afraid someone would be watching her, or even worse, that whoever she was chasing was long gone.

A few people milled about, dragging poles and lining them up along the ground. Others slogged along in teams, carrying heavy flagstones. They dropped the stones and slid them into place, creating a meshwork across the street.

Now, there was not only the threat of the Spider. Someone in Aonark was gathering feathers, and they had attempted to murder Darstrid, the Raven clan's new jarl.

47

MÄRREN

Firelight from the Dragon city shone through the storm, its stone walls standing high over the tundra. Märren and Uisge trudged along with the caravan as the wind bit at them and snow whirled about, the daylight nearly spent. At dawn, the Dragon warriors had rounded up the captives who survived the last bitter night and discovered that Märren and Uisge's chain had been broken. The warriors quickly replaced it and set off, but this far north, winters days did not last long.

"Are you planning on somehow becoming a citizen of this city and then a Dragon warrior?" Uisge asked. "To obtain your scale?"

"She doesn't know what she's doing."

"She never has. Her choices always lead to greater and greater suffering."

"She's encountered a dragon and a giant and survived. This city is nothing."

Ancient runes engraved into the walls of the city stared back at her, defiant, making some of hers burn.

"I don't know what I'm doing," Märren said. "I just put one foot in front of the other and keep going."

Uisge fell silent as they approached massive twin gates. A guard above held a torch high, leaning over and peering through the snow.

"Who's fool enough to be out there at night?" The guard bellowed into a horn to amplify his voice, which carried but was partially sheared away by the wind.

The berserker in the caravan cupped his hands to his mouth and hollered back. "We're returning from offering sacrifices to Surtr."

A short silence followed.

"With living thralls?" the guard asked, incredulous.

"Open the buggering gates! It's me, Raidn, berserker of the Dragon."

A thud sounded, and the gates groaned. One swung open just enough for a score of local warriors to jog out. The warriors fanned out before them as Raidn waved his men and the caravan into the city. The local warriors parted, allowing them to pass. Once they had all entered, and the gates were shut and barred, the wind died and the berserker faced the dozen surviving captives, his warriors surrounding them.

The berserker's sunken eyes narrowed above his braided black beard, his face reddening. "You lot did not march fast enough to appease Surtr and attain glory, as was intended." He paced before them, stopping in front of Märren and Uisge. "And because of it, he'll wake sooner the next time. You'll live another day, but when the jötunn shows signs of stirring, you will trek north again. You will be the first to be offered. Until then, you shall live in shame. As thralls of Torank." He glared at Märren.

Märren tugged on her iron collar but did not lower her gaze as the voices raged. Her lips parted on their own.

"Do you have something you wish to say?" Raidn snapped at her. "*Thrall.*"

Märren kept quiet, although she yearned to ask him for an opportunity to bear a scale.

"Here, her existence will be miserable."

"He'll let his men have their way with her, until she is fodder for the fiery jötunn."

"She's in no worse of a situation than before."

Raidn stepped closer, his face a finger's distance from hers. "What is wrong with you?"

"The cautious guest who comes to the table speaks sparingly," she replied, her voice barely audible. "Listen with ears. Learn with eyes. Such is the seeker of knowledge."

"Do *not* utter the Hávamál at me!" He spat at her. "Take them away and put these dishonored to work with the other thralls."

In Märren's mind, a rune of power on her chest smoldered with firelight. "I've seen where Surtr keeps your dragons."

Raidn froze.

"They despise their confinement and what the jötunn takes from them," Märren continued. "I would ask you for a full scale, and in return, I would join your people. Your berserkers. We can then use the dragons against the giant, ride them and overthrow the jötunn."

Raidn's jaw dropped in surprise as he cocked his head, allowing her words to rattle around in his mind. He growled, a deep guttural sound, and drew his axe, pointing it at Märren's face, his skin flashing and looking segmented—like scales.

"*We*?" He sputtered, exasperated, smoke rising from his mouth and nostrils. "A scale for you?" He scoffed. "The fiery jötunn cannot be killed. The Dragon herself proved that feat impossible." He snarled, and his fist tightened around the shaft of his axe as he raised the weapon, heaving with fury before curbing his rage. "No. I won't kill you here. Not even for that grievous insult. A quick death must be what you desire. But it would be too easy." He turned to a warrior beside him. "Have this lot perform all the tasks the other thralls despise the most, but keep them healthy enough to survive until Surtr wakes again. We'll stake them out in front of any others we gather, to ensure they're charred and devoured first. They'll save a dozen of our people."

"Aye, Master Raidn," one of the warriors said as he and the rest grabbed Märren, Uisge, and the others and shoved them deeper into the city.

"This night, they do not sleep," the berserker said.

For the remainder of the night, Märren and the captives scrubbed out the latrines with a brush and bucket of water. Uisge gagged and retched from the reek of shite as simple soldiers watched over them, keeping a safe distance.

Märren's voices ran rampant, and she turned inward, cleaning and working for hours, lost to the outside world. She worked under a barrage of verbal assaults—nothing new—although the torment never came easy. Hours dwindled away.

A hand gripped her shoulder. A warrior wearing a section of a scale on his brigandine looked down at her in bewilderment. "Do you not tire?"

Märren's fingers and hands were bleeding onto the handle of her brush. The sun had risen. The warrior speaking to her had not been watching her when she first began her duties. Nor had the soldiers in the distance. Shifts had been traded without her realizing it. Uisge sat slouched against a stone wall with the others, their heads hanging with exhaustion.

The warrior hoisted Märren to her feet, wrinkling his nose at the smell of her. He pried her hands from the brush and held her by the wrists, her palms facing up.

"I appreciate your efforts, but you must remain fit enough to be a worthy sacrifice," the warrior said. His blond beard was sparse, his jaw rigid. He was probably older than thirty winters, although he had a young-looking face. "Or Raidn will have my head. And you must work as a thrall till then." He turned and shouted something at those behind him.

A boy in a tunic came running and passed the warrior a vial. "Here's the tincture, Yrstl."

Yrstl faced Märren. "This'll sting." He dumped acidic-smelling liquid over her hands.

Märren nearly screamed, but she bit her lip, wincing, her hands clenching and quivering with pain.

"It's just vinegar," Yrstl said, a hint of sympathy seeping into his tone as he studied her. "It's what we use on any warrior or soldier who trains too long and blisters. It'll harden the tender skin you've exposed."

He gently wrapped her hands with cloth and tied off the ends.

"Thank you," she whispered.

"Take better care of yourself."

"I am Märren."

"Take better care of yourself, Märren." He gripped her around her upper arm and shoved her away.

Märren stumbled, her legs cramping after sitting in one position and working all night. Uisge staggered to his feet and joined her.

"You lot should get to the thrall house." Yrstl pointed at a structure in the distance. "Throw some buckets of water over yourselves and eat whatever dagmal you can. You've got a long day of work ahead of you before you're allowed to sleep."

Uisge's feet scuffed the stones as they walked and neared the building in question, where people in stained tunics and iron collars wandered about.

48

CAËTIN

"SHE WAS FOUND DEAD," HALFNR SAID WHEN CAËTIN APPROACHED the great hall, the torches around the longhouse hissing in the rain. Hildm followed close behind her, the girl's head bowed in subservience, her hands still in fetters.

"Darstrid?" A blade of pain twisted in Caëtin's gut. She had found no other trail to follow in pursuit of the missing feathers, and Darstrid had no longer been at the site where Caëtin had found her bleeding.

"Aye."

Huginn winged past, shrieking her outrage.

Sanre shifted beside Halfnr, gripping her axe's handle, and said, "Her body was taken to the temple."

"Then Taknhal is acting jarl?"

Sanre nodded. "He's ordering the Raven warriors and Knights Black to march south to confront the Spiders at our border. There's been several bloody fights between those who followed him and those who followed Darstrid but no deaths. Not yet."

"Fucking imbecile," Caëtin said. "None of the Knights Black

who are still loyal to me will leave Aonark. It'll be a death sentence for anyone who goes."

"I wouldn't follow that fool even if he hatched from one of Muninn's eggs," Halfnr said.

"Good." Doubts about what was to happen to the Raven people rained down on Caëtin. "If Taknhal and the others depart, perhaps we should leave this city for the Spiders. Everything I attempt is for naught, and the worst outcomes prevail. I'm done being a sword for a jarl."

"Don't give up on Aonark," Halfnr said. "Please. Not yet. You're all that's holding this city together. Don't turn your back on whatever's left, no matter what you've endured at Uktr's hand. No matter what you'll endure from Taknhal. If you do, the Spider will have won."

Caëtin bit her lip.

"She with you?" Sanre asked, nodding at Hildm, who hunched in the rain, her tunic sodden.

"Aye," Caëtin said.

Sanre raised an eyebrow. "A Spider thrall? Even among the Raven people, she'll be difficult to hide unless you wash that black paint off her face and out of her hair and change her clothes."

"Aonark's karls will want her head," Halfnr added.

"As long as she stays with me, I'll keep her safe." Caëtin faced the girl. "She is devoted to her god, but she may know something that could help us."

Hildm did not acknowledge the suggestion or their conversation. Caëtin approached the great hall's doors, but Sanre held out a hand to stop her.

"Your brother is not in there," Sanre said.

"Then where is he?" Caëtin asked.

Sanre pointed south. "At the southern walls, amassing our warriors and knights."

Caëtin cursed and hurried away, running through the streets as Hildm struggled to keep up. The number of people working to secure the ground of the city had greatly diminished, and more than a few shouted obscenities at Hildm as they passed. Soon, Caëtin neared their destination, and inside the southern walls, ranks of warriors stood at the ready as more poured in through the gates. Caëtin shoved her way through them, standing tall and searching for Taknhal as Hildm clung to her cloak. Just inside the gates, her brother spoke with those who were entering. She marched up to him.

"Don't do this," Caëtin said.

Taknhal turned and studied her. "We cannot allow the people of the Spider to invade our lands. We should confront them—show our strength and drive them away long before they reach Aonark."

"You'll all die, and then Aonark will fall."

Taknhal indicated the incoming warriors. "You also believed that the work I did in Sparsgard wouldn't be beneficial, and yet warriors from all the villages in our lands now march to Aonark alongside their people. Our numbers swell."

Caëtin's eyes closed as she tried to control her response. Of course the staged massacre had worked, but she had not been willing to sacrifice innocents in order to achieve the objective. However, the ruse seemed to have worked better than she thought possible.

Taknhal turned his broad back to her and spoke with a jarl who had entered the city. Her pale blade seemed to thrum and then pulse with a heartbeat of its own, thumping against her side with agitation. She could kill Aonark's newest jarl right here and be done with this disastrous plan of his.

She clenched her weapon's hilt and drew the blade a handsbreadth from its sheath, her breath catching and rasping in her throat. Such an attack would be considered cowardly and would approach what Taknhal had done to the people of Sparsgard, but it would save the lives of all of these warriors and potentially their city. The biggest difference between her killing Taknhal in cold blood and what Taknhal had done was that the Raven people would see her do it. She would not be able to say it was someone else's crime.

The savagery of Uktr entices me again... Caëtin's arm shook, but she stayed her hand. "Someone in Aonark killed Darstrid and is stealing Muninn's feathers." *Pray it isn't you.*

Taknhal slowly pivoted around to face her again. "I heard about our sister's fate. Do you know who the murderer is?"

"I was hoping that you could tell me."

"What's that supposed to mean?" A spark of anger lit his eyes.

"The only reason you've risen past drink and stand here sober before our legions and as jarl is because Darstrid helped you."

"Darstrid was overly fond of drink as well, but it no longer matters. I loved her, in a way you and I have never loved each other."

"How many feathers do you carry?"

He opened his cloak to reveal two flight feathers. "Darstrid and the *gyðja* ordered the knights and warriors to carry as much as we're able. Better to prepare now rather than try to distribute Muninn's remains when the Spiders are beating down our gates." He allowed his cloak to settle closed over his chest. "But that's not why you've come, is it? I am now jarl of Aonark and the Raven clan, and you believe I killed our sister to obtain this power. But unless you're going to accuse me of murder here in front of all these knights and are ready to challenge me, be off."

"I'm not certain of anything. Not yet."

"Then take heart in what you can. More than a few of the warriors and Knights Black who were loyal to Darstrid won't obey my commands. They wish for you to be jarl and have sided with you."

"That's hardly consolation for Darstrid's death."

He gritted his teeth. "Speak with Uktr. He may know something about the murderer and smuggler of god parts. He has long suspected such a traitor. Find out who it really is. As soon as dawn breaks, I march south with this army."

"I pray you don't lead these people to their deaths."

"If we're slain, I hope it's not because you refused to join us with the last of your warriors and Knights Black."

A wheel of disbelief spun inside Caëtin. "And leave *no one* to defend Aonark? You're mad."

He shrugged. "Perhaps those who are frightened of our enemies should stay behind the city's walls."

"*You* should stay out of my reach, because if I find that you had anything to do with Darstrid's death, there'll be no safe place for you." She heaved for breath and turned to the masses. "If there's any more fighting between our knights, rangers, and warriors, it'll only make the Spider stronger. Keep your anger in check. Until you can release it on our enemies."

Sunlight brightened in the east, and ranks of Raven warriors mounted their horses and rode out of the gates, the Knights Black marching after them, heading south. Huginn squawked in protest.

Caëtin strode into the great hall with Hildm right behind her. Uktr and Grimmurk sat at a table before the central fire, drinking from horns and feasting on fired meats. Grimmurk bellowed with laughter and pounded a fist on the table before noticing Caëtin.

"You talked Taknhal into this, didn't you, Father?" Caëtin said more than asked.

Uktr regarded her, runnels of drink running through his beard. "To take the battle to our enemies rather than hide behind walls waiting for the Spiders to lay siege on our city?"

"Aye."

"No. Your brother once had the mental capabilities of a sack of raven shite, and that was on a good day when he wasn't deep in his horns, but he's becoming a shrewd thinker. The attack was his decision."

"It's what you would've done."

"Of course."

"And now that Darstrid is dead, Taknhal controls most of the knights and warriors."

"It's the way of our Viking people. The way of all the clans."

"And Darstrid's murder means nothing?"

"Since you are her sister and do not carry the pressures and commitments of the jarl, I'd hope you wouldn't sleep until she was avenged."

Caëtin shot Grimmurk a dark look. "While her father drinks with his last friend and reminisces of old times?"

Uktr's cheeks reddened. "You've tied my hands. You and Darstrid. You undermined my authority. I cannot send warriors out to do my bidding, and I'm too old to run around the city searching for answers and interrogating witnesses."

"Don't trouble yourself, Father. I will avenge her." She glared at both men at the table. "No matter who is behind it."

A few breaths of tense silence followed.

"Your Spider thrall would make a good sacrifice before battle," Grimmurk said, eyeing Hildm, who scooted behind Caëtin.

"She's *my* thrall."

"And don't fret about your children while you're away." Uktr smiled. "The servants always take good care of them. At least when they're visiting me, which is often."

Caëtin's stomach dropped. Was that a threat? If this man could kill his adopted daughter, he could kill a grandchild who was not his own blood. Uktr had never had a conscience.

"I'll be watching them, Father. And I'll make sure they stay away from the great hall." Caëtin exited the longhouse with Hildm and found Halfnr, Sanre, and the rest of Knights Black who were loyal to her waiting outside.

"Wake all the warriors and karls remaining in Aonark and have them continue placing flagstones across the city," Caëtin said. "But make sure that priority is given to the construction of the longhouses over and around the temple. Then round up the new arrivals from the villages and let them know that they're required to assist us in every endeavor. Each covered street and floor could be the one that saves Aonark. Halfnr and Sanre, come with me." She waved the two over as the rest of the knights and warriors departed.

"And what're we to do?" Sanre asked.

"Halfnr, take two knights with you and fly south. Now. Watch over Taknhal and his army. Let me know when anything happens."

Halfnr dipped his head and strode away.

"Sanre," Caëtin continued, "join me and Hildm. We'll be looking for any evidence not washed away by the rain. Anything that could have been left around where Darstrid and Halvi died."

She led her companion and thrall to the side of the great hall and began scouring the area.

49

BELFEDRN

"Hold both squares on your body but not in your mind," Belfedrn said to Thelira after they had docked their longship and marched northward into Bear territory. She wore her square of Fenrir as well as Dradn's, which was Belfedrn's idea. He hoped to ease her into wielding more magic. "Feel that shaking sensation in your skull, the power. You crave it. You desire nothing more than obtaining a full pelt."

Thelira growled and tore the longbow from her back, nocking an arrow faster than any man or woman without godly enhancements could hope to. She sighted quickly and loosed. The projectile screamed through falling snow and slammed into a trunk, sending splinters flying. The thick-armed longbow, which could not be drawn by someone with mortal strength, hummed. Thelira grinned and turned to Belfedrn, pride welling in her eyes.

Dradn cheered. Kesg grunted in surprise.

Belfedrn struck Thelira across her gut with the shaft of his spear. She groaned and doubled over, stumbling back. He advanced, shield raised, spear jabbing at her until she twisted and leapt aside. She parried another strike by using her bow to knock the spear away, saving herself from being skewered. Then she drew her seax and hacked off the tip of the spear before lunging at Belfedrn. She pressed her weapon to his throat, panting for breath as a line of blood formed around her blade and Belfedrn's flesh.

Belfedrn shoved her away and she slammed into a tree as he snapped, "You would've already been dead, basking in the glory of increased power and one fine shot. The enemy berserkers and warriors would've flayed you."

"Let her have her moment," Dradn said.

Belfedrn wheeled on him. "You'll have your chance soon enough! It's my task to train two warriors to become Ulfhednar, and if your shite abilities get you killed, it'll be my fault." *And my heart will crumble. Like with Deyja, whose death I cannot accept, whose father I may one day have to face in the afterlife.* "Now focus, and stop letting the power swell in your minds so it affects you like drink and mushrooms." He turned to Thelira, who glowered at him as she clutched her midsection. "If you allow the god magic to take you to a place of calm and confidence, and you find yourself at peace with the world, you'll die. You are not a god. None of us are. The only difference between the Ulfhednar, or any berserker, and you warriors is our ability to tolerate that power and wield it rather than wallow in it. To do as we do, you must have the resolve to give all that magic up at any moment."

Thelira rammed her seax into the tree she had been shoved into and stormed off, tearing both squares of Fenrir's pelt from around her neck and flinging them at Dradn. They landed in the snow near his feet.

Perhaps she's stronger than I thought. She parted with both pieces with less difficulty than Belfedrn ever had. If her frustration and anger with him did not get the better of her, maybe she could one day wear a full pelt.

"You know you can be a blazing arse, right?" Kesg said.

"I'm trying to help them survive." Belfedrn's eyes closed. "Am I worse than any of those crotchety old fucks who trained us?"

"You are the embodiment of those crotchety old fucks."

Athna stepped closer as Dradn bent over to pick up the pelt pieces. Athna shook her head and muttered to Belfedrn, her tone thick with irritation, "You haven't taught them to respect the power and remnants of Fenrir. They discard them like old tunics."

"I've never trained anyone before." Belfedrn rubbed his eyes, weary of pretending to be an instructor. "I don't know what I'm doing, but I focus on what I had the hardest time with—letting go of the power."

Athna's tone did not soften. "These adolescent warriors won't be able to control their abilities if they're always thinking they should rid themselves of their god parts."

"I'd be more than happy if you took over their training."

She scowled. "These two pups are your burden."

"Then stop telling me how to train them."

"Not a chance." She stalked ahead with the remainder of the pack.

Dradn donned both squares of Fenrir, their power causing him to shudder before he jogged to Belfedrn.

"Should we wait for her?" Dradn asked, motioning in the direction Thelira had gone.

"She's a Wolf warrior, if not more. If she can't track us without her pelt remnant, she's of no use to anyone."

Dradn pursed his lips but trod along. "You don't have to be so hard on her."

"So when we find ourselves battling the Sea Serpents or Bears or anyone else, she gets killed? Is that what you want?"

He swallowed. "Of course not."

"Am I any easier on you? Please tell me, since everyone

seems to have an idea on how I should be teaching you two now that the trainers in Nistreel are dead."

"No. If anything, you're harder on me. I think you take it easier on her because she's a woman."

That felt like a shield strike to the gut, but Belfedrn hid his pain. Dradn was probably right. Belfedrn pushed Dradn further, struck harder and faster, connected more often. "Damn the dead gods." If Thelira were to be killed, Belfedrn would ask himself if he had taken it too easy on her, if it was his fault that she had died in battle—if he had treated her like the daughter he never had. Lyrne's death was partially his fault. He could not bear a second wound akin to that one, and so he would not allow himself to imagine Deyja dead with the other trainees. The boy he vowed to protect had to be a captive of the Serpents, and Thelira would have to live well beyond Belfedrn's time in Midgard.

A cry pierced the cold day, coming from ahead. The answering shouts of several Ulfhednar followed. Dradn looked to Belfedrn with concern, but Belfedrn sprinted through the trees. He leapt over logs and arrived at a clearing where a man as broad and towering as any he had seen swung a maul in whistling arcs. The Ulfhednar surrounded the man, but he was full of rage and roared, his weapon swiping about in a deadly dance. A bearskin covered his head and shoulders.

A Björn—Bear—berserker.

The berserker raged, attacking wildly. "A jötunn! And now Wolf raiders in our lands!" He lunged at Eakthr, swinging his maul.

Eakthr leapt back, dodging the blow and prancing about.

The berserker raged as the Ulfhednar stood around him with their weapons lowered. Whenever the Bear berserker came close to any of them, they leapt out of harm's way and the others advanced a step so the berserker would turn on one of them. It took almost an hour before the raging berserker's trance broke and he slowed, his maul drooping, attacking slower, chest heaving for breath. Strong was the fury of the Bear.

"We haven't come to your lands as enemies." Vard held a hand up in hopes of pacifying the berserker.

The Bear man growled and swung again with renewed vigor, continuing his onslaught for a few more minutes until he tired a second time. The berserker glared at Belfedrn, hate boiling over in his eyes, blue rune tattoos riddling what little of his face was void of hair as well as the shaven sides of his scalp.

"We've come to speak with you," Belfedrn said. "About the jötunn."

The berserker snarled before he stilled and blinked, looking at each of them. After a few heartbeats, he said, "Have you seen the jötunn who hides like a craven thief?"

Belfedrn kept his tone as neutral as he could. "We haven't yet seen this giant, but we may be able to aid you."

The berserker straightened. "You won't have any more luck than me in finding the icy bastard. And why would a Wolf wish to aid a Bear? We've had our... differences."

"We could help you track this giant. We've raided each other's lands in the past, but we've never arrived with the pretense of peace. Never have we deceived the Bear. It has always been honorable pillaging and battles. On both sides."

The berserker studied them while continuing to try to catch his breath. "This jötunn doesn't leave footprints. No trail at all. And he recently destroyed a nearby village. Slaughtered everyone there, including women and children." He spat. "Bugger his gods and his cowardly arse."

"He cannot evade the Wolves."

Eventually, the berserker relaxed. He rubbed his beard, his head and face covered with untamed hair. "Name's Aegmor. I won't make no decisions concerning you Wolves, but since you will not fight me, I can take you to my jarl. You can try to convince him of your worth."

"That's all we ask."

Aegmor did not move. "As long as you tell me why you have come to our lands offering aid."

"We have a giant of our own, so to speak." Belfedrn sighed. "After years of the Sea Serpent and Wolf clans living side by side in peace, the Serpent ambushed our people. We never expected such a raid. Many Wolves were killed, and we were forced to flee."

"Then in exchange for helping us find the jötunn who torments the Bear—and only *if* you can locate him and we kill him—you're hoping the Bear warriors and berserkers will join you in taking revenge on the Serpent's people?"

"Aye. Revenge and reclaiming our homelands."

Vard stepped closer to Aegmor. "Any surviving Wolves have probably been enslaved as thralls, providing food and shelter and beds for the Sea Serpent bastards."

Aegmor nodded. "I can't promise anything, but I can take you to my jarl." He waved them after him as he tromped through the snow and into the woods.

Belfedrn followed, and his ears perked up. Someone behind the pack was watching and moving. Their subtle scent told him it was Thelira. Hopefully she was over her anger.

The pack trudged along at the crawling pace of a Bear berserker plowing through snow.

"We cannot waste this time," Belfedrn said to Dradn, who cast him a look of uncertainty.

"More training?"

"Of course."

As they trekked onward, Dradn practiced hurling his spear. The weapon flew farther than he had ever thrown it with the aid of only one pelt square. When the spear struck a trunk, the weapon impaled its wood, sinking deep.

The boy grinned. "I'm getting better."

"That you are, but you're not yet Ulfhednar quality," Belfedrn said. "Consistent precision only comes with thousands of throws."

Dradn grunted and trudged on, retrieving his spear. He stalked sideways, forward, and backward in the snow, sighting targets and hurling his weapon. Finally, before night fell, Aegmor led the pack to a snow-covered village where smoke rose in dark clouds from a longhouse.

"You must leave your weapons outside the village," Aegmor said, "and if that frightens you, you can go back to your woods."

Aegmor entered the village and headed for the longhouse, and the pack laid down their arms and followed him inside the structure. Scents of roasting meat and tubers hung thick in the air, burning Belfedrn's nostrils and making him salivate. A beast of a man with a braid of gray hair tromped between tables, shouting at those who sat gnawing on bones and drinking from horns. The beast-man slowly pivoted his bulk around to face Aegmor.

"Jarl Gron," Aegmor said. "The berserker's trance came upon me, and I ran out of the village in madness, hunting for the jötunn. I was... unsuccessful but unafraid of taking on the task alone and of dying. However, these Wolves came upon me with no intent of raiding or seeking battles for glory and honor. They offered to assist me in tracking down the jötunn. I thought it best if they speak with you."

Gron scrutinized the pack as Vard stepped forward and said, "Thank you for allowing the people of the Wolf into your house, Jarl Gron."

Gron grunted. He bore many rune tattoos similar to Aegmor's, including a plethora of them on the sides of his scalp.

"I haven't granted you permission to stand inside my great hall. Aegmor may be my finest berserker, but he has taken some liberties here and stepped beyond his rank. He doesn't know the Ulfhednar when he sees them. I do."

"They can help us find the frost giant," Aegmor added.

"This giant camouflages with snow." Gron paced before the Ulfhednar. "He travels in storms covered in wind and sleet and is rarely seen. Only his axe and face sometimes appear just before he slaughters our people. He is nothing more than mist and illusion, a craven jötunn who wields Seidr magic."

"Given the long history of skirmishes and raids between our clans, the Wolves have not ventured into Bear territory and have avoided discussions with your people for many years," Vard said. "But these are different times. When greater foes lurk around us, we're no longer each other's enemy. Such foes grow stronger now, and if they had their way, they'd wipe our peoples from Midgard." He paused to allow his words to sink in. "As one of Fenrir's berserkers, I have many reasons not to trust the Bear—for acts I should still bear grievances for. You probably feel the same about us. But I would gladly set all that aside to help rid you of your jötunn if, in return, the Bears would vow to help us cleanse our lands of the Sea Serpent warriors and berserkers who have defiled them. I promise you that your jötunn will not elude us."

"And how are you so certain of that?" Gron pointed at Vard and Belfedrn and continued speaking before they could answer. "Don't feign confidence in hopes that I'll spare your lives for entering our lands without permission, you dogs. It's not fitting for the Ulfhednar to be deceitful even if you can be treacherous. The Bear and Wolf do not cooperate. Neither in hunts nor war. It's unheard of and might as well be a law that harkens back to the old ways in the time of the Great Bear and Wolf War."

Vard's cheeks burned as if he could barely tolerate the jarl's insults. Eakthr giggled and hopped in place while Athna's face darkened and firelight shone from her fingertips.

"Then let there be new ways," Belfedrn said. Gron's insults were nothing more than wind compared to what the Sea Serpents had served them. "We have not come to fight or trade insults. I am Belfedrn, the second of the pack, and I assure you that I can pick up the scent of any giant and track him to his den."

"Unless his only smell is of ice and snow," Gron replied. "That is all this one leaves behind."

"I will smell more." Belfedrn stiffened as determination swelled like a river within him. A hint of doubt muddied that water, but he ignored it. "Or you can have me as a thrall. I *will* hunt down this jötunn."

50

MÄRREN

MÄRREN FELL INTO LINE BEHIND SO MANY OTHERS WHO WORE IRON collars and scooped up slop that was supposed to be oats, quickly slurping it off their fingers. Uisge took a spot behind her with the rest of the captives who had been with them in the caravan.

"Aye, you there," someone within a local group of thralls said. A hulking man with muscles bulging atop his shoulders stalked toward them, his scalp shaven. "You're new here." He sniffed and tilted his head, his neck popping. "And you smell like ripe shite. You've had latrine duty. Get the fuck out of here. Wash yourselves, and maybe then you can return for any dregs that're left over."

The other captives cowered and backed away, but Märren did not budge. The thrall maneuvered around the table holding the food and approached her. She ignored him, and he grabbed her by the hair, her scalp burning like fire as he yanked her back and hurled her to the ground. She hit the dirt with a thud but did not cry out, the voices in her head taking on a distorted waver and ringing. Uisge snarled, and the thrall turned, towering over her companion, making Märren realize just how small of a man Uisge was—shorter than her and no broader.

"Get out!" The thrall pointed at one of the entryways to the roofed area they stood under. He shoved Uisge so hard that Uisge sailed backward and hit a wall.

"This leader of the slaves senses that she's different and not worth as much as the rest of them." The slits between scales on the dragon's neck lit up with firelight.

"She's nothing. At least the Wolves tolerated her because she's of their blood, but no one else will." The wolf paced around in Märren's mind, his head hanging as he licked his lips.

"She has a purpose, and she's done more than anyone could ask trying to achieve it." The silhouette of the child ran around a tree. In Märren's thoughts, a row of wicked runes on her ankle glistened.

Märren slowly climbed to her feet as the angry thrall loomed over her, and she shuffled outside and found an area with buckets of water. Uisge joined her, limping, their fellow captives already at work scrubbing themselves. Uisge picked up a bucket and emptied it on his head, dowsing himself while fully dressed and reveling in the bath. Märren shivered with cold as she stripped off her leathers and then her undergarments. It would not be wise to wear wet clothes for hours. Not this far north.

Uisge continued washing himself with bucket after bucket, watching Märren as her arse and small breasts were revealed but then taking less notice of her than the water he was bathing in. Märren dumped a bucket on herself. The water hit her like a cold fist, stealing her breath. She quickly followed it with two more, rinsing until her hair was bronze again and then wiping around her thrall collar. She dressed in her undergarments and scrubbed her pelt, leathers, and Eimri's pouch until they were clean.

"I cannot defeat such a man," Uisge said, jerking an elbow in the direction of the thrall feeding area. "I'm small and not a powerful creature. Not when I am out of my element."

"But in water, you're strong."

He shrugged. "I'm deceitful. That's really my greatest asset. It'd be best to avoid him."

Märren caught sight of another man watching her from a distance. It was Yrstl, the Dragon warrior who had spoken to her at the latrine and rinsed her bloodied hands with vinegar. The warrior quickly glanced away, attempting to make it seem like he had not been interested in her bath.

Once she was fully dressed, she headed back toward the roofed area. Uisge strode past her and under the shelter. From the shadows of a corner, the hulking thrall stared at her as he chomped his oats.

"Now you don't stink, whore," the thrall said as Märren hurried by, "and the show wasn't too bad either. Not great, but not bad."

She and Uisge waited at the end of the thrall food line and had to use their fingers to scrape enough gruel together for a few mouthfuls. Uisge offered his clumps to Märren.

"You have to eat too," she said.

"I don't eat this shite," Uisge replied.

She glanced at her scarred wrist. "I won't be able to feed you here. Not until nighttime, anyway."

"Then eat as much of this crap as you can." Uisge dumped what he had managed to roll together into her palm, and she wolfed it down.

"She'll never be able to feed the uisge and perform all the work of a thrall."

"Neither of them will hold up."

"Uisge will aid her, and she will feed Uisge."

"Megtr, stop!" Yrstl stood at an entryway to the shelter along with a score of Dragon soldiers, shouting at the hulking thrall, who was shoving a smaller man around and leering at him. "It's time to begin your work."

Megtr shoved the man over and shrugged before following the other thralls out into the city. The morning air was so cold it was brittle, with snow sifting down from the clouds. Märren trailed the thralls through the city where karls stacked sacks of food and sold weapons and tools. The soldiers divided up the thralls and led each group in different directions. Yrstl led Märren and Uisge's group to the walls where piles of boulders were stacked.

"The smiths are here." Yrstl pointed to several karls holding hammers and chisels. They worked at stones, shaping and then fitting them into crumbling sections of the walls. "This day, you'll be assisting them."

Yrstl stepped out of the way and allowed the thralls to shuffle forward and begin hefting rocks and rolling boulders. The smiths directed them and gave them mauls and picks to break the boulders into smaller, workable pieces. Märren and Uisge took turns hammering away at a stone. When Märren struck it, the maul's shaft vibrated and stung her raw hands. They worked for hours, and Märren sank into her own head. The sun climbed and then fell across the sky before Yrstl passed by again. He paused and approached Märren.

"Your hands aren't bleeding too badly?" He grabbed Märren's wrists and turned her hands over, inspecting the bandages he had placed. Blood seeped through the wraps. "Come with me. We must change these, or tomorrow, you won't be able to hold anything."

Uisge cast her a wary look, and Märren hesitated.

"Come." Yrstl tugged her away and led her to a covered area with benches. He unwrapped her bandages, taking care to peel them slowly from her palms. Fibers stuck to her blisters, her skin red and weeping bloody fluid, everything stained with vinegar. "This looks terrible. We'll use water this time."

He motioned to a bucket sitting near their bench, and after Märren washed her hands in its water, Yrstl unwound more bandage material and began wrapping her palms.

"You'll retire to the thralls' quarters and rest," Yrstl said, "you and your comrades who arrived last night, though they don't work as hard as you. I'll pretend they earned it."

"Thank you, warrior." Märren looked up at him, searching his face for signs of treachery, sexual interest, or some other motive. He avoided eye contact. "If all the thralls here are destined to be sacrifices, why do they work so hard?"

His lips thinned. "They don't have much of a choice. Work or the whip. But not all of them will be sacrificed. At each waking of the giant, straws are drawn. Only a few thralls are taken each time."

"Me and those who arrived with me are destined to be next."

He nodded. "So I've heard. Do you intend to run? Or resist? Because neither will save you."

"I intend to release the dragons."

He chuckled, then paused and studied her. "You are mad."

"So I've been told."

He swallowed, his eyes closing, his voice barely a whisper. "I *knew* it. From the moment I first saw you working in the latrines. My sister carries the darkness of the mind."

Another? "And where is she?"

He hesitated. "Dead."

"Oh. I'm sorry for your loss." *He said 'carries.'*

"She died not long after the darkness began. It took hold of her, and she couldn't care for herself. No one else could, either. These lands are too harsh for anyone who requires a caretaker. Everyone must fend for themselves and Torank. There is no other way. It's for the best."

Märren bit her lip.

"She should die like this man's sister."

"She should've died when the darkness first claimed her."

"Your threats wound her, but she presses on through all of them."

"Do I remind you of her?" Märren asked.

Yrstl's gaze ran across her face and hair. "In some ways. In others, not at all."

"Then—"

"Go," he said. "Back to the thralls' quarters. Sleep. And take your companions with you."

51

BELFEDRN

The Ulfhednar stalked around what was left of the Bear village. Nothing was burned, but the houses had been smashed to splinters, everything flattened. Thelira and Dradn accompanied Belfedrn, Thelira having rejoined the pack after they exited Jarl Gron's longhouse. After an hour, the siblings wandered off, searching other areas.

"Can you pick up its scent?" Aegmor asked, walking beside Belfedrn, the Bear berserker's rage barely contained, the whites of his eyes streaked with red vessels.

"There isn't anything obvious." Belfedrn sniffed the air and around the remains. There were no bodies anywhere.

"Well, this is the most recent site of the jötunn's destruction," Aegmor said. "You won't find a fresher scene, and if you cannot track him, all of us"—he gestured at the score of Bear berserkers and three times as many warriors waiting around the village—"will kill you Ulfhednar. To do so won't be without honor. You swore you could find us the giant."

"I cannot detect anything," Vard said to the Bear jarl who stood nearby, "but Belfedrn has the keenest Wolf's nose."

"This jötunn masks his scent well." Belfedrn paced about. "But give me a bit more time before you raise your weapons."

"Whose idea was it to make the tall skinny one our second?" Kesg asked. "His promises are going to get us killed."

The other Ulfhednar dispersed, their noses working, ears listening. Athna and Eakthr circled the area, searching but probably realizing this errand would not be as simple as they had hoped. Belfedrn prayed to Fenrir's remains that he would detect something. Anything.

Another hour passed, and the Bears grew restless and paced about, grumbling to each other.

"This giant hides himself well," Belfedrn said. "Nearly as well as Sea Serpent magic can conceal a troll's scent. But there's a small tell here." He stood near the outskirts of the village and stared into an old forest, waving his hand through the air to bring more of the peculiarity to his nose. "A particle of something is off amid the ice and snow and overpowering fragrance of the woods. I believe it's frost, but not Midgard's. It must've come from Jötunheim."

Vard hurried over and sniffed but shook his head. "I hope you're right. I cannot detect a thing."

"It's here." Belfedrn pointed into the trees. "And it leads that way."

"I don't think I would have noticed," Eakthr said and giggled, high stepping in glee, "but now, I smell it too. It's an inconsistency in the snow, but only with one flake in every tens of thousands."

Vard shrugged. "Then we hunt. For the Wolves!" He stepped toward the forest.

"Not so fast." Gron gripped his shoulder and held the Ulfhednar jarl still as easily as Belfedrn might hold back a child. "I've noticed that two of yours don't wear the full pelt." He nodded in Dradn and Thelira's direction. "They're not Ulfhednar."

"We've taken two of our surviving warriors into training," Vard replied.

"But they are not berserkers." Gron gestured at his three score of warriors. "We have brought warriors as well, but even I know the pack of Fenrir is only as strong as its weakest. These two will get your pack killed. Against this jötunn, we need everyone at their fullest strength, except for those who'll endanger the others."

"Then you'd have these two remain behind?" Belfedrn asked, initially relieved by the suggestion, although his emotions quickly shifted. Leaving Dradn and Thelira alone in an area where a veiled jötunn roamed terrified him.

"Aye."

"I won't stay behind." Thelira marched up to them. "I am an Ulfhednar. You said so yourself, Jarl." She glared at Vard.

"As family," Vard replied, "but not in ability."

"I'm coming as well." Dradn joined them. "For the Wolves. I am one of you."

"Not without a full pelt, you aren't," Vard said. "You are companions of the pack, but neither of you are a berserker. You're not pack members."

"I'll follow you anyway," Thelira said.

"I won't allow it." Gron's voice was deep and carried an edge of finality. "Not in my lands. If you do, my berserkers will slay you. You stay behind."

A moment of tense silence settled over them.

"There's a way for at least one of..." Belfedrn suddenly stopped, afraid that what he was thinking could turn for the worse.

"What is it?" Vard asked.

Belfedrn refused to answer.

"Tell me," Vard demanded. "Now."

Belfedrn swallowed a lump and turned away. "I carry an additional full pelt. I don't wear it, but it's in my pack. It was meant for my cousin, but she refused the Ulfhednar's call. Before the troll encounters, I left it for her and then found it at her hut when I went to check on her after. She was not there."

Vard looked between Thelira and Dradn. "One last pelt of Fenrir, then. One last Wolf berserker—if either of you are worthy."

"I cannot allow this," Belfedrn said.

"They will duel." Vard clenched his spear. "It's the way of the pack. You cannot shelter them simply because you've come to think of them as your young."

Remorse pulled Belfedrn's eyes shut. He had known this would eventually happen, ever since he had taken that damn pelt. But how could he have left the last remnant of Fenrir behind? *Curse all the old gods, the dead beast gods, and this land.*

"Both of you have already traveled to the Wolf's den," Vard said to Dradn and Thelira. "You are warriors of the Wolf. That is a mighty accomplishment. One to be proud of. There is no dishonor to be had here, but there will be a chance for one of you to gain the highest of distinctions."

Thelira faced her jarl, pride welling in her eyes. Dradn did the same, standing a little shorter than his sister.

Belfedrn cursed the gods again and paced before the two, understanding his duty as second of the pack. He had to initiate the ritual. "Which of you has obtained the ears of the Wolf from Fenrir's den?"

"I," they both answered.

"Which of you has obtained the eyes of the Wolf to see in darkness?"

"I," they both said again in unison.

"The nose of the Wolf to detect all smells?"

"I."

Both of them still. But these first questions were merely formality, a ceremony harkening back to the old ways. "The paws of the Wolf for stealth and agility?"

"I."

"The call of the Wolf to communicate with the pack?"

"I."

There was one last question. The only one that mattered. To determine if any warrior could—after years of harsh training and discipline to the pack—become an Ulfhednar. "Which of you has obtained the rune of the pack so that you can become one of its members and grow stronger together?"

"I," they both said.

Belfedrn's eyes shut again.

"Then a duel it is," Vard said. "What will be your weapons?"

"Thelira can wear the full pelt," Dradn said. "She deserves to become Ulfhednar."

"Nay, boy," Vard barked at him, making Dradn cower in surprise. "To best complement the pack, the better of you must wear it. Kindness and generosity are admirable traits, but the Ulfhednar cannot choose its members based on these, nor on an opinion offered by someone outside the pack. Such graciousness is reserved for karls and kinder, better folk than we'll ever be. We must battle in this world the gods left us, and these lands are not a kind mistress."

"I'll wield the bow," Thelira said. "And axe."

"And you?" Vard asked Dradn.

"The shield and spear. And seax."

Vard clasped each of their shoulders. "Then both of you are already armed. Take your positions."

Thelira faced Dradn, backing away as Dradn did likewise, a look of hostility and determination etched into Thelira's expression. Dradn's demeanor was more apprehensive as sweat beaded on his forehead.

"Now," Vard continued, "as in the ways of the old gods and those who are dead, I must state that if I believe either of you take it easy on the other because you wish for your sibling to be victorious, you'll both lose favor with the Ulfhednar. You cannot give less of yourself even for those you love. The pack would be weaker because of it, and you'll both be stripped of your warrior's furs."

Dradn's jaw clenched.

"Now—to first blood," Vard said. "This cannot be any simple scrape, but pray it isn't a death wound either. Trust in the strength of your opponent to defend themself. Hold nothing back. Glory and honor await only one of you. Fight!"

More than a few of the Bears approached and hollered with excitement as the Ulfhednar silently formed a circle around the combatants. Thelira nocked an arrow, dancing and weaving about, hunting for an opening in Dradn's shield defense. Dradn stalked her, trying to close the distance between them without exposing himself and while keeping an eye on where she was aiming.

Thelira loosed. Her arrow whistled across the short distance, ramming into Dradn's shield with a thud. The arrow pierced his shield, its broadhead sticking through the inner surface and angled toward his head, although it did not nick his flesh. Dradn stumbled and nearly fell, the reality of the situation and how dangerous it was, including how dedicated Thelira had become, dawning on him.

Dradn quickly recovered and made a mad dash for Thelira as she nocked another arrow. At the last moment, he pulled his shield to the side and thrust his spear at her. Thelira threw herself out of the spear's path and loosed. She tumbled into the snow, barely avoiding the blow. Her arrow streaked past the edge of Dradn's shield, flying wide but slicing his shoulder as it passed. Dradn grunted and glanced at his wound. Blood welled from beneath his fur. Somewhere nearby, Kesg gasped.

"A grazing blow," Vard said. "Not enough to drop a child of the Stag. Continue."

Dradn snarled and reared back, hurling his spear at his sister. She ducked and sank deeper into the accumulation, disappearing in the white. The spear buzzed as it flew toward her location, the sound ending abruptly as the weapon pierced snow and ice and thudded against something hard, its haft thrumming.

Belfedrn suppressed a gasp and stopped himself from running to Thelira. Athna placed a hand on his arm and said, "She'll be fine. You've trained them well. At least in the short time you've had."

"And they were already warriors," Belfedrn muttered, attempting to reassure himself. *But she bears no shield.*

Dradn ripped his seax from his belt and approached warily, his voice tense when he spoke. "Thelira? Are you injured?" He kicked through the snow she had ducked into, which rose above his knees.

Nothing moved.

He couldn't have killed her instantly... It would've had to have been a perfect throw at her heart or throat while she was concealed.

Off to the side from where Dradn was focusing his attention, the snow erupted, and Thelira's torso popped up, her fur and helm covered in white. She loosed almost immediately but hesitated for an instant while adjusting her aim. Dradn stood frozen in shock as her projectile hurtled toward him, tearing a chunk of muscle from the side of his neck. Blood spewed in the arrow's wake.

Fuck.

Dradn dropped his seax and grabbed at his wound. Thelira

pounced on him, drawing her axe and knocking him over backward, landing on top of him and ramming the blade of her weapon against his *brynja*, directly over his heart. She then snapped her axe up against his throat, her eyes wild with the hunt.

"Halt!" Vard shouted, raising his hands. "The last arrow shot was a killing blow if I've ever seen one." He pulled Thelira off Dradn and grasped the young man by the wrist, heaving him up. "You're lucky she's your sister and a forgiving warrior. Not all Wolves are so kind when their opponent stands frozen before them."

Vard removed Dradn's hand from his wound and inspected it as Belfedrn rushed over, trying to mask his concern.

"He'll be fine," Vard said. "But not because he defended himself well."

Dradn's head and shoulders slumped in shame. His shield fell from his grip and sank into the snow. Belfedrn removed a roll of bandage material from his pack and began wrapping the young warrior's neck.

"You cannot allow yourself to be taken by surprise." Belfedrn shook his head, anger and sadness pouring through him. "Not ever. You would've been killed."

52

CAËTIN

THE ROAD IN THE AREA AROUND WHERE HALVI DIED WAS A SMEAR of footprints and mud. Caëtin paced about, cursing the dead gods, wishing all of them had buggered the Spider before it too had perished. Huginn hopped about on the street, pecking at things here and there.

"We could try to find someone who goes by the name of the Axe," Hildm said, her voice barely a whisper. "That's the name Halvi mentioned before he died."

Caëtin paused, recalling the words, unsure if such a nickname would help them.

Sanre crouched, wiping at the wall and inspecting something before sighing and standing. "We don't have anything else to go on."

"If I don't want to hear that it's impossible, how likely is it that you could find all the people in or around Aonark who call themselves the Axe?" Caëtin asked.

Sanre's lips pulled to one side in thought. "I'll send a few soldiers and warriors deep into the city. To ask around. Maybe someone's heard something. There can't be too many self-proclaimed tough bastards who think they deserve that title. But if there are, we'll know soon enough. I don't think any of the hundreds of fighters who carry an axe would go by that, or they'd never know when someone was referring to them." She paused. "I'll choose soldiers who can blend in with the karls of Aonark, and warriors carrying parts of Muninn will demand respect."

"Do it." Caëtin continued her search for anything as Sanre burst into ravens and flew away.

Whoever killed Halvi and took Darstrid's feathers left nothing behind, not even a remnant of the feather the boy must have been given to ease his addiction. Caëtin retraced the path Halvi would have fled along, making for the site where Darstrid died. Hildm quietly followed. Huginn was much louder but also came along. Once they arrived at the location, Caëtin bowed her head, paying reverence to the earth here, her thoughts turbulent. The area was so plain. So simple. Not the site where someone who was a member of the Knights Black *and* a battle Seidr of the Raven should have fallen.

Hours passed as she hunted about and Hildm inspected several crates as well as the ground and walls around them.

An unkindness cawed and swirled into the alleyway, their cries ear-splitting before they merged into Sanre, and she said, "The day grows late."

Caëtin grumbled. "I'd like a shred of evidence before I fly south to stop Taknhal's army, accuse him of murder, and kill him."

"He had the most to gain with Darstrid's death."

"But he may not be a complete fool. He probably had someone else interact with Halvi and pass a feather along to him. I need to find this person and get their confession." Accusing someone of being the smuggler or their accomplice and bringing them to the Raven's bridge to sign a confession would serve a purpose, but the irony of the idea and how Caëtin detested such acts was not lost on her.

"Sanre." A man rushed toward the knight, his worn cloak flapping open and revealing twin axes at his belt.

One of the soldiers Sanre sent into the city.

Sanre and the soldier discussed something quietly before Sanre faced Caëtin and said, "A man who uses the name 'the Axe' has purportedly frequented an establishment called the Tainted Feather. It's beyond the walls, in the lower city."

"A tavern?"

"A whorehouse."

"Huh. Never heard of it."

Sanre raised an eyebrow at Caëtin, probably unsure if her manner was facetious, and slipped the soldier a few coins. "I'll take you."

The soldier departed as Sanre led Caëtin, Huginn, and Hildm away, making sure to take a route that would not pass by Muninn's temple and reveal to Hildm what they were doing to conceal it.

"Should I be surprised that you know where the Tainted Feather is?" Caëtin asked.

Sanre cast her a pinched look full of offense. "Do you believe I'm so unattractive that I'd need to pay men to hump me?"

"If anything, I was assuming you went there to make some extra coin. A knight's wages aren't as good as they used to be."

Sanre shook her head and paced on. They wound through rain-muddied streets where karls and thralls worked to reinforce the ground.

When they reached the southern gates, Caëtin flashed her pale sword with its feather, and to the soldiers there, said, "We need to pass into the lower city. Now."

After realizing who she was, the soldiers scrambled about and opened a man-sized gate within the larger city gates. Sanre slipped through, leading the rest of them out of Aonark. They traversed many streets and descended a hillside facing west, where a hint of sea stench rode in on the wind.

Signs rattled on posts, and firelight streamed through cracks around doorways, the houses here having fallen into disrepair more so than in the parts of the city where Caëtin typically resided. Ahead, two men muttered to each other. They stumbled as they walked, both of them holding horns, their breaths rank with drink even from a distance.

"The Tainted Feather?" Sanre asked as she approached the men.

One of them brushed greasy hair out of his face and leered at her, grinning. Sanre pushed back her Raven's cloak, revealing her feather and axe. The man's grin fell flat. The other pointed down a cross street. Sanre veered in that direction, and Caëtin glared at the men as she and Hildm passed, wondering if they were karls who were not helping to strengthen their city or if they were of noble blood and thought such work was beneath them.

Sanre stopped outside a longhouse with a faded sign. At one time, runes had probably spelled out the Tainted Feather, but the markings had worn thin and were barely discernible in the wood. Sanre shoved on the door, which opened easily. She stepped inside, and Caëtin and Hildm followed.

Portions of the hall were curtained off with thin fabrics that could be seen through with the torchlight burning behind them. Beyond the curtains, lone figures sat on beds. Only an area near the far end of the hall seemed to be occupied by more than one person, given the groans and rhythmic pounding arising from there. At least most of the Raven people were out in the city trying to do what they could to save Aonark.

A woman in a draping shawl sashayed toward them. "How may I help you women?" Curiosity pitched her tone.

Caëtin stepped forward and jingled her purse. "I'm looking for someone."

"I am Vrithn," the woman said. She was thin and looked like she had seen fifty winters. "Many someones enter these doors, but they often leave their names and identities outside."

"This is important. It involves Aonark's safety."

"I see."

"Have you had a patron who calls himself the Axe?"

Vrithn cocked her head and placed a long finger against her chin, her eyes focusing on something near the ceiling. "Men often use the same names here. Strong names."

Caëtin pulled two silvers from her coin pouch and offered them to the woman.

Vrithn moved to take them but hesitated. "Who's asking?"

"Two of the Knights Black." Caëtin opened her cloak to display her feathers and blade.

The woman gawked and reached out. "Are those truly Muninn's feathers?"

Caëtin stepped back. "Aye. Do not touch them."

Vrithn snatched her hand back. "I meant no offense. I've just never seen the remains of Muninn before." She did not blink. "Now I understand what people mean when they say you can feel the feathers when they're nearby."

"Believe me," Caëtin said, "there's a steep price for carrying the parts of a god. We won't live as long as you."

The woman smirked.

"You should accept my coin and tell us all you know," Caëtin continued. "I need to find the Axe, and I'll do whatever is necessary to learn of his whereabouts. Time is running short."

The woman swallowed and grabbed the silvers. "There's a man who frequents my establishment who calls himself that. But I warn you, you may not like what you find, and I'd appreciate it if you never mentioned my name or that you were here."

Does that mean that Taknhal did not have an accomplice and it was all his doing? "I'll mention no names, and the sooner I know what you do, the sooner we'll leave." Caëtin paused. "Do you know the Axe's true name?"

"Nay. I've no interest in names. Only coin. But I'd be able to recognize him."

"Is he in that last stall there?" Caëtin indicated the thumping and moaning.

"He's not here."

Because he traveled south... "Do you know where he is?"

She shook her head. "But at night, he also frequents another establishment that's not far from here." Vrithn pointed southwest. "The Whispering Beak."

"Another whorehouse?"

"A tavern."

"Finally, a tavern. If the Axe shows himself here again, I trust that you will immediately send word to Caëtin of Muninn and no other."

The woman's lips thinned. "I'll send a runner to Aonark's great hall."

"And make sure they only speak with me."

Vrithn dipped her head. "Of course." She gave Caëtin directions to the tavern.

Caëtin exited the longhouse and strode through hissing rain, Sanre at her heels and Hildm close behind. They wound along a couple streets, most of which were empty except for an occasional passerby who hurried through the night. Beside them, the Vkum River snaked through the city, the rain turning its surface into a torrent of ripples and fragmented moonlight. Caëtin led the others to one of the only bridges in the area and crossed to the other side of the Vkum.

"There." Sanre pointed to a longhouse with a sunken roof. Firelight shone dimly through gaps in its walls.

Caëtin tried its door, which opened. Inside, a few men sat at tables under shadow, drinking. No laughter or conversations carried, the only sound, the clanking of horns being set on tables. A serving man and woman roamed about, horns in hand while wiping down tables with greasy rags.

"Take a seat." The serving man motioned to a dark corner. "We're nearly empty this night. Too much work and fear running about Aonark. Especially in the lower city." He looked Caëtin up and down, probably noticing by her cloak that she was not from near here. "They say if any part of the city is to be sacrificed to the Spider, it'll be ours. Fodder and all that."

"If the Spiders come to Aonark, the people of the lower city will be brought into the fortified portion of Aonark, and if the walls are breached, everyone's lives will be at risk."

"But the best protected places will be the great hall and Muninn's temple. Then the areas around them. The people of the lower city won't be housed there."

I can't argue with that. "We'll take two meads." Caëtin headed for the table and took a seat. Sanre and Hildm joined her.

They waited until the servant returned carrying horns, and Caëtin slid two silver coins across the table.

"A copper will cover the first round," he said, although his fingers quivered.

"This is for information," Caëtin said in a low tone. "I need to know about someone who comes in here."

The man tensed, and he set down the horns, spilling liquid over their lips before raking his fingers through his beard. "Who?"

"A man who calls himself the Axe."

The servant pursed his lips. "Aye. He comes here often. I don't know much about him though. Other than he drinks until he's piss drunk, always tries to fight someone, and sometimes stumbles out of here before he collapses. When he can't manage that, we have to drag him out into the street."

Then it probably isn't Taknhal. He's often in the same state but in the great hall. "Do you know his name?"

The servant shook his head. "He just likes people to call him the Axe."

"Where does he live?"

"Somewhere around here I suppose, though I don't know."

Caëtin took one of the coins back. "That was hardly worth two silvers."

The servant stuttered, "I-I... that's all I know. I could tell you a lie to get the other, but once you figured out what I'd done, you'd come back here and gut me."

"True enough." Caëtin passed him the second silver, and he scooped both of them up and whisked away.

"Now what?" Sanre drank and wiped at her mouth with the stump of her forearm.

Caëtin sighed and sipped at her mead, its sweetness heavy on her tongue. Not close to the best mead she had tasted, but not terrible. A man in a torn tunic emerged from the shadows nearby, and he sat down at the far end of their table, furtively glancing about.

"Name's Kruh," he said, his drink-soaked breath stinging Caëtin's eyes. He was thin and haggard, and the dim light made it difficult to determine his age, but he had to have been nearing sixty winters. "I know the Axe."

Caëtin leaned closer. "You do?"

"Indeed."

"And?"

"And you got any more coin?"

Caëtin pulled a few silvers from her pouch, laying them on the table before her. She pressed a finger down on one coin. "I'll only give this for information that will aid us."

"Oh, I have that and more."

Caëtin slid one coin over.

Kruh took it, his eyes shining as he did so. "We grew up together, the Axe and me. His name's Brooth."

"Where is he?"

"Haven't seen him here or at the Tainted Feather for a bit." Kruh eyed the rest of the coins.

Caëtin pushed one more across the table. "Then where would he be?"

"If he ain't here or at the Tainted Feather, he's probably passed out or with a new woman. And both of those situations would mean he's probably at his house."

"Where does he live?"

Kruh hesitated. Caëtin passed over another coin.

"I can offer directions, but I won't take you there," Kruh said. "The Axe will kill me if he finds out that I told a soldier anything about him."

Caëtin scooted closer to him. "If you're lying, and you send us somewhere just to get a few coin to spend on whores and drink, I'll find you and carve their worth out of your belly."

Kruh startled, but he recovered quickly, his head wobbling when he spoke. "No need for that." He quickly explained where they could find the Axe's house. It was not far.

"You know anything else about him?"

"We grew up together." Kruh smirked. "The damn lot of us always wanted to become berserkers—or I guess they're called knights and rangers these days. At the least, we wanted to be warriors. To carry the remains of Muninn. Never could though. Me and the Axe always had to settle for mercenary work, use our brute strength and all that."

"If you couldn't bear part of Muninn, you still could have become soldiers."

He chuckled. "Nah. Got to get up too early for that, and

getting up early when there's still drink in your head is the shites."

"Thank you for the conversation." Caëtin stood.

"There was only one of our lot who made it far," Kruh said offhandedly.

Caëtin's interest sparked. "And who was that?"

Kruh scratched at his bald scalp, his face wrinkling with confusion. "One of the boys when we was young. Always went by Hairchest, but that wasn't his real name." He shook his head. "I can't remember much about him. He left decades ago and hasn't come back since."

"Did he know the Axe?"

"Sure. He knew all of us when we was young."

"Was his real name Taknhal?" Sanre blurted.

Kruh's eyes widened for an instant and then narrowed. "That sounds familiar, but I ain't sure that's it."

"If you remember, let us know," Caëtin said. "There'll be more coin in it for you." She passed over two more silvers, downed her mead, and departed.

53

BELFEDRN

Thelira knelt before Belfedrn, the shield she now carried emblazoned with the open-mouthed wolf heads of the Ulfhednar. Belfedrn pulled the pelt meant for Märren from his pack, unrolling it with a flick of his wrists, its power humming in the air around them. The small scrap he had stolen from the sanctuary flung out with it.

Vard bent over and picked up the strip between his fingers, studying it. "What is this?"

"Maybe the last shred of Fenrir," Belfedrn said, snatching it back and stuffing it into his pouch.

"There's still power in it." He studied Belfedrn with curiosity. "It hasn't been desecrated."

"It's barely a sliver."

Vard grunted before shifting interest to more pressing events, although he would not forget.

Belfedrn faced Thelira, gathering his thoughts and dismissing his worries over being found out as a thief. For now. "You kneel as a warrior of Fenrir." His voice became so thick with emotion—pride for Thelira and remorse for Dradn—that it choked his words. He draped the pelt over Thelira's head and shoulders, and she gasped and shuddered before falling still. Its power would be surging through her, a feeling unlike anything she had experienced before. "And as you did with the warrior's square of his hide, take Fenrir into your body. The Wolf's den is already behind you—conqueror of other realms. Rise before me."

Belfedrn stepped back as Thelira stood, draped in her new pelt, head bowed. The Ulfhednar banged spears against shields, chanting in the old tongue. The old words meaning "for the Wolves" echoed and rolled through the empty village like ghosts.

"Welcome to the pack, Ulfhednar." Vard strode forward and placed his palms on either side of Thelira's shoulders. "I know you will strengthen us and make us proud. Do not worry that you were invited so quickly. Your place is well deserved."

Thelira nodded and pushed back the hood of her new pelt, gazing at the jarl and then the pack members around her while Dradn stood behind the Ulfhednar circle, his shoulders sagging. Thelira took up the shield with wolf heads.

"All right," Gron said. "Enough of the bullshit formalities. She's an Ulfhednar. Now let's track the jötunn."

The pack pressed together, and Thelira started to ravenously devour meats from her pack.

"Before arriving here, we also sought the aid of the Boar people," Vard said. "We should send for them."

"I've already sent messengers," Gron snapped. "If those frolicking Boar fucks can ever tear themselves away from their music and drunken stupors, they could aid us, but I won't wait for that fateful day. We'd all likely die of old age before then. We move onward, but that boy warrior stays behind." He pointed at Dradn in disgust and then eyed Belfedrn. "We can't have him getting himself and another of you killed because you feel obligated to protect him."

"I ask that we may leave him at your village," Belfedrn said. "The pack cannot abandon its young in an area a giant recently attacked."

"Belfedrn." Vard gripped his shoulder. "We hunt."

"Only I can follow this giant's scent." Belfedrn shook off his grip. "And I won't hunt until Dradn is safe with the Bear people."

"You would defy my order?" Vard stepped closer, glaring at Belfedrn, challenging him like an alpha wolf.

"I would." Belfedrn met his gaze. "For this."

"Aye." Vard backed down. "I understand. For our young."

"We don't have time for foolish coddling," Gron said. "I won't allow it."

"Then take your Bear berserkers and warriors in the direction I showed you," Belfedrn said. "I'll run back with Dradn and return soon."

Belfedrn moved toward Dradn without awaiting an answer. Gron grumbled and ordered his warriors out into the woods. Belfedrn inspected the bloodied bandage on Dradn's neck and tugged him away.

"We must run like hunting wolves," Belfedrn said.

"Leave me here," Dradn replied. "I don't care if I die fighting a giant alone. At least it would restore my honor."

"Don't be a fool!" Belfedrn shook him. "You are a Wolf warrior. The last of your kind. That is something to be proud of, but if you're ashamed of it, I'll lash you myself. One day, we may find more of Fenrir's remains, and if not, a pack member will die. Given what we're about to do, this may happen sooner rather than later, and if one of the pelts of the dead is not desecrated, it'll be passed on. Either to you—if you're deserving—or to another who is powerful enough to carry two."

"I don't deserve a pelt."

"Then one who is able will take up a second. I'd prefer that to a downtrodden boy bearing something he doesn't believe he's earned." Belfedrn shook him again. "Now come."

Someone behind Belfedrn cleared their throat, and Thelira's scent came from that direction. She stepped forward, swallowing a lump of meat, head bowed as she placed her forehead against her brother's.

"Take heart, Brother," she said. "I used trickery to defeat you. You'll never let that happen again. Not ever." She squeezed the unwounded side of his neck. "One day, you'll be in the pack by my side, but until then, take this." She slipped her small warrior's square of pelt over her neck and placed it around his. "Now you command two squares, and not only when we're training. You can slowly grow accustomed to more power. It may be better this way. Mine"—she shook out her arms—"is invigorating but overwhelming."

"Aye, Sister." Dradn squeezed her neck in return. "If I am ever to lose in combat, I pray it will only be to you."

Thelira kissed his forehead and wheeled about before jogging toward the pack.

Belfedrn tugged Dradn along, and they loped away, bounding over the snow like wolves. They ran for Gron's village, their lungs burning. When they reached its outskirts, the karls and a couple warriors there caught sight of them and approached.

"He is to remain in the safety of your people until we return with the frost giant's head," Belfedrn said.

The closest Bear warrior, who also had a tattooed face, grinned. "May the spirit of the Björn guide you. We'll watch over your young."

"Then I'm grateful to you and your people." Belfedrn bowed to the warriors, shoved Dradn toward them, and bounded away.

It was not long before Belfedrn arrived at the edge of the

forest where he had scented the giant's trail. Within the trees, the Ulfhednar's path was difficult to identify, but the Bear warriors and berserkers left not only a swath of crushed snow but also mangled vegetation. Belfedrn sniffed as he followed the Bear's trail, searching for the subtle scent he had detected prior —almost more of a feeling than a smell. Soon, he came upon the Bear warriors and ran past them.

"The one with the nose has returned," Aegmor said.

Gron huffed. "And sooner than I thought possible."

Belfedrn passed the berserkers and found his pack, who were in the lead but had stopped. Eakthr stood upon a precipice overlooking a cliff and ravine. Far below, a river rushed through rock and ice.

"I've lost whatever I was following." Eakthr rubbed vigorously at his head and flicked his nose.

Athna said, "Well, thankfully, Belfedrn has returned."

Eakthr studied him with a pained squint and waved him forward. "Can you smell anything?"

"I sure as shite cannot." Kesg paced about.

"You can't smell your own arsehole when you're licking your hindquarters," Belfedrn said.

"Don't judge me"—Kesg's nostrils flared as he sniffed about —"or the methods I use to keep myself sanitary. I do what I must for Ylsga. And maybe it's because my arsehole has no scent."

Ylsga shook her head.

Belfedrn stepped onto the precipice, inhaling a gentle wind as snowflakes floated by. A sense of calm and peace should have suffused these woods, but an underlying dread lingered. He walked along the edge, crouching and then standing on his toes, sniffing at trunks and needles. The Ulfhednar waited on him as the Bears caught up with the pack.

"It's here." Belfedrn pointed down the cliff. "Leading that way."

"How do you expect us to climb down that?" Kesg asked, shaking his head.

"With this." Ylsga drew coiled rope from her pack and slapped Kesg on the back with it before turning to the Ulfhednar. "Gather all the rope we carry and tie it together. We scale downward."

"Wolf people aren't built for climbing or rappelling down cliffs." Athna looked over the precipice.

"Bears should be better equipped than wolves for this sort of thing," Eakthr said, wrinkling his nose.

The rest of the Ulfhednar moved quickly, knotting their short ropes and cinching one end around a boulder. The Bears joined them and offered much longer ropes. Once they finished tying them together and anchoring them, Athna tugged on one, testing it as she bit her lip with apprehension.

"Down you go." Gron waved his warriors onward.

The Bear warriors stowed their weapons on their bodies and slowly descended, using their legs against the cliff face as they eased the rope around their waists and through their hands, their bulk moving slowly but steadily downward. Their berserkers followed their warriors, and soon, it was the Ulfhednar's turn to descend.

Belfedrn attached his shield to a strap on his back, tucked his spear through it, and studied the descent. He followed Thelira, who moved quickly, keen to test her newfound abilities. Her passion combined with this venture could prove dangerous, far more so than any danger awaiting Dradn. Belfedrn used his feet to walk down the cliff, searching out footholds as he slowly eased his grip along the rope. Vard followed him, moving even slower.

Once the Bears were halfway down, they grew braver, kicking away from the cliff and rappelling, dropping swiftly. Thelira watched them before mimicking their movements and plunging after them. Belfedrn cursed under his breath and opened his mouth but stopped himself from saying anything to her about being careful.

Eventually, when Belfedrn reached the ravine, the Bears were ready and waiting. He sniffed as he trekked along the base of the cliff where snow and ice formed mounds, a stream raging through a nearby gully.

"The scent grows stronger." Belfedrn tracked the subtle odor wafting through the air, moving upstream toward the highest peaks, where a waterfall flowed over a sheet of ice that weaved down the mountain.

The Ulfhednar and Bears trudged after Belfedrn as he climbed over hills of snow and frozen water. He halted in the vicinity of the waterfall, its frigid spray showering the area. Within the mountain, a massive crack parted stone, reaching halfway up the cliff's height. The scent was strongest here, flowing out of the crevice.

"Your giant resides in there." Belfedrn pointed.

Vard held up a hand to stay any who were eager to charge ahead. "Bears, please allow the pack to enter first. We'll move silently, find this creature, and see if he's sleeping. We'll call you in to help before we attack."

"Nay, Wolf jarl," Gron said. "My fighters will move in and kill the jötunn now. He's trapped. Forward!" He swung his arm in an encouraging sweep.

Aegmor roared and plowed ahead, plunging into the crack, and the rest of the Bear berserkers and warriors hollered and stampeded after him.

"No giant could sleep through that," Belfedrn said to Vard. "Do you think we should wait and prepare for it to come storming out?"

"No." Vard grimaced. "If they kill this monster, they may

claim that they're not obligated to fulfill their end of our bargain."

"They wouldn't do that," Kesg said. "Not after we led them here."

"Either you don't know their people, or you don't understand our history with them after the Great Bear and Wolf War," Ylsga told her mate.

54

MÄRREN

Märren scraped a hearth clean while the other thralls and Uisge moved about the interior of a longhouse, picking up horns and wiping away the grime of food from tables and the floor. The inhabitants of this house were not present, which was proving to be the norm when the Dragon thralls were sent to offer services to the wealthy and powerful—those who were most often provided with free laborers.

A fortnight had already passed since Märren had arrived in Torank, and she had performed a multitude of tasks across the city. She rubbed her healed and callused palms together.

"She'll toil as a thrall for the remainder of her days."

"Then she'll be staked to the ice and fed to the jötunn. Any foolish dragons waiting for her will be disheartened. Even if she tried to free them, she *could never accomplish such an inconceivable feat."*

"She takes each day as it comes while the darkness within her lingers and grows stronger. And yet still she is not broken."

Once Märren finished cleaning the hearth, she headed up the longhouse's stairs. On the loft, bedding and clothing were strewn about. She sighed and gathered up blankets and furs, the prattle in her head running nonstop.

Someone grabbed her around the neck from behind and squeezed. She gasped, dropping the bedding and clawing at their arm. Her assailant's grip relaxed as they grunted in pain, and she whipped around. Megtr, the hulking bald thrall, glared at her.

"I'll pull each of those claws from your fingers," he said. "Right after I'm done raping you."

Märren retreated a few steps.

"Then every other thrall man here will have their turn," he added. "You should've given yourself up to one of the strong who could protect you. Your puny mate is weak."

Märren crouched, preparing to strike Megtr or wrestle with him if need be. Whatever it came to. Someone leapt onto Megtr's back, wrapping an arm around his face and punching the back of his head. Megtr reached around, flailing and trying to grasp them, although he could not pull them off. Instead, he rammed his back and his attacker into the nearest wall.

Uisge groaned, and Megtr smashed him again. Märren cried out and charged, kicking and punching at Megtr's knees and groin. She landed a boot on his shin and a fist on the soft part of his crotch. He bellowed with pain.

"Stop whatever's going on up there!" a soldier shouted from below. "Or I'll come up with my axe and end it."

Megtr doubled over as he grabbed at his genitals and snarled. "You'll make up for this pain with pleasure, Wolf whore." He jerked his chin to indicate her furs.

Uisge crawled out from behind him and waved for Märren to head downstairs. She quickly skirted past Megtr and descended with Uisge at her heels. The soldier who had shouted at them paced about the hall, already having lost interest in their commotion. Scuffles amongst the thralls were not uncommon.

Märren began cleaning one of the tables the others had not yet made it to, and Uisge joined her. After some time, a middle-aged woman with a gaunt face wandered over and scraped at hardened food bits on the table between wiping down its surface. She casually worked her way closer to Märren.

"Are the rumors true?" the woman asked without looking up from her duties. "That you and those you lead, those who arrived with you, have already been sacrifices?"

Märren cast her a side glance, unsure why she was being furtive. Thralls could talk as they worked, as long as the soldiers did not think it was so much that it was slowing their tasks. Märren also wondered why this woman believed that she led those who had been captives.

"Aye," Märren finally answered.

"And you escaped Surtr?"

"Barely."

"How?"

The runes for fire lit up inside her head, turning with her thoughts. She would exaggerate the event and her deeds, which in her current predicament might prove useful. As long as the truth was never revealed. If it were, she would look like a mad fool. "When the jötunn feasted on others, our chains melted and broke. We ran into a dragon's den."

The woman continued cleaning for a while before asking, "And you believe you can free the dragons and kill the fiery giant?"

"I plan to." The voices in her head raged.

"I've been here for a few years, which is longer than many of the thralls."

Märren paused her work, gauging the woman and her intentions. "How do you survive in this situation? I don't see the point."

"It's either keep at it or be whipped. So I would say pain, I guess. Pain keeps me going. It also destroys me."

"Then you're stronger than any warrior or berserker I've known."

The woman forced a disbelieving grin. "There's nothing we thralls can do to those who wield the power of the gods. Not even if we cooperated with one another. Each of us must still serve what fate our god laid before us."

Thoughts of Fenrir circled in Märren's head. She had spurned her Wolf god and all she had been offered to come here.

"Fool."

"Of all her terrible choices, that was the worst, the reason why she suffers so much."

"She chases what no one else will."

"I've never drawn the straw to be sacrificed, but my luck cannot last," the woman added. "All the friends I've ever managed to make have been sent to Surtr."

Märren recalled a poem from the Hávamál and sucked in a deep breath. "The first aid is song, which will bring thee assistance in all woes and in sorrow and strife." She sang quietly in the lilting high-pitched style of her people. The woman joined in, humming with her, their melody bright and free. For a moment, no one could touch them.

But the moment did not last long. A few soldiers strode into the longhouse, led by a warrior—Yrstl. "Finish up," Yrstl said. "You thralls will be needed at the smithy for the next few days." He walked down the center of the hall, noticing Märren as he passed. "All is well?" he asked her.

Märren nodded.

"Your hands are shaking." He pointed at the rag she held.

She remained quiet.

"What is it?" he asked.

"An incident with Megtr, but it's over."

"Ah. I'll keep an eye on him. There'll always be a leader among the thralls. It can't be helped when putting people together, but if he's harming others or creating a situation where less work gets done, I'll put a stop to it."

"Thank you, warrior."

A grin tugged at his lips before he forced it down, and he waved his soldiers into action. "Gather up the rest of the thralls." Once the soldiers dispersed around the chamber, he stepped closer to Märren and whispered in her ear, "I wish I could help you, but Raidn would never allow you or your husband to be spared from the next sacrificial offering."

Märren kept her head bowed as she scrubbed the table. "Uisge is not my husband. He's a companion. I do not have a husband."

"The best I can do is make sure a certain other thrall is also sent. If you desire it."

"Don't take any risks for me."

"I want..." He sighed. "I understand your burden, at least as well as someone who doesn't carry it can. I..." He reached out and almost touched her arm but caught himself.

A thrumming pressed against Märren's skull. She ignored the distraction and glanced back at him, catching sight of the cause of the thrumming—a wedged portion of a red scale on his brigandine. "Did the scale help your sister deal with her darkness?"

Yrstl cocked his head, his eyes wandering over thought and memory. "She was never meant to become a warrior. But there was another—a distant relative who supposedly carried the same darkness. Family stories say that she became a Dragon berserker, but her scale must not have done anything for her because she went mad and died soon after joining their ranks."

Märren shuddered. "It cannot be. The scale has to have the ability to control the darkness."

"I'm sorry. Where did you get that idea?"

"From my father. And an ancient Seidr man. They told me it may be the only thing that could help me."

"'A wolf pelt can't even cure you,' her father said. 'Like with your mother, there's no remedy for your illness. Not unless you can achieve the inconceivable, like wielding the power of the Dragon herself. A Seidr man may have told me that. Or I dreamt it.'"

"He was speaking in metaphors. She is a fool."

"No! A Dragon scale is her cure."

A chisel of empathy broke Yrstl's statue-like expression.

"The only thing that can aid me now is returning to the dragons' dens and riding one of those creatures out of the mountain," Märren whispered.

Yrstl noticed where her attention was focused—on his chest. "Don't be tempted by the impossible. Only berserkers of my people can ride a dragon, and only a select few can carry a full scale of our god. You'd need years of training to even attempt it. Even then, bearing a scale will warp most people's minds, and the vast majority of trainees have to accept their fate and remain a soldier. Without dedicating yourself to such instruction, you'd succumb to the effects of a god remnant and die within hours of picking it up."

"She'll never ride a dragon."

"She'd never even be able to bear the dust of the Dragon's scales."

"She's been trained! In her formative years, she was taught by the Ulfhednar instructors. She just never took up a pelt."

"And the dragons cannot be freed," Yrstl continued. "Not even while Surtr sleeps. Some of the berserkers in the past attempted to do this after the giant first imprisoned the creatures. Surtr woke when the gates in the mountain began to open."

"So the portcullises can be raised?"

Yrstl shook his head. "Don't consider it, unless it gives you hope. If you have nothing else to lean on, you may as well carry that for the rest of your time in Midgard."

"You said the gates began to open. How?"

"There's a wheel and chain running to each portcullis. They were built by my people long ago."

"And where are these portcullis wheels?"

Yrstl bobbed his head in thought. "I believe they'd have to reside outside each gate. Maybe in a nearby alcove in the mountain. You probably didn't see them at night when retrieving eggs."

"How did you know that I retrieved eggs?"

He cocked his head. "I was there. I escorted you to the portcullis and back out. I allowed you to go to Surtr's fire that night. To survive the storm."

She tried to recall Yrstl's face in memories from the time, but she had paid no attention to the warrior escorting her given it had followed a confrontation with Surtr and a dragon.

Yrstl grimaced, his face with its sparse blond beard making him look to barely be thirty winters. He kept his jaw rigid, appearing stern. "You may plot as you desire. Take heart while you can."

"Thank you for your kindness," she replied. "I'll carry it with me. I... haven't often experienced decency from men, and other than for my current comrade, not since my mate first took an interest in me."

"What happened to your mate?"

"Nothing. He merely lost the desire to be near me. I proved to be too much of a burden."

"Then he's still alive?"

"He was Ulfhednar, so he may be. But most of my people have been slaughtered."

"Ulfhednar?" The word slipped past his lips in disbelief. "They are... I am sorry for your loss." He squeezed her shoulder and joined his comrades as they ushered the thralls out of the longhouse.

The middle-aged woman Märren had been speaking with followed the soldiers. Uisge trailed her, and Märren hurried to catch up with the woman as they stepped outside and headed for the smithy. Megtr shoved past Märren, nearly knocking her over as he chuckled.

"Don't forget what's coming to you," Megtr said.

"Walk on, Megtr!" Yrstl shouted from somewhere off to the side, and the thrall huffed and strode ahead.

The soldiers escorted them through Torank—a city of stone—which still looked foreign to Märren. All the cities and villages she had seen before had been built of wood. The Dragon's defenses here would be stronger than any she had known, a place of safety if need ever arose.

"Try to avoid being noticed by him," the middle-aged thrall woman said to Märren while gesturing at Megtr. "He's attracted to every new woman and usually rapes them many times before losing interest. The less you fight, the faster he moves on."

Märren contemplated her advice as the roar of smithy fires and rising black smoke neared. "What's your name?" Märren asked.

"Årn." The woman brushed dark but graying hair from her face.

"And how did you end up here?"

"My people are the Sea Serpents. I was a proud karl once, but I strayed too far after Surtr awoke."

"I was a Wolf."

"And your mate?" She glanced at Uisge. "He looks different from you."

"A wanderer without a homeland."

Årn nodded, as if she had guessed correctly. "Megtr controls the thralls through intimidation and fear, but if you could somehow rise above him…" She shrugged. "I've heard rumors of your wit and bravery, with how you led the others to escape Surtr. You could give us thralls something no one else ever has."

"And what's that?"

"Hope."

55

CAËTIN

THE DOOR TO BROOTH'S HOUSE WAS WARPED AND DID NOT CLOSE completely. Caëtin shoved its planks, but it held fast. She knocked and waited.

No one answered.

She rapped her fist on the door again. "Brooth, we're coming in one way or another. If you're piss drunk, you best crawl over and unbar your door."

Nothing. She summoned the power of Muninn's flight feather for strength, but Sanre reared back with her axe and smashed her weapon into the door. The door burst open, swinging inward.

A dying oil lamp sat on a table, its flame barely bright enough to light the interior of the cramped room. A single bed was stuffed against the far corner, and someone lay atop it. Caëtin drew her blade and edged closer.

The man lying there did not move. Caëtin tapped him with the tip of her sword. He did not appear to be breathing, either. She shook him and felt his neck.

Dead.

"Bugger the bloody gods who left us." Caëtin kicked over a

stool, which crashed into the far wall and shattered into pieces. "The only trail we could find has led us to a dead end."

Sanre crept closer.

Hildm shuffled into the house. "Was he murdered?"

"I'm certain he was." Caëtin searched the body. The man had a graying red beard and was stoutly built. He must have been at least fifty winters old—similar to Kruh. His chest was crushed, his ribs caved in, both of his hands shattered, along with his knees. "And he was tortured."

"Then we have nothing but speculations about Halvi and Darstrid's killer." Sanre searched the interior but did not react to anything.

Caëtin clenched her jaw. "We cannot stop here."

"But we have no other names."

"There's still one living man who probably hasn't told us everything he should have. I'm tired of playing by Uktr's rules when he asks it of me and then suffering at the hands of my conscience when I cannot stomach the viciousness of it. My patience is spent. Come." Caëtin strode past Hildm and exited, heading for the Whispering Beak, a maelstrom of dark thoughts whirling within her and pulling at her conscience. She knew what she had to do but did not like it.

When she stepped inside the tavern, she searched its shadowed tables. A man sat near to where she and her companions had taken their seats. She stalked closer. The man lifted his head, his movements sluggish, his eyes bobbing as he tried to focus on her.

Caëtin grabbed him by the arm. "Kruh."

Kruh flinched and tried to pull away, but his attempt was weak, his breath smoldering with drink.

"Would you step outside with us?" Caëtin asked.

"Why? I already told you everything I know."

"I have a few more questions, and I don't think you'd like it if anyone in this tavern overhears our discussion."

Kruh leaned against her grip, but Caëtin jerked him to his feet as the servants and other patrons watched. Sanre stepped behind Kruh and helped usher him outside. Caëtin shut the tavern door behind them and dragged Kruh to the side of the longhouse. She spun him around and slammed him against the wall. Hildm muffled her cry of surprise.

"Which of your childhood friends became a warrior or berserker?"

Kruh trembled, his eyes darting between Caëtin and Sanre. "Was the Axe not at his place?"

"We found him," Caëtin said. "But he was already dead."

"Dead?" His eyebrows shot upward.

"Aye. Tortured."

Sanre grabbed Kruh's wrist and slammed it down on the remains of a crate beside them. She pinned his hand down with her stump and hefted her axe.

"No!" Kruh tried to pull away, to fall down even, but Sanre held him fast. He could only slump to his knees. "I can't tell you."

"Break his hand," Caëtin said, unable to resist and adopting Uktr's methods once again, this time for the truth. She would likely regret it later, but wrath swam through her blood. She silently vowed not to fully succumb to Uktr's methods and kill the man.

"No! I don't know who it was."

Sanre brought the backside of her axe down on his hand, crushing bones in a burst of sickening cracks. Kruh screamed, and his head dipped forward. Caëtin shoved him against the wall again and smacked his cheeks.

"Who was your friend?"

Kruh sobbed. "I..."

"Take a finger from his other hand."

Sanre let his crushed hand go and grabbed his other, pressing it against the longhouse wall.

"Any names?" Caëtin asked.

Kruh wailed.

Sanre chopped, severing his first finger near the base of his hand. Kruh screamed, his cry carrying over the thrum of the rain. The sound of the tavern's door swinging open followed, and both servants and a couple patrons soon appeared near the corner of the building, watching through the downpour.

"Who was it?" Caëtin asked. "Or we can keep at this until you're no longer able to hold a drinking horn."

Beating wings sounded, and Huginn dived, landing on Kruh's face, flapping wildly and shrieking. Kruh screamed and screamed.

Caëtin let the raven have at him for a few heartbeats. "That's enough." She held out her arm, and Huginn landed on it, cocking her head and studying the man she had attacked.

Kruh spit and sobbed, his face pale, eyes wild with fear as he stared at the raven, many beak holes on his face bleeding. "That is Muninn's harbinger." He trembled. "The dead god is punishing me."

"Tell me what I need to know," Caëtin said, "or Muninn's raven will take you to the bridge herself."

"He became the jarl..." Kruh's head drooped, and he went limp.

A fist of surprise struck Caëtin. "Uktr?"

Sanre shook Kruh, but he did not respond.

"Bring him back inside." Caëtin grabbed him by one arm, and she and Sanre lugged Kruh past the onlookers, his knees and shins dragging through the mud. Once inside the tavern, they set him on a table, and Caëtin dropped her coin pouch on his belly. The people who had ventured out to watch returned, and Caëtin jingled the pouch and said, "Take care of him until he can manage to take care of himself."

The woman servant nodded, her eyes wide with fear. Caëtin strode past them and out into the night, Huginn still on her arm. Her comrades followed.

"He could've lied," Sanre said. "Simply to end his suffering and his fear."

"True, but he said 'jarl,' and Taknhal couldn't have been his childhood friend. Kruh's too old to have grown up with my brother."

Sanre paced in silence for a few breaths. Hildm stood with hunched shoulders, her head hanging and fetters clinking when she shifted her weight.

"Did your father come from this area of the city?" Sanre asked Caëtin.

"He took the throne by force, I know that, but he never spoke of his childhood."

"Maybe we should torture Uktr until he confesses." Sanre ran her hand over the head of her axe, which was again hanging at her waist.

Caëtin's mind turned as she stroked Huginn's neck. "Or take him to the Raven's bridge. We didn't have time for an inquisition with Kruh, but I will do so with Uktr. If I must, I'll interrogate him and then Taknhal." She rubbed the raven's beak clean. "I should've put more effort into advancing my inquisitor skills rather than the other magics."

"We fly?"

Caëtin regarded Hildm. *She cannot see the temple.* "Nay. We'd be leaving the Spider girl to die at the hands of our people. Take her to the great hall. On foot. I'll meet you there."

Sanre nodded and tugged on Hildm's arm. At first, the girl resisted, hesitant to leave Caëtin's side, but Sanre quickly convinced her with a less than gentle heave.

Caëtin became the unkindness and flew over the river and walls into the city proper, accompanied by Huginn, circling downward and landing outside Muninn's temple in human form. The night had grown late. Tools and scaffolding the karls, thralls, *goði,* and *gyðja* had been using to build the walls of a few longhouses surrounded the temple. Caëtin passed under the scaffolding and approached the doors, where two *gyðja* waited. These women unsealed the temple without a word.

"Send for Igendrn." Caëtin stopped before entering. "Wake him and have him bring me however much of Muninn's draught is available, as quickly as he can."

The *gyðja* nodded, and one rushed inside. Not long afterward, Igendrn exited.

"Are you here to help us?" Igendrn smirked as he motioned to the longhouse walls that were under construction. "So late in the night?"

"Anything for Muninn," Caëtin replied with a heavy dose of sarcasm. "Or at least for her remains. But I can't right now. I need more draught. The last for a while, I hope."

"I wished that your coming was born out of physical desire, not the need for draught." He gave her his best enticing stare. "Who do you need it for this time?"

"I'll keep that to myself. For now. The draught must be strong, but not so strong that I won't wake for days."

Igendrn handed her a flagon, his fingers lingering on hers. "Made by the high *gyðja.* You should visit again soon."

"There's too much to do."

"All the more reason to seek Muninn's clarity. And..." He did not wink, but his sentiment was clear.

"Soon." Caëtin took the flagon, but because of how heavy it was and how easily it would spill, she walked to the great hall.

56

BELFEDRN

VARD MOTIONED FOR THE ULFHEDNAR TO FOLLOW THE BEAR fighters into the crevice in the cliff, and Kesg and Ylsga led the pack inside.

Bear fools! They'll get us all killed. Belfedrn trailed the others, keeping Thelira behind him. No torches burned inside the mountain, but his Wolf eyes quickly adjusted to the darkness. He spotted some of the Bear warriors at the rear of their company. The passageway of cracked stone twisted and descended, leading them deeper while the odor of Jötunheim grew stronger.

Yelling erupted ahead, echoing along the walls, the clash of steel and banging of shields answering. A deafening roar blasted through the cavern, throwing Belfedrn's hood and hair back with its gust. Then a much stronger wind arose. Whirling snow and ice whipped around a corner ahead, flinging Bear warriors aside in its wake and smashing them into the surrounding stone.

"Clear the way!" Belfedrn threw himself and Thelira against the nearest wall as the blizzard barreled toward them.

Massive footfalls and the hint of feet composed of frost thundered past, a finger and a nose poking from a white haze. The giant hurtled through the cavern and out into the world beyond.

"Don't let the jötunn get away!" Aegmor came tearing around the corner ahead, blood streaming from his mouth and one of his nostrils as he spat out fragments of teeth.

More of the Bears charged after him. Some of those who had been thrown against the walls shook their heads and staggered to their feet. Others did not move. Belfedrn sprinted ahead of the Bears in pursuit, and the Ulfhednar howled as they joined him. When he reached the chasm's opening, rivers of snow were avalanching down from the cliffs, piling up at the entrance and threatening to trap them inside.

Belfedrn covered his head and lunged through the plummeting snow, the avalanche smashing into him and almost burying him before he tumbled and rolled through the other side. A towering mass of whipping snow and ice stood beyond the crevice. An almost indiscernible hand reached out, scooping snow from the cliffs and feeding the avalanche. Thelira plowed through the icefall, followed by the rest of the Ulfhednar. Bear berserkers and warriors began to trickle through as the avalanche intensified, and these fighters carried heaps of snow on their heads and shoulders and stumbled under its weight.

"Troll attack formation!" Vard cried, and the Ulfhednar growled and charged at the snowstorm.

Thelira loosed arrows over Belfedrn's shoulder as he ran. Thoughts of Lyrne and what happened to her hammered at his berserker's trance. He yelled over his shoulder to Thelira, "Once the giant stops creating avalanches, dig out the Bears!"

The jötunn continued pounding at the cliffs, adding to the rivers of snow and ice, blockading the crevice and trapping two or three score of warriors inside the mountain, or at least slowing their progress as fewer Bears burst out. He was smart, the brute, reducing the number of biting ants who would swarm him.

Belfedrn altered his course, again taking the flank position and veering for the closest rope. An alternate attack on this beast may prove helpful. He climbed as fast as he could while the rest of the Ulfhednar struggled against raging winds, shielding their faces from chunks of ice as they speared at what could have been the tendon on the rear of the giant's ankle. Others hacked with axes. Aegmor dived into the white, his axe swiping wildly as his berserker rage took control. Gron and the rest of the Bears manifested similar behavior, drooling and roaring like savage beasts.

Belfedrn climbed faster. In their trance, the Bears would fight with every part of themselves given to battle, and they would not stop until the last drop of their strength had been spent or they died. Unfortunately, this did not mean they would fight wisely. They probably would not focus on the tendons that could fell the jötunn and may not think to target other vital areas, if there were any around their adversary's feet. Belfedrn scrambled higher, reaching a level midway up the blizzard's height. A hint of a cheek and then a finger and a massive club of stone and ice intermittently revealed themselves within the storm.

The giant roared and reared back, turning away from the cliff and swinging at the masses of warriors who were attacking him. The Ulfhednar leapt away. Athna growled, her magic hand burning, and flaming chunks of earth and rock rose from the ground around her, taking on the form of a wolf. She commanded her magical creature at the monster, and the wolf hurtled toward the giant, burning and howling. The Bears continued their feral attacks that were interrupted only when they ducked or lunged aside. Then they bellowed in rage and charged in once more. A club swept out from the storm again, and crunching sounded before many Bear berserkers and warriors flew through the air and across the ravine, some landing in the icy stream while others were hurled into the cliffs, their flights ending abruptly in sickening thuds.

Belfedrn ascended faster, slipping and stumbling against the mountainside before pausing and waiting. The club whipped around and disappeared into the spiraling storm again. The tip of an ear and a beard of frost emerged. Belfedrn summoned the power of his pelt, all that he could, and leapt. He sailed through the air and into the haze. The white and its swirling particles blinded him before he struck something hard and cold, his hands scrabbling about for holds. He grasped onto what he was searching for—a tuft of hair within a beard—and his hands stuck to it, almost freezing his grip closed. He kicked and climbed upward as the giant continued swiping at his attackers and barely noticed Belfedrn, only flicking his head with annoyance.

Belfedrn's fingers turned numb, and he had to work harder and harder to unclench them. When he reached the top of the jötunn's beard, the hoarfrost-encrusted hairs of the creature's mustache became visible in the storm. He climbed toward a nostril and reached around, ripping his spear from its place on his back, his fist freezing closed around its shaft. He scaled up the giant's nose and leapt higher, his spear angled for what he could not see.

In the heartbeat before his weapon struck, an icy-blue iris came into view, darting around, scanning the area below. Belfedrn's spear punched into the jötunn's eye, impaling the outer layer and sinking into soft liquid beneath. The momentum from Belfedrn's leap slammed him into the creature's cheek, and he grasped the hoarfrost-covered eyelashes on the monster's lower eyelid. Liquid burst from the puncture he created and drained over him.

The giant roared, the cry a frigid blast that rang Belfedrn's ears and skull while he prayed that Thelira was freeing the trapped Bears so they could drop this beast. Belfedrn strained and ripped his spear free just as a massive palm appeared, swatting at him. He leapt for the periphery of the hand—the thumb—catching it and wrapping his arms around the appendage, hugging it tight as the hand slammed into the giant's face. The beast pulled his hand away to inspect his palm, probably hoping to see the squished remnants of a human there. The jötunn may not find what he wanted to, but he would see Belfedrn. Then the monster would flick his hand, and Belfedrn would go flying.

Belfedrn let go of the giant's thumb and leapt for his beard again, latching on with his free hand and burying his spear into as much of it as he could. At this stage of exhaustion, and with numb hands, Belfedrn was not sure if he could release the spear even if he wanted to.

The giant pivoted his hand from a position of palm facing him to palm away and repeated this, his movements coming quicker as he must have realized his attacker was not dead. Belfedrn rammed his spear into the nostril above him. The weapon sank deep, and a rush of blue blood erupted, coating Belfedrn in its freezing river. Belfedrn cursed and flung himself aside, his hand burning with pain as he forced his grip open, releasing his spear. The jötunn bellowed and wiped at his nose while Belfedrn crawled into the hair on his upper lip. The creature's hand searched about his face, probing and prodding. Belfedrn cringed and pulled himself deeper into the hoarfrost mustache.

A couple breaths later, the frost giant teetered as if one of his legs gave out. The beast hollered and leaned over, swiping with his club-bearing hand as he crashed into a cliff. Belfedrn tore his axe from his belt, his hand burning like fire as he scampered up the outside of the jötunn's uninjured nostril and leapt for the creature's other eye. He grasped onto a clump of lashes, pulling and kicking himself higher until the beast's iris came into view. The pupil contracted as it tried to focus on what emerged before it—on what was coming.

Belfedrn chopped the giant's eye with his axe, hewing into it and then tugging to carve downward. The resulting cry from the giant was barely audible over the pounding in Belfedrn's skull and the high-pitched ringing in his ears. The jötunn teetered but braced himself against the mountain. Then the monster's other leg gave out, and he pitched forward. Belfedrn hung before the gushing eye as the beast plummeted, its frosty hair streaming around him in tendrils. Belfedrn released his axe and grasped at the locks, taking hold. This flung him from the giant's face, and he clung to its hair as it waved out away from and then behind the beast's face during his descent.

The monster smashed into the floor of the ravine. The impact tore the hair out of Belfedrn's hands and he went flying, smacking into piles of snow before his back struck something hard and cracked. Only white surrounded him as everything settled, the chaos of the ordeal dwindling away. He winced and grunted in pain. His back ached, and the burning in his hands faded as they grew numb again. A similar sensation of lack of feeling spread from his toes up his feet and legs. He had heard of men who had lost sensation in their limbs after breaking their spines. He struggled to move.

Many heartbeats passed as he heaved for breath, terror surging through him. *Let me die with honor rather than live as an Ulfhednar who cannot fight.*

Light poured in through a hole in the snow above him as hands flung away more snow and ice. Dradn reached into the opening he had created and grabbed Belfedrn by the wrists. The young Wolf heaved, grunting as he hauled Belfedrn out. As Belfedrn emerged, Dradn lost his footing, and they rolled down a mound, coming to rest side by side at the bottom and staring skyward.

"Are you all right?" Dradn asked.

Belfedrn blinked back tears. "You're not supposed to be here."

"I couldn't stay behind while the last of my people died."

Then you are worthy of the pack. "You must obey orders, or the Ulfhednar cannot rely on you."

"I'm not part of the Ulfhednar." Dradn looked over the blood and gore covering Belfedrn along with many hoarfrost crystals stuck to the grime. "Are you injured?"

"I can't feel my hands or feet."

A breath later, sharp pain bit into Belfedrn's upper leg.

"Ah!" Belfedrn bellowed in surprise.

"Your back isn't broken." Kesg was also there and yanked the tip of his seax from Belfedrn's thigh before cinching down a bandage over the wound he had created. "But your frostbite is worse than mine."

Kesg tore off Belfedrn's gloves and rubbed at his fingers, two of which had turned black at their extremities.

"Those two will have to be removed," Kesg said, "but you'll live." He and Dradn worked on removing Belfedrn's boots.

Bear warriors continued their tumult of roaring and chopping into the neck of the jötunn, who lay strewn along the side of the stream, the swirling blizzard around the monster fading to drifting flakes. The beast lay still and was pocked with smoldering burns, probably due to the work of Athna, unless the Bears had another battle Seidr.

A familiar figure—but not one Belfedrn expected to see—moved about, commanding Boar berserkers who were digging through the wall of snow outside the crevice and releasing more trapped Bears. The Boar people could dig like no others, which they usually implemented in survival situations while searching for food, but this would do. Most of the Bears had already been released, or their bodies had been uncovered from the avalanche. At least another score of their warriors lay in bloody heaps around the ravine, more probably dead inside the chasm. Several berserker bodies lay among them, as well as at least two Ulfhednar.

The Boar jarl strode to Belfedrn and grinned down at him, her axe enameled in blood and dripping.

"You made it," was all Belfedrn managed to say.

"It's quicker when you come over the falls." She pointed to a plethora of ropes dangling over the frozen waterfall. "You should've waited for us."

"I tried."

She looked him over. "Those frost jötunn are colder than a witch's tit floating in ice in the North Sea." She prodded near his groin with the toe of her boot. "As long as you haven't lost your prized appendage, you'll be well enough."

57

MÄRREN

UISGE TUGGED A LINK OF CHAINS OVER HIS SHOULDER AND BRACED against them, leaning into their weight and dragging them through the streets of Torank, headed for the city's northern gates. Behind him, Märren hauled her own chains. These links would no doubt become shackles and be used to bind the next group of sacrifices to their stakes and each other, and these chains were thicker than the previous ones Märren had endured. Thicker and heavier.

Once they reached the gates, they dropped the chains in a heap, and Megtr and many of the other thralls loaded them into carts. It would probably not be long before Surtr awoke again. No rumors had carried through the thralls suggesting that anything had happened, but the city was preparing for something. Sacrificial offerings seemed most likely. How many other thralls would be chosen and sent with the previous survivors remained unknown, but the number could depend on how many people the other Dragon cities and villages sent with the caravan.

"Well done." Yrstl strode past as twilight settled over the city, the score of soldiers in his entourage looking less impressed than their leader. "You thralls have worked hard this day, and your efforts do not go unnoticed."

"He's the only one who thinks our work is meaningful," Uisge whispered.

Märren nodded.

"She wants to place her hopes in him, but those dreams will be ripped away."

"He's a Dragon warrior. Her enslaver. He cannot understand her and her darkness."

"He is kind, unlike all the others."

"There are extra rations waiting for you," Yrstl continued, positioning himself between Märren and Uisge and the other thralls. "Return to your quarters for a celebratory nattmal."

The thralls released half-hearted cheers and slogged away with hunched backs, the soldiers guiding them.

"I need to speak with you," Yrstl said to Märren, his gaze flicking over to Uisge.

"I'd be happy to return to a big meal," Uisge said. "I can only guess what news you're about to share." He grimaced. "Nothing good is waiting for us."

Yrstl stepped aside and allowed Uisge to pass, and the warrior mouthed, "Thank you," to him.

Uisge cast one last glance at Märren and followed the thralls. Yrstl waited until the others were gone and then walked off, heading away from the thralls' quarters.

"What is it?" Märren hurried after the warrior.

"I won't speak of it here. We must go behind closed doors."

Märren swallowed with apprehension as she followed him to a single-chamber house. He opened the door and stepped inside, waving her in.

"Surtr has woken."

"There will be no escape this time."

"Everyone believed that the first time."

After Märren entered, Yrstl closed the door behind her. He sighed and took off his helm, setting it and his weapons on a table where a vat of steaming stew waited. He used a bowl to scoop out some of the vat's contents and offered the meal to her.

Märren accepted and sipped at the stew, its broth thick. It burned her tongue on the way down and was full of meats and vegetables, which she was not accustomed to since her arrival in the land of fire and ash. Its savory taste was more delightful than her favorite—fired venison and mountain berries—but probably only because she was so hungry. Yrstl dug through a crate on the table and lifted out a bottle of wine, then filled two horns. He offered one to her.

She hesitated.

"Surely you're parched," he said.

"I am, but strong drink often worsens my troubles." She knocked on her skull. "A clear head is good company. Drink is a dangerous friend."

"Aye. The Hávamál. You quote the words of the old gods." He poured the contents of a jug into another horn, passed it over to her, and pointed to a chair before refilling her bowl with stew. "In case you prefer mead instead. Please, sit."

Märren devoured three bowls of stew and drank the horn of mead before leaning back against the chair and relaxing, her eyelids growing heavy. Yrstl studied her, barely able to tear his attention from her.

"There's news from the north." His head drooped as he studied his boots.

"Surtr has awoken."

"Aye. Once the caravan arrives at Torank, Raidn, the warriors, and I will march those who arrived with you and the thralls who draw the marked straws north. We display as much of our power to Surtr as we can by carrying parts of the Dragon with us."

"Little good that does your people."

He grunted and poured himself another horn of wine. "You're certain you don't want any? This may be your last chance for any sort of comforts."

"My last horn of mulled wine..." She picked up the waiting horn and sipped at its spiced and earthy liquid. It had been years since she had tasted anything like it.

After drinking half of the horn, a tingling ran through Märren's head, and her muscles relaxed.

Yrstl smiled. "It's the least I can do for all you've endured and for what you accomplished, even if Raidn tells all those listening that escaping Surtr's hunger was cowardly. They need to punish you and make a show of it for the others."

"To make sure it doesn't happen again."

"Aye. If you believe a sacrifice fighting for her life and the lives of those with her is deserving of punishment."

Märren sipped.

"There's someone I want you to meet," he said.

Märren nearly dropped her horn. "Who?"

Yrstl stood and removed a rug from the ground, grasping a handle in the floor and lifting a door. Darkness lay below. Märren leaned forward.

"Erstyk," Yrstl said. "Come. She's here."

Nothing happened for several breaths, then shuffling arose. Footsteps ascended stairs. A young woman as wan as death emerged, her thick hair in tangled knots around her head, her eyes darting about.

Märren's heart fluttered. "Your sister?"

"Aye."

"You said she was dead."

"That's what I tell people. So they will leave us alone and not come blaming her every time a blight strikes the crops or Surtr awakens or a child dies."

Märren stood as Erstyk stepped into the chamber, muttering to herself, her back hunched. She scratched at a rash on the side of her face. Yrstl grabbed her hand to stop her.

"It's the woman I told you about, Sister." Yrstl guided her to the table and sat her down.

"You keep her in the ground?" Märren asked.

"That's where she likes to be. In the dark. She says it quiets the voices."

Märren knelt and took Erstyk's other hand, stroking it. "I see your pain." She looked into the woman's eyes, familiar with the way they darted around, the way they listened to all the voices that never quit. Doubts. Anger and hate. Violence. Apprehension concerning every choice in life. "I hear them too."

Erstyk's eyes stopped darting around and focused on Märren, although they still vibrated.

"Seeing this woman is like looking into Märren's future."

"There is no escaping the darkness. Not for her or anyone."

"Märren has battled against it and thus far has prevailed. She's nothing like this other woman."

"You are stronger than any who have not had to deal with the darkness," Märren said. "No matter what those voices tell you. No matter how often others who have no notion of them tell you that you are weak."

Erstyk's hand twitched in Märren's grip, squeezing only enough to be noticeable.

"They tell you that you are nothing," Märren continued. "That you cannot accomplish anything. That you do not deserve to live. Sometimes you believe them. After so many years, who would blame you? And yet you still resist. The strength of dragons flows through your blood."

Erstyk stopped blinking and stared into the nothingness. A subtle grin pulled at a corner of her lips.

"There's one voice in there that brings you comfort amidst

however many dozens of others you may hear." Märren touched her cheek. "Sometimes this one may be silenced by the rest, probably much of the time, but it is the only one you should listen to. Hear them now!"

Erstyk blinked several times, and she turned her head, focusing on Märren and then Yrstl. "Yrstl?"

"Erstyk!" He grabbed his sister and embraced her, pressing his head to hers. "You're here."

She nodded.

"It's been some time since we last shared a conversation," he said.

"Too long. The darkness had claimed me. Where is Mother?"

Yrstl's head drooped. "We've talked about this. Let us focus on the present."

Erstyk nodded and sipped at the stew her brother offered. He almost passed her a horn of wine but paused, glanced at Märren, and furtively moved the horn aside. They talked for some time. Yrstl smiled and laughed more than once. Erstyk managed to consume half a bowl of stew and flashed a couple smiles before she slumped onto the table in sleep. Yrstl allowed her to rest for a while before he picked her up and carried her down below, returning shortly after and closing and hiding the door in the floor.

He sat across from Märren, a grin on his lips, a distant look of relief and contentment hanging in his eyes. Eventually, he focused on her.

"Thank you," he said and drank deeply. "We've not had such conversation in far too long... at least years."

She nodded.

A moment of silence passed, their gazes locked, the room warm and fuzzy. Märren leaned forward and took Yrstl by the hand, grinning at him. He tensed and nearly pulled his hand away.

"He does not desire her."

"No man would. She'll never find that kind of pleasure again. Unless it's with that beast of a creature who follows her."

"Everyone deserves enjoyment, and Yrstl has taken an interest in her."

"I should get you back to your quarters," Yrstl said.

Märren nodded. "You should, and yet you brought me here." She stood and shuffled closer to him, gazing into his eyes.

He reached up and touched her hair, and he ran his fingers through her locks, which seemed more radiant and bronze than usual. "You are beautiful and strong."

"He lies so he can bed her."

"The same as her mate."

"He..."

Märren sat on his lap and took him by the cheeks, pressing her lips to his. He inhaled deeply and kissed her back, his hands sliding up her legs to her arse. She pulled at his tunic, but his brigandine was drawn tight. He jerked the brigandine over his head and yanked her fur off her shoulders, his fingers fumbling at her leathers. She aided him by removing her tunic and then her leggings as he watched in anticipation, excitement celebrating in his eyes. She slid off her undergarments as he struggled with his leathers and everything else. Beneath it all, he was corded with muscle, svelte but not thick or broad—similar to Wolf men. A look that made her desire swell.

Once they were both naked, he stared at her, his gaze lingering over her breasts and then the scar runes she carried, all those markings she had carved into her flesh. He reached out a finger and traced the runes for love on her chest.

"Do they hurt?" he asked.

"They bring me comfort and strength."

She pushed him back into his chair and lowered herself onto him. He groaned as she worked her hips and tossed her head back, her hair tousled. She pulled her hair onto the top of her head and held it there, and his eyes closed as his hands ran up and down her body, feeling every portion of her from her upper legs to her chest and everything between. His breathing quickened as he grasped her under her legs and stood while she continued her motions. He carried her to the bed and set her on it. There, sweat beaded on their skin, and their bodies moved to the beating of their hearts and rush of their breaths as they spent themselves.

Time seemed to stand still, and Yrstl rolled off her and lay on his back, his chest heaving as he stared at the ceiling. After a few minutes, he pulled her close and draped an arm over her.

"It's just like the capriciousness of the gods to do this," he said. "To bring you to me only to have you taken away so soon. I—"

Märren pressed a finger to his lips to silence him. "Do not speak of such things. This night is ours. No one can take it from us." Energy and vigor coursed through her as Yrstl's fled. She ran her fingers through his thick hair and shushed him when he tried to speak again. He squeezed her tighter, and she turned around and pressed her back against his chest.

They lay there in their embrace until their sweat dried by the heat of the hearth fire, its comforting crackle the only sound in the world. Shadows danced on the walls in slow peaceful motions, and Yrstl's breathing became a quiet snore.

Märren eased his arm away from her breasts. He groaned and shifted, and she paused, waiting until he fell asleep again. Then she stood and dressed, her attention drawn to the table, although she kept trying to ignore what was there. After donning her fur and pulling it tight around her shoulders, her gaze slipped past the horns and bowls and empty vat of stew on the table, focusing on Yrstl's belt and the sheathed seax tied to it.

"She's vile. She helped one as afflicted as she is only to use this man's weakness against him."

"Then the filthy whore used her body to entice the warrior. In hopes of killing him and escaping."

"She wouldn't use the weapon against him, unless..."

Märren wrapped her fingers around the seax's handle, and she slowly drew it from its sheath, creating no more than a whisper. Its blade reflected firelight and glowed orange. She turned to Yrstl, and a stone of regret tugged at her heart. If she were to carry out what she was planning, he would likely be killed, unless while he hunted her down, he hid the fact that he had been fooled by her.

She stifled a sigh. She could have grown accustomed to such a considerate mate, as kind a man as any she could hope to meet in Midgard, and after her upbringing and past mistakes, only the tender-hearted piqued her desires. Here lay a man who could one day understand her. Unfortunately, she had found him in Dragon territory, and the discovery might as well have been a wicked blade shoved into her side by the gods.

She cursed under her breath, working through the remorse she would feel before even creating a need for the emotion. She should not feel too terrible for what she had to do. Her mate had done the same with her—used her for pleasure and then left. She wished this situation had involved her mate instead of Yrstl, but why should she be bound to offering others better than she received? If her actions served herself or Eimri and could save her life, she should follow through with them.

Still, a hardened kernel of guilt solidified in her gut and squeezed. He had been—*was*—a good man. There were few like him. But a man was not what she or Eimri needed. Not now.

She picked up Yrstl's brigandine from the ground, turning it over until its wedge of red scale stared back at her. Her pulse hammered in her ears. Her skull hummed. Saliva gathered in her mouth.

Märren squeezed the seax, using its tip to pry the scale from the warrior's *brynja*. After working quietly and carefully, she peeled the edges of the scale away from its steel frame. Some substance was also adhered to the scale's backside, sticking it to the armor, and she had to use the blade to cut and pull it free.

The scale gleamed in the light like a mirror of blood, seeming to waver like liquid, its call pulling at her every desire, begging her to accept its power.

"A piece of the Dragon's scale."

"It cannot be."

"She holds it!"

In her head, Märren's Dragon scar runes flickered. She cast Yrstl one last glance that was filled with as much love and remorse as was stored within her shallow reserves, but the scale quickly drew her attention again.

She was enthralled by its beauty but would not open her mind to the Dragon's powers. Not yet. Doing so would bring her to another realm. She could not face that world while her body lay in this house.

She crept to the doorway, silently opened it, and fled into the night.

58

CAËTIN

CAËTIN AND SANRE ENTERED THE GREAT HALL, HILDM MEEKLY following. Both Uktr and Grimmurk sat before the hearth, drinking, the firelight dancing across their faces and dark cloaks. Uktr turned, his expression distant and clouded. He squinted, studying Caëtin, his hair mussed from sleep.

"Disldryn?" Uktr asked.

"Greetings, Father," Caëtin said with as much loving conviction as she could muster. "Taknhal ran off with most of our warriors and knights, who currently despise each other, but some of us remain to defend Aonark. For the moment, all is well." She approached their table and poured the contents of her flagon into a horn.

Grimmurk glared at her. "Is that better tasting mead?"

"Aye," she said. "The best." She reached over and filled Uktr's ornate drinking horn with the draught.

Uktr took a drink without noticing anything out of the ordinary.

Grimmurk sniffed at his comrade's horn and grimaced. "It smells like shite."

Caëtin took the first horn she had filled and sipped from it.

"Drink up, Father." She gave Uktr her best loving smile. "Grimmurk, it'd be best if you avoided imbibing any of this. I already have someone who can watch over us." She indicated Sanre.

Uktr drank deep. Grimmurk shook his comrade's shoulder, but Uktr did not stop.

"It's *gyðja* draught, isn't it?" Grimmurk asked.

"Indeed." Caëtin's smile dropped flat. "My father and I are going to have a discussion on the bridge."

"And if I can convince him not to join you?"

"Then your guts will be dangling below your bullocks." She unsheathed her blade and held it low beside her leg. "I'm done with any secrets my father has kept."

Grimmurk glowered and sipped from his untainted horn, his fingers straying toward the axe at his waist.

"Don't." Caëtin's blade flashed up, and she pressed the tip of her weapon to his throat. "Not here or at the bridge. Sanre will be watching."

Grimmurk chugged the rest of his horn's contents and wiped his lips with the back of his hand. "You'd best prepare for what you're about to encounter. It's not easy to take another member of the Knights Black to that world, especially not one as powerful as Uktr."

"I'll keep that in mind." She finished her drink and pulled up a chair, sitting and leaning back.

Uktr's head had already dipped and rested on his shoulder, his eyes closed. Grimmurk turned his back to Caëtin and stared into the fire. A vast weight pulled at Caëtin's insides, siphoning her soul into another world.

She woke in the midst of blurred surroundings that resembled ethereal banners. These ranged in color from browns to dull reds to whites. The sun burned with an icy blue halo, frozen in the sky, while the glacier-encrusted mountains blazed with fire. A strong hand gripped her by the shoulder and spun her around. Uktr glared at her as wraiths rushed past, the wind they created streaming her cloak and hair out before her. Her father raised an axe as black as the Raven and swung it at her head.

Caëtin fell back, lifting her hand, her pale blade clutched tightly as she parried the strike. The power of the blow knocked her down, and Uktr towered above her, vigor and strength so thick within him that he seemed like a different man. His chest heaved as he raised his axe. A raven soared past Uktr's face, momentarily distracting him.

"Father, stop!" Caëtin rolled aside and came up in a crouch.

"You're not powerful here, Daughter." He sneered. "Those who are near death but haven't crossed over are stronger in this world. Surprise." He strode toward her. "Perhaps this is what I wanted all along."

Caëtin scampered back, lifting her blade in defense. "You will answer my inquisition. No matter how powerful you believe you are. And you will *not* kill me."

Uktr laughed. "You've brought me here to steal my thoughts and dreams. In Midgard, I may not have realized it, but now I understand your intentions. *I* am still jarl of the Ravens!"

"You are not jarl any longer. And you'll answer my questions, or you'll suffer me."

Uktr snarled and lunged, swiping with his axe. Caëtin leaned aside, parrying and knocking his weapon wide. Power flared within her, and her cloak billowed in the ghostly wind. All of her feathers became exposed, as well as Muninn's claw, which curved around her throat like a necklace. Uktr's eyes shot open. He hesitated.

"No." He shook his head. "It cannot be. There are no paladins of Muninn. No one more powerful than a berserker, a Knight Black. There hasn't been for an age."

Caëtin slowly advanced, and Uktr retreated one step and

then another. She raised her pale blade, which glowed like white fire.

"You'll answer me." She pointed the blade at him, using its tip to part his cloak. One long flight feather rested against his chest. "I am a paladin of Muninn, and I demand it of you here, on the Raven's bridge!"

Uktr trembled, and his axe fell from his hand.

"What did you do to Darstrid?" Caëtin asked.

"Darstrid..." His eyes turned dark and cloudy. "She was my daughter. One whom I came to prefer over you."

"Then why did you have her killed?"

"I... She..."

Wraiths hurtled past on their journey, their numbers swelling and greater now than ever before. Something else came with them, a presence—a feeling only Muninn could pass on to her. Caëtin whirled about to face a wall of wraiths as this something plowed through them.

Hildm's face appeared between roaming souls, her skin smeared in black paint, her expression taut and terrified. Huginn was perched on her shoulder. She pointed behind Caëtin and screamed, her fetters clanking as her body emerged from the mist.

Caëtin spun around as an axe of flames chopped downward at her, wielded by another man who appeared within the spirits, attacking with the beaked strike of Muninn. Caëtin lunged back and to the side. The axe swiped close to her head, severing a lock of dark hair that turned into a feather as it fell. Recognizing her attacker drew a gasp of surprise from Caëtin as she readied herself and Grimmurk stalked out from a cluster of wraiths, coming toward her. Hildm whimpered and disappeared.

Of course her father's closest comrade would also be a Knight Black of immense power, even if Caëtin had never seen him use magic. And of course he would find a way to appear at

Uktr's inquisition. She had never seen either of these men this way before. They had been old for as long as she could remember. Grimmurk's cloak billowed, and against his chest, three feathers spun in the wind.

"It was *you*," Caëtin said, circling Grimmurk. "Not Uktr. You are the smuggler. You had Darstrid killed, and you murdered the Axe—Brooth. And Halvi. You're the one who gave that boy another feather. It was also you who grew up in the lower city with Kruh and Brooth."

Grimmurk spat at her feet.

"Answer me!" she cried.

He grinned. "That boy was begging for another chance to touch Muninn, and you and Darstrid had already usurped the throne from Uktr. You both betrayed your own father, the man who took you in and cared for you when no one else would. You don't deserve to be called his daughters. Not after all he's done for you."

"Taknhal best resembled the jarl you once worshipped nearly as much as a god. Taknhal would be most like Uktr."

"Aye. Darstrid was always too concerned about relations with the other clans and building trade and wealth rather than raiding. And you are no better, with your attempts at parleys and negotiations. Either of you as jarl would weaken the Ravens. You would weaken us!"

Caëtin continued circling her father's advisor. "So you had your closest comrade's daughter killed to preserve a world you thought we still needed. And to accomplish the deed, you stole from Muninn."

"I'm saving the Raven people!" His face turned purple.

Strong arms wrapped around Caëtin from behind, pinning hers to her side. Grimmurk lunged forward, swinging his axe.

Caëtin exploded into an unkindness, her ravens parting around the weapon. The birds shrieked, flapping out of her father's grasp and ramming back together just to the side of Grimmurk as she performed the beaked strike. Her blade slid between Grimmurk's ribs, puncturing his chest but not sliding deep before he leapt out of reach. Blood streamed down his brigandine.

"I also command all of Muninn's magics, you old bastards," Caëtin shouted.

Grimmurk doubled over, grunting in pain as he tried to face her and raise his axe.

"Stop!" Uktr lunged toward them, his eyes welling with emotion. "Please, Daughter. I beg you. Let him live."

"He killed Darstrid," she said.

Uktr's posture broke as he stumbled closer. "Grimmurk is the only person still alive who sees me how I was—a valiant berserker. A man to be respected for my abilities as well as my wits. He is my last and only friend."

Caëtin restrained herself from impaling Grimmurk again, the tip of her blade poised at his head. "Because *you* killed Freydeg, your other friend."

"My daughters and sons see me as a feeble old man with an ailing mind," Uktr said. "But none of you will experience anything close to what Grimmurk and I have shared. You can't. There was too much, and it was a different time. You will find your own heroes, your own lives, and I will no longer be part of either. The sun sets on my horizon. But please, don't take all that I have left. Not before I go. I will leave soon enough."

A rush of empathy stemmed Caëtin's fury, and her muscles relaxed a little. "Did you order Grimmurk to kill Darstrid through that addicted boy?"

"Nay." Uktr shook his head. "But Grimmurk's reasoning is sound. It's what I would've done in my younger years, if I had known. Grimmurk and I are two souls who should not be parted, and he'd do anything for me. I'd do the same for him."

Caëtin gritted her teeth. "If I spare him after all he's done, he cannot carry flight feathers. Not anymore. Neither can you. A single under feather to keep you both satiated and alive is all, unless the Spiders are beating down our gates."

Uktr stared at the swirling ground but did not protest. It was enough that it stayed her hand from delivering a death blow to her father's comrade, was as much as she had ever seen Uktr capitulate to anyone.

"However," she continued, "Grimmurk can no longer carry an axe and kill those he wishes to when he wishes it. What I'm about to do will not reach your level of brutality, Father. It will be at my discretion. It's what must be done so I don't have to fear his axe cleaving into my back."

She stepped around Grimmurk, swiping with her blade at his raised arm, cutting into his flesh and severing his axe arm from his shoulder with a spurt of blood. Her weapon continued to shear through the thickness of the wind in this realm before it struck the ground and carved deep as Grimmurk bellowed in pain. Then, with one hand, she ripped Uktr's feather of Muninn from his neck, but it disappeared in a puff of smoke.

Uktr trembled and his shoulders sagged. All that he was had been broken. He fell apart into a squawking unkindness, and the ravens flew on over the bridge and into the haze and the wraiths. Grimmurk collapsed to his knees, holding his wounded stump of an arm, his head hanging.

Caëtin slowly stepped away from him and closed her eyes.

She awoke in the chair before the hearth in the great hall. Sanre stood watching the three of them, and Hildm cowered behind her. Grimmurk groaned in pain as he clutched his bleeding stump.

"He drank the rest of Uktr's draught before I could stop him," Sanre said, jerking her chin in Grimmurk's direction. "I wasn't sure what was going to happen, but I didn't think it would be that." She gestured at his missing arm. "Hildm thought one of us should visit the bridge, and I wasn't going to leave her to watch over us while we were defenseless."

Caëtin grimaced at the thought. "Grimmurk is the murderer we sought and the man who stole the feathers from Muninn. He's the boy Kruh was saying became jarl just before Kruh passed out. Perhaps Kruh was going to say the 'jarl's advisor.' I'll give him the benefit of the doubt." Recollections of what she had done to the man circled in her thoughts—the torture-assisted confession that had ended up deceiving her. Treading down Uktr's route had led to further confusion.

Uktr's eyes fluttered, but when they settled and remained half-open, he stared absently into the fire, drool stringing from his lips.

Caëtin stood, sympathy striking her anew as she looked upon the former jarl, the man who had taken her in after her parents died. The man who had raised her as his own. It had not been an easy or kind upbringing, but it molded her into who she was now. She shoved back Uktr's cloak and plucked the flight feather from his chest. Then she grasped Grimmurk by his long gray hair and jerked his head back, lifting his beard and revealing the three feathers he wore. She removed them all but did not allow their power to seep into her. It would be too much. She would return them to the temple.

"I'll have a *goði* bring an under feather for each of you," Caëtin said to them. She turned to address Sanre. "I must fly so that a healer may arrive before Grimmurk bleeds to death. Inform the warriors and knights that Uktr and Grimmurk are to be confined to the great hall. They are not to leave its walls. Ever."

Sanre nodded. "And what shall I do with your thrall? If you leave her anywhere in Aonark, someone will kill her."

"Break her shackles and free her. In the bridge world, she

saved my life. Send her to work with my servants. To help care for my children. But arm the other servants and order them to watch her closely. If she tries anything suspicious, have them kill her." The reality of a Spider having visited the Raven's bridge was terrifying, although if Hildm had not, Caëtin would have been killed. "But if anyone harms her without cause, I will kill them myself."

Caëtin gave Uktr one last glance and paced toward the exit, becoming ravens before her tears could spill in the hall.

59

MÄRREN

MÄRREN CREPT INTO THE THRALLS' QUARTERS. TWO SOLDIERS caught sight of her, and the bigger, more aggressive of them strode forward. The other grabbed his companion's arm and whispered something in his ear.

"Where were you?" the bigger soldier asked.

"With Yrstl."

The soldier shot his comrade a knowing look and grinned, then motioned to Märren. "Get inside."

Märren entered, stepping over sleeping thralls who lay under blankets or a rare fur, all of them pressed together for warmth. She reached the corner where she and Uisge slept and shook him. Uisge grumbled. She shook him again.

"Leave me be, or I'll eat your liver." His voice was choked with sleep as he shoved her away.

"Uisge," she whispered. "Wake."

"What is it?" He sat up and glanced around in confusion, then focused on her. "You've returned. Then we're to be sent north to Surtr?"

"The jötunn is awakening, but there's something I must do before we march and I cannot do it when others are watching."

"You need me to help you with this... errand?"

She lifted her pelt, revealing the wedge of the Dragon's scale. Uisge sucked in a breath of wonder.

"Is that...?" He reached out.

"Aye." She covered the scale again before he could touch it. "But I wield none of its power. Not yet. I must take it into myself. Accept it."

"Do whatever you need to do." He sat straighter, casting wary looks around them. "Before it's too late."

"I'll be here but absent. I have to depart Midgard, and I need you to look after my body while I'm away."

"Where are you going?"

"To the Dragon's den."

He swallowed. "Will your body make noises?"

"Possibly. Probably."

"Can we sneak out to some dark corner of the city?"

"I don't think so. The soldiers are alert, and there are many stationed around the quarters."

"Lie under the blanket with me. I'll keep a hand clamped over your mouth and try to hold you still."

Märren lay down and slid her back against him. "Don't let me catch the guards' attention. Or Megtr's."

"I'll try my best. Do you know what you're doing?"

"Nay. My childhood and adolescent years were spent training with the Wolf to bear a pelt. They prepared me for the Wolf's den. I was supposed to obtain as much of the dead god's magics as I could before the beast there found me. Fenrir's beast would kill me unless I could escape with whatever I'd acquired."

"And what do you know about the Dragon's lair?"

"Nothing."

Uisge scoffed.

Märren closed her eyes, and Uisge pulled a blanket over them and wrapped his arms around her. She hugged the scale to her chest, feeling its thrumming might, and opened her mind to the god remnant like the old Wolf trainers had taught her—like Belfedrn had once done and explained to her. The scar runes covering her body shook and burned, all of them lighting up in her mind. A shock of power struck her like an axe to the chest.

Märren fell through darkness.

Her stomach rose into her throat as she plummeted into another world, spinning, spiraling, flipping head over heels. She struck the ground with a smack and attempted to regain her senses while the horizon tilted. A small light shone in the sky far, far overhead, but there was no way to reach the aperture she had fallen through. She glanced around. Unforgiving stone and earth sprawled away from her, creating a tunnel, its confines lit by firelight.

The only path.

Märren felt along her limbs. Nothing was broken. The fall had not dislocated anything or harmed her more than the jarring thud of the impact, but this was not Midgard. Rules she took for granted might not apply here. Except for death. That law was governed similarly in both realms. Those of the Wolf who died in the Wolf's den died in Midgard as well and were lost to both worlds. Maybe Helheim took them. Or perhaps they became trapped in some other realm.

Märren crept forward through passageways resembling a cave with irregular walls, which crooked and twisted deeper into the Dragon's lair. Fire crackled, burning in the stone ceiling at intermittent intervals.

Memories flooded her, all her training from when she was young and eager to become a Wolf berserker returning in waves. She had to hurry. To find and claim the runes. Only then would she be able to command each power of a dead god's, and she had to do so before—

A guttural growl sounded in the darkness, and an atavistic

fear surged through her. She hurtled on, nearly twisting her ankle on uneven ground. Whatever beast lurked in the Dragon's den, protecting the god's powers, would not have been killed in the past wars. In Fenrir's den, the deformed wolf or giant—depending on the account of the warrior or berserker who had caught sight of it and was able to return to Midgard—was still there, ready to devour any who sought what no human should. A traveler to the den attempted to collect what they could and flee the realm before the mutilated beast caught and killed them, but a person only had one chance, one visit they could ever make.

The scuff of claws and a tail, and perhaps scales, dragged along the passageway behind Märren. She sprinted on, careening around sharp bends. The tunnel divided into two with one route leading up and the other down deeper into whatever mountain this was.

"Up is a chance to escape before the beast consumes her."

"She'll never command the power of the Dragon. She should give up now."

"She's come so far. To give up without obtaining at least one power would be devastating. After all she's done..."

Märren swallowed her terror and delved deeper, charging into the passageway leading downward.

"If she dies here, who knows where the Valkyries will take her."

"Probably to Valhalla for attempting this mighty feat."

"No! Not Valhalla. She cannot go there."

Märren flinched at the thought, and her stomach cramped.

She barreled down another stretch. The sound of slapping footfalls diminished but did not fade completely. Perhaps she should flee this place at the next opportunity. If dying in the Dragon's lair was considered as glorious and honorable as dying in battle, this was not for her, something she had not considered. It had all seemed so distant before, so unreal and unobtainable.

But this was what she had yearned for. For so many long years, she had turned Belfedrn and all her kin down, shunning the pack itself, for this one chance. She had done so for herself and Eimri, but she could not abandon her daughter by being taken to Valhalla, not even for this.

"Do not pass on your one chance at wielding the power of a scale," a feminine voice in her head said, although it was unfamiliar, its figure veiled.

She ran on for what felt like hours, the pursuing creature never tiring or falling too far behind. The passages led nowhere. Every so often, the tunnels would branch with another fork leading upward, an escape for the sane and those who had had enough to return to Midgard bearing nothing to show for their efforts.

Märren's lungs burned, and her legs ached, her feet pounding as she ran. The path she chose kept her ahead of the beast who hunted her, but it was not leading her to any runes. She slowed her breakneck pace and glanced about. There had to be some trickery here. The Dragon was better known for treachery than even the Wolf, also for wisdom and malevolence and dark cunning. Things would likely be different here than in Fenrir's den.

She reached out and ran her hands along the walls as she continued her flight, feeling for something she could not see. The clattering drag of claws and a scaled tail drew closer, as well as a rasping breath that sounded in the darkness. She glanced over her shoulder.

The firelight in the area she had run through winked out. Only shadows and darkness waited there, and they came rushing closer like a tangible creature. Märren cried out in fear and hurtled onward, and her right hand fell into a nothingness. She halted and entered the wall there, slipping through stone and dirt as if it were mist.

Only darkness lay ahead. She felt her way along, hurrying. A roar blasted through the caverns, ringing her ears. The slapping footfalls quickened, turning into the hidden passageway in pursuit. A light glowed ahead, and she darted toward it. There, sitting upright on a pedestal was a scale as red as blood—a full scale as large as her torso with a glowing rune on its surface.

Märren hurried for it, reaching. When her fingers clamped around the scale's edge, it disappeared and power rumbled through her. Her bones shook, and her skin hardened, taking on the texture of stone or similar—of dragon hide—and segmenting into scales.

She gasped as thrumming magic lashed through her chest and limbs. Then the sensation faded to a whisper, residing somewhere within her but locked away. The beast pursuing her rushed closer.

A faint light shone in the distance, on the far side of the pedestal, one path leading up and out of the lair, the other onward. Märren's legs were still shaking, her arms tingling as she ignored the exit from the realm and ran on through shadowed caverns, the walls narrowing in on her as she went. She stepped beyond an archway, and a vast chamber sprawled away into the distance, portions of it lit by firelight, although stalagmites and stalactites curtained off sections.

The huffing breath of the creature pursuing her drew closer, its rasp loud and grating. A gleam of firelight shone beneath the scales of the beast's neck. Dragon fire. Wings scraped against walls that were tight for Märren, but somehow this beast fit inside even though it rose ten times taller than her.

Firelight flashed, and an inferno blasted from the creature's maw. Märren leapt to the side, scurrying around a stalagmite and hunkering down against its base, cowering and covering her head. Flames rushed past in a deluge of fire, sizzling, making the air around Märren take on its scalding heat. She trembled and tucked her head between her knees as sweat streamed from her brow. The voices in her head raged.

The fire died, the air sweltering and smoking. A roar followed, and Märren sprinted away, veering around a cluster of stalactites. The far end of the chamber shimmered with orange light. She rushed toward it, but another, fainter light caught her attention.

Far to her left, another pedestal waited. She glanced over her shoulder. The dragon was coming for her.

"If she thinks she will gather all the Dragon's powers, she'll certainly die and have gained nothing."

"While losing Eimri in the process."

"She has already come farther than any Wolf could have dreamed."

She wheeled to her left, sprinting for the pedestal, tripping and stumbling, her strides lengthening to catch herself as she almost sprawled onto her face. She reached out to stop herself from falling and grabbed the lip of the pedestal, quickly regaining her senses and leaping for the floating claws and a rune atop it. Just before she touched them, the talons disappeared, but strength surged through her hand, which stretched and extended outward as if to strengthen a weapon in her grasp. But she did not carry her axe.

Dragon claws.

She kicked off the pedestal and hurtled on, again passing on a tunnel that would allow her to escape the lair, but she had not run fast enough. Fire blasted again, creating a wall of flames in her path, the wall rushing toward her. She could not stop. Could not avoid it. The voices screamed, and the child said something that struck her like a blade.

"The Dragon's hide."

Märren searched for the first power she had obtained, delving into her bones, and her skin hardened, segmenting once again. She barreled through the fire, heat rising but unable to scorch her. She erupted from the other side, and her magic fell away, exhausting her, the ends of her hair smoking.

"She cannot do that often, or it'll tire her and she'll be caught and devoured."

She neared the glow at the far end of the chamber. There, molten rock and fire flowed over a rock overhang above a cliff, creating a waterfall of lava. At the base of the cliff, lava pooled and flowed in streams, which caused the temperature to soar and pull sweat from her skin.

Märren felt for the magic of the Dragon's skin again, but it had fled too far from her exhausted mind. She would not be able to use it again so soon, though she doubted it would save her from running across or through molten rock anyway.

A deep growl sounded just behind her, and she ran on in the only direction she could—straight at the falls. Heat pounded against her in waves as she neared and glanced up. If she could scale the wall on either side of the cascading lava, maybe she could avoid the monster chasing her. She felt for the Dragon's claw, but its magic was also buried and had only given her the sensation of empowering a weapon in her grip. She grunted in frustration as she reached the bank of a lava stream and jumped. Patches of fire burned along its surface, and the heat seared her flailing boots before she landed on the other side, scrambling for the cliff face.

She leapt as high up the stone wall as she could and began grasping for hand and footholds, pulling herself up in small increments. The beast's breath drew closer. She reached overhead but found nothing else to grasp onto, and instead, glanced back. The scarred and spiked face of a monstrous dragon with flaming red eyes leered at her, its body draped in shadows. Its wings unfurled as it sucked in a breath.

Märren reached as high as she could, scrabbling for a hold,

her attention drawn to the falls of fire. The lava flowed over the lip above, creating a gap between the falls and the cliff. She hesitated for only a heartbeat before hurling herself from the wall and landing on her feet, although they gave out under the impact, and her knees struck stone. She ignored her shooting pains and bleeding flesh and sprinted for the gap between the falls and cliff as dragon fire blasted the area where she had been, crackling and charring everything.

She slipped behind the falls, its heat causing welts to rise on her cheeks. Behind the flowing lava was an opening—an archway in the stone. A pedestal with flames burning atop it and forming a rune waited there. She grabbed the symbol's fire, taking it into her body. Her lungs burned like hot embers, causing her to wail in pain.

"She's taken the Dragon's breath."

The monster pursuing her shrieked, its muzzle erupting through the lava falls, smoke billowing from its snout. Märren plowed on through the archway, ignoring another opening with steps leading upward. The archway opened into a chamber composed of stone bricks, resembling the inner walls of a castle. Similar to the walls of Torank. But ancient runes were engraved in the bricks. The air turned cool, much cooler than the last chamber. Torches burned in sconces on the walls. Behind her, the beast lumbered forward.

She dashed on and arrived at diverging paths leading to her left and right. The shimmer of gold and silver shone to her left. Piles of coin, bracelets, and jewels glinted. Her muscles tensed. The passageway to her right ended in a dull glow.

It's a trick. Vast enough quantities of gold and silver could possibly buy her a dragon, but they were probably not something she could bring back to Midgard.

Märren tore down the darker path to her right as dragon fire gushed through the tunnel behind her. She briefly closed her eyes and barreled on. The light grew brighter.

Another pedestal. This one held what appeared to be a miniature skull of a dragon, horns and spikes protruding from its bones. A glowing blue rune was engraved in its forehead.

"It's more treachery."

"She'll never be able to bear a second skull."

"It's the Dragon's wisdom."

Märren snatched the skull, and it disappeared, burning her arm. Her mind thumped and swelled, the taste of bloody meat filling her mouth. The idea of ancient truths, of knowledge concerning Midgard and other realms, seeped through her like fleeting memories.

One passageway beyond led onward, and another up and out. She ignored the escape route and ran on, glancing over her shoulder. A cloud of flames surrounded the monster, lighting up its underbelly and lower jaw as it lumbered toward her. Its eyes smoldered. She fled through twisting corridors, descending deeper and deeper into the Dragon's lair, the air growing warmer, heavier.

She burst into a vast chamber where piles of gold and jewels created mounds. Firelight danced around the periphery, forming shadows and monstrous shapes. Märren shivered, her boots clinking over rivers of coin as she trudged through hoarded treasure. Open chests spilled goblets and silver crowns decorated with rubies and emeralds. She reached down and grasped a handful of coin. Such wealth could buy peace and land for all her kin.

The creature pursuing her roared as it advanced, its smoke spewing into the chamber. Märren dropped her loot as she climbed onto a pile of treasure and tried to run, but coin and necklaces slid under her feet and spilled, briefly causing her to lose her footing.

She hurried for the far end of the chamber, ascending and descending mountains of treasure. She fell and tumbled down one slope, scrambling up another as pounding feet rammed through the riches, the creature unfazed by the treacherous footing. The end of the chamber neared—a dead end. But there, one last pedestal loomed over the piles of treasure. A dragon's open maw and tongue sat upon it with a rune floating between its teeth. She clawed her way up the pedestal's shaft, fighting for handholds before grabbing its lip and kicking herself upward.

She grasped the maw, and it swirled into firelight and rushed in through her lips, burning her tongue. Her throat felt thicker and more powerful. A deep groan that sounded like it carried from the mouth of a beast escaped her lips.

The Dragon's voice. Märren shivered with awe. A narrow passageway opened in the wall ahead.

"Look behind you."

A roar erupted, the power of it flinging Märren off the pedestal and into a pile of treasure below. She rolled down an incline and scrambled about to get her bearings. The face of a twisted old dragon leered down at her, teeth flashing, eyes burning.

Then she saw what she had been hunting all along—not another pedestal but an idol to the Dragon's power, a glowing red rune. The same symbol she had carved and tattooed on her chest. This rune was positioned behind the skull of the monster looming over her, and it burned like fire.

There was at least one last power to obtain. She glanced at the tunnel leading to freedom and then again at the creature. A face of malice glared back at her, baring teeth, smoke spewing from its nostrils, more hatred than all the creatures of Midgard could carry billowing from it.

"Another trial."

"This one impossible, a folly meant to deceive. To lure the greediest and most ambitious to their deaths."

"She desires this rune more than any other."

Märren called upon whatever strength she had left, and a voice came from her throat that was unlike anything she had uttered before. Her echoing cry blasted through the chamber. *"Forn ormr, uggr mér nei. Hlýða minn tala. Iak em hjá ykkr."*

The monster hesitated. It blinked. Märren leapt for its spines, clambering upward as she swung her feet and kicked, scaling the side of the beast's jaw, then climbing up its face. The monster roared, rearing its head back, flinging Märren higher as she reached for more spiked holds. She grasped a horn rising from the back of its head and heaved herself up as the creature shook its head, its claws rising to tear her away. She swung her leg over the dragon's neck and planted herself on the spiked scales there, hugging the rune to her chest. The creature's spines that were beneath her impaled her legs, drawing blood and piercing deep into her flesh with sharp pain.

Märren cried out as the symbol disappeared and a rush of power smacked her in the chest, cracking ribs and blasting the air from her lungs. She only realized one thought as the monster's claws ripped her from its neck, shredding her back, blood leaking from so many parts of her.

Dragon rider.

She hit a pile of coins with a thud, gazing upward through her darkening vision, the scarred monster snarling over her. The creature lunged, biting into her flesh, devouring her.

60

BELFEDRN

Music hummed as Belfedrn paced through throngs of dancers and drunken Bear and Boar warriors as well as karls from the Bear village they had returned to. A warrior cheered and stumbled, bumping into Belfedrn's bandaged hands, which made him wince and his knees buckle. He had lost one joint from a finger on one hand and two joints from another on the other hand to the black death of frostbite, but he could have lost far more to the giant.

"Jötunn slayer!" Aegmor clapped Belfedrn on the back, hollering for the hundredth time and gulping down a horn's contents as he eyed Belfedrn's bandages. "For centuries, tales will be told of how you sniffed out one of Jötunheim's beasts and rode its frozen beard to the ground. Your hands were probably frozen to the giant so you couldn't let go even if you'd wanted to, but we'll leave that part out, starting tonight!" He guffawed, squeezing Belfedrn's shoulder harder. "And you did all this after putting out both of the jötunn's eyes!"

"It may've been the Bears who killed the monster by cutting its throat open," another Bear berserker added with a drunken grin, "but that'll be a lesser story. One forgotten when those here die. You'll hence be known as the Wolf who hunted down a giant."

"Or the Giant Sniffer!" Aegmor bellowed and smacked his comrade on the backside.

"The monster wouldn't have fallen without the axes of the Bears and Ulfhednar working together on its ankles." Belfedrn grinned and patted them in return. "All will remember that."

The berserkers cheered and drank more. Belfedrn paced. In the distance, the Ulfhednar stood with more Bear and Boar berserkers outside a longhouse, feasting on wild boar and drinking heavily. The Ulfhednar's conversations were more reserved than the others, but this was due to the Wolf's hunger and how much they were swallowing between breaths. Flutes and pipes played dancing music, and many of the Boar people sang an old song of victory, belting out lyrics in drunken pitches, little of which Belfedrn could understand.

Dradn sat at the edge of the shadows, sipping from a horn as he stared into a bonfire. Belfedrn ached to comfort the young man, but first, there was a more pressing matter he had to bring up with the jarls. Too much time had already passed in traveling to this village and celebrating.

Near to the Ulfhednar, Gron, Vard, and Onunith drank and discussed something between themselves. Belfedrn approached, and Gron stepped aside to allow him to enter their circle of conversation.

"The mighty hero," Gron said. "Let glory and honor rain upon you, Ulfhednar."

Belfedrn dipped his head in acknowledgment. "What still awaits us is far closer to my heart."

Vard clenched his jaw, glancing away.

Onunith cleared her throat. "About that... There's something we've been discussing with your jarl."

Belfedrn's chest tightened. They could not renege on their

vows now, not after what the Ulfhednar had risked helping their people. Two Ulfhednar had died, and the pack was ever weakening, but Deyja could still be alive.

"What could possibly have changed—" Belfedrn began, his anger rising before Vard cut him off.

"Just listen to them," the Ulfhednar jarl said.

Belfedrn snarled. "A battle still rages in our lands, our trainees taken as thralls. Suffering and slavery abound while we are here celebrating."

"Life is a constant battle," Onunith said nonconfrontationally. A simple statement. "Finding enough food, shelter, and coin to survive is nothing less than war. You may consider protecting your people and loved ones the highest of priorities, but the battles of life never end. You only have to choose which battles you believe are worth waging, and you must celebrate in between, or you'll go mad."

Belfedrn stepped toward her. "This is not what we—"

"Bear and Boar messengers have come with word," Vard said. "Things have changed."

Belfedrn's heart sank.

"It's not that we won't aid you, Wolf," Gron said. "I'm not the king of the Bear lands, but I am jarl of its second-largest city. I'll grant you Aegmor—my finest berserker—and half of what is left of my berserkers and warriors, but I need the others to remain here and protect our lands."

"The giant is dead," Belfedrn said. "What do you need protection from?"

"The Sea Serpent and Spider have made an alliance." Onunith stared into the distance as she drank. "I'll offer you the same support that Gron has, as well as my axe, but like him, I have a king. I can only offer some of my berserkers and warriors. I cannot leave my village vulnerable when there's a growing threat from the Spiders in the south and now the Sea Serpents to the west."

"Then you should march with us and help us take back our territory." Heat rose in Belfedrn's cheeks. "Now. It's been far too long already that those Serpent scum have walked our lands. Worked our people. Slept in our beds."

Vard rested a placating hand on his shoulder. "What they're trying to tell you is that with our current number of Ulfhednar and a few score of Bears and Boars, we'd fail, and many lives would be lost. The Ulfhednar would be no more. Nearly all the Sea Serpent fighters from their isles swarm our lands, and the Boar scouts say that there are a few Spider legions who have sailed in and joined them. Currently, the Spider numbers are few, but it proves that those clans have formed an alliance to crush others."

"Then we sail to the undefended Serpent Isles instead?" Belfedrn said his next words with as much of an insulting tone as he could muster. "Or are you giving up, too, Jarl?"

"I'm not giving up on anything," Vard snapped. "But we must think before we act, or the last of the Ulfhednar will fall and we'll be nothing more than legend."

"Then we ask the Bear and Boar kings to provide enough warriors to fight our common enemy," Belfedrn said.

"Nay." Gron bit his lip, taking part of his beard into his mouth. "My king would be grateful for what you've done, but he'd never give you enough berserkers to ensure the victory you seek. Especially since his messengers will know that the Spider and Serpent people are raiding and claiming lands. There aren't even that many Bear berserkers to begin with."

"Then it's time to form an allegiance between the Wolf, the Bear, and the Boar," Belfedrn said. "To crush our enemy while we still can. If we try to defend ourselves alone, they'll slaughter us one by one. You've seen what it's like when we work together

—we feed off each other's strengths and shelter one another's weaknesses."

"We've already sent messengers to our kings," Onunith said. "I don't expect mine to see it your way and accept the risk of losing their lands while marching to war with the Ulfhednar and the Bears." She glanced at Gron. "No offense."

"Nah," Gron growled. "My king feels the same about the Wolves and Boars."

"If you desire war," Onunith said to Belfedrn, "there's a better option. The Ravens are poised to be the next to fall to the Spider army. So if you wish to die sooner, you could seek out the Raven people and join them."

"The people of Muninn are wicked and untrustworthy," Belfedrn said.

"Aye." Vard nodded his agreement. "Their magic is as dark as the Spider's."

"And the Ravens are now pinned between the Spiders in the south and the Sea Serpents in the north." Belfedrn growled. "Those two clans have been plotting this war for years."

"Then remain here with the Bears," Gron said. "Until our king decides what we shall do."

"What do you think he'll decide?" Belfedrn asked.

Gron shrugged. "I'd be willing to wager that he'll amass the warriors and berserkers from all the villages and have them gather at Grondnshroud—his city—where they'll remain until war comes to us or he sends them to it."

"And how long will it take for these fighters to gather?" Belfedrn clenched his fists and cracked his knuckles with impatience.

"It'd take near the turning of a couple seasons to amass and supply all our warriors for war." The jarl drank. "There hasn't been the need for such a large-scale legion in decades."

"The Ravens will have fallen long before the turning of a

couple seasons," Belfedrn said. "And we'll have lost another potential ally." He cursed to himself. "It's already too late to stop the Spiders and Sea Serpents, and we'll never find vengeance." He exhaled slowly. "I'll march to Raven lands. Alone, if needed."

"You won't go alone," Vard said. "I've lost as much as you. And you're right—if the Ravens fall, the Spiders and Sea Serpents will rule the west before the Bears and Boars begin to act. I know both of their kings. Neither would be willing to aid the other until it's far too late." He addressed Gron and Onunith. "We'll take every berserker and warrior you can spare, and on the morrow, we will march to Aonark to offer the wicked Raven a deal."

61

BELFEDRN

BELFEDRN SAILED SOUTH WITH THE ULFHEDNAR. A DOZEN BEAR berserkers and a score of their warriors filled more longships, and about as many of the Boars, including Onunith, sailed with them. Belfedrn was glad to have them, except he was never comfortable around Onunith and tried to avoid her. Especially at night. At least until she had taken a Bear berserker or warrior, or sometimes one of her own, to bed. Then he could roam camp without worry. Kesg had thought the situation hilarious until one night Onunith approached him instead of Belfedrn. Kesg quickly rushed away, leaving Belfedrn to scramble for an excuse and hurry after him.

Many days passed as they sailed through Bear and then Boar territory before they were forced to dock and travel by foot at the meandering pace of the other clans' peoples, who believed that sauntering was pushing themselves. They swept westward into Raven lands, avoiding Wolf territory and thus reducing the chance of alerting any Serpent scouts. More days came and went as they traversed the sodden lands of Muninn's people, rain or a mixture of snow always falling.

They passed a cairn, whether natural or stacked by ancient

man, Belfedrn could not tell. He knelt and placed a pebble he had carved a rune into at the cairn's base.

"Why do you always do that?" Dradn asked. "There are no gods left."

"It's a sacrifice for the spirits and land wights. There are still many of those residing in these lands. I can feel them. Especially here."

"You still believe in those creatures? Most of the warriors I trained with said they were myth."

"Just because the old ways are nearly lost doesn't mean that they are wrong. Maybe you, too, could learn to see the spirits."

"I'm no *goði*."

"You don't need to be a *goði* or use Seidr magic to see or speak with them. I'm hardly either of those." He nodded to where Athna paced. "She's more closely linked to the Seidr than any of the Ulfhednar, and she doesn't leave offerings."

"Then you probably don't need such creatures to wield their strange magics of fortune and fate either."

"You never know what you'll need."

They trod along.

"The advantage of a pack member wielding the spear is their range with the weapon," Belfedrn eventually said, realizing the young man should already know this, but Belfedrn had no other words to comfort or distract him from his depression. Thelira strode ahead of them with the rest of the Ulfhednar. "Also, a spear can easily be thrown, but if you do so, you better make sure it wounds or kills your attacker because you'll be unarmed for a moment. Your enemy knows this. So use the weapon to your advantage—as a warning to keep them back and as a deadly blade before they get within range with an axe or sword."

"But its weakness is its shaft." Dradn held his spear overhead as if absently going through the motions and using it to block an attack. His vigor had still not fully returned after the duel with Thelira. "An axe can chop right through it and split my skull."

"Use your shield for defense and a spear thrust against anyone charging you. But your axe or seax should always be close, in case your spear splinters."

"And if my shield shatters?"

"Pray to Fenrir. And move swiftly."

Dradn's shoulders sagged. "It's a curse that Fenrir was the god who died in our lands." Dradn's tone was melancholy.

"And why is that?"

"Because his magical remnants are fur and hide, which are easily defiled, their powers lost. If either of the pelts of the Ulfhednar who fell when battling the giant retained their power, I could've taken one."

"It's a blessing and a curse." Belfedrn paused. "When we lose a fighter, most often we lose their pelt, but then our enemies cannot take it and try to use it. A scale may not be cut so easily, but as you saw with the Sea Serpents, their relics can be stolen and maybe one day used against them."

"If one could ever bear the parts of two gods."

"Impossible. But an enemy who was trained in the arts and hadn't yet taken up a god remnant could do so with a pelt." His thoughts strayed to Märren and her dreams of bearing a Dragon scale. He had always hoped she would one day achieve her desires, since she would not join the pack, but she was probably long dead. Like Lyrne. Like Deyja. Like so many of the Wolf people.

Dradn grumbled something under his breath.

Belfedrn clapped him on the back. "You've handled your second square of pelt without difficulty. You may not have noticed, but I have."

Dradn straightened a little.

Belfedrn continued, "I've often wondered if the slow route to bearing more of Fenrir's might would be easier and thus make a berserker stronger and live longer than one who takes it all at once and flares brightly only to snuff out in a few decades."

"Has that been tried?"

"Nay. Men crave power and cannot wait to take it up, no matter if in the end they succumb to its addicting pull. This is the way it's been since the gods fell."

The top of the sun dropped below the horizon, and a soft wolf cry rang out, a sense of warning carrying with it. Belfedrn rushed toward the call. A stream ran through an area of mud and dead grass, a single alder rising from its bank. Multiple spear hafts were planted in the ground, and horse heads were impaled on their spikes.

Eakthr crept closer, inspecting the rotting eyes and blood stains on the shafts.

"Who or what would've done this?" Thelira asked.

"Someone who wants to summon the land wights in this area." Belfedrn pushed past her. "Remove the heads. They call to the spirits. To anger them. They're sacrifices and draw not only wights but also entice dark elves and dwarves."

Athna strode toward the offerings, her hand burning with the white fire of Fenrir. She touched each stake, and the wood burst into flames, quickly engulfing the heads. No smoke rose from her fires.

"This land will soon be cleansed," Athna said as twilight faded, leaving her white flames to burn brighter. "We can rest here for the night."

The Bear warriors who caught up with them and watched shared worried glances. Many of the Boars knelt and drank from the stream, and then Onunith and her people gathered kindling and wood to start a fire. Belfedrn wandered away into a copse of birches, overturning rotting leaves and grass until he found what he was looking for—Seidr man's fungus. He plucked one from the earth and dropped it into his mouth, slowly chewing as he sat against a trunk. Consuming one of the mushrooms felt like the right thing to do, which probably meant he was figuratively lost and did not know what path to follow. He leaned his head back against the tree, his eyelids growing heavy.

"You're not doing that shite again, are you?" Kesg said. "Here?" He grumbled and stalked away.

Time crawled by before the hair on the back of Belfedrn's neck spiked. Something entered the copse, moving silently through the brush. The wights had come. He drew his axe, clutching it to his waist as he slowly slid himself up the trunk of the birch.

Dradn stepped into the open, moonlight silvering his hair and stubbly chin.

Belfedrn relaxed, returning his axe to his belt. "Here." He waved the boy over and offered him one of the mushrooms.

"What is this?" Dradn's face wrinkled in disgust.

"A mushroom."

"I see that."

"Eat it."

"It's not one of the edible types I recognize."

"It's edible but not nutritious. That's why you don't know it. It's to help you see the spirits."

Dradn cocked an eyebrow at him.

Belfedrn sank back into the grass. "Do what you will, but I've already partaken."

Dradn stood there for some time before placing the mushroom in his mouth and slowly chewing. He grimaced and stuck his tongue out.

"Ignore its taste," Belfedrn said. "You have to swallow it for it to open your mind to the other worlds around us."

Dradn gulped down a lump and sat beside Belfedrn, who leaned back against the birch, breathing shallowly.

"They're already here." Belfedrn pointed to the far end of the copse, where a figure composed of dull light moved through the branches.

Dradn lurched, his body so tense he did not breathe.

"Don't let them sense your fear," Belfedrn whispered. "They are wights and spirits. Some are friendly but many are not, and the unfriendly kind realize when they've gained the upper hand."

Dradn trembled as he squeezed the handle of his seax. The first visitor became more distinct—a humanoid of tree and leaf. This woman smiled at Belfedrn and winked before passing on through the copse without a word.

"Do you see her, too?" Dradn asked.

"Aye."

"Then we both can't have lost our minds."

Next came a water wight from the stream, her skin rippling and translucent. She sat across from them, never taking her unblinking eyes from Dradn.

"Speak to her," Belfedrn whispered.

Dradn's lips did not move, his posture rigid, reminding Belfedrn of himself the first time he had seen Lyrne naked. "I... can't."

"She's engaging with you, not me."

Dradn's jaw worked a few times before any sound came out. "What were the horse heads for?"

The spirit giggled, running her hand across her legs. "They weren't of my doing or the doing of any of those here. The Spider broke the Horse."

"They broke the Horse clan?" Belfedrn asked so only Dradn should hear. Dradn relayed the question.

"If that is the clan whose people bore the hoofs of the fallen Horse god." The water wight stood and stepped closer to Dradn, who leaned as far back against a trunk as he could, pressing himself against its bark. “In a world without gods, there’s nothing to separate the people of Midgard and the spirits.” She laid a hand on his cheek.

Dradn gasped and jerked, smacking his head against the tree.

“Many of the bright elves have come and gone,” the wight said, “but some remain, with their songs and poetry and dancing. However, they can be vicious warriors when they need to be.”

Dradn nodded furiously. Belfedrn prodded him, attempting to remind him to remain calm.

“Meanwhile, the dark elves and dwarves have taken a liking to these lands”—she glanced around, holding her palms upward —“this beautiful and yet viciously violent Midgard. However, they did not appreciate the sacrifices made in their honor. Or at least the dwarves did not. The dark elves enjoyed it very much.”

“Ask her about the Spiders,” Belfedrn whispered. “If they’re plotting to tempt the dwarves and dark elves to their cause.”

Dradn’s lips parted with a dry click. “Are the Spider people working with the dwarves and elves?”

The wight giggled again. “‘Working’ is something all but the wights do.” She patted his head.

A short and stout silhouette appeared, seeming to rise between two of the trunks near the edge of the copse. Belfedrn’s hackles spiked, and he found his seax in his hand. The silhouette held an object—a weapon of some sort—reaching out and seeming to offer it to Belfedrn or Dradn. Neither of them moved. The wight beside them grinned through watery lips. Eventually, the silhouette set down the weapon and slowly receded into the grass and earth, vanishing.

“What was that?” Dradn’s voice was tense and breathy.

“I told you that the dwarves and dark elves took notice,” the wight said.

Dradn sat up on his haunches, trying to see what the silhouette had left behind.

Belfedrn grabbed him by the shoulder, stopping him from rising, and said, "Be wary, warrior. Whatever is offered by a dwarf comes with a price. They do not give away what they craft for naught. If you take it, you will carry a debt. One you will have to repay."

Dradn shrugged off Belfedrn's grip and crept past the wight, her smile unchanged. He stopped where the dwarf had been standing and stooped, inspecting something there before cautiously reaching for it.

"Do not take it just because you feel like it'll fill an emptiness inside you," Belfedrn said. "You are still a warrior who bears two pelts and may one day join the Ulfhednar."

Dradn straightened, lifting an axe by its handle. Runes engraved in its head glowed with an eerie blue light.

"It's beautiful... Magnificent." Dradn held the axe aloft and rotated it around, its runes blinding in the dark. "A weapon fit for a god."

Worry created a pit in Belfedrn's stomach.

The screeching of ravens sounded overhead. Belfedrn lurched and staggered to his feet, the effects of the mushroom still weighing on him, the wight suddenly gone. He hurried out of the copse, following the cries. Beyond the trees, birds flew past, darkening the moon.

Belfedrn ran for the nearest clearing, waving his arms, shouting. He threw back his head and howled with all his might.

The Ravens have come.

62

CAËTIN

Caëtin stood atop a battlement overlooking the Vkum River as it flowed to the southern walls and out into the lower city and world beyond. Several days had passed since Taknhal had departed with most of Aonark's fighters.

"Release her," Caëtin said.

Sanre blew into a horn, its blast radiating over the city and all watching. The onlookers fell quiet, and a small ship floated down the Vkum, winding through the city, its white sail emblazoned with flying ravens. The wind shoved into the sail, pushing the boat along. People lined the banks, watching as the vessel passed, Darstrid's body lying on clumps of rowan, bowls of sacrificed herbs and flowers and weapons beside her. She was wrapped in her cloak, only her face showing, staring skyward with open, dead eyes, axe in hand and placed over her breast. Huginn flew over her, matching her pace.

"My sister, the feared battle Seidr," Caëtin muttered under her breath. "Probably the shortest-lived jarl in the history of Aonark. May you feast eternally in Valhalla where Grimmurk and the Spider cannot touch you."

Another horn blast rang out. "Open the gates," Sanre called.

Soldiers at the base of the walls turned wheels and used poles to heave open the river gates. The ship passed through, and a woman in black stood along the walls above the waterway, singing high notes brimming with melancholy. Her cloak lifted in the wind, resembling wings. The beauty of her tone, and her lyrics in the old tongue, stabbed Caëtin's heart. The boat drifted beyond the walls and out of Aonark, and Caëtin's eyes burned with tears.

"Light them," Caëtin said, and Sanre trumpeted her horn.

Archers along the walls drew their bowstrings and dipped the wrapped heads of their arrows into braziers. The heads of the arrows ignited.

"Loose." Caëtin watched the boat leave her home forever, her heart heavy.

Sanre sounded the horn one last time, and the archers loosed their flaming arrows, the projectiles streaming high and falling in magnificent arcs before plunging into the ship. Fires flared, and smoke rose, smearing the horizon. The flaming vessel drifted away and into another realm as the singing woman reached a crescendo of lyrics and emotion.

"Sleep, feast, love, and drink well, Sister." Caëtin's vision blurred as she raised a fist to her breast and pounded her chest. "And hold your blade tight as you walk the soul road and cross the Raven's bridge. We did not always see eye to eye, but I loved and trusted you more than any other in our family. Soon, I'll join you."

All those standing along the battlements followed Caëtin's lead, pounding their fists against their chests, creating a hollow drumming sound that accompanied the high notes of the singer. Huginn cawed. Until everything faded into smoke.

At twilight, Caëtin strode along the southern walls. The catapults and trebuchets there had been prepared for war, and nearby, boulders were piled high, waiting to become projectiles. The sparkling Vkum River swept southward beyond the walls and lower city, the smoke of Darstrid's passing washed away by rain.

The Spiders could arrive at Aonark by land or water, but no fires glowed on the horizon and no smoke rose in the direction of any surrounding villages. Caëtin stared into the night, her thoughts a tempest of worry and doubt. In a time of madness and rage, perhaps Taknhal was better suited for leading the Raven clan. Maybe Grimmurk had saved their people from Caëtin's mistakes.

A cloud of ravens soared overhead and spiraled lower, swirling together beside her. Halfnr appeared in a flurry of feathers, bowing his head.

Caëtin's stomach sank. "What news?"

"No war yet rages, and our ranks were undisturbed when I left Taknhal, but my unkindness spotted a lone Ulfhednar man in our lands."

"An Ulfhednar in Raven territory?"

"Aye."

"And he wasn't in a pack?"

"Nay."

"Must have gotten lost hunting squirrels," she said. "If one of the Ulfhednar wished to remain hidden, you'd have a hard time spotting him. There could be more of them."

"Your suspicions are probably accurate. The berserker emerged from the brush as my ravens flew over. He even howled."

"Announcing his presence." Her thoughts tumbled. A trap from yet another clan? Or could the opportunity be nurtured into the alliance the Ravens needed? Huginn landed on her arm and cocked her head, blinking as she dropped an object from her talons. It clattered and rolled about on the walk—a rune stone. Huginn's beak gaped, as if attempting to speak to Caëtin, encouraging her with her body language and gift to go investigate the matter. It must mean something. Caëtin steeled herself, trusting her companion. "Take me there. He may wish to speak with us."

"We should bring more knights."

"I doubt the Wolf people would ever bind themselves to the Spider. Given their history, the Wolves would be even less likely to join those bastards than we would. And time isn't on our side. You're certain it was an Ulfhednar and not a Spider warrior? A recluse?"

"Absolutely, unless my raven eyes and ears lied to me."

"I hope your senses aren't aging too quickly. Take me there. Now."

Halfnr dipped his hooded head again and collapsed into ravens. Caëtin joined him, and they soared east—a strange direction for a Wolf to have arrived from. They flew on as night descended, their eyesight poor in the dark. Halfnr led her in slow swooping circles, the landscape below a wash of moonlight. Nightfall and empty branches made Caëtin's unkindness want to roost, and she had to remain vigilant so she would not succumb to the temptation.

Their circles grew wider as Halfnr searched about. A flash of flame appeared within a copse in the distance but quickly snuffed out. Halfnr's ravens flew toward it and landed near the base of a tree, merging into his human form. Caëtin joined him, standing and glancing about in the dimness, ready to become her unkindness in an instant if need be.

Nothing moved, and she crept onward to where a lone man in a pelt sat, placing offering stones around a birch tree.

"You are Ulfhednar?" Caëtin asked.

The man did not even flinch. "Aye. I'm Belfedrn Nvutsson. I hoped that the Raven would come."

"Did you hear us arrive?"

"Indeed. My wolf eyes saw you circling in the sky. I also smelled you before you came through the trees."

Do I smell that strongly? "You stink as well, dog. What're you doing in Raven territory?"

"Your scent is not unpleasant. It's just there, like anyone's." He paused. "I was looking for your berserkers... or Knights Black, if that's your current title for them, and your warriors. Or the jarl who commands them."

"This is not the time to cross our borders without welcome. Your presence could be construed as a threat."

"I am no threat to you."

"Are your people aligning with the Spider?"

"The Wolves would never do so. The Spider and the Wolf are ancient enemies."

"But there are ways to coerce people into alliances."

Belfedrn sat in silence for a moment before looking over at her, the skin around his eyes painted, black lines running down his cheeks. He was tall and lanky with corded muscle, his hair and beard brown but streaked with gray. He stared into her eyes without blinking, acting surprised—like men sometimes do when taken aback by the attractiveness of a woman.

Caëtin hid a smirk. Maybe she would have a subtler and unexpected way to maintain the upper hand with him.

"The Sea Serpents raided our lands and drove us from them," he said.

"If you're seeking solace, you've come to the wrong place."

"I'm not looking for shelter or protection. I came here to offer your people aid in return for helping me drive the Serpents from our lands and reclaiming those who were taken. Right now, you're surrounded. To the south, Spiders roam. In the north, there are Serpents. Together, they will crush the Raven."

"How many Ulfhednar do you have with you?"

"Less than a dozen."

She scoffed in disbelief. "Then you might as well have brought a child with a wooden sword to an axe duel."

"I've already sought aid elsewhere. There are also two score of Bear and Boar warriors accompanying us, along with another dozen berserkers from each clan."

Caëtin's thoughts collided. "You've managed to convince some of the clans to work together?"

"Only after we helped rid the Boar and Bear people of their frost giant problem. Are you one of the Knights Black?"

"Aye. I'm Caëtin Harekrsdóttir. Where are these other fighters of yours?"

"Come." Belfedrn stood and motioned, encouraging her to follow him. "They're eager to meet you, but tonight, they're feasting."

He said those last words with annoyance, as if he were tired of feasting. Caëtin kept a hand on her sword's hilt as she and Halfnr followed Belfedrn out of the copse and across a field where rain drizzled upon them. They entered a ravine where a few sentries were barely visible in the darkness, and Belfedrn led them upstream toward the roar of a waterfall. Firelight flickered in the night, the smell of roasting meat and bread clinging to the air.

"Come and eat." Belfedrn waved her on. He paused before a semicircle of Ulfhednar, indicating one older man, as the Ulfhednar eyed her and Halfnr. "This is Vard, my jarl."

Belfedrn introduced the other Ulfhednar and some of the Bear and Boar berserkers, although Caëtin did not care to learn all their names. She accepted a horn of mead and turned back to Halfnr.

"Return to Taknhal's army and keep watch over the situation there," Caëtin told her knight. "Let me know if anything changes. If on the morrow, I don't find you or one of my messengers doesn't reach you, tell the knights that the Ulfhednar have become our enemies."

Halfnr eyed the warriors around them, his face hooded, then burst into ravens, squawking and taking flight. More than a few of those watching flinched or lurched back. One shorter and stockier Ulfhednar cried out in surprise, his voice high-pitched with horror.

Vard laughed. "Sit, knight of the black. Eat and drink with us. Let us talk."

63

CAËTIN

CAËTIN RUBBED HER BLEARY EYES AS SHE SAT UP, THE SUN ALREADY high and shining down into the ravine. The mead, need for recovery from the Raven's magics, and the late night without much sleep must have gotten to her. Or, like Darstrid, the additional god parts she carried were affecting her, but she was unaware of the change.

Nearby, some of the Ulfhednar snored, but Belfedrn did not. He paced, wringing the shaft of his spear while speaking to a young man and woman who were arguing with him and each other.

Family? In her experience, it was usually family who argued the most heatedly without resorting to violence. Thoughts of Treln and Lythi and what they were doing without her right now tugged at a thread of guilt.

"I appreciate the food and drink," she said to Belfedrn, interrupting his discussion with the younger warriors, "but I must return to Aonark. Travel on to the gates of my city, and I'll welcome you and your fighters in to help defend her." *Though you'll never know the whereabouts of Muninn's temple.*

Belfedrn's lupine eyes wandered. "So you've decided?"

"I have."

"And if we defeat the Spider," he pressed, "then I have your word that the Raven people will aid the Wolves in removing the Sea Serpents from our lands?"

"If by that time the Sea Serpents haven't already come from the north to crush us all, then aye."

Belfedrn nodded as a muscle at his jaw bulged.

The shrieking of ravens rang out overhead, and an unkindness soared over the ravine and into the gully. Dread swallowed Caëtin as the Ulfhednar stepped back to give the ravens room to land and become Halfnr.

"Caëtin." Halfnr glanced at those around them. "Thank Muninn you're still here. There's a complication concerning Taknhal's army."

Caëtin's heart clenched. *No one could've predicted such a thing.*

"I spotted a massive army of Spiders sweeping in from the west, heading toward Taknhal and his legions. Our enemies must know their path and where they're heading."

"Did you inform my brother?"

"Indeed. I spoke with him first, but he wouldn't consider returning to Aonark. Not from my suggestion alone. He sent out scouts to confirm what I saw while his army finds a place to hole up and prepares for battle."

"How many Spiders are there?"

"At least thrice the number of Taknhal's fighters. And I fear any widows were in hiding, as I saw them early this morning after the sun had already risen."

"Fucking imbecile! He'll get them all slaughtered."

"It seems that way."

Caëtin's mind turned over possible options. She retrieved a burned-out ember from a fire and found a flat rock where she drew the rough outline of Raven territory in ash. "Where is Taknhal?"

Halfnr took the ember and marked a location in the south, near to the Horse border.

"And this Spider army?" Caëtin asked.

"Here." He scribbled a black 'x' on another area.

Caëtin marked Aonark's location with a rune. "In light of this, even if Taknhal realizes he erred, he shouldn't attempt to return to Aonark now. The Spiders could easily intercept his legions during their retreat. His Raven fighters would be massacred."

"Without his knights and warriors, Aonark will fall."

She groaned. "At this point, it probably would be for the best if they found a spot that's advantageous for defense."

"Does your jarl command another, smaller pack?" Belfedrn, along with several other Ulfhednar who had taken an interest, stood behind them, studying their diagram.

Vard nodded. "A sacrifice for the lives of the many."

Caëtin whipped her head back around to the map. "A sacrifice to distract the Spider... To give them someone else to fight so the larger army can return to Aonark?"

Belfedrn used his seax to point at the locations. "If you had a small pack in this area"—he planted the tip of his weapon on a spot northwest of the Spider's current location—"they could get the Spiders' attention and draw them off course. But this pack would have to engage with your enemy long enough for your army to reach your city."

"This pack couldn't be too small, or they wouldn't last long enough," Caëtin said as she brushed her hair from her face. "And no matter what, they would all die."

"A sacrifice," Vard reiterated.

"I have no jarl other than the fool leading our people to their deaths." A wave of nausea sloshed up Caëtin's throat before she could shove it down. The Wolf's idea was sound and could be her people's only chance for survival. But whom could she send?

These Wolf and Bear and Boar people would never volunteer for such a task—not that they would ever arrive at the designated location far to the west in time to pull off the ploy. The sacrificial band of warriors would need to be able to fly or already be near the city.

The world tilted around her, and she braced herself against the rock. There was only one option. It was almost unthinkable, reprehensible, but it could potentially save most of the Raven army, if Taknhal would agree to return to Aonark and help defend their city. Even before Darstrid had died, Caëtin had far fewer loyal fighters than Taknhal. After that incident, most of those who had followed Darstrid pledged their axes and swords to her brother.

"Halfnr..." Caëtin swallowed and stood, clasping his forearm. "I do not ask this lightly, and I wish it could be me instead of you."

The knight nodded, his eyes draining of emotion. "I understand. You must return to the city."

She squeezed his arm. "But first, in light of this, I'll speak with Taknhal and make sure he sees reason before we risk everything. If you don't hear any further commands from me, take all the Knights Black and warriors from Aonark, all those who are still loyal to me, and lead them west. To loop around and attack the Spiders before slowly retreating and drawing our enemies farther from Taknhal. I fear it's the only chance our army has."

"You'll be risking nearly as much as the rest of us, and you'll do it for those who chose to follow another over you." He inhaled slowly. "When the knights and warriors I bring with me are gone, you'll have no more fighters. Taknhal will command all of them."

Guilt and shame clawed at her insides. "But if we don't..."

Halfnr dipped his head. "It must be done."

Caëtin turned and addressed Belfedrn and Vard again. "If my Raven fighters do what you suggest, you will likely die as well. After the Spiders slay those who are distracting them, they'll soldier on toward Aonark in pursuit of Taknhal's army. The Ulfhednar and your Bear and Boar friends probably won't reach the city before the Spider people do. We're far to the east."

Vard rubbed at his shaven chin. "I see. Should we head back to Boar territory?"

"No." Belfedrn grabbed his jarl's arm. "We can't let this go on any—"

"If you pledge yourselves and all those with you to our cause, and you travel fast enough, I'd be willing to meet you here." Caëtin poked a finger at a location on the map more easterly than Aonark. "Then, depending on where the Spiders are and how they're moving, we can sweep around and enter Aonark from the north. Or, if the Spider army's position won't allow it, you can flee Raven territory and leave us to our own problems."

"And where is 'here'?" Belfedrn nodded at her finger. "Do we just wait in the spot where we think it is and pray for ravens to fly overhead?"

"There's a crumbling old ruin of a dwelling in a hillside. No one resides there. You'll see the hills from afar."

Vard and Belfedrn shared a quiet conversation before the pack leader said, "Aye. Look for us there."

Caëtin gripped Halfnr around his upper arms and said, "If Taknhal still wants to fight the Spiders in the open, I'll come and stop you from walking into the face of death, my friend."

"I'll see you again in Valhalla." He broke into ravens, whose cries deafened the ears of those around them as they soared in the direction of Aonark.

Caëtin's unkindness landed and merged into her human form as the veiled sun dropped low in the sky. Rain fell in buckets.

Many Knights Black and Raven warriors argued, pointing at one another with fingers or weapons, but they made way for her, and she marched through their ranks and said, "Stop fighting amongst yourselves! You're only helping the Spider." She grabbed one agitated knight by the neck and shook him as easily as a man could shake a babe. "Your chance to fight will come soon enough!"

The quarrels died out as she passed.

The army had taken a position atop a hill, which provided sweeping views of the area. Nearby, hobbled horses grazed uneasily, their ears flicking, tails swishing, any sound or gust of wind making them jerk their heads up and snort.

"Taknhal!" Caëtin hurried along until she arrived at the center of the Raven army.

Taknhal sat upon a mound of stones there, his chin resting on his fist. He slowly turned his head toward her, his eyes bloodshot. "Have you come to gloat? Or to die with us?"

His words and defeated tone pierced the fiery walls of her wrath, settling her angst a little. "Then you know what it is you face?"

"I've seen them. I can fly, in case you've forgotten. The Spiders will reach us before dawn, when their widows are at their strongest."

"You can still save your sorry arse."

He scoffed. "If the knights fly away from this terror and leave all our warriors to die, we'd be cowards."

"You can take your warriors with you."

His eyes narrowed. "How? These Spiders know where we are. They're headed straight for us, and they'll reach us long before we make it back to Aonark. This hill is a finer place to do battle than any other location nearby."

"I've done something and you cannot undo it. It's too late. To not take this opportunity would be even more cowardly than flying away and would waste all the lives around you."

He stood, bewilderment or anger rising in him. "What have you done?"

"The last of the warriors and Knights Black who are loyal to me now march from Aonark. They'll sweep west and attack the Spider army from behind while feigning expectations of victory, drawing the fight toward the sea as they slowly retreat but never give up."

"They'll be butchered like pigs."

Caëtin steeled herself. "I realize this. I did not make the decision lightly."

"And any Ravens who are poisoned will be turned into mindless fighters for the Spiders."

Caëtin tensed. In her rush to act, she had not thought of that possibility, but it would not change what had to be done. She could find no sarcastic words to ease her suffering. Not now. But without such a response, her emotions broke through. Tears blurred her vision.

"Then you accept that your army must return to Aonark," she said. "Your warriors will depart now, as fast as their mounts can carry them."

"And the knights will fly overhead and keep watch?"

"As long as they don't stray too far west and give away our ruse." She paused in thought. "The Spiders must have scouts underground—to have known about your army's location without being spotted—but the Spider people cannot travel as swiftly as our knights can fly. Not until they take Aonark and Muninn's remains from us."

Taknhal wiped the streaming rain from his brow and beard as he called to those around him. "Ravens—we ride for Aonark!"

64

MÄRREN

Märren jolted awake. There was only darkness and stuffy air as she gasped for breath. Her lungs burned. She was still clutching something tightly to her chest—a wedge of a Dragon scale.

She threw aside a heap of blankets and a couple furs that were covering and concealing her. Uisge was no longer holding her and was not in the vicinity. Shouts carried from beyond the thralls' quarters, and Märren slowly stood, her knees trembling. She felt along her inner thighs, where so many spines had impaled her flesh and made her a dragon rider—at least in her mind. Her skin there was intact. No blood.

The voices of thralls rang with shock and fear. Märren slipped her portion of a scale inside her leathers and rushed out of the quarters. There, the slaves stood around a large trough where two horses were drinking. Dragon warriors had joined them and were staring at something in the water. Märren shoved her way closer. In the trough, Megtr's body floated idly, his eyes open and dull as he stared into falling snow. His abdomen had been ripped open and emptied of organs, but only the brown lobes of his liver floated beside his head. His other organs were missing.

Märren spotted Uisge, who looked reinvigorated, and sidled over to him, pulling on his sleeve and saying, "This was your work."

One corner of Uisge's lips lifted in a wry smirk. "If there's any chance for the plan you've been laying out to succeed, you'll need the thralls to listen to you, and he would have made that difficult. I never liked him anyway. Did you?"

"You left me alone when I was inside the Dragon's lair?"

"You were making so much noise that Megtr came over and started asking questions. I had to distract him, or you'd be found out. I took him out for a walk. Then I found my element." Uisge smiled and licked his lips. "After that, distracting the others wasn't difficult. As you can see."

"Get back inside your quarters, thralls!" a warrior shouted, waving his axe at them as Dragon soldiers drove them away.

Märren stepped under the roof with Uisge and took a position in the center of the chamber, fighting against the incoming tide of people so she could maintain her spot even though others shoved against her. Some of the thralls who had already been at the city when she arrived grumbled slurs—dog, whore, stinking bitch, or worse.

Once the thralls had been forced back into their quarters, she spoke loud enough that most of them should be able to hear her, but not so loud that her voice would carry outside. "The time for drawing straws is near."

The thralls' murmuring halted, and all eyes turned toward her.

"Megtr ought to shut your mouth," a man called.

"She saved us from the jötunn," another said.

"Megtr is dead." Märren folded her arms across her chest. "You have no leader now, and placing your trust in a thug hasn't gotten you anywhere. You're still a Dragon thrall waiting to be sacrificed."

The man who had spoken against her curled his upper lip but did not make a retort.

Märren's gaze met Årn's. Årn tensed and swallowed with apprehension as Märren spoke. "I'm informing you of this now, because other than me and those who arrived with me, we don't know who'll be taken. I hope none of you will be offered to Surtr." She paused. "But if the villages do not deliver enough sacrifices for the caravan and you must go, why not fight back?"

"You think you can escape the fiery jötunn a second time?" another man, this one with a haggard white beard, barked. "This time, they'll make sure you arrive early, and they'll be prepared for any attempts you make. We have no hope."

"We do. As long as we don't submit and convince ourselves otherwise. We've"—Märren gestured at Uisge and herself—"been considering different strategies that could save us a second time."

She quickly explained how the portcullis gates imprisoned the dragons inside the mountain. She had come to suspect that Dragon warriors must have initially closed those gates, probably at Surtr's command, because it seemed unlikely that the giant had operated them. Soldiers outside began shouting as she was mentioning the wheels that controlled the raising and lowering of the portcullises and a plan. The soldiers' torches neared their quarters, and early morning light fell across the city.

"If you're taken to Surtr, don't allow yourselves to be staked into the ground," Märren said. "Delay it any way you can. I'll shout when it's time for us to act. Be ready and move swiftly. Our lives will depend on how quickly you respond."

"Line up and file outside," a soldier said as he appeared under their roof, his torch casting creeping shadows around his eyes. He glared at the thralls, his attention focusing on Märren. "And you—be silent."

Märren submissively lowered her head as the thralls muttered and did as they were told. Märren and Uisge took their spots in line. The thralls marched out one by one, only pausing near a warrior who held out something for each of them.

"Take her," the warrior who was offering whatever it was in his hand said, pointing to a straw a woman was holding.

Soldiers grasped the thrall by both of her arms and hauled her away from the others. She wailed and burst into tears. "No! No!"

The line moved quickly, and when the warrior noticed Märren and Uisge, he said, "Take these two as well. They were with the other cowards."

Soldiers yanked the two of them away from the rest and shackled their wrists, placing them beside the thralls who had arrived with them and those who had drawn the marked straws. One of the unfortunates was Årn. After the allotted number of thralls had been chosen, Raidn, the berserker who displayed his full scale of the Dragon, marched up to them.

"She came so far only to succumb to the same death she once avoided."

"She's a blind fool of a cunt. She came back to these lands of her own volition. She did this to herself and the uisge. She cannot rid herself of us."

"She has a plan."

Disbelief wrenched at Märren's gut, followed by a flood of gloom. The voices had not fled her...

Before she spiraled into despair, a twinge of hope pierced the darkness enveloping her. She did not yet bear a full scale. Maybe once she took up that more powerful complete piece of the Dragon, she would be cured.

"Time to join the caravan." Raidn marched before the line of thralls as most of them quivered and begged or sobbed. "Be proud of what you must do. Your sacrifices strengthen the Dragon's lands, as well as those who are meant to live on."

Horses pulled supply carts past them, and soldiers, warriors, and berserkers ushered the thralls through Torank and beyond its walls. Once outside the city, the berserkers and many of the warriors mounted armored horses.

Such lowly mounts for people who at one time rode dragons.

Årn glanced back at Märren from her place in the sacrificial line. Årn's face was wan and tense, and Märren winked at her in hopes of instilling courage. The warriors drove the thralls on toward a caravan composed of a dozen shackled thralls who were awaiting them.

Another warrior came running out from the gates of Torank. *Yrstl.* His hair was strewn about, but he was fully armored, his cloak wrapped around his brigandine where the empty setting for his wedge of scale would be. He stopped near Raidn and stood rigid.

"Is there a problem, warrior?" Raidn asked Yrstl.

Yrstl tamed his hair while glancing around at the thralls until he spotted Märren.

"She's to go north," Raidn said, "as was intended. She gets no special treatment."

Yrstl stepped toward her.

"Don't concern yourself with any thralls, warrior," Raidn snapped. "No matter how comely you may find them. You've made that mistake before, remember? Now, I ask again—Is there a problem?"

Yrstl glanced between Raidn and Märren, grabbing at his chest in the area of his missing god remnant. He would have known the scale was gone as soon as he had awoken. His mouth slowly opened, but no words came out. He shook his head and stood straighter.

Whips cracked. Carts creaked and rolled forward, and horses whickered as they joined the caravan. After they journeyed north for some time, Yrstl rode his long-haired steed closer to Märren, falling into line beside her.

"I am sorry for what I had to do," she muttered.

"Give it to me," he said, his voice trembling. "It'll kill you, although your longing for another will be unbearable."

"Like yours is now?"

"If I do not get it back, I'd look forward to death at the hands of Surtr. So I'm not dishonored by my people. I don't want to, but if I must, I will use force to take it from you."

"If you create a commotion, your comrades will realize what happened."

"Aye. But if I take it from you, I'd be held in higher regard than if I hid the theft and was later found out."

Märren pondered his predicament. "Is the addiction strong enough that if you did not get the piece back, you'd as soon die and leave your sister alone?"

He rode along for several strides without answering. "She passed. I speak the truth this time."

Märren's throat clenched.

"After I woke, I went below," he continued, "hoping that she had somehow taken my wedge of scale. I thought she was sleeping peacefully. She was not whimpering at all, but she was no longer breathing."

Guilt suffused Märren, and the voices cackled with glee. "I am... so sorry. I was only trying to help her."

"You did. She had never looked so peaceful as she did when I found her. I'm grateful you were able to meet her and press her darkness back for one night. But I cannot allow you to bear my god remnant."

Märren reached into her furs and clutched the portion of the scale, her desire for it burning, the voices thundering in her skull. She furtively passed it to Yrstl, who could not mask his surprise. Belfedrn had once told her that only berserkers could willingly part with a divine remain.

"My plan to free the dragons depended on me having a scale," she said. "And so with my passing of this to you, I trust that you will aid us."

He grunted as he tucked the scale piece under his cloak. "Once we arrive, I don't know if there's anything I can do."

A deep yearning struck Märren, a sensation that a piece of herself was suddenly missing, along with a need to fill the void created by the god part. She trudged north through keening wind and sheets of snow.

65

BELFEDRN

Belfedrn pressed on, leading the Ulfhednar and the dragging Bear and Boar warriors across Raven territory, rain spewing down upon them, the midday sunlight a muted gray. Over the past days, Caëtin should have been able to convince her jarl to return to their city while sending her loyal berserkers to their deaths. Flying as ravens, she should have had ample time to do all that and arrive at the ruins where she had suggested they meet.

Caëtin's dire situation and the weight of the decisions she had been forced to make burned in Belfedrn's guts. He was thankful that Vard had never ordered him to choose between such irrevocable options. Perhaps he was not strong enough to be jarl.

"Why are they so sluggish?" Dradn glanced over his shoulder. "Do they not understand the importance here or the danger of traveling so slowly?"

Belfedrn huffed. "The Boar and Bear are not built for covering a lot of ground. Maybe if we had the Horse and Stag people with us, it'd be different."

"But those people wouldn't be as helpful if the Spiders show up and it comes to blades," Thelira added. She walked on the opposite side of Belfedrn as Dradn, the siblings' bond not yet healed.

"The Ravens are said to carry powerful Seidr magic." Dradn ran his fingers over the axe at his hip, the one he had accepted from a dwarf. He was rarely not touching it. "Maybe if we aid them, one of them will take you to the Raven's bridge and you can speak with your lost mate before we return to Nistreel."

Belfedrn's mind turned. The idea had been lurking in his head for fortnights, but he had never paid it much thought. At the Raven's bridge, he could speak across worlds. *Another benefit of befriending the Raven.* But he should let Lyrne feast in peace. He should not trouble her with the woes of Midgard. Hopefully, one day he would join her and his longing would cease. However, putting the idea into words pulled at a tender cord, and his thoughts followed that line for too long. He could also find out if Deyja was there with her or if the boy could still be alive.

A lanky man appeared on a hilltop in the distance, peering down at them before lifting his head to the sky and its dwindling sunlight. He emitted a low, familiar howl, the call summoning a sense of urgency.

Eakthr.

"We haven't traveled far enough." Dradn marched faster.

"Ulfhednar, go on ahead and find Caëtin." Vard waved them onward. "I'll wait for our new comrades."

"Be wary," Belfedrn said to Vard. "And keep a few of the Ulfhednar with you. So each of us can maintain the might of the pack."

"Aye." Vard motioned for a few of the pack members to stay behind and for the others to accompany Belfedrn. "Go."

Belfedrn loped off, setting a swift pace. Thelira, Dradn, Athna, Ylsga, and Kesg trailed him. Eakthr kept ahead of their pack, scouting about. They ran for hours until the sun dropped into the west, and they crested a hill. On the other side stretched a valley sodden with mud and winding streams. The hills on the far side of the valley rose steeply, and near their base stood the stacked stones of a dwelling.

The ruins. Belfedrn sniffed and hurtled down the hillside, the others at his heels as sunlight faded and moonlight slowly clawed its way through the clouds. He scanned the skies for ravens—nothing. They crossed the valley, their boots sopping wet, and reached the ruins where they paced about, searching.

"Caëtin?" Belfedrn called.

No one answered. The premonition of land wights and others from the realms of elves and dwarves lay thick. He knelt and placed a rune stone at the foot of a crumbling archway. The others stalked around its deteriorating walls.

"Maybe she needs more time," Dradn said.

"To fly here?" Kesg grinned with mockery.

"The Boars and Bears slowed us down." Thelira surveyed the hill beyond the dwelling. "Maybe she has already come and gone."

"We wait at least until dawn," Belfedrn said. "If she hasn't arrived by then, we'll rejoin the others and inform Vard. We can decide where to go from there."

Belfedrn passed through a gap in the ruin's walls and came upon a doorway that stood ajar, the chamber beyond leading into the hillside. He ran a hand across the door—sturdy, and its hinges were still intact. Beyond the door and inside the earth was a square chamber with a hearth. Tussocks of grass poked through cracks in its stone floor and walls. He entered and meandered about, finding two smaller chambers that adjoined the main one. After completing a quick search and noticing little else, he exited and returned to the outer walls.

"We have no way of knowing if the Spiders wiped out the

Raven army." Eakthr kicked a pile of rubble. "Or if the Spider people are now moving toward us."

"You want to be sent out to scout around," Belfedrn said.

Eakthr nodded vigorously. "The rest of you can wait here, but I think it'd be best for the pack to know who or what may be coming."

"Send him," Athna said. "Something here doesn't feel right."

Eakthr crouched, awaiting Belfedrn's dismissal. The options weighed heavy on Belfedrn as he said, "You'll be weak when you're alone."

"But I'll be able to move swifter," Eakthr said.

Belfedrn cursed under his breath and looked to Kesg and Ylsga for their opinions.

"Might as well send him." Ylsga shrugged. "There's not much going on here."

Kesg wobbled a hand and grunted with indifference. "I don't give a fuck about him."

"Go," Belfedrn said.

Eakthr giggled, leaping into the air and sprinting away. He ascended the far hillside, traveling west under the cover of night. The remainder of the Ulfhednar sat beneath a partially collapsed roof of the dwelling and ate from their packs. Soon, their heads were nodding.

Sometime later, the screeching of ravens carried overhead, the shrill cries piercing the hum of the rain and making the Ulfhednar lurch and snarl as their adrenaline spiked. Beating wings flew closer, and something landed outside the ruins. Belfedrn exited the covered section and stepped beyond the walls.

Caëtin stood there with a grimmer expression than the one she wore when she first came to speak with him. Her black hair shone in the moonlight, her pale face beautiful and haunting, her wing-like cloak waving, rain dripping from her every lock and curve.

"You made it." Belfedrn smiled in an attempt to ease whatever worries were tormenting her.

"Where are the rest of your comrades?"

"Leagues behind. They travel slowly."

"Too slowly." She entered the dwelling, anger and anxiety sheeting from her as Belfedrn followed. "The Ravens don't have a choice now but to seek the aid of the Ulfhednar and the companions you've made. We just lost the best of our Knights Black and warriors merely to pull off a ruse to save those who wouldn't listen to reason."

"Then the larger Raven army made it back to your city safely?"

"That's still to be determined. They ride and fly for Aonark, the Spiders in pursuit but unable to head them off."

"I'm sorry. As an Ulfhednar, I understand—"

"You understand very little. Right now, there's a small band of Spiders sweeping this way. I've been tracking them since they broke away from their main legion, after my friends attacked from the west. Hence my delay. I flew past this group once I realized where they were headed. Somehow, they seem to know your whereabouts."

Belfedrn's heart thumped. "Maybe they possess another sense or are more in tune with Midgard—like how spiders feel the vibrations of prey in their webs."

Caëtin shrugged.

"Eakthr... he left not long ago," Belfedrn said.

"I saw him when he emerged from the brush to get a better look at my unkindness, and I landed and warned him. He should be returning soon."

"If it were only the Ulfhednar, I believe we could move undetected by the Spiders no matter the method they use to sense others, but we cannot do so with a troop of Boars and Bears lumbering along with us. Maybe this band of Spider warriors is headed for them."

"Perhaps. But instead of guessing at their intentions, you should be thinking about where you can find safety."

"Should we be concerned about this band of Spiders?"

"One made up of widows—their berserkers—who will arrive in the night? Aye. They're not afraid to die, and their powers are immense. If you run, maybe you can make it back to the Bears and Boars before they fall upon you, but then you'll be surrounded by the Spiders in the open. In the darkness. I fear you'll lose many of your warriors that way. Those you've worked so hard to obtain."

"And if we stay here?"

"It may be a better option, though I can't promise to know anything for certain. If the Ulfhednar shore up in these ruins and draw the Spider band into a miniature siege, your new comrades can come up behind them and crush them between the two of you. And this way, the Spiders won't be able to ambush your comrades in the dark."

A rush of fear surged through Belfedrn. Somehow these Spider people had felt like a distant threat, not one the Ulfhednar would have to focus on while seeking revenge on the Sea Serpents. "I know little of the Spider's abilities. Is remaining here the most reasonable option?"

"Unless you can all fly like ravens."

Belfedrn grunted. "You should flee and save yourself. If we eventually arrive at the gates of Aonark, then you can let us in."

"I've promised my assistance here in return for your warriors helping with our Spider problem. I'll stay."

Eakthr came sliding down the hillside and hurried through the archway, heaving for breath.

"Eakthr," Belfedrn said. "You are the swiftest of us. If you're able, race back to Vard and the others and inform them of what we know. They'll need to press on through the night to arrive here and help us defeat what's coming."

Eakthr nodded as his breath rasped in his throat.

"If you're too weary, I'll send Athna," Belfedrn added.

"I'll go," Eakthr said.

"You must take Thelira and Dradn with you."

"I'm not leaving." Thelira met Belfedrn's gaze. "I'm Ulfhednar now, and I'm not abandoning my pack."

"I'm not leaving either, Fath—Belfedrn," Dradn said. "Either we survive this, or we die together."

Tense silence reigned. Belfedrn could order them away. He should, for their safety.

"And what if the Spiders go chasing after Eakthr and he has only Dradn with him?" Ylsga asked. "It'd be better not to divide what's left of our pack. No more than necessary."

"My mate is wiser than you, you fool." Kesg stepped closer to Belfedrn. "Eakthr is swift and sly. Alone, he could outrun the Spiders and remain unseen. A young pup of a warrior crashing along behind him will draw attention."

Belfedrn pondered their situation, despising all of it—everything that had happened since the Ulfhednar had set out to hunt down a few trolls.

"You'll need Athna's magics here," Eakthr said. "I'm still fresh enough to run all night. I'll return with able warriors who will slaughter those who are coming."

"Have them come bearing as many torches as they can carry." Caëtin dug flint out of her pack.

"I send you off, again," Belfedrn said to Eakthr.

Eakthr dipped his chin and darted away into the night.

"We'll draw the widows here." Belfedrn paced. "We can feign that we're traveling, and when we spot them, we'll duck inside the ruins and the chamber with the door. If they have more berserkers than we do, it shouldn't matter in that cramped space where the fighting would be in small numbers."

"Prepare now." Caëtin withdrew a torch from her pack, struck a spark, and lit it. "With how quickly the widows move and how slowly the Bears and Boars travel, I fear that we'll have to hold out until morning. Light as many torches as you carry, but keep them hidden inside that chamber you mentioned."

"We have little need for torchlight," Athna said. "Our Wolf sight is more than enough."

"Then you do not carry torches?"

"No."

"Damn this buggering insect and its offspring!" Caëtin kicked a wall, surprising the pack members with the quickness of her anger.

"But I have fire when I need it." Athna snapped her fingers, and white flame writhed across her palm.

"Then gather all the sticks and kindling you can find in this sodden mess." Caëtin marched out of the dwelling, and the Ulfhednar followed. "Make whatever torches you can. Firelight may be the only thing that holds these widows at bay and may be the only reason we survive long enough to see the dawn."

66

MÄRREN

TIME DRAGGED BY UNDER UNENDING SNOWFALL BEFORE THE GLOW of the mountain of fire and the great flames of Surtr showed through the murk.

"Now is the time for bravery and truth." Raidn trotted his steed past the line of thralls, shouting over the wind. "Your anguish will soon pass, and great things await you in the next life. Midgard will be nothing more than a blink of an eye in the era of your existence. Your sacrifices won't go unnoticed. The Dragon people respect each and every one of you, and we thank you for all the work you have provided and for what you must do. For facing the fiery giant and standing against him with courage so the Valkyries will take you to Valhalla."

The thralls trod along without response.

"You may be asking yourself—why me?" Raidn continued. "But this opportunity is a gift. If you were to toil for others all the long years of your life, you would one day lie dying, asking yourself—what have I done? What have I accomplished? Did my life matter? Would you not wish it then to return here for honor and a chance for glory, to relive this day and look Surtr in the eye? To challenge the god slayer himself and know that you did not feel fear. That you stood upon the same ground as the Dragon herself, and *you* did not break!" He whipped his horse around and rode back along their line. "That your names will be written in history and remembered as those few who were brave enough to save a kingdom. So you could reside in Valhalla for all eternity!"

Cheering erupted from the Dragon warriors and soldiers as they beat axes against shields.

Raidn's words stoked a tingling fire inside Märren, but her rational thought quickly extinguished the sensation. This berserker was a good speaker, and he could probably convince soldiers to throw their lives away for a cause, but when that cause was not beneficial to his audience or their own kin, he merely sounded foolish.

The longing still pulled at her like lead weights, and the voices had grown stronger.

"But who is the bigger fool?"

"She who allowed herself to be brought back here? Or Raidn?"

"She's no fool, but she recognizes one when she hears him speak."

The warriors drove the thralls toward the inferno blazing at the base of the mountain. Heat throbbed against Märren's face, bringing with it a rush of memories—the jotunn rising, the fear, chains breaking, a dragon.

"Spread out!" Raidn called, and the warriors and soldiers pulled massive stakes from the carts as others whipped at the thralls, forcing them into a semicircle around the blaze.

Uisge cast Märren a frightened, questioning look, his brows pulled high.

Märren glanced around. Many soldiers and warriors waited nearby, not too close to Surtr's fire, but those bearing stakes approached.

"She's waiting for the giant to rise."

"Without Surtr's aid and fear, her plan will be ruined."

"She adapts as well as any in Midgard."

Yrstl stepped closer to Märren and pounded on a stake, hammering it deep, its metal ringing and causing the single link it had been wedged into to groan and bow. He passed by her carrying another stake to place on the other side of Uisge.

"Your chains are weakened," he whispered. "It's all I'll be able to do against a giant."

Märren's dread amplified. She had needed the thralls to make their escape before they were staked in, but if Surtr had not risen, the warriors would simply chase them down.

Now is the time. "Thralls!" Märren shouted and crouched, her voice piercing and carrying over the howling wind and crackling of the flames. The soldiers closest to her lurched in surprise, and the great fire wavered, flickering, its base swirling. "Run! Now!"

Märren pulled against her bonds. Some of the thralls who had not been fully staked into the ground made a mad dash away, although not all of them did. The chains quickly turned taut, slowing their escape or stopping them in their tracks with a jerk, and the soldiers regained their senses. Some warriors continued hammering in the stakes while others ran after and hauled those thralls who had fled back into a circle.

Surtr stirred, the charred limbs of a humanoid bathed in fire revealing themselves as his flames lengthened and writhed.

"Finish pounding in the stakes!" Raidn bellowed at his warriors so they would not flee.

Yrstl hurried over to the next position, jammed a stake into the ground, and hammered at it. Surtr rose, unfurling, his great sword clutched in a flaming hand. The giant lumbered closer, shaking the earth. The Dragon warriors wheeled about and fled, led by Raidn.

Uisge knelt and sprawled out onto his belly. Snowmelt seeped outward from under him, reaching toward Märren. "Lie flat in the water. And stay silent and still."

The other captives shrieked and cowered. Some pulled against their bonds, trying to flee. Others became petrified with fear, but none of them were lying flat, most of them huddled and covering their heads. Märren followed Uisge's lead as the pool engulfed her, its icy sting not as painful as it should have been. Even in this position, she could not look away from the advancing giant.

Surtr snatched up his first victim, a man off to Märren's right who had been thrashing about and wailing. The thrall ignited, and the links around him turned red, then orange and yellow. Distant cheers sounded. Märren was pulled upward as the giant lifted the man toward his mouth, uprooting the stakes around them before the deformed link turned orange and bent, distorting its ovoid shape as it opened. The remaining links closer to Märren plummeted, and she crashed onto her stomach.

She crawled toward Uisge, sliding through the water and compacting snow beneath.

"If you can't run from a jötunn, run at a jötunn," she said.

Uisge glanced over at her. "I'm afraid you're not jesting. Is that something from the Hávamál?"

"No. But it sounds like it should be."

"You may want to die, but burning at Surtr's feet would hardly be better than burning in his hands. Unless you mean to attack him."

She shook her head. "There's no chance for victory. Not against that."

Surtr used his sword to cleave through a sacrifice's chains before dropping his weapon and plucking up several more howling people, a few in each hand. They burst into flames, blackening before his eyes.

"The Dragon people are behind us," Märren said. "There's

nowhere else to run. We'll have to tear out the stake on your far side."

"And break that chain as well."

"We'll only have to wait for that to happen."

Surtr finished off the loudest of those to Märren's right and turned toward others to her left who were howling. He strode closer, his hand dangling above Märren as she pressed herself deeper into the pool while lying as flat as she was able. Water washed up inside her nose and rose over her head as Eimri's skull dug into her hip.

Intense heat passed overhead, scalding her, and something jerked at Uisge's chain but relaxed again. After a few heartbeats, Märren surfaced, her skin stinging with heat. Surtr was devouring the man to Uisge's left, the chain between them broken, the stake there pulled free and lying on its side.

"Run." Märren splashed through the water, flailing to find her footing as she pushed herself up while sliding about.

Uisge stood, turning to face Surtr's heels but hesitating.

"Run past him!" Märren jerked on the chain between them. "Toward the mountain."

Uisge hesitated, glancing between the giant, the mountain, and the Dragon warriors in the distance, weighing his options. Märren rushed past him, veering toward the jötunn, lifting the remaining links on the far side of her collar and coiling them around her shoulder.

"Run, thralls!" Märren cried as loudly as she was able. "Flee toward the mountain! It's our only chance."

Uisge ran with her. Some of the thralls—probably those who had heard her speech in Torank and whose stakes had been uprooted—charged after them. The slack ran out of the chain links between fleeing thralls and some who remained behind, the power of many jerking the few unmoving off their knees. These men and women smacked into the ground and slid atop the ice as they cried out and were dragged away. More groups of bound thralls followed while some remained in their original circle, sobbing and trembling.

Shouts of outrage rose behind them, erupting from the Dragon warriors in the distance. The ground boomed and shook as Surtr turned. The giant roared.

Märren glanced back as Surtr looked about in confusion before lunging after her—the person who was closest to him. The ground quaked under his footfalls, and Märren charged along even faster, the melting snow making for treacherous footing. The Dragon people's cheering rose to a crescendo.

Märren and Uisge raced on as fast as they could, and Uisge helped steady Märren while they fled across the meltwater of the terrain. However, their chains weighed them down, slowing their pace and exhausting them quickly. A ball of fire whooshed past Märren's head, crashing into the ground to her right and blazing there.

"Fuck the gods!" Uisge bellowed.

Märren darted toward the flames, and when she was near, she veered around them to use them as cover. Another fiery ball came screaming toward them, flying from Surtr's palms. When she glanced over her shoulder, fire nearly struck her full on, but Uisge jerked her aside, using the chain running between them. She flew off her feet and sailed toward him, landing hard and sliding across ice. Fire still caught her and ignited her hair, tunic, and leggings as she cried out, the flames burning. Uisge dowsed her head and then her body in meltwater and yanked her to her feet. Her singed hair released a pungent odor, a bronze lock blackened and shriveled.

Märren shook off her terror and ran, angling to her right and then left, avoiding another projectile, and after this attempt, Surtr focused on those who were now closer to him. He began devouring the thralls who had not fled and had not been dragged off.

In the distance, Raidn kicked his mount's flanks, but the horse shied away and would not run toward the jötunn. Instead, the Dragon warriors and soldiers gave chase on foot, quickly covering ground between their ranks and the thralls who were weighted down. Some of the mounted warriors managed to kick their horses into a gallop, although these steeds angled away from Surtr, giving the giant a massive berth. This put them farther away from the thralls than their running comrades.

Märren planted her feet into the ice with each stride and propelled herself forward. A score of thralls ran behind her and Uisge, most of them linked together. The captives dragging on the chains behind that group skidded back and forth under their tow.

The first warriors on foot rushed around Surtr, although the giant lunged over and swiped up two of them. These men did not ignite.

The magic of the Dragon.

The jötunn devoured the warriors, savoring those who were not charred before roaring and swinging his weapon at the people around him—mostly warriors and soldiers in pursuit. The horses screamed, their eyes rolling as they bucked and fled.

As Märren rushed across the tundra toward the mountain, the first warrior caught up to a thrall dragging on the chain at the rear of the group behind them. The warrior grabbed the woman, attempting to pull against the momentum of their ranks, but he was jerked off his feet and hauled along. A couple more warriors gained on and overtook them, each grabbing a sacrifice. At least one warrior buried his axe into a thrall's head. The warriors attempted to stop each of their captives but were dragged along, although their added resistance slowed the group's flight.

"Halt, you buggering cowards!" one of the warriors holding on to the chains hollered as he bounced around in their wake.

Other warriors neared, but the one who yelled hit a snow berm and rolled away.

Märren barreled toward the nearest glowing cavern in the mountain. "Orstenshard! We're coming to release you."

She angled away from the entrance and portcullis, slowing and searching about in the dim light for a wheel to open the gate. Uisge spun about and charged toward the other sacrifices who were nearing. He unwound some of the links from his shoulder and allowed the thralls to rush past, jumping on and wrapping his chain around the neck of a Dragon warrior. Uisge pulled the chain taut, and the warrior's eyes gaped, his tongue sticking out and turning dark.

The thralls came to a halt at the base of the mountain, and two more warriors who had been dragged along stood. Several others were still in pursuit and came hurtling closer. Uisge and the rest of thralls fanned out, preparing to face them as Märren returned to hunting for a wheel along the cliffs.

"She won't find one."

"They're concealed."

"Not night, not even death, can hide it from her now."

She spotted a narrow alcove in the cliff and slipped inside. Attached to an inner wall was a great wheel, the moonlight barely making it visible. She grasped it and pulled, but its steel only groaned. A lever stuck out of the rock beside it, and she yanked the lever downward before trying the wheel again. Still nothing but creaking.

"Help me!" Märren called.

Årn and another thrall joined her. Together, they heaved and loosened the wheel, the protest of rusted steel and chains screeching. Behind them, the din of a scuffle arose, and someone screamed in death. Others yelled. Thudding followed.

Märren pulled harder, and the wheel spun, the clinking of chain links rattling around them. A crack followed, answered by a shriek that blasted her ears. A beast as large as a keep slunk across the snow behind them, emerging from the mountain with a great thumping of wings. The beast roared. Fire flashed in her breath, and she rose into the night, crying so loudly it quaked the mountain.

Answering shrieks echoed in the night.

67

BELFEDRN

BELFEDRN ROAMED ABOUT THE VALLEY JUST BEYOND THE dwelling, never taking his eyes from the hillside. He had ordered Thelira and Dradn into the stone chamber with the door. Everyone would be safest there, and given what Caëtin knew about widows, firelight would be their best weapon and defense.

Overhead, a flash of movement tore through the darkness and across the hillside. Belfedrn's hackles prickled, and he howled and pointed, his Wolf eyes unable to see enough detail to make out what approached.

Strange. And frightening. His vision had never let him down before. His hands shook as he gripped his spear and sniffed.

The Ulfhednar stalked about as Ylsga called to the others in their acted lines, "There's an old dwelling here."

When Kesg spoke, his tone sounded so staged that an infant would not likely be fooled. "We should seek our shelter there for the night."

"Aye." Belfedrn tried to carry on as casually as he could, hoping anyone listening paid as little attention to his incompetent friend's words as the pack typically did. "We should all get some rest. We've a long road tomorrow."

More shadows weaved through the brush on the hillside, descending quickly, moving inhumanly. Belfedrn's heart bucked as he ushered the others in through the archway.

"Do you think they'll come?" Kesg asked.

"If they're not deaf and blind, then, aye, they will," Belfedrn said. "Although your acting won't have fooled them."

"Unless they're too cunning to fall for this ploy and have some other plan." Caëtin waved them toward the chamber within the hillside as she tripped over rubble, her eyesight clearly inadequate in the darkness.

Once they entered the chamber, which was lit by Caëtin's torch and a fire burning in the hearth, Caëtin slammed the wooden door closed and barred it with a beam. Braces on the walls held the beam in place. The others wedged a few logs they had scrounged up against the door.

"Now we wait," Caëtin said and stomped her heel. "On a thick but cracking stone floor. With walls that are no better off. If Spiders can burrow into this place, we'll find out soon."

Kesg paced about the chamber and the two smaller adjoining ones, cursing while running his thumb along the blade of his axe. "The sun cannot rise fast enough."

The din of rain dumping on the stones outside and the crackle of the fire carried on. Belfedrn leaned his spear against the wall beside the door, in an easy position to grab and skewer anything that tried to break through. Then he wandered the interior with Kesg as time crawled by.

"What if they don't come for us?" Dradn's breathing had turned shallow and quick.

"Then they'll reach your comrades before morning," Caëtin said. "And all will not be well. They *must* come here first. They cannot ignore the threat of Ulfhednar showing up and tromping about in the lands they seek to claim." She slid her back down a wall and sat, staring blankly into the hearth, shivering a bit, her eyelids heavy as if she were exhausted. She drank deeply from her waterskin.

Thelira placed a hand on Dradn's shoulder and said, "They will come, and we will hold them off until the sun rises and their widow powers ebb."

A sharp clap sounded just beyond the doorway.

Everyone lurched. A stilted silence followed. Belfedrn clutched his shield tighter and grabbed his spear, taking a knee before the doorway, bracing the butt of his weapon against the inside of his foot, preparing for someone or something to splinter the door and charge through.

"They know we have at least one fire burning." Caëtin stood, drawing a sword with a blade almost as pale as her skin. Her cloak flapped open, revealing a row of raven feathers strung around a chain on her neck. "They're assessing and planning their attack."

A stone struck the door. Something scuttled around outside.

"I hope these bastards rot in Helheim." Dradn's hand quivered on his axe, and the weapon's runes glowed with a bluish light.

"Let them keep this up all night," Caëtin said. "This is easy. The longer they take trying to frighten us, the closer we come to sunlight."

The door rattled, juddering against its stone frame. Belfedrn steeled himself, expecting an axe to start chopping through the wood. The firelight behind him dimmed, and someone bellowed with fear. He whipped around to find a mass of typical-sized spiders scurrying up the wall toward the torch. Other spiders were already climbing the torch's shaft and were snapping and burning as they reached the fire. When each arachnid burned, ten more rushed up around their flaming companion. With their sheer numbers, they began smothering the flames.

Caëtin lunged and tore the torch from the wall, waving it

about and sending spiders flying into the corners. "They're trying to extinguish the light."

Belfedrn glanced back at the door, realizing the pounding there had merely been a distraction. "They control little spiders as well?"

"It's not something I've seen." Caëtin used her sword to scrape clumps of arachnids from the torch's handle and stomped on them.

The hearth fire snuffed out, the crackling of insects in those flames subsiding as the chamber was thrown into shadows and the dim light of a single torch. White flames bloomed along Athna's hand. A wave of insects scuttled from the hearth into the chamber. Athna flung fire at them.

A plank in the doorway splintered, the head of an axe punching through. Belfedrn tensed. The axe was ripped back, and an eye within a hooded face leered through the gap. Belfedrn jabbed with his spear, but before its tip connected, the face... collapsed, or fell into a thousand dark pieces.

Belfedrn yanked his spear back and cautiously crept closer to the door. Spiders poured through the crack beneath the door and the gaps between it and its frame. He yelled and pointed, stomping what he could. Thelira and Dradn joined him, their boots smashing and crunching through the arachnids.

Kesg howled in fear, and Belfedrn spun around. The insects swarming around the hearth piled on top of each other, forming humanoid legs, then a torso. In a few heartbeats, a man wearing black armor and a red cloak stood before them, wielding a barbed axe.

A widow.

The widow swung his weapon at Ylsga as she skewered him with her spear. His axe shattered Ylsga's shield, carrying past as she ducked. Their adversary groaned and doubled over, Ylsga's spear buried into a gap in his armor and impaling his waist.

Kesg roared, using two hands to raise his axe overhead and chop downward. He cleaved the widow's head in two.

A rush of wind brushed against Belfedrn's back, and when he spun around, a widow woman formed and stood before him. Caëtin screamed, shaking her torch hand just as the light extinguished and plunged the chamber into darkness. The eyes of the widow before Belfedrn barely shone in the dark, and Belfedrn dived aside, expecting a strike.

The whoosh of a blade passed overhead, and at the far end of the chamber, Athna shrieked, the last of the light—the flames on her hand—snuffing out.

"The widows are too powerful in the dark!" Caëtin said somewhere behind Belfedrn as he rolled to his feet. "And I cannot see a thing!" The knight's blade whistled around in a flurry of defensive maneuvers.

Scuttling from more spiders clambering through the doorway followed while Belfedrn's Wolf eyes adapted. He lunged at the widow, who became less visible, less distinct, his spear leading the way. His weapon glanced off his enemy's arm, although he had not even struck her armor. Thelira's arrow whistled past and hit the widow's neck but fell without piercing her flesh.

Dradn roared and swung his axe at her, the runes on his weapon a blur of faint light. The widow raised a sword to parry his attack, and the weapons clashed in a flash of sparks, the axe bending her blade and hooking it as Dradn jerked her weapon toward him. The widow released her sword rather than be pulled toward her attacker and stumbled as she pivoted and leapt backward, flying across the chamber and hitting the far corner with her back, where she scrambled up the wall like a spider, her form blurring even more. Near the ceiling, she paused, assessing the situation, her breathing quiet but audible to Wolf ears.

She thinks we cannot hear her. Nor see nor smell her in the dark. Belfedrn howled his sentiments, knowing the Ulfhednar would understand. Although it was difficult to visualize much of the widow's details, she resembled a dark smear in the chamber. She resumed her climb with her back against the wall, reaching the ceiling and clinging to it as she scuttled out toward Belfedrn. His Wolf's ears picked up her almost silent movements and aided him in determining her location.

Belfedrn glanced around for Athna, who shook her magic hand vigorously, trying to fling away a mass of spiders that swarmed over her flesh and suppressed her Wolf's flame.

"Help her!" Belfedrn shouted, gesturing in Athna's direction.

Dradn and Thelira rushed to assist her as Belfedrn knelt and awaited the widow as she crawled across the ceiling. He kept his spear angled at the door in hopes of deceiving her. Thelira and Dradn grunted while trying to help Athna free her magic.

The widow reached an area directly over Belfedrn and paused. He prayed to Fenrir that her skin was not always stronger than steel when she was cloaked in darkness while also hoping Dradn and Thelira would work swiftly.

The widow dropped, a seax in her hand at the forefront of her descent. Belfedrn jerked his spear up while planting it against the ground and leaning as far to the side as he could.

Faint white light lit up the chamber.

Belfedrn's weapon impaled the widow's belly as she plummeted. Her eyes went wide as she slid down the length of the spear, blood leaking from her midsection as she swung wildly with her seax. Belfedrn released his spear and rolled away.

The widow hit the ground with a thump, Belfedrn's spear standing straight up from her back and lacquered in blood. Belfedrn ripped his axe from his belt and sprang closer, chopping into her neck and rending flesh, burying his blade deep before attacking again and again. Blood gushed, flinging from the head of his axe as it worked.

The widow went limp.

Caëtin assisted Thelira and Dradn with removing the remainder of the spiders from Athna's hand. As one, the arachnids fled into the hearth, scampering up the walls and disappearing. Caëtin retrieved her torch and used Athna's fire to relight it. Then the Raven knight relit the hearth, her chest heaving as she faced the Ulfhednar and took in the dead widow on the floor.

"Your Wolf eyes may end up aiding us more than I thought possible," Caëtin said. "Even if there are so few of you left." She faced Athna. "And your flame is the only light they couldn't snuff out completely. It may be why Belfedrn was able to kill that widow." She studied the battle Seidr's hand. "Did the spiders bite you?"

Athna grunted, dimming her fire and scrutinizing her ungloved flesh. Hundreds of punctures covered her hand.

"Is their bite deadly?" Dradn stepped closer.

"I've seen what their poisoned blades can do," Caëtin said, "but I don't know about the small spiders."

"I feel nothing more than stings." Athna shook her hand, and flames rose across her exposed skin. "If their venom hasn't seeped beyond my arm, the Wolf's fire should cleanse my flesh."

A few tense breaths of silence passed.

"Where are the rest of them?" Belfedrn peered through the shattered plank in the doorway. "They couldn't have given up so easily."

"Maybe they were testing us." Caëtin sidled closer to him. "Learning our strengths and weaknesses. Or perhaps you killed their leader, or they sensed the coming of the Boars and Bears and realized they have more enemies they'll need to understand."

"It's nothing." Ylsga shooed Kesg away.

"Let me have a look at it, woman." Kesg tried to inspect her shoulder.

"It's only a scratch." Ylsga shoved him away. Her shield lay in splinters on the ground.

Caëtin sheathed her blade and approached them. "If you were cut, we should have a look. Their poison... it can change anyone."

Ylsga grumbled but turned so Caëtin could inspect her injury—a small gash on the side of her shoulder. Black tendrils encircled the portion of the wound that was visible through the rent in her garb.

"Remove your fur." Caëtin yanked Ylsga's pelt aside and then had the Ulfhednar lift her arms so Caëtin could remove her *brynja* by sliding it over her head. Caëtin pulled aside her undertunic.

Black tendrils reached for Ylsga's neck, crawling up from the cut. Caëtin staggered back.

"We can still cleanse her wound," Kesg said. "With fire."

Caëtin and Athna shook their heads, and Caëtin said, "The only thing I've seen stop the creeping rot is amputation."

"You want to remove her shield arm?" Kesg snarled. "No. I won't let you."

"Losing her arm won't save her now. The poison is in her blood and has reached her shoulder near her neck."

"No." Kesg growled, veins standing out on his temples. "No. That isn't so."

"What can we do?" Belfedrn asked.

"Let her go." Caëtin could not meet Kesg's glare. "She'll become one of them. A mindless soldier for their army."

"That's a lie!" Kesg spat, pointing at her. He turned to his mate and wiped vigorously at her wound with a bunched cloth, trying to clean it of the black vines.

"If we don't, she'll turn and attack us."

"No, she won't." Kesg scrubbed harder. "I'll watch her. Wait..." He squeezed and plucked something from the nape of her neck and held it out—a single black spider with a red underbelly. "Its head was buried in her skin."

Belfedrn shuddered.

"The person I witnessed save herself only had one of her ravens affected." Caëtin seemed to be in the midst of an argument with herself as she ran a finger along her blade. "She cut off her hand and had no spider."

"Then you don't know!" Kesg sobbed. "You won't touch her. The spider is gone, and she'll be fine."

"Maybe the Spiders knew she was cut and fled because they're waiting for her to kill us for them."

Kesg sobbed harder.

Ylsga shook her mate. "Get a hold of yourself, Ulfhednar." She then spoke to everyone. "If you can't kill me now, you will keep an eye on me, and if I start to become affected or act out of sorts, do what must be done. Right now, I do not feel ill, and it's only a scratch. Not all poisons overcome their victims, but if I notice anything, I'll warn you. And if you're still too weak to act, I'll kill myself. Then I'll see you all again in Valhalla."

Kesg crumpled against her, shaking.

68

MÄRREN

ORSTENSHARD BLEW FIRE AT THE BASE OF THE MOUNTAIN BEFORE circling around and landing, crushing beneath her talons several Dragon warriors who fought against the thralls. Bones crunched, and armor cracked. Their death cries were brief and muffled.

In the distance, Surtr faced the mountain and bellowed with rage. He began jogging toward them, the earth thumping as he swung his sword in mighty arcs.

"The fire giant comes to smite the last of my kin," Orstenshard said to Märren. "Release the others." The dragon sliced through the chain links binding the thralls, freeing Uisge, Årn, and most of the rest of them. "I used fire to mark where the gate wheels are in the mountain. Hurry! I'll distract the giant."

Orstenshard flapped her wings, propelling Märren away, and Märren raced for the closest dragon fire that burned on the mountainside. Orstenshard lifted from the ground and wheeled into the air, streaking toward the giant, breathing flame. She continued her ascent while nearing Surtr to keep out of range of his sword.

Near one of the fires that Orstenshard left burning, Märren

spotted another recess in the mountainside. She ran for it. Årn and Uisge followed, but she waved Årn on.

"Find another fire marker," she said. "We need to release all the dragons as quickly as possible. Have the thralls split up and free all they can."

Årn nodded and darted away. Märren slipped into the alcove and found another wheel. She grasped it and heaved with all her might, but the wheel was jammed. She cursed and again yanked a lever downward, grabbing the wheel and lifting herself into the air, using her weight. Uisge assisted her, and the wheel grated slowly and then rotated. They kept the wheel spinning as dragon roars erupted. A massive beast—this one as green as a forest—came lumbering past, unfurling its wings, the leathery segments billowing like all the sails on a drakkar ship.

Märren rushed out of the niche in the mountain and sprinted in the opposite direction as most of the thralls were headed. In the distance, Surtr swung his blade wildly as more dragons came barreling toward him, blowing fiery breaths that did nothing other than distract the jötunn and make him angry. Märren and Uisge located another wheel and released another dragon, and more wings filled the sky.

Surtr bellowed at the thralls and charged toward them and the mountain. Dragons wheeled above the giant, dipping and biting and clawing. Surtr slashed at them, but he did not slow his thunderous approach. Wings beat, and feet thumped into the ground beside Märren as she ran for the next alcove. Orstenshard glared down at her through fiery eyes, scrutinizing her. A few other dragons landed behind Orstenshard, flanking her.

"You've obtained the rider's rune," Orstenshard said. "Typically, I wouldn't take anyone who wasn't carrying a full scale of the Dragon, but we're pressed for time." She lifted a foot, unfurling her claws. In her grip were three wedges of scales—from the warriors the dragon had crushed. She held them out.

Märren trembled as she grabbed them all.

"She's taking too much."

"Her greed will kill her now."

"The power of the Dragon courses through her."

Orstenshard lowered her head. "Climb on."

"I've wanted nothing more," Märren said, "but against Surtr, we'll fall. It's why the Dragon failed. Your breath doesn't harm him."

Märren turned to a dragon beside Orstenshard who was as pale as winter ice but with blue undertones. She had seen this dragon as well as others breathing at the jötunn.

Märren spoke over her shoulder to Orstenshard. "Do not take my decision as an insult. If Surtr's fire doesn't burn you, attack him with teeth and claws. Wound him in any way you can, but I cannot ride you. If we were to attack him up close, his flames would kill me."

"If she pursues this end, she will *die."*

"She won't survive her first flight, and she'll lose Eimri forever."

"She'll ride to victory and glory."

The dragon before her had spikes like icicle spears and sniffed at her before lowering its head. Märren gripped onto two of the spikes and yanked herself up the side of its neck, climbing and quickly settling behind its head. Her legs sank between the scales, melding with and becoming part of the creature. No spines pierced her flesh, but an intangible bond shot through her, the other end of the line connected to the dragon's mind.

Surtr resembled a flaming mountain as he stormed closer, swiping at the dragons who swooped overhead attempting to slow him. The thralls screamed and fled. Orstenshard beat her wings and took to the air, gushing fire at the jötunn as she screeched. Märren's dragon lifted off the ground, the wind gusts from his wings thumping against her.

"Freydaskarde," Märren said, the dragon's name floating in

her mind like a core memory. The dragon wheeled beneath her, the wind tearing at her hair and cloak as they rose. Märren leaned over, gripping on tightly, although she quickly realized that maintaining her balance was second nature and her legs had welded to the creature's scales. "Unleash your breath on the jötunn."

Freydaskarde roared. "You do not command me, rider. It is I who make the decisions. You're a passenger meant to aid me."

A dozen dragons flew at Surtr, clawing and biting. The giant's sword cleaved through two of them, severing a wing and slicing clean through another's body as easily as a Wolf blade could cut through human flesh. The dragon who lost its wing spiraled downward. The other fell in halves.

Orstenshard breathed her fiery breath, which engulfed Surtr, and she hurtled into her own flames and those of the giant's. Her claws and teeth flashed, impaling the jötunn. Where she rent Surtr's charred flesh, flames erupted. The jötunn roared in pain, his empty hand reaching out and snatching Orstenshard around the neck.

Dragons can *wound him.*

A dozen other dragons of a myriad of scale colors swooped in, focusing their claw and bite attacks on the giant's back, shoulders, and arms. Surtr raised his blade.

Märren's heart clenched. "Breathe!"

Freydaskarde swiftly banked right, bending Märren's torso far to the left, then soared at the giant, but they were still too far away for his breath to reach its target. "Don't command me. That is a rider's first mistake."

Surtr's blade fell, severing Orstenshard's neck. As if in slow motion, the dragon's head fell to the earth, reminiscent of how her god had died at the hands of this jötunn. The giant cried triumphantly, throwing his arms back and bellowing as he brought the severed neck to his mouth and bit into its flesh.

Blood spurted and sizzled in his fire, smoking as it ran down his chin and chest.

"Her plan to kill the giant is flawed."

"She'll only succeed at getting the last of the dragons killed."

"She won't!"

"*Iak feikinstafir yðr,* Surtr!" The scale pieces inside Märren's furs grew hot, and the Dragon's voice erupted from her throat, her rage carrying in those words. Her shout became a force, a blast that rolled out and struck the giant.

Surtr lurched back, wavering as more dragons descended upon him with their claws bared, rending and biting. Gouts of fire punched through cracks and slashes in the jötunn's skin as he bellowed in rage. His sword flashed, cleaving and hewing through more dragons, who dropped around him.

Freydaskarde hurtled closer, and Märren belted out more of the Dragon's voice, this time fire spewing from her lips and startling her as her flames crackled in the night. *The Dragon's breath.* She was partly scaled now. Far more Dragon than Wolf.

Freydaskarde weaved around Surtr's flashing sword, inhaling and expelling a breath of white wind filled with icy shards. The breath struck Surtr with the keening howl of a blizzard, shoving him back a few steps as he bent over at the waist, hollering in pain. The dragons fell upon him again. He tore into them, snapping bones, burning any that would burn, sword arcing through the air.

In Märren's mind, Freydaskarde's thoughts became her own. Märren and Freydaskarde inhaled and focused on Surtr's weapon hand as they expelled their breath. The gale struck the jötunn's fist with full force, dousing the fire there and covering his charred flesh in frost. Surtr roared, looking at his hand in disbelief as the dragons continued to tear into him.

Freydaskarde whipped past the giant, flying on before wheeling about and veering for him again. Surtr hacked down more dragons and pivoted to face the icy one that had caused him so much pain. The fire on his hand broke through the frost, smoldering before growing stronger, the flames leaping higher. He raised his blade.

Two red dragons attacked from behind, burying their teeth into the flesh of his wrists and latching on, pulling his arms wide. Freydaskarde barreled on, and Märren leaned over the dragon's scales, steeling herself as they rushed closer to the jötunn. The ice dragon exhaled again, washing Surtr's face and chest with his breath, dimming the giant's fire—especially the flames around his neck. His flesh there turned white. Freydaskarde's maw gaped, and he crashed into the jötunn, sinking his teeth into the giant's throat.

Surtr reeled backward and toppled. His arms flailed, making the dragons clinging to them whirl in circles. One of the beasts was flung away before the jötunn struck the earth with a boom. His fire flared around Freydaskarde and Märren, singeing and then burning the dragon's wings.

"Release him!" Märren said.

"I won't." The dragon's thoughts echoed in Märren's mind. *"Not the jötunn who slayed my god. My mother."*

The fires grew stronger as Freydaskarde shook his head, shredding the giant's flesh. Surtr's flames licked at his wings and underside, the heat rising and pressing a heavy hand against Märren's face. But her flesh did not burn. Her skin was scaled now, segmented and hardened. Fire resistant.

The other dragons landed on Surtr, attacking as the giant writhed and tossed some aside like flying rodents, kicking others and shattering ribs and wings. His sword flashed and cleaved through more. Freydaskarde expelled another breath into Surtr's torn-open throat. The giant gasped, and the dragon bit deeper. A crunch sounded, and Freydaskarde ripped his head back, bringing a hunk of flesh with him.

Fire spouted from Surtr's neck, and his head fell back, his sword dropping and landing at his side with a clatter. More intense flames spewed from his body, and Freydaskarde shrieked in pain and lifted off him. The dragon hovered above the giant with Märren watching in awe as Surtr burned like a bonfire, lighting up the sky.

The flames dwindled and faded, leaving nothing more than a sword as tall as a keep, its blade black before frost settled over it in sheets of white.

69

CAËTIN

AHEAD, THE NORTHERN WALLS OF AONARK STOOD UNDER MISTING rain. Caëtin paced toward the city with the Ulfhednar, the Bear and Boar warriors trailing behind.

After the encounter with the widows, the Ulfhednar had eaten more meat than she had seen anyone eat in five to ten meals, stones' worth of food, but afterward they were reinvigorated. No more Spiders had attacked them, and the following morning Caëtin led her new companions on, pushing them hard. She felt less weary and cold than if she had flown the distance.

When Caëtin neared the walls, Huginn dived toward her and landed on her arm, tapping Caëtin with her beak. Caëtin smoothed over her feathers as she shouted up, "Open the gates. It's me, Caëtin Harekrsdóttir."

A soldier peered down at her. "Why don't you fly in like the Knights Black? Are you a captive of this horde?"

"Nay. The warriors with me have come to aid our cause. Let us pass."

"Warriors from other clans?" He stared, dumbfounded.

"As long as there's no indication that the Sea Serpents will be immediately arriving from the north, open the gates."

"The Sea Serpents? Should we be worried about them as well?"

"Aye. We've much to discuss."

The soldier motioned to those below him, and the grating of bracing beams being removed sounded as he said to her, "Taknhal has returned with his army."

No shite? Relief washed through her. The danger Taknhal had put himself and his army in was deep, but at least they had not been massacred, unlike her knights and warriors.

The soldier continued, "The Spiders were pursuing Taknhal but turned about once it was clear his army would make it to the city before they could be overtaken."

One of the gates parted, and Caëtin entered but waited there for her new comrades to join her. Ranks of Raven warriors in black surrounded the area, stepping back to make way. No one was arguing, the atmosphere somber. The Ulfhednar slipped in, their faces painted black, shields emblazoned with wolf heads strapped over their pelts, spears pointed skyward as they glanced around the city in wonder. Then came Aegmor under his Bear hide, his maul resting against his shoulder, his berserkers and warriors following. Next was Onunith, in her Boar skin, stout and powerful, eyeing all the Ravens with a smirk. After the rest of the Boars entered, the gates shut, and the Raven soldiers hurriedly replaced the bracing beams.

"Ravens," Caëtin called to those around her. "Serpent legions have taken hold of the Wolf's lands. Here along the northern walls, you must also remain vigilant, and if you see any signs of an approaching army, alert the masses who are on guard in the south. I'll have a few of the Knights Black fly north and watch our borders as well." She paused, waiting for her words to sink in. "Show our new comrades about Aonark, and find them a longhouse, where they will be staying. They're here to aid us against our enemies. We must prepare. It will not be long before the Spiders and the Sea Serpents come."

The Ravens broke ranks and approached the new arrivals, grasping the forearms of the Ulfhednar, Bears, and Boars while offering words of thanks and praise for coming. Then the Raven's people began to lead the others away.

"The Ulfhednar, Aegmor, and Onunith are to come with me," Caëtin said. "Together, we shall visit my jarl."

Dradn quietly argued with Belfedrn, but Belfedrn grabbed him by the neck and tugged him along, saying, "You'll stay with the Ulfhednar from now on."

A Raven warrior approached, dipping his head to Caëtin as he said, "Last I heard, Taknhal remains at the southern walls. He's been there since his return. Don't look for him in the great hall."

Caëtin patted the warrior's arm and marched away with Huginn, wishing she could fly to the far walls. If she were not a Knight Black, perhaps she would have been forced to learn patience and to accept slower forms of travel. She led those she requested to remain with her through Aonark, much of the streets lined with flagstones and poles. Karls toiled vigilantly, wiping brows, backs hunched as they paused and watched Caëtin and the strange outsiders.

They neared the great hall. Caëtin had no intention of going inside or seeking out Uktr or Grimmurk, but as they passed, one of the two warriors standing guard outside nodded to Caëtin. Caëtin paused, disbelief swirling in her mind as she turned and approached them.

"Sanre?" Caëtin asked.

"I'm still watching over the great hall and those who are inside." Sanre dipped her hooded head. "As you asked."

"Then Halfnr didn't take you with him when he and the rest of my fighters left to go distract the Spiders?"

"Nay. He asked me and Sigr to stay behind because he thought you may need at least two of us, if he wasn't going to be around anymore."

"I do need you." Caëtin rushed up and embraced her and then patted Sigr's bald and scarred head as Huginn squawked. "I'm thankful that Halfnr realized two more would not turn the tide."

"It's good to see you too, Caëtin." Sigr nodded, his eyes moist. "But the others..."

"They will not return," Caëtin answered.

Sanre pressed her forehead to Caëtin's while squeezing her shoulder. "Then our comrades sacrificed everything we could ask of them. They're now feasting in Valhalla."

Caëtin shuddered, hoping it was true. "And the Spider thrall and my children?"

"They're inside."

Caëtin's apprehension surged. "I did not want them anywhere near Uktr."

"Taknhal demanded that, for the time being, all of his extended family reside in the great hall. The command did not seem nefarious."

But a threat had been made before. Caëtin eyed the longhouse before her hands seemed to move of their own accord and shoved its doors open. "Wait here," she said to those she was escorting. "This will only take a moment."

Huginn flew off, and Caëtin's feet took her inside. Children ran amok as servants milled about.

"Uktr?" Caëtin called.

Her father sat at the central table before the hearth, staring absently into a corner of the ceiling, drool stringing from his lips. Grimmurk had been talking to him in quiet tones but turned to look over his shoulder at Caëtin, his glare brimming with resentment as he rubbed at a bloodied bandage covering the stump of his arm. He was pale, and he slouched.

"If you haven't heard," Caëtin said to Uktr, "I was forced to sacrifice many good knights and warriors to save Taknhal and allow him and his fighters to return to Aonark."

"Cowards." Grimmurk shook his head.

Caëtin's feet continued moving on their own, and she had to stuff down her desire to stride closer and cleave that man's skull in two. She glared at him. "You're only alive because of my father's request. I can slay you at any time."

Grimmurk snarled but turned away, gazing into the fire.

"Mother!" Lythi casually walked up to Caëtin, a whimsical grin pulling at her lips.

Caëtin wrapped her daughter in her arms, lifting her off the ground and squeezing her. "You're all right, Lythi?"

"Of course." She returned her mother's embrace.

"Where's Treln?"

Lythi glanced about and pointed down the way to where a group of boys were fighting on the floor. Caëtin stormed over. Treln shoved another boy down and landed on top of him, rearing back and punching him in the face. His nose cracked, and blood erupted. Caëtin rushed for her son, but a servant she did not recognize yanked Treln off the other boy. Caëtin grabbed her son from the servant and spun him around, kneeling and glaring at him.

"What are you doing?" she asked. *If I don't put a stop to this behavior, he'll surely end up like Uktr and Taknhal.* But she did not know if the best method would be to reprimand him more harshly or show him more love.

"Mother?" Treln blinked a few times, and his eyes turned misty. "The boy I punched said you were here."

She shook her son, hoping to fling the foolishness out of

him. "Why do you go about fighting all the time? You have to stop this and start acting like an adult."

"I want to be the strongest knight, like you." A tear trickled down his cheek. "And it's what the Raven leaders do. The men anyway." He indicated the boy he had been hitting. "And he said he saw you walk in, but I didn't. Then he said you would've made a bad jarl, so his father had to take the throne from you or the Ravens would all be dead."

She glanced at the child—one of Taknhal's boys.

"He said you sent your warriors on a foolish errand and got them all killed," Treln added.

Caëtin bit her lip to stifle her emotions as she smoothed his hair. "That boy has everything turned around. I'll explain it to you later, and that communication should come before fighting." She stood and addressed the servant who had pulled Treln off the other boy. "Take my children to my house. I don't want them..."

She could no longer speak, was taken aback as she recognized the servant—Hildm. The Spider girl no longer wore paint on her face, and only her hair was still black, her tunic plain and gray. She was clean and dry and looked like any other adolescent girl.

"Thank you for stopping him," Caëtin said. "The other servants rarely ever break up the boys' fighting. They fear they will be reprimanded by Uktr."

Hildm dipped her chin. "It seemed right."

"Gather my servants and have them take my children to my house. Stay there until this war is over or I tell you otherwise. I don't want them around Uktr or Grimmurk. If Taknhal has a problem with it, he can speak to me."

"Certainly." Hildm grabbed Treln and Lythi and got the attention of the servants around her, most of whom shot her hateful looks.

Caëtin relayed her orders to the servants and knelt again and kissed Lythi. "My lovely daughter. I'll take you out to hear the owls and wolves soon." She turned to her son. "Stop fighting with your kin. The Ravens are all in this together. I'll return once the Spiders are defeated."

Treln hung his head as the servants gathered and ushered her children away. Caëtin followed them, exiting the great hall and slamming its doors closed behind her. She nodded to Sanre and Sigr, waved when her children glanced back, and led her new companions on to the southern walls. She barely spoke, only mentioning major areas of the city they might need to know, and although she wanted to see how far along the long-house cover for Muninn's temple had come, she avoided passing it by.

Eventually, they approached the southern walls, and Caëtin ascended a stairway to the battlements. Warriors bowed their heads in acknowledgment and stepped back, making room for her and her companions.

"Taknhal is that way," one said, pointing as she strode along.

As Caëtin neared, Taknhal spotted her and said, "The Raven fighters owe you a great debt. If not for you, we wouldn't be here guarding these walls."

"It wasn't me," she said. "It was the sacrifice all my knights and warriors made. Pay homage to them. I'm not dead. At least not yet. And we won't know if guarding these walls will be beneficial until after the Spiders have arrived."

Taknhal cast her a wry grin. "Either way, the Raven people and my warriors are in your debt. And their animosity for each other has vanished." He looked behind her. "You bring others to aid our cause?"

"Aye. The Ulfhednar and many Bear and Boar berserkers and warriors have come to Aonark. Sea Serpents now occupy the Wolf's lands. These are the last of the Ulfhednar." She gestured at Vard and Belfedrn and those trailing them. "They will help us in return for our aid against the Serpents, if we should survive. I assured them we would honor that bargain."

Taknhal assessed Belfedrn and then Vard and the others and pursed his lips as he rubbed his beard. "If we should survive the coming of the Spider, we shall then offer you all the assistance we can."

Vard and Taknhal clasped each other's forearms to seal the agreement.

It is settled. Caëtin stared southward across brown hills rolling into the distance as rain turned to sleet. Her heart burned with memories of Halfnr and those who had been loyal to her—loyalty repaid with death. The best she could hope for now was that the Ravens could resist the coming tide.

Huginn's familiar shrieks rang overhead. A scream sounded behind Caëtin, making her jerk in surprise and rip her blade from its sheath as she whipped about.

Ylsga wrenched her axe from the head of a Raven warrior, who dropped like a stone as she swung next at Belfedrn's back, her axe biting deep into her companion's *brynja* and flesh. Her Ulfhednar victim bellowed in surprise, dropping to his knees. Ylsga's eyes had turned wild, the creeping blackness writhing up her cheeks and encircling her nose and eyes, her silver hair waving as she moved with quick, calculating strikes. She swung at another Ulfhednar, but he leapt aside. Her blade smashed into his shield and broke off a plank of wood, sending it skittering away.

Spider poison has taken her... without any warning of its coming.

Kesg wrapped strong arms around Ylsga, pinioning hers to her side as he yelled at her. "What are you doing?"

"Ylsga!" Athna ran to her comrade and lifted Ylsga's chin, looking into her eyes.

Ylsga snarled and growled at her, gnashing her teeth while kicking at her.

"You brought these warriors here to kill us." Taknhal pushed past Caëtin.

"No." Caëtin grabbed him and held him back. "They slayed a few widows, and she was cut by a poisoned blade."

"Then she must be killed."

The Raven fighters around them backed away, forming a circle as most of the Ulfhednar moved in to better restrain Ylsga. She struggled against Kesg's grip, wearing him down even though she did not seem to tire. Eakthr, Athna, and a couple others bound her thrashing hands and feet while Thelira and Dradn rushed to Belfedrn, who wavered on his knees, blood streaming from under his pelt and pooling around him, his face pale.

"She must be set free from this possession," Vard said once she was bound and Kesg laid her down, where she continued to bite and roll about before Eakthr held her still with his foot, snarling over her. Black vines had crawled up her jugular vein on the side where she had been wounded.

Dradn and Thelira yanked Belfedrn's pelt aside to assess his wound, but the older Ulfhednar reprimanded them and stood, pulling away, wobbling.

"What if there's a cure?" Kesg's face had drained of color, and tears dribbled down his cheeks, his hand clenching and unclenching his spear.

"There's no cure for such magic," Vard said.

"You don't know that!" Kesg snapped.

Somewhere far away, Caëtin thought she could hear the Spider god and Envinkia laughing.

"I will do it, my friend." Belfedrn stumbled forward, pale, seax in hand. "Do not watch. Remember her for how she was."

Kesg shoved him back. "No! If she must be killed, I'll do it. I owe her that much. But... can we not keep her in some dungeon, locked up until we speak with a Seidr man and woman?"

"We've already spoken with the *goði* and *gyðja* on this matter, as well as our Raven Seidr," Taknhal said. "We did so after experiencing something similar. To learn if there was a way to prevent the poison from taking control."

Kesg's cheeks flared red as he heaved for breath.

"I don't claim to know much about Spider magic," Taknhal continued, "but none of the people we spoke with believed there would be any way to prevent the poison from consuming a victim. Other than for amputating an affected limb. They did not know of any method that could negate or reverse its effects. None had prior experience with this poison, but as of right now, this is all we know."

Silence followed as sleet dropped around them and Kesg stared at Ylsga, who sputtered and thrashed about. Belfedrn stumbled, bracing himself by planting his spear's shaft on the walk. Dradn grabbed his arm, but Belfedrn shook him off.

"Let her go." Belfedrn gripped Kesg by the base of the neck. "Ylsga is no longer in this body. You'll find her again one day. In Valhalla."

"You just want to kill her for attacking you," Kesg sputtered, dropping his spear.

Belfedrn squeezed his comrade's neck. "She is my friend, you fool. I do this to let her go, because you can't. Because *she* asked for this. It should be one of us who does it. But if this were Lyrne, I'd be in the same state and would ask this of you." Belfedrn teetered before regaining his composure.

Tears rained from Kesg's eyes. Onunith stepped forward, offering her axe to Kesg. He tentatively took the weapon and raised it over his head, staring at his mate. He paused, shaking. His hands fell, but not with a blow. The axe dropped at his side as he shook with emotion, sobbing.

“I’ll free her.” Aegmor stepped closer, hefting his maul.

“No!” Kesg held up a hand. “Please. Not with that. You’ll crush her beautiful skull. Let Belfedrn do it.”

Dradn offered Belfedrn an axe engraved with runes, and the young warrior said, “Use this. Its magic could free her soul of any curse.”

The Ulfhednar accepted the weapon without consideration as he wobbled and paled further, blood streaming from underneath his cloak. He spoke in the old tongue—words Caëtin barely recognized, their power carrying around them and emitting a still calm. Caëtin turned away, unable to witness yet another mercy killing. Too many of those already plagued her. She stared southward, her fury rising, while she wished the Spiders would come so she could unleash her wrath upon them and rid this world of the Spider and its magics.

The chunking of an axe hitting flesh and then stone sounded behind her.

After the deed was done, Belfedrn collapsed in a pool of his own blood, his pelt soaked through. Dradn and Thelira cried out and ran to him.

70

MÄRREN

Freydaskarde landed outside the Mountain of Fire, heaving for breath, blue-tinged blood dripping from his neck. Märren placed her hands on the weeping scales.

"Are your injuries grave?" Märren asked.

"I do not believe so," Freydaskarde said, his voice hoarse and ringing of exhaustion. "With proper care, I should heal, and you will tend to my wounds."

The sharpness of the dragon's tone caused Märren a shudder of fear.

"Do not believe that you as a small human can command me." Freydaskarde glared back at her with an icy eye. "My kind are not brainless, unlike your mounts with hoofs who wield ten times your strength and speed and cannot think to unseat you and go their own path. You are a rider, which means you are here to aid and assist me—an offspring of the Dragon—with tasks I cannot otherwise accomplish. Any decisions that affect us are mine to make. You are bound to me! Not the other way around."

Märren could not respond. She had never thought this

would be the case, that these mighty creatures would only want her for assistance and that they would govern her.

"Ha! A jarl with scales."

"What she has fled all her life. And now that she's chased down her desires, she only manages to embrace her own weakness... again."

"She is not weak. She bears parts of the scale. She's a dragon rider."

"Where do these other voices in your mind come from?" Freydaskarde asked.

Märren did not know how to answer that. "They've occupied space there for as long as I can remember."

Three other dragons landed around them, the creatures in no better shape than Freydaskarde as they struggled for breath, their wings sagging. Märren looked skyward, hunting for more of their kind. There were none. A dozen dragon bodies littered the area around where Surtr had fallen and more burned in the last of his flames.

"So many are lost." Märren's heart crumpled under a crushing fist of guilt, and a strange yearning crept up from some dark recess inside her. "I caused this."

"It was not your doing, rider," Freydaskarde replied. "You released us from a prison that we endured for far too long. I would've gladly given my life to escape and slay that monster. Amongst your feeble kind, you've proven worthy of your title."

"But there are so few of the Dragon's offspring who have survived..."

The sunrise lit up the eastern horizon in pink and orange, and a group of thralls timidly approached.

"She lives!" Årn pointed up at Märren, gesturing frantically, hopping up and down. "And she sits upon one of the beasts. She's a dragon rider!"

The thralls all fell to their knees in reverence, bowing their heads. Only Uisge remained standing, smirking and tossing back his damp locks as he gazed upon her.

"The first dragon rider in centuries," Årn cried.

The clatter of others approaching sounded behind them, and Freydaskarde craned his neck around. There, Raidn sat atop a warhorse, axe drawn, urging his mount closer as the horse shied and attempted to run away. A score of Dragon berserkers and twice as many warriors flanked him.

"The dragons have been released." Raidn's voice was airy with disbelief. "And where is Surtr?"

"Surely you saw him fall," Märren said, and her bizarre yearning turned to a blazing wrath, excessive for the current situation. "But if not, you couldn't have missed the inferno when he burned out."

"Surtr cannot be killed," Raidn said. "He slayed the Dragon herself."

"The fiery giant took her by surprise while she slumbered." Freydaskarde's voice rumbled. "And she did not realize her breath was useless against him until it was too late. Now her remains lie in the lands of her offspring." He flicked a wing toward the distant mountains.

Raidn dismounted and stood before Freydaskarde, looking up. "A mere thrall sits upon you, dragon. I am one of the Dragon's berserkers." He grasped the edges of his cloak and yanked it open, revealing his chest and the full scale covering his brigandine. "Only berserkers may become dragon riders."

Freydaskarde scoffed and shook his head. "She obtained the rider's rune from the lair of the Ormr."

Raidn's gaze flicked to Märren, his mouth falling open. "But... she's a thrall. She cannot have visited the Dragon's lair."

"She has!" Freydaskarde snapped, lowering his head and staring into Raidn's eyes, the beast only a few handsbreadth from the berserker's face.

"Take it from him," Märren whispered, the dark desire in her churning, her rage boiling.

"Certainly," Freydaskarde said only in her mind, and then to Raidn said, "You will give your scale to her."

Raidn ran a hand over his chest. "I-I cannot. I earned this god remnant. I am of the Dragon clan. Of her blood. Her grave lands are my home. That thrall does not belong here."

"You were merely lucky enough to be born where she fell under Surtr's blade." Freydaskarde snarled. "You did nothing to free her offspring. Instead, you fed the giant—the slayer of your god—while bearing her scale, pretending to be her follower and basking in her power while serving her greatest enemy. You're weak. Much weaker than the one who rides me, and if you weren't wearing a scale, I'd have devoured you already."

Raidn retreated a step, his axe hand shaking.

One of the warriors stepped forward, a man with a sparse blond beard and young-looking face. Yrstl. He approached Raidn, unafraid.

"You should honor her, Raidn," Yrstl said. "She is the first rider, and more Dragon than any of us who failed to free her offspring. We should all follow her and the last of the dragons!" Yrstl waved a hand in Märren's direction.

The other berserkers and warriors shared bemused glances, but they bowed their heads in reverence.

"Give her your scale," Yrstl said.

Raidn hesitated.

Freydaskarde flashed his teeth, which were blackened by Surtr's fire. "Before I devour you and have to spit it out of your mangled corpse."

Raidn used a seax to slowly pry the scale from his brigandine. Once it was removed, he lifted the scale up to Märren, and she accepted it, allowing the power of the Dragon into her body. Its force hit her with a smack, punching the air from her lungs and making her gasp before she could recompose herself. She clutched the scale to her chest and removed the other wedges, holding them out.

Raidn scowled. "I don't want a warrior's paltry piece of the Dragon. Not even three of them. I'm a berserker. I obtained the rider's rune. I *am* a rider!"

"Then you'll have to earn another," Freydaskarde said, "before you will be accepted as a rider of one of my kin and serve them."

"These wedges are for Yrstl," Märren said. "I wasn't offering them to you."

Yrstl accepted the pieces, opening his cloak and revealing the wedge he carried. The one Märren had returned to him. "I hold no grievances against you, Märren First Rider. I may not be able to bear all of these, but I will find worthy warriors."

Märren smiled. "I'm sorry that I stole yours, but it was necessary."

"After seeing this"—Yrstl spread his hands to indicate all that had transpired—"I cannot argue with you."

A short, black-bearded berserker beside Raidn pried his own scale from his brigandine. "Take mine, Jarl," the berserker said, and Raidn ripped the scale from the berserker's hands and pressed it into the emptiness on the front of his armor, gasping.

Raidn straightened, inhaling deeply. He patted the berserker on the helm. "You'll be rewarded for your loyalty." He glanced down the line of berserkers and pointed at one man near the end. "Remove your scale and give it to Thranst." Raidn motioned to the berserker who had given the scale to him.

The berserker at the end of the line hesitated before slowly detaching his scale, demoting himself to nothing more than a soldier, and handing it to the man who had given his scale to Raidn.

"Now, Thranst and I, and one more berserker, can ride the

remaining offspring of the Dragon." Raidn looked past Freydaskarde to the last three dragons.

"If they accept you," Freydaskarde replied. "They may, as you have achieved the right, but I would not expect them to be overly welcoming of you and your kin. You'll have to earn your bond and your place under their command."

Raidn's eyes closed, and he bowed. "I accept this fate. The failure of my ancestors to see what could've been has cost you and your kin far too many years, but I only followed what I knew, what those before me allowed. I was not a berserker when Surtr trapped you." He indicated the dead dragons. "And this strategy was not without cost."

"Agreed." Freydaskarde spread his wings. "The cost was high but worth our freedom. The offspring of the Dragon have been caged for too long. It's time for us to fly again."

The berserkers and warriors genuflected.

"Rip their scales from them," Märren thought to her mount, realizing her intentions were extreme but not caring to curb her emotions.

Freydaskarde lashed out, biting the newly scaleless berserker in half, creating a geyser of blood. Then the dragon whipped his tail, smashing into two other berserkers and hurling them away. The thralls gasped, and the warriors retreated in fear. Freydaskarde paused his assault, his laugh a deep rumble in his throat.

"I would kill them all, but we'll need Dragon fighters soon," the dragon said in Märren's mind. *"The full scale you've taken should satiate your yearning."*

Märren cringed at the sight of the devoured berserker's legs that lay on the ground, bleeding. *"What has come over me?"*

Freydaskarde chuckled. *"It is the aftereffects of using the Dragon's magic."*

Märren gasped and clutched her scale. *"This anger and yearning to possess something—everything around me—is so terrible compared to what I've heard of the Wolf's hunger."*

"You are not Wolf. And if you were, you are no longer. You are Dragon." Freydaskarde backed away from the frightened warriors, the delight in his tone not concealed. *"The feelings your kind view as wicked grab hold of you now and sink their teeth deep. You also lust after treasure and desire to hoard it. Malevolence and greed. Those are the human words for what you experience."*

Märren trembled, and a wave of bile washed up her throat. "No. I don't need such things."

"But you will, after every battle when you use the Dragon's magics. There is no escape, and if you do not satisfy the sensations, they will never release you. Just pray that when a battle is over and things have settled, some enemies still surround you. Like in this situation. You humans have trouble dealing with the aftereffects when you plunder from and kill your comrades."

Guilt flooded Märren, but as she held her new scale tightly to her chest, her yearning and rage ebbed. She stared into the distance in shock. She could run and hide from this, from where her fate had brought her, but then she would be turning her back on everything she had achieved. Everything she had ever longed for.

"Yet another fault she has obtained."

"She cannot ever do good. Especially not for herself and those she loves."

"She has done more for these people and the dragons than anyone in centuries."

The voices are still here... The realization struck her like an axe to the back, and she almost broke into tears. Her father had lied to her, again. He had sent her on a wild errand that should have gotten her killed many times over, but she prevailed. And although her father had passed, in a way, he still lived, his voice haunting her as the wolf in her head. A voice she could never forget. The vilest of them all.

"Now!" Freydaskarde scrutinized all those before him, making Märren lurch with surprise. "Are there any more jötunn who have come to and remain in Midgard?"

No one answered.

"We seek to reestablish the land of the Dragon in Midgard and reign as the Dragon herself intended—what she wished for her offspring," Freydaskarde continued, "but we cannot do so while any jötunn reside here."

Raidn stood before the dragon. "There are rumors of another. In the cold regions to the east. In Bear and Boar territory, but a recent messenger claimed that it has fallen."

"There's a third." Årn slowly approached Freydaskarde, her eyes wide with awe. "One who hides and is kept secret. It is the reason I fled my homeland. A jötunn of lightning haunts the Serpent Isles. He too demands sacrifices and is the reason why my people have been hunting thralls and raiding."

A flash of truth floated in Märren's mind. The Dragon's wisdom told her that Årn spoke honestly. That meant this woman was Sea Serpent, and her people were now Märren's primary enemy. But Årn was not wicked.

"Then we must slay this last jötunn or send it back to Jötunheim," Freydaskarde said. "We will not rest until the last of their kind have been driven from Midgard."

"But," Märren began, "now that I've freed you and obtained a scale... I've never thought this far before... I wish to return to my home and aid any of my people who have survived the recent raids and pillaging. My kin."

"You have much to learn about the Dragon," Freydaskarde said. "I thought I made this clear—you ride and care for me. You do *my* bidding."

Märren's fury returned, but it was different this time. It was her own. "I released you, and you refuse to come to my cause?"

"I will not make any promises to a human."

Märren gritted her teeth. "You require riders to care for your injuries, in addition to warriors and berserkers who will fight for you. There are far too few of your kind left. Look how many of your kin Surtr brought down. If you will not aid me, I will not ride you and care for your wounds while we remove this last jötunn. Not even if you threaten to devour me."

Freydaskarde glared back at her. Breaths came and went, neither of them capitulating.

"We should strike a bargain with this woman, Freydaskarde," a dragon as blood red as Orstenshard said. "For now. She is the first of the last riders—Märren, if her name rings true. If not for her and what she had to do to get past Surtr and the Dragon people protecting him, we'd still be imprisoned."

"First the giant," Märren said, "if that is non-negotiable, but then we travel to Wolf territory."

Freydaskarde tossed his head with agitation. "We shall work in tandem like in the days of the old riders, when the Dragon herself ruled these lands." He grunted. "We will agree."

Märren hid her relief and elation.

"We fly to the Serpent Isles and reclaim Midgard from the jötunn." Freydaskarde reared up. "For the Dragon."

"First we should search the dens," the red dragon said. "Orstenshard and the other females may've been hiding their last."

Freydaskarde settled and nodded. "Aye. Be quick."

The four dragons lumbered toward the mountain and slipped into different caverns. Märren hunched low as her ice dragon weaved through the corridors of Orstenshard's den, sniffing. A tingle of anticipation rose in Märren's mind, and she knew the feeling was not her own.

They arrived at the dead-end chamber where Orstenshard had been sleeping. There, against the far wall, packed together in a nest of dirt and stone, sat four scaled eggs. Freydaskarde reached out and scooped them up, handling them as tenderly as a man would a newborn. Then he whipped about and exited. The dragons searched every cavern.

In the end, the dragons formed a circle, displaying eggs that were a myriad of colors. A dozen eggs had escaped Surtr's hunger. The dragons conversed in words Märren could barely understand.

"... lay the young..." The green beast's dialogue came and went in thundering cracks.

The black dragon said, "Each will be raised and cherished..." before meaning was lost to an incoherent rumble.

"As in the times of old," the fire dragon added, its words twisting into a coherent voice. A line of runes running from the base of Märren's neck to her ear flared in her mind, and the dragon's reverberating words became clearer. "Oaths have been laid. The unhatched gathered and hoarded. Our most precious treasure."

"We will need the humans," Freydaskarde said. "To provide care for them."

A stabbing pain struck Märren, and she felt for Eimri's skull at her hip. Still there. Always there. *I shall raise one of Orstenshard's offspring.*

"It'll be a child without a mother."

"Like Märren, a mother without a child."

"She'll name it Eimri."

Freydaskarde tilted his head and eyed Märren as best he could. "You'll be a fitting caretaker for a dragonet. Another use for you." He faced the others of his kind and said, "We shall leave the unhatched here in the heat of the mountain and return for them when the last jötunn and threat has been removed from Midgard. I'll demand that some of the berserkers remain behind and defend our young, as it was in the days of old. But we'll need the rest of the Dragon warriors to accompany us. Take on your riders. We fly."

The other three dragons turned about to face the berserkers and lowered their heads. Raidn climbed onto the fire dragon, Thranst and another berserker onto the remaining two, one that was black, the other green. The berserkers settled into their positions, looking less comfortable than Märren, probably because the dragons had not yet opened up to them.

"We fly to Torank to gather all the Dragon soldiers and warriors and order them to prepare to sail," Freydaskarde said.

Märren pointed at the five berserkers who were left without a mount and questioned Freydaskarde in her mind. *"Is that a sufficient number to guard the mountain and the eggs?"*

"It will have to do. For now."

"Then we kill this giant who has caused such suffering for the Sea Serpents and thus my kin," Märren said, wanting to reaffirm their bargain.

"Wait!" Yrstl hollered. "The Dragon cannot allow their new First Rider to remain in irons." He strode forward, staring at Raidn. "You must remove her collar."

Raidn studied Märren before addressing his fighters. "Break her shackles."

A few warriors stepped forward, pulling stakes and hammers from their packs.

"Step down," Raidn said to Märren.

"I will only do so if all the thralls are to be released from their irons."

Raidn grimaced and exhaled slowly as he considered it. "It shall be done."

Märren scaled down Freydaskarde's neck and awaited the warriors. One woman held a steel spike and angled it at her, and Märren cocked her head to the side, kneeling and bracing her collar against one of Freydaskarde's spines.

"There are no stumps or stones to be used instead," Märren said.

The warrior nodded in understanding, looking upon Freydaskarde with awe and fear before jamming her stake into a loop in the collar that housed a bolt. She hammered the spike, and the bolt punched free. Märren stood, pulling her collar open and flinging it aside.

"I think you deserve to have this back." Raidn reached out, offering Märren a double-bladed axe. Her axe. "It's befitting of you now, First Rider."

The warriors broke the remainder of the thralls' collars, freeing them. Freydaskarde slid his neck closer, and Märren climbed back onto her scaled seat, grasping the haft of her axe, her fingers falling into familiar grooves. Power flowed through her arm and out of her fist, into the weapon. The Dragon's strength surged inside her, and the magic of the Dragon's claw settled into the iron of her weapon.

Märren jabbed her axe into the air and shouted, crying out with all her might.

The thralls and berserkers and warriors raised fists and blades, yelling back at her, banging axes against shields, chanting. "The riders have returned! THE DRAGON RIDERS HAVE RETURNED!"

For all of Midgard, PLEASE READ!

First of all, I put A LOT of thought into this book's ending and whether or not to contain a big battle with the Spider clan. After discussing it with my alpha readers and editors, I decided against including the battle and events that have to happen prior since the first book in the series would then be around 1,000 pages long. The battles the story is building up to will be included in the next book. This first book in the Forbidden Runes series may feel like a cliffhanger ending. I sincerely apologize for that but hope you have engaged with the characters and world enough to want more. If so, I will write it.

Now that I've explained myself, I'd like to add my feelings on this story and world. I loved diving into a Norse-inspired world, as there is so much myth and lore to immerse myself in. It has become part of who I am, and I sincerely hope it has also become part of you!

It's hard to match the vast fantasy worlds of the Norse, as Tolkien must have realized, and there's much left to tell, but with the ever competitive world of writing, an author has to find stories that resonate with readers. If this story receives many glowing reviews and becomes popular, it will move to the forefront of my endeavors. If it does not, then it will be shuffled back while I work on other ideas.

To keep Märren and Caëtin and Belfedrn alive and striving toward their goals, please rate or review this work on **AMAZON!**

Now, with all that I am, I want to thank you, reader, for taking the time and risking your imagination on *The Hunger of the Dragon.* Without readers, books and most stories would be lost, and without your support, I could not continue to write and dream.

Please, if you enjoyed *The Hunger of the Dragon,* consider rating or quickly reviewing it on Amazon. Every single review is important and aids me in practicing my art and standing out among millions of other books by encouraging other readers to take a chance while also showing Amazon the book is worth promoting. A review is the single most powerful thing a reader can do for an author—if not for Märren, Caëtin, and Belfedrn, and the unfolding story I've only just begun (although I've outlined so much more). Reviews make all the difference in the digital book world where each year hundreds of thousands of authors battle for your attention and a place in your heart.

Creating this world and its characters and connecting with readers through story is an incredible feeling and the reason why I write. As weird as it may sound—I want to get out of bed each day to continue this dream, and I would be honored if you could help guide me along the path of honing my craft and making this dream come true.

My vow and oath to you, reader, is that I will always continue to treat my skills like a blade and continue to sharpen them, and I will not stop looking for stories to bring into our world.

One last plead.

PLEASE hear me out.

If you enjoy or love a book but don't post a review or even rate it, Amazon believes it didn't give you the emotional response it was hoping for. This is especially true for indie books, which is a realm that is getting more and more difficult to compete in.

I began my writing career decades ago but only started self-publishing at the end of 2017. Releasing books now is growing exceedingly more difficult, and I need all the help I can get.

YOUR HELP!

"For the Wolves!"

A fan of all those who still dare to read and tread the worlds of imagination,

Ryan
R.M. Schultz

Please Review and/or Rate Here: ***The Hunger of the Dragon***

GLOSSARY

Midgard: The Norse-inspired world of this story where the gods and beast gods have all perished in a war involving each other and the giants. The gods' remains are piled in the lands where they fell, thus giving rise to the different clans and powers harnessed by those people.

Character Names

Aegmor (EEG-muhr): A Bear berserker. Male.
Årn (OHRN): A thrall in the Dragon city of Torank. Female.
Athna (AHTH-nah): The battle Seidr of the Ulfhednar. Female.
Belfedrn Nvuttson (BEL-feth-ruhn NVOOT-sohn): One of the three main characters. An Ulfhednar of the Wolf clan. Male.
Caëtin Harekrsdóttir (KAY-eh-tin HAR-ek-ers-DAH-ter): One of the three main characters. A Knight Black of the Raven clan. Female.
Darstrid (DAHR-strid): One of Uktr's adopted daughters. A battle Seidr and Knight Black of the Raven clan.
Deyja (DAY-ya): Young trainee of the Wolf clan who Belfedrn vowed to protect. Male.
Dradn (DRAY-thin): Young warrior of the Wolf clan. Thelira's brother.
Eakthr (EEK-thr): The thief of the Ulfhednar of the Wolf clan. Male.
Eimri (EEM-ree): Märren's dead daughter.
Envinkia (EN-vink-eeya): The jarl and queen of the Spider clan. Female.
Freydaskarde (FRAY-dahsk-ahr-day): Ice dragon. Male.
Freydeg (FRAY-thig): One of two of Uktr's surviving but aging warrior companions. Male.
Grimmurk (GRIM-urk): One of two of Uktr's surviving but aging warrior companions. Male.
Gron (GRAHN): A jarl of the Bear clan. Male.
Halfnr (HALF-ner): One of the Knights Black of the Raven clan. Male.
Halvi (HALH-vee): A captive boy who attempts to steal a feather of Muninn from a Raven berserker.
Hildm (HILL-them): A young captive from the Spider's clan who had been training with her people to be a warrior or berserker. Female.
Huginn (HOO-gin): Caëtin's befriended raven, whom she named after one of Odin's ravens.

Igendrn (IG-eth-ren): A *goði* of Muninn for the Raven clan. Male.
Jestorg (YEHS-torg): The 'venerable' white wizard who commands ice trolls.
Kesg (KEHSG): An Ulfhednar of the Wolf clan and Belfedrn's closest comrade. Male.
Lyrne (LEER-nee): An Ulfhednar of the Wolf clan. Mate of Belfedrn. Female.
Lythi (Lie-THEE): Caëtin's daughter.
Märren (MAH-ren): One of the three main characters. She is haunted by voices in her head and is part of the Wolf clan. Female.
Megtr (MEHG-ter): A thrall in the Dragon city of Torank. Male.
Onunith (OHN-oon-ith): A jarl of the Boar clan and a berserker. Female.
Orstenshard (OHRS-tehn-shard): Fire dragon. Female.
Raidn (RAY-thin): A berserker of the Dragon clan. Male.
Sanre (San-REE): One of the Knights Black of the Raven clan. Female.
Surtr (SUHR-ter): The fire giant ruler and guardian of Muspelheim.
Taknhal (TAHK-en-hal): One of Uktr's adopted sons and a Knight Black of the Raven clan.
Thelira (THEE-lihr-ah): Young warrior of the Wolf clan. Dradn's sister.
Treln (TREL-n): Caëtin's son.
Uktr (OOK-ter): Jarl of the Raven clan and a Knight Black. Male.
Uisge (OOSH-geh): A water wight of the fjord.
Vard (Varth): Jarl of the Ulfhednar of the Wolf clan. Male.
Vegask (VEHG-ahsk): A jarl of the Sea Serpent clan.
Ylsga (ILS-gah): An Ulfhednar of the Wolf clan. Mate of Kesg. Female.
Yrstl (IRST-el): A warrior of the Dragon clan. Male.

Terms and the World of Midgard

Alfheim (ALF-hame): The world of the bright elves, who enjoy music, poetry, art, and magic.
Aonark (Ay-OH-nark): The Raven clan's largest city.
Arvakr (AHR-vah-ker): Old Norse name for a horse that pulled the sun. In this story, the term refers to the Horse god or clan.
Asgard (AS-gard): The world of the gods.
Björn (BEE-yoorn or BEE-yern): Old Norse word for bear. In this story, the term refers to the Bear god or clan.
Brynja (Brin-YA): Old Norse term for armor, which was often chainmail but could be lamellar or other types.
Dagmal (DAHG-mahl): Old Norse term for the day meal that was eaten in the morning as breakfast. One of two meals in the day.
Djarkar (DEY-yahrk-ahr): In this story, the name refers to the Spider god and its clan members.

Dvalinn (DVHA-linn): Old Norse name for a stag who lived around Yggdrasil and ate the tree's branches. In this story, the name refers to the Stag god and its clan members.

Fenrir (FEN-rir): The wolf giant and god who was chained.

Goði (GOH-thee): An old Norse male priest.

Gyðja (GIHTH-ya): An old Norse female priest.

Hávamál (HAW-vah-mawl): An old Norse set of poems from Odin that offered worldly wisdom, advice, and insights on proper conduct.

Helheim (HELL-hame): The world of the dead. Hel, who is a melancholy giantess, presides over it. This world is inhabited by those who died of old age or disease and not those who died in battle.

Hildisvini (HILL-dis-vee-nee): Old Norse word for boar. In this story, the term refers to the Boar god or clan.

Hrafn (HRAH-fen): Old Norse word for raven. In this story, the term refers to the Raven god or clan.

Jarl (YARL): Old Norse term for the chief of a clan or region. This word was adopted by the English, giving rise to the title of earl.

Jörmungandr (YOOR-mun-gahn-der): Old Norse word for the serpent who encircles the world. In this story, the name refers to the Sea Serpent god or clan.

Jötunheim (YOH-tunn-hame): The world of frost giants. A land of pure chaos and disorder.

Jötunn (YOH-tunn): Old Norse term for a giant.

Karl (KARHL): Old Norse word for a freeman or freewoman.

Midgard: The land of humans.

Muninn (MOO-nin): The dead raven god who was once a raven of Odin's.

Muspelheim (MOO-spell-hame): Primordial world of fire and home to the great fire giant Surtr.

Náhvalr (NAH-vahl): Old Norse word for narwhal. In this story, the term refers to the Narwhal god or clan.

Nattmal (NAHT-mahl): Old Norse term for the night meal that was eaten in the evening as dinner or supper. One of two meals in the day.

Nidavellir (NID-uh-vell-ir): The world of dwarves who love craftsmanship and magic. Also referred to as the land of the dark elves.

Niflheim (NIF-el-hame): The primordial world of ice and mist, which was inhospitable even to frost giants.

Nistreel (NIS-tree-el): The Wolf clan's largest city.

Ormr (OHRM): Old Norse word for dragon or serpent. In this story, the term refers to the Dragon god or clan.

Raven's bridge: In typical old Norse mythology, this was a 'Rainbow bridge' termed 'Bifrost' (BIF-roast). It forms a bridge between Midgard and Asgard and was protected by a guardian.

Seax (SEE-axe): A single-edged knife or short sword typically used by Vikings as a secondary weapon and a tool.

Seidr (SAY-ther): Relating to dark magic similar to a witch's or druid's.

Skål (SKUHL): A term in old Norse that meant 'bowl' or a drinking vessel. Often used as a friendly greeting before drinking. Similar to 'cheers.'

Sparsgard (SPARS-guard): A small village in the Raven's lands, near its southern border.

Thrall (Thrahl): Old Norse word for a slave.

Torank (TOHR-anhk): The Dragon clan's largest city.

Ulfhednar (OOLV-heth-nar): Old Norse title for highly trained berserkers of the Wolf.

Ulfr (OOL-ver): Old Norse word for wolf. In this story, the term refers to the Wolf god or clan.

Valhalla (val-HALL-uh): A place in Asgard. It is a celestial hall where the souls of dead Vikings who died in battle reside and feast, drink, and fight for sport.

Vanaheim (VAH-neh-hame): A fertile and magical world of lesser gods called the Vanir.

Vkum River (VKOOM): A river that flows through Aonark in the Raven's lands.

OTHER BOOKS BY R.M. SCHULTZ

The Forged and The Fallen

Novels
Through Blood and Dragons
Through Fire and Shadow
Through Ashes and War

Novella
The Taming and The Betrayal

(Amazon Affiliate Links)

ACKNOWLEDGMENTS

I wish to thank the following people for all their help and sacrifices in turning this story into a book.

To Matt Schultz for reading and editing the first sorry version of every book I write and making the story shine.

To Jason Weersma for cheering me on from the beginning.

To Laura Josephsen for the most detailed questions and concerns I'd ever consider.

To Sarah Chorn for the additional dive into the nuances.

To each and every reader in the Sky Sea Council and the Small Council. Without your support and insight and reviews, I couldn't have come this far.

ABOUT THE AUTHOR

After reading Tolkien, R.M. Schultz wrote his first 100,000-word fantasy novel as a freshman in high school. When he's not saving animals, he has continued writing across genres for over two decades but always includes fantasy elements. R.M. Schultz founded and heads the North Seattle Science Fiction and Fantasy Writers' Group and has published twenty novels.

R.M.'s books have won multiple awards, including bronze and gold medals for fantasy. One his series is being adapted into a video game! The game is slated to be released in the Fall of 2025. He has written and performed several songs—calling them dragon shanties—for the world that will be included with the music played for the game.

And someday, he hopes to be knighted by George R.R. Martin.

www.rmschultzauthor.com